The One and Only

Julia Ash

ISBN-13: 978-1-7320816-1-1

DEDICATION

To my husband Rick,
for embracing my writing journey!

෨ ෬ ෨ ෬

*"When I dare to be powerful—to use my strength
in the service of my vision,
then it becomes less and less important
whether I am afraid."*

~ Audre Lorde

The One and Only

THE ELI CHRONICLES
Book 1

Julia Ash

1

Wednesday, June 23, 2032
The White House Situation Room: Washington, D.C.

WHILE ATTENDING THE Special Warfare Council meeting, in an atmosphere buzzing with urgency over the escalating bacterial threat, Ruby Spencer's mind drifted. Her eyebrows tensed. Had she instructed the babysitter—the first since Gabby was born, to lock all the doors? Including the glass sliders?

Sitting beside her at the conference table, Clay gently nudged her with his elbow, giving her the is-everything-okay look.

She nodded, barely perceptible, but enough to answer her husband's question. Truth was, motherhood had made her cautious. Or maybe the state-of-the-world had sparked the uneasiness that hid beneath her skin, behind her smile. Warning of things to come.

The SWC needed the best minds acutely focused on the fight ahead. But she was no longer in the game. Keeping her newborn daughter healthy and safe was all she could think about. Which meant the high-risk days of analyzing the horrific bacterial-anomaly as a Council microbiologist were waning.

Glancing at her husband again, she hoped he would understand her resignation. She'd tell him soon.

Only half-listening, she nodded as President Newton admitted world leaders were bracing for World War IV. Civil unrest was percolating. And legislators continued to press for a shock-and-awe response to the crisis, even though the President believed the SWC was making headway on the microscopic battlefield.

1

Soon, talk in the room became muffled, as if Ruby were wearing earplugs. Only her thoughts about society's unraveling were enunciated in her mind. The chronology of events was easy to remember, since most coincided with major milestones in her life. Like a week after her engagement, she was struck with an illness at lightning speed, dropping her onto the kitchen floor before she ever registered a symptom. Millions became sick from the mysterious pathogen, including animals of every species. As health organizations scrambled to identify and treat the infected, time ran out.

Except for her.

She was the lone infected-victim to survive the first outbreak.

She'd never forget when she and Clay chose a wedding date. On the same day, she learned *how* she'd skirted death from the bacterial agent, labeled F8. Her blood, and only hers, had overwhelmed the infection by generating powerful dendritic cells and antibodies. Miraculously, she possessed the key to a cure. A cure she helped develop.

Even though immunizations ended human infections, animals suffered and were nearly annihilated. Humankind catapulted toward starvation. In fact, two years ago, the future looked bleak, broken. But she and Clay refused to relinquish their dreams. So they got married.

As the President briefed the Council about "chatter" amassed by counterintelligence agencies, Ruby stared blankly at a vase of yellow roses. She remembered how hope had blossomed months after they wed. How the promise of better-times pulsed through her veins. Made her feel alive, enthusiastic. Because fifteen-months-ago, the Chinese manufactured and distributed a meat-supplement as humanitarian aid. And even though she and Clay had avoided the product in their quest to eat home-grown vegetables and grains, they'd celebrated hunger's defeat, deciding to conceive. To embrace the hope. Secure the future.

But a year ago, when her pregnancy-test indicated positive, society shattered. The meat product was a Trojan horse, delivering microscopic-bombs: nanorobotics called Remote Electronic Detonators, to be exact. REDs were programmed to discharge in the brain. One-billion unsuspecting people were no longer hungry when the ingested devices exploded, instantly killing them, along with the forty-seventh President of the United States and most leaders in the Federation of Independent Nations.

She clenched her teeth. Anger festered over lives lost, over a world made fragile. Vulnerable. An unstable planet that her daughter would inherit.

She seethed over the man responsible for the F8 bioweapon and RED atrocities: former Chinese President Huo Zhu Zheng, the madman who launched World War III against humanity. All in a perverse attempt to emerge as *the* supreme ruler of a unified world.

At least Huo had gotten justice—in a flavor he understood.

Now, with the war over, the SWC met every week to stitch the world back together. But rips in the fabric were spreading. Huo's bioweapon had mutated in animal carcasses, morphing into a freakish pathogen: Zoonosis Mutated Bacteria or ZOM-B. Freakish was understated. By a long shot. Because infected humans died and reanimated shortly thereafter, giving rise to a cataclysmic oxymoron: the living dead.

How was the Council going to kill an enemy already dead?

And even though Ruby had leapt head-first into the fight to save humanity—from the beginning, the moment she gave birth and locked eyes with Gabby, her heart beat for one reason: to shield her three-month-old from the horrors of ZOM-B.

"Your thoughts on my suggestion, Ruby?" President Newton asked, narrowing her eyes as she glanced around the table. "Let *her* make the decision, people."

"Decision?" Her heart sputtered. She felt as if she were back in high school, when her teacher called on her, knowing she'd been daydreaming. "If you wouldn't mind, could you recap your suggestion? To ensure I'm...I'm understanding correctly?"

Clay smiled.

"I'd like to send you and Clayton to Taiwan. Pretty simple," the President said, raising her eyebrows. "You'd visit the temporary Naval base to observe what's left of China's Huo Zhu Zheng. More importantly, you'd consult with an interdisciplinary team of scientists, onsite at the base, to analyze tissue samples taken from captive zombies. And while you're on the island, I'd like you to inspect the burnt ruins of Shifen, a small mountain-village: the only area on the island affected by the bioweapon mutation. Our satellites scanned the remains—thoroughly I might add, but you'd be searching for artifacts which may have been missed." She huffed. "Clearly some members disagree with my suggestion."

Ruby's heart hammered in her chest. "But...I mean, can't another team go?"

"Have you not been listening?" President Newton asked, as if scolding a child. She exhaled slowly, perhaps cleansing herself of frustration. "As an experienced microbiologist who specializes in bacterial anomalies and pandemic prevention, you are the perfect fit. Who better than one of the dynamic duo who developed the cure for F8, using her own unique blood? If anyone can help us learn how to stop ZOM-B, it's you." She glanced at Clay. "And your husband will offer support as you deem necessary."

She hated when the President treated him like disposable luggage.

"The other-half of the dynamic duo," Ruby protested, "is sitting across from me, and he's not a parent of a newborn. Why not send Em, instead of us?"

Emory Bradshaw was her best friend in college, not to mention the highest-regarded microbiologist in the world. With two PhD's from Johns Hopkins, one in microbiology and the other in immunology, number-one in both programs, as well as the youngest ever to accomplish this feat, he was the "think" behind the SWC's think-tank. More importantly, other than Clay and her parents, she trusted Em with her life.

"Em is working on a high-risk project in the lab," the President answered. "In contrast, your assignment has minimal risks. Besides, you'll get back in the field where you love to be. And it's only for a long weekend, five days roundtrip."

Ruby was caught off-guard. While she'd been recounting the fall-of-society to sharpen her arguments for resigning from the SWC, the President wanted to send her and Clay halfway around the world. Leaving Gabby!

"Wait," Clay said. "How can you say the assignment has minimal risks? We barely have the resources and assets to keep *this* country operating at a rudimentary level. Won't Taiwan be in worse shape?

Even though it was spared from the bioterrorism and nanorobotic attacks—except for Shifen, the island *imports* everything. It must be unstable."

"Quite the contrary," the President argued. "Huo prepared long before he executed his take-over-the-world scheme. His people and all-important allies weren't stricken by attacks, so their labor forces are intact. Although China imports three-quarters of its energy and crude, it does so from its allies. The pipeline from Russia to Kazakhstan to China is still operable, as are pipelines from Saudi Arabia and Africa. You'd be visiting a safe zone, resembling our former country. Traveling to a place without restrictions. Frankly, I'm envious."

For a second, sitting in the air-conditioned room, paneled in cherry from wall-to-floor and illuminated by inset lighting, Ruby wondered if Taiwan might reflect the same visual-normalcy as the Situation Room. And normalcy might ease the tiredness, the anxiety that pressed on her chest like dead weights.

How great would it be not to have electricity shut down each night? Or not to be rationed at the grocery store? What if there were no limits at the gas pump or at charging stations? And no driving restrictions?

Flying to Taiwan, in fact, would be remarkable. Receiving government approval for air travel was as common as seeing a flock of birds, a herd of cattle, or a nest of rabbits. It just didn't happen. Not after the original bioweapon—the F8 bacteria—was unleashed.

Could the normalcy of Taiwan help ease her fears? Help her restore balance in her life?

No one spoke as members glared at her, waiting for her response.

Her mouth salivated thinking about water. What if she could drink as much as she wanted, even for a few days? Or do laundry when needed, instead of having restrictions? She thumbed the filled glass in front of her, wet and cool, glistening with beads of condensation. The ice cubes bobbed as if playing at a pool party. Guzzling, she downed the entire glass, letting the water cool her parched throat.

"With their mastery of desalination," the President said, having watched her gulp, "the Chinese and Taiwanese have plenty of fresh water, too. Your thoughts?"

Ruby glanced at Clay. He raised his eyebrows and tilted his head forward. He was leaving the decision to her.

"We appreciate your confidence in us, Madam President, but we respectfully decline. Gabby is so young. Our responsibility is with her."

Luther Pennington, the Council's chair, slapped the conference table. "Yes!" He turned, softening his features from elated—like he had won a bet, to caring and looking fatherly. "I'm so relieved. You're making the right decision."

His reaction surprised her. Why would the chair display relief? Wasn't like they were friends outside of the Council. And he was curiously opposed to the President's idea—which seemed reasonable. Something didn't add up.

"Out of curiosity, Dr. Pennington, why are you against our taking this assignment?"

"Yes," the President added. "Explain your reasoning. I'm all ears."

"I'm simply supporting her decision as a mother. *Their* decision as parents." He squirmed in his chair, fiddling with his pen. "With a third of the population destroyed in Federation countries, raising little ones is paramount. Is it not?"

"Sweet Mother of Jesus," the President snapped. "We're talking about less than a week. Five short days, *including* travel. I'm sure Ruby and Clayton have friends who can care for the child without causing irreparable harm. Besides, who else could we send from this Council to evaluate the accuracy of the base's findings? In case no one's noticed, we have a potential Extinction Level Infection!"

"Regardless, I agree with Luther," one member blasted. "Too risky for her to go."

"No disrespect intended," another member chimed, locking eyes with her, "but bravery alone can't ensure your safety. You need to stay on domestic soil."

Bravery? Now she was really confused. "But you said Taiwan would be like traveling back in time. Back to when the world was *safe*. So how did bravery become a prerequisite?"

She looked at the Secretary of Defense; her eyebrows raised. He would resolve the mixed messages. After World War III, he awarded her with the Medal for Valor—the highest public-safety recognition...for bravery. The medal was displayed within a frame, hanging above the fireplace mantel at home.

"*Is* Taiwan safe?" she asked the Secretary.

"The Federation of Independent Nations, over which we preside," Henry Kilgore answered, "constantly monitors Taiwan and mainland China. FIN affirms these regions are the safest on Earth. And the Taiwanese and Chinese are not hostiles; they were victims of Huo like the rest of us. Therefore, I concur with the President's assertion."

She was baffled. Why would some members be over-the-top concerned about her safety?

"Em: what do you think?"

"I say go. If President Newton, Secretary Kilgore, and FIN assert that Taiwan is safe, then it's safe. And Gabby will be fine for a long weekend. Think of the trip as a honeymoon. Because when the world first unraveled, you and Clay couldn't take one." He winked. "I'm sure President Newton will put you up at a posh hotel—all the food and drink you want. With electricity twenty-four-seven and a low-risk assignment to boot, why say no? Hell, I'd go in a hot minute, if I wasn't knee-deep in a project. You deserve a little fun, girlfriend. Go for it."

"Fun won't sway me."

He nodded, like he understood. "Your eyes on the cellular diagnostics are vital. We need you. The world needs you. I'm just saying...what's the harm in having a little fun while you're there? A brief R&R with your man. Some time to refuel. It's all good."

"Maybe we should consider the assignment." She looked at the President. "I'll discuss your request with Clay. We'll let you know."

As much as she wanted to, she couldn't deny that a honeymoon sounded tempting. Maybe the trip could even help her overcome irrational fears that were getting harder and harder to shake—that were keeping her and Gabby indoors. And what if she made *this* assignment her last? Certainly her departure from the Council would be a little less abrupt.

Besides, if leaders with the best intel were encouraging her to go, how dangerous could Taiwan be?

2

Saturday, July 10, 2032
Northern Taiwan

WITH HER HUSBAND'S encouragement, Ruby accepted the SWC's assignment. Fifteen days later, she and Clay delivered Gabby to their best friends, before hopping on a government jet at Dulles International the next day.

After a sixteen-hour flight, they landed early-morning, rested, in humid-hot Taiwan.

Energy hummed through her veins. This trip might get her back on track. Might get her feeling positive again.

When they walked into their massive suite at the Mandarin Oriental, a luxury hotel in Taipei, a vase of pink roses was waiting for them on the dining room table. The attached card was from the President, reading: *You'll always be America's "one and only," Ruby. Thank you both for your service to Country and humankind. Good luck!*

She smiled. She hadn't been called *the one and only* in a while. A reporter had pegged her with the title during the F8 pandemic, after she'd survived the infection. The nametag had stuck. Until ZOM-B. Her blood offered no protection against the mutated pathogen. Nor did anyone else's.

Being tagged with a label wasn't new. Born Ruby Pearl Airily, she had been called her mother's little superhero for as long as she could remember. *By land, by sea,* and *by air,* her mother would say. Turns out, she had a knack for outrunning death, for surviving the impossible. Maybe she had first earned the label in utero, after the blood transfusion. Besides saving her life, no doubt the transfusion had contributed to her blood's unusual complexities, though she'd never know for certain. It wasn't like blood bags came with business cards from their donors.

Regardless of when or how many near-death experiences she had survived or the number of titles she'd earned over her twenty-seven-years, she was quite ordinary.

If she *had* developed into some sort of superhero, things would be different. Like today. Today she would've shielded herself and Clay from the Taiwan heat. Of course, the minute they left their hotel, their T-shirts bled sweat. Which proved that the only items capable of saving the afternoon were the water bottles stuffed inside their backpacks.

From the hotel, she and Clay flagged a taxi to the Taipei Police Department to pick-up handguns, temporarily issued with a three-day permit, under the auspices of FIN and the U.S. government.

Taipei Main Station was their next stop. They jumped onto the MRT line, headed for the Ruifang Station. Even though the train was antiquated, she felt so alive, so free. The rattle from the tracks woke her senses. Looking beyond the railcar window, the city's heartbeat pulsed. Stores were open, cars zipped along roads, electronic billboards flashed, people scurried like ants. The President was right: Taiwan reflected America's former self.

They arrived at the bustling Ruifang Station, northeast of the capital. The only outward sign that something unspeakable had happened ten-months ago was the abandoned ticket-booth for the Pingxi Line, a single-track railway that once transported passengers to touristy attractions—including Shifen.

The Pingxi shutdown also meant she and Clay had to switch transportation modes. From the station, they walked to the town's public health office where their government-assigned escort, Chia-hao, was waiting. The English-speaking guide had been commissioned—by the American Consulate in Taipei, by order of President Newton—to drive them to Shifen where they'd inspect the burnt ruins.

Inside the vehicle, sitting behind the driver, Ruby ran her fingers over the holster's nylon fabric. Despite being on assignment in one of the safest locales, it couldn't hurt to carry an added layer of protection. They were, after all, heading to a village which once swarmed with zombies. But five minutes after Chia-hao turned onto the 106 County Road, her issued pistol did little to quell her anxiety. Guns couldn't fix everything.

Being the sole vehicle on a normally congested mountain-road only fueled her unease. She shivered, maybe from the air-conditioning. Most likely from the road-closing signs appearing more frequently.

Chia-hao weaved back and forth around fallen rocks and tree limbs littering the pavement. Weeds had forced their way through the baking asphalt. On each side of the road, brush and tall grasses swayed with the wind. Eight kilometers from Shifen, their driver reached into his glove compartment and retrieved a surgical facemask. He stopped the car to position the mask, knotting the straps behind his head.

From the front passenger-seat, her husband glanced over his shoulder at her, his eyebrows raised, like maybe she knew why the driver was covering his nose and mouth.

She shrugged.

Chia-hao looked up at the rearview mirror. Beads of sweat swam on the driver's forehead, crisscrossing as they descended and moistened his facemask.

"ZOM-B bacteria aren't airborne," Clay said. "We're safe, especially in Taiwan."

"Safe?" Chia-hao's voice was muffled behind the fabric. "The fact that the bioweapon mutated into ZOM-B is more than a bad omen; it is darkly prophetic. Add this to contaminants already depleting the vital energy of our human bodies, which we Taoists call Qi, and more death, and *un*death, are certain. Inevitable, in fact."

"How does the facemask help?" he asked, sounding like he hoped to appear earnest rather than condescending.

Chia-hao put the car in gear and resumed driving toward Shifen. "Since the portal to health is through our mouths, I am filtering what enters. Besides, our breathing is a beacon to the undead. Even though humans are polluting themselves, we are still *alive*. Zombies need the living to replenish the life-force consumed by their infection. To replenish Qi."

"Fair enough." He combed his fingers through his black hair.

Around a blind bend in the road, the sedan's tires screeched and skidded over the pavement. As the tires bit the road, Ruby raised her arms to absorb impact. She slammed into the driver's front-seat.

Clay immediately turned to her. "Are you okay?"

She nodded, scooting to the middle of the back seat, to get a better view through the windshield. A twelve-foot-high chain-linked fence, topped with rows of barbed wire, loomed in front of them. The fence stretched past the vehicle on both sides, getting lost in the mountainous forest, beyond where she could see. A padlocked gate was centered in the road. The entrance was adorned with several signs displaying a black skull, beneath which, two bones were crossed to form an "X." Each sign's canary-yellow background made them impossible to overlook.

"No guards?" Clay asked the driver.

"No need. The Taiwanese people, including the aborigines, want to stay far away from this place." Chia-hao's knuckles were white, as his fingers clutched the steering wheel. "This is my first time here. If I could have refused this assignment, I would not have come."

Ruby sensed his fear, smelling it in his rancid sweat. "But you'll wait while we look around, right?" Being stranded on the deserted road, leading to a town which had been cremated—residents included, would *not* make her day.

"Be assured, Mrs. Spencer: I will wait." Chia-hao exited the vehicle, heading for the gate.

She and Clay opened their car doors and stepped onto the roadway, shutting the doors behind them. The pavement's heat radiated through the soles of her hiking boots. Bringing her baseball cap proved to be a good choice. Unclipping the cap from a belt loop on her shorts, she pulled her ponytail through the cap's back opening, above the adjustable rear-strap, and wiggled the cap into place on her head.

After grabbing their backpacks from the trunk and hoisting them onto their backs, they joined the driver at the gate. Chia-hao's hands were shaking. He fumbled to find the padlock key on his supersized keyring.

"How much farther down the road is Shifen?" she asked.

"About five kilometers, or three miles. Stay straight until you're alongside the river on your left. Take the first right and you'll find what's left of Shifen Old Streets."

She tapped her smartwatch on her wrist. "Remember to videoface or vext—you know, voice text—if you need to contact us. You added our numbers, right?"

After slightly bending at the waist in an upper-body nod, Chia-hao opened the gate. They walked to the other side and headed down the road. The gate squeaked shut behind them. No doubt Chia-hao would find security in his car—facemask in place.

The breeze felt cool on her T-shirt and she loved the sound of wind shuffling through tree branches. The leaves danced. Yet her skin prickled with worry.

"Do you think we'll find anything?" Clay asked.

"Hope so—something to shed light on the living dead. Or at least what happened before the fire."

"Glad we came? I mean, it's good to get out of the house, right?"

"Not sure yet. Because being separated from Gabby is not something I want to get used to. But have you noticed? I've been less gloom-and-doom. Maybe focusing on our assignment, on the science, is helping me."

"That, and you're dealing with your fears head-on—resisting the impulse to shelter-in-place at home, until the crisis passes. Which is more like existing than living. So what you're doing takes courage."

"Let's not get ahead of ourselves. I'm fighting this feeling that something bad is going to happen. While we're here."

"You're worried?" He reached for her hand. "We've got this. Together."

"What if we get *separated*? In a country that's unfamiliar? I don't think I could survive."

"You? The quintessential survivor? You've got nothing to fear."

"Except being alone. Every time I survive, I end-up *the one and only*. Left with guilt and sadness. I can't lose you or Gabby." She blinked, fighting back tears. "I can't be left behind."

Her heart sputtered, and she urged herself to get a grip. Filling her lungs with air, she hoped to dilute the anxiety. She'd been making progress and didn't want to regress.

"Hey. I'm not going anywhere," he said. "Neither is Gabby. But don't forget: being the one and only isn't always bad. Your blood saved the world."

"Until it didn't."

"There was no way of knowing the bioweapon would mutate. And by the way, you're doing that thing you always do."

"What *thing?*"

"You underestimate your significance."

"Not always. Don't forget my obsession two years ago. About being kidnapped? About being ransomed to the highest bidder for my blood? At the time, I was the only one capable of stopping the pandemic. Isn't *that* accepting my significance?"

"Different," he said, striking a stone with his boot and sending the small rock bouncing across the roadway. "The things you obsess about come from fear, not confidence."

"So tell me, how would confidence look?" She winked, hoping to seem playful, to encourage more frankness. After all, one reason she'd accepted this assignment was to help mellow her fears. To bring balance and some normalcy back into her life.

"Confidence is acknowledging you were born to save others. Embrace your gift. Of all the people I've ever known, you're extraordinary. You have real purpose on this planet."

"Can't my purpose be with you and Gabby? What I want is to be the *we*, the *us*, the *they*. An ordinary, safe family. If we get home, I'm hanging up my stint on the SWC."

She couldn't believe she blurted out that she was leaving the Council. All the mental rehearsing…wasted! She paused for his reaction. He might be annoyed. Worse, disappointed. Say she was hiding from her gift. Giving into her fears.

"If…*if* we get home?" he questioned. "You mean…*when*. Hey, we're like Dorothy, Toto, and Kansas; nothing can keep us apart or away from home. Not for long anyway."

"Did you hear what I said? About resigning from the SWC?"

"Of course. And I trust your instincts, as long as they're not driven by fear. But no matter what, I'll always have your back. Now trust *me*. We'll get home safely."

"All we need is our ruby slippers." She smiled. "And a healthy dose of confidence."

"You got it, babe! Emerald City: here we come."

She loved him, so deeply that words were insufficient. She'd already experienced two years of marital bliss, with the man who was her childhood best friend and high school sweetheart, no less. She had to pinch herself sometimes, to remember she wasn't dreaming. Her relationship with Clay was a perfect fit: the *we*. And now they had a baby: the *us*. Bottom line, Clay was right. She needed to regain her confidence. Her fear of losing everything was irrational.

Although the assignment would intrigue her professionally, and the amenities would pamper her alone-time with her husband, she still couldn't wait to board a plane for home on Monday. With or without ruby slippers.

They stopped in their tracks. To their right, twigs snapped. Leaves rustled.

With her heart shifting from first to fourth gear, her right hand hovered over the holster and loaded nine-millimeter. She held her breath, staring into the distance, into the shadowy forest. The crunching of underbrush and breaking of twigs grew louder. On the edge of the woods, bush tops in the thicket shook, announcing that something was on the move. Something was heading their way. With nervous fingers, she unsnapped the strap on her holster.

The tall grasses parted.

Her lungs inflated with fresh air. She held it, before slowly exhaling.

A family of sika deer, with tan coats and white spots, emerged from the dense vegetation. The healthy buck had velvet on his antlered rack. Unaffected by their presence on the neglected road, the buck, doe, and fawn strolled by, nibbling on weeds between the asphalt cracks, crossing the blacktop and entering the woods on the other side.

She resumed walking. "I keep forgetting Taiwan dodged the F8 pandemic. It's strange to see animals free-roaming. Healthy."

"Lucky for them, Huo didn't attack his people or wildlife."

"It's hard not to be envious. Because those deer are thriving. The island clearly offered protection—a buffer from the bioweapon. And without animal infections, the Taiwanese were spared from the mutation. I wish that were the case in other parts of the world."

"Not everyone here fared well. Remember where we're heading. And don't forget about the former Chinese President. Huo's failed one-supreme-ruler scheme left him *undead*."

"Serves him right."

"I'm not looking forward to seeing the zombie-bastard tomorrow." He kicked another stone across the pavement. "Here's what I don't understand: if Huo protected his populace against his own weapons-of-mass-destruction, how did one isolated village manage to contract the ZOM-B mutation? Wouldn't the F8 bacteria need to be present *first?*"

She briefly stopped walking and looked at him. "The Secretary of Defense thinks Huo intentionally infected the villagers to test how the ZOM-B pathogen affects humans."

"Kind of what our government did to Huo, once he was our POW."

"Except Huo wasn't innocent," she said. "With so many deaths on his hands, the least we could do was infect him with his own bioweapon mutation."

"Do you think he knew F8 bacteria would mutate into ZOM-B?"

"Maybe. Maybe not. But when you play God, there's always a price to pay."

"Let's hope we can figure out how to kill Huo's undead sorry-ass with minimal collateral damage. With zombiism on the rise, we need surefire solutions. Ones that don't deplete anymore natural resources."

She pointed to a metal sign displaying an arrow to the Shifen Waterfall and then glanced at her smartwatch. "The village is sixteen minutes ahead, by foot."

Thunder rumbled overhead. Clouds were thickening. A gust raced across the road, bending the grasses and marking its path.

They walked under a deserted overpass. When they emerged on the other side, the smell of burnt wood greeted them, even after so much time had passed. The odor wasn't strong enough to irritate her throat, but it was unpleasant nevertheless. And the fact that the air likely contained zombie-ashes, swirling with the breeze, didn't help.

On the outskirts of Shifen, only blackened tree trunks remained, sticking up from the ground like singed toothpicks. The charred remnants of what was probably the visitor center was on her right, though there wasn't a surviving sign, standing like a tombstone to confirm it.

With a downward view of the village, she saw the exposed framework of buildings and houses, hollowed by fire. On their last day, the intact structures had probably served as coffins for their undead inhabitants.

A breeze slapped at her back, as if impatiently pushing her nearer. Nearer to the villagers' story—one violently reduced to soot and ashes.

"This is no Emerald City," Clay whispered, as if he might disturb the dead.

She stopped. "Listen."

3

Saturday, July 10, 2032
Shifen, Taiwan

CLAY STOOD ON a raised slope in the roadway, studying the charred ruins below. Swirls of dust strutted around scorched frameworks of two-by-fours. The wind whistled like construction workers on break, approving of the scenery passing by.

"I'm not hearing anything," he said to Ruby. "Just the wind."

"Eerie, right? Hard to imagine this was a popular location, teeming with tourists." She dismounted the backpack from her shoulders, swinging the pouch to the blacktop. Unzipping the pack, she rummaged through its contents as he watched. "Here." She offered him a bandana.

Taking the blue scarf, he covered his nose and mouth, tying the ends behind his head. "I guess Chia-hao had the right idea after all."

"Zombie-dust," she said, as she positioned her red scarf, knotting the ends under her ponytail. "Protecting our Qi can't hurt."

"Amen to that."

As they continued to walk, he marveled at how Ruby reminded him of his mother: determined, yet conciliatory; smart, yet relatable; and beautiful, yet natural. That's not to say she didn't lack confidence. Sometimes she trusted others more than her own instincts. The very trait that had compelled his parents to let Mr. Shoemaker drive after an evening out. The same Mr. Shoemaker who savored Manhattans. *The* Mr. Shoemaker who drove onto the highway with Clay's parents in the back seat, going the wrong direction, against traffic. And that's when his normal teenage-life came to a crashing halt.

No denying that he and Ruby also shared a mutual weakness: their peculiar fear of death. While most people were afraid of dying, they feared *surviving* after those whom they loved-or-knew had perished. He had survived his parents' death. She had survived multiple tragedies over her lifetime—almost too many to list. Early on, each of them wondered if their own deaths would've been easier. But what his wife didn't know, what he kept from her to ease her anxiety, was his own lingering obsession. Because every day—every single waking hour—he feared losing his new family. And he would never, could never, survive life without them.

Ruby and Gabby were his world.

Still, his wife never accepted she was special, extraordinary. But he knew. There was something unparalleled about her and he was grateful for it. She was *his* one and only.

When the Keelung River flowed next to the road, he turned right onto Shifen Street, heading toward the center of town. Before their trip, he and Ruby had Googled the village, the way it looked pre-fire. Shifen was someplace he would've visited with her—back when the village had a pulse. Stores and eateries had sandwiched the railroad tracks, showcasing colorful awnings and signs, like lures on a hook. Now, only tracks and gray-stone pavers remained. And dust. Lots of dust.

"You think we'd see some skeletons," she said, scanning the landscape facing north. "Maybe the intense flames destroyed them."

"Maybe." But he had his doubts. He'd seen a show on National Geographic about forest fires. In the open, fire traveled with the wind, seeking new fuel. And even when a fire raged, which this one clearly had, it rarely stayed in one place long enough to reduce human bones—of an entire village—to ashes. So where were the bones?

Behind him, he heard flapping, like a flag. He turned and eyed a kongming sky-lantern, latched to the top of a metal pole, fluttering in the wind. Shifen was famous for releasing the miniature hot-air balloons into the night sky.

"Strange how one thing can survive utter devastation," she said.

"You've been there before. It means the lantern-sock has purpose.

Let's take it back with us."

They walked south along the tracks. As they neared the pole, the images on the sock came into focus. Ghoulish faces—eyes wide, mouths open, exaggerated teeth—were drawn on the fuchsia fabric, along with Mandarin writings. Gave him the creeps.

Using his hands as a stirrup, he hoisted Ruby. She climbed the flagpole and unclasped the lantern-sock, before lowering herself like an inchworm.

"Did you hear that banging sound?" she asked, as her feet touched the ground. She stuffed the sock into her waterproof backpack and looked at him.

"No. From which direction?"

"North, I think." She pointed up the railroad tracks, from where they'd come. "The map on my watch shows an elementary school in that direction, over the hill."

"Let's check it out. Because there's nothing left to examine on this street."

"It hurts me to know that precious children were lost here."

"Same. ZOM-B has no age restrictions. Or heart."

As they walked north and climbed the hill, the banging became steady, rhythmic. Louder as they neared.

Unlike Shifen Old Streets which had been reduced to dust and ashes, some structural remnants remained of the school, like it had been bombed instead of burned. A four-foot-high, white-brick wall sealed the perimeter of the campus. The bricks were topped with steel pickets, some still coated in green paint. Land elevation blocked the view on the other side of the fence.

The school's entrance was foreboding. An expansive brick-casing secured the steel-barred doorway that reminded him of an entrance into a prison cell, not that he'd ever seen one up-close. Industrial-sized locks dangled from thick chains.

"Guess the government didn't want anyone going inside," he said.

"More likely, they didn't want anyone *leaving*."

Leaving? What kind of screwed-up government would infect villagers, including women and children, and then lock them inside an elementary school? Then again, it wasn't like he didn't know the ending. It was like watching remakes of *The Titanic*—the ending never got better. So why was he looking for threads of humanity, of decency, when nothing could minimize the atrocity? Bottom line: the residents of Shifen were used as an experiment and then burned. Nothing made the outcome bearable.

The banging was more like a dog's tail thumping against a door, at evenly spaced intervals.

"Here," he said, picking a low-point in the fencing where several picket prongs had broken off. "Let's enter here." He got a running start and leapt onto the wall. In a seamless movement, he turned sideward through the pickets, pushed off, and landed on the other side. The ground beneath him shifted like an unsettled pile of stones and twigs. Glancing at the ground, he struggled to balance. "Damn it!"

"What?"

Before he could warn her, she climbed onto the brick wall and looked down. Her eyes grew wide with alarm. She saw what he saw. Under his feet and blanketing the lawn near the fence were bones and skulls of every shape and size. Heaped together. Yellow teeth were still anchored in jawbones, looking like they might chatter at any moment.

Ruby jumped back, out of his sight. He climbed onto the wall, wedged himself between the pickets, and landed by her side. His wife was already on her knees, her bandana clutched in her hand, heaving her lunch onto the ground.

"Let it out," he urged, rubbing her back.

He couldn't believe how stupid he'd been to encourage her to accept President Newton's assignment. Recently, her fears about Gabby's safety had been isolating her. She rarely wanted to leave the house. In fact, the last SWC meeting was the first she'd attended in-person, since the baby was born. Up until then, if she participated at all, she'd join the meeting from home via videofacing. So he had rationalized that traveling to one of the safest places would help ease her fears. What the hell was he thinking?

Seeing the bones sparked a blast of clarity. No country, no human—including Ruby, was immune from ZOM-B. He had led her to this dustbowl, to what was once zombie-central, and the risks were greater than he'd imagined. Proof was on the other side of the fence.

Unzipping his backpack, he grabbed a water bottle and handed it to her. Rinsing her mouth with the first swig, she spat the water out. She guzzled the rest, chin up and head back, before lowering her face so he could see her eyes. They were always more intense—greener—when she was upset, like a current ran through them, making them glow. Strands of her hair, those freeing themselves from her ponytail, peeked out from the edges of her baseball cap.

It killed him to see her cry, and he wiped tears from her cheeks. "Listen: you stay here. I'll check out the school and be right back. Promise I'll find some artifacts."

"Can't let you do that," she said, sounding stubborn, as though she was quickly recovering. "We're a team and we have an assignment. Besides, I need to restore my confidence, right?" She placed the emptied bottle in her backpack and zipped it closed. "Seeing the bone graveyard overwhelmed me, that's all. I need to focus on being a scientist, to remember our observations can help."

Spanning their years together, he had learned when there was wiggle room to sway her and when an amoeba couldn't squeeze through. Her change in tone meant she was resolved to continue, and he respected that.

"Any observations so far?" he asked.

"Notice there are no bones on *this* side of the fence? Which means zombies can't process information between the frontal and motor cortexes. The undead are strong and can move; we've witnessed that on videos. But they obviously can't combine thinking and motor skills to solve problems, like climbing fences. Even when they're faced with annihilation."

"Good observation."

"Some of the school is intact. Maybe we can find more clues."

His wife tied her bandana behind her ponytail again. Climbing the wall, she maneuvered herself between the pickets, leaping onto the bones. A puff of dust lifted and swirled away in a miniature ash-tornado. He followed her as she headed toward the back of the dilapidated building, where cinderblock walls remained.

The steady rapping continued.

Now that they were closer to the sound, Clay felt uneasy. He unholstered his nine-millimeter, catching Ruby's look of confusion.

"Precaution. That's all."

He may have underestimated the risk involved in the assignment, but he sure as hell wasn't going to place his wife in danger by being caught off-guard.

She nodded, continuing to walk toward the back of the structure.

"There," he said, pointing to a black metal door. "The sound's emanating from behind that door. But let's inspect the area first, before we try and open it."

The thumping stopped. Only the whistle of the wind averted the silence.

They walked around the enclosed space, the size of a closet, examining the cinderblock walls which were intact. As they moved, the thumping resumed, only faster. With more force.

"What could that be?" she asked.

"Maybe an animal, like a dog, was scavenging for food and got trapped. Because I don't think a zombie could've survived incineration. Do you?"

"The lantern-sock survived."

He eyed her as she pulled the pistol from her holster and cocked the action.

"Stand back and I'll swing the door open," she said. "I'll move to the side, so shoot if you need to. Nod as a green light."

He readied his pistol and dipped his chin.

The door couldn't have been locked because he watched her easily open it.

"What the…" He jolted back in defense, his heart pounding in his chest. Not only was he assaulted by a stench of rotting flesh, but a male zombie—an actual *zombie*—with flaking gray skin and shredded clothing like a river birch, was advancing on him. The bastard's teeth chattered, rapidly clicking together, before releasing a deep guttural-moan, like a pocket of stale air had raced up his rusted windpipe and irritated his vocal cords. His eyes were like tar.

Backing up, his mind froze, like even his brain synapses were in shock.

"Shoot!" she yelled.

Of all the times to stumble on debris, he had to do it now. As he fell backwards, though, he managed to fire a shot, striking the zombie's lower torso. But the undead never hesitated, not for a second. Maybe the caliber was too small? One thing was clear: the *pop* of the discharge instantly stimulated him, like he had downed two cups of joe in a blink of an eye.

"Again," she cried.

This time he wouldn't miss. Scooting backwards over the rubble by pushing with the heels of his boots, he increased the distance between him and the zombie. Because if he didn't, the freak was going to drop on him with those gnashing teeth. Taking precise aim, he fired at the zombie's heart. Hitting its target, the aberration stopped for a moment. But the ghoul didn't drop. He resumed his forward motion. What the...

"Move out of the way," she ordered.

Clay rolled to the side as Ruby whistled. The zombie stopped, turning to face her. Raising her pistol, his wife fired at the zombie's skull. On impact, the undead toppled on his back, onto the concrete slab. His limbs violently twitched for a few seconds, before stilling completely. Black goo splattered around him.

Thank God her shooting was always drop-dead accurate.

As Clay rose to his feet, his wife holstered her pistol and engulfed him in a hug. He clutched her, bringing her head against his chest. "Now *that* was unexpected," he said, grateful that his clumsiness hadn't resulted in her getting hurt. "We've learned something else."

"Don't fall shooting a zombie?" She delivered a crooked smile.

"Funny. Not funny ha-ha, but funny like crush-me-when-I'm-down and need my wife to rescue me! Thank you, by the way."

"Aw, you're welcome." She released him. "To answer your question: we've learned that they drop when shot in the head. Come to think of it, that makes sense. Since the motor and sensory strips appear to be the only areas of the brain still functioning, if you destroy their brains, you kill them. Once and for all."

Stepping over the zombie, they walked back to the closet.

A ceramic coating glazed the interior steel-paneling. "This closet is fire-resistant," he said, rubbing his hand along the smooth but sooty finish.

Under a metal chair, Ruby reached for a journal. From his vantage point, the edges of its pages looked charred.

"The pages are brittle," she said, slowly flipping through the journal. "But look...the Mandarin writing goes from meticulously neat to sloppy and illegible toward the end."

"Maybe our ruby slippers?"

"Absolutely." She grabbed a plastic baggy from her backpack and placed the journal inside, zipping the baggy closed before lowering it into her backpack.

Lightning flashed like a strobe.

"We'd better head back or Chia-hao will worry," she said.

"I'll videoface him." Clay attempted to voice-activate his smartwatch, but the black screen remained. A digital voice notified him that the device had no signal.

Ruby touched her device's screen, but it relayed the same message.

The sudden lack of telecommunications reminded him of Huo's reign of terror, after the lunatic had commandeered the airwaves, releasing high-pitched frequencies to activate the brain-implanted nanobots—the REDs—in unsuspecting victims. Clay's body temperature elevated, as if it could get any higher. Would the mental and physical triggers associated with World War III ever ease up? As was the case with his wife, PTS was under his skin, constantly itching.

Black goo oozed from the zombie. The thick liquid looked alive, escaping from the body and creeping, like reaching fingers, inching over the concrete. He had been told the tar-like goo left a zombie corpse in search of a new host. Talk about getting the creeps—like on steroids.

Clay retrieved lighter fluid from his backpack and doused the body, setting it ablaze.

When they exited the school—leaving the zombie engulfed in flames, the clouds ripped open. On the 106 County Road, he and Ruby walked in a downpour, making the trek slow. They neared the fence forty-five minutes later. The sedan was waiting. At least the guy had kept his word. As they approached, Chia-hao unlocked the padlock. He looked relieved to see them and nodded a greeting as they walked through the opened gate.

After they found refuge in the car, Ruby removed the lantern-sock from her backpack. Pointing to the writing on the fabric, she asked their driver to translate.

The gap between Chia-hao's eyebrows narrowed. "It says," he started cautiously, as if saying the words out-loud might make them real, "*The world is damned. Death is rising.*" The guide locked eyes with her. "Did anything else happen that I should know about?"

Clay peered through the windshield—blurred by the rain, wondering if a billow of smoke might had tipped-off their driver that they had lit a fire, that something clearly had *happened*. But no smoke. Maybe he'd heard the gunfire?

"Well..." Ruby started.

"No. Nothing," he interrupted, before she answered. "Shifen was burned to the ground as you suspected. Only the lantern-sock survived."

Knowing his wife as he did, she would've trusted their driver with detailed information about the zombie and journal. And did they really know Chia-hao's motivations? Or his boss's or government's? No, best to reserve the debriefing for the POTUS.

Chia-hao had no more questions. His shoulders relaxed. But for the entire drive back to the Ruifang District, the guy wore his surgical facemask, probably thinking he and Ruby were contaminated from the village of zombie dust.

Which wasn't far from the truth.

4

Saturday, July 10, 2032
The American Consulate: Taipei, Taiwan

LIEUTENANT COLONEL QUINTON Oxford sat at his laminate wood desk—on a non-cushioned, fold-up chair—in a cramped office (as in shoe-box small), with a Walmart fan recycling stale air. Ironic, since he had earned enough chest candy in the Marine Corps that dear, boring Aunt Betty could have sewn him a quilt the size of Russia. After all, he was the proud recipient of the coveted Medal of Honor, for fuck's sake. As well as the Distinguished Flying Cross. In fact, symbols of excellence in the form of ribbons and medals were plastered all over his Service Dress Blues: exceptional meritorious service, distinguished heroism, exceptional performance of duty…blah, blah, blah. And for what? He had risked his life in combat for an extra four-hundred-greenbacks a month? If he had known the MOH only yielded chump change, he might have left his wingman pilot bleeding-out in the streets of Aleppo after their single-seat F/A-18 Hornets were shot down.

And what really pinched his balls was that Ambassador Jon Jeffries who sat in a leather high-back chair, with swivel and tilt, behind a mahogany desk resting on an oriental, enjoying an AC unit blowing cool air, had served a four-year stint in the Navy, behind a desk. Well, ain't that something.

Of course, he had opted to finish his longstanding career as a military attaché at the American Consulate in Taipei. But a man like him got bored easily. And embittered.

26

He eyed the time before unstrapping his government-issued smartwatch and shoving it into the desk drawer. Did the National Security Council, Homeland Security, and the International Security Agency really think he didn't know that he could be traced at any time? Or have his conversations recorded? Or that the agencies were itching to do both because their trust in him was eroding like a riverbank during the monsoon? It twisted his gut that he answered to idiots who were on a higher paygrade.

At 1400 hours, he would receive a call on his personal, encrypted cellphone—archaic, but effective—in the center of Zhuchang Park, near the consulate. Outsmarting his superiors was the only thing that gave him a hard-on anymore. Well, almost.

After adjusting his Navy hat, leaving his office, and locking the door, he walked past "Jonny Ambassador's" door and into the reception area, nodding at twenty-something Patti Davis who was working the front desk. He wondered if her panties were moist and what they smelled like. Maybe he'd find out soon, before the opportunity slipped away forever.

Outside, he walked with his back straight and stiff, like he was a general. Marines Wyatt and Insley, who both showed promise, were manning the gate. But he already knew that. They were his men. Men who would die for him and his cause. And they weren't the only ones.

Wyatt and Insley saluted and he returned the gesture, touching the brim of his hat.

"Sir," Corporal Wyatt said. "Let me get the gate, sir."

Ox nodded, smiling internally, but wearing sternness. This was why he hadn't retired. He loved the power of the military. Because in what universe would he be shopping in a grocery store among civilians, letting people treat him as though he were average, just another dickwad trying to find a ripe peach. The optics were bullshit. He'd never return to civilian life. Which is why he had nothing to lose.

After a three-minute walk, he sat on a bench in Zhuchang Park, with two minutes to spare. The breeze had picked up and the thick air felt like an afternoon thunderstorm was in the works. Would Vladimir Volkov, the Russian President, be ready to execute his end of the deal?

The cellphone rang. He pressed the touch screen before holding the device to his ear.

"Ox here."

"My friend!" Vladimir said, as he talked and laughed simultaneously.

The man was jolly Old Saint Nick—long white hair and a rounded belly, but ticking with the heart of a troll, waiting under the bridge to strike the unsuspecting.

"Good to hear your voice," Vladimir continued. "Now to business: has the girl arrived in Taiwan?"

"Affirmative. She's here with her husband, as expected."

"Are we on-schedule for their arrival in Moscow on Monday? My staff is anxious to examine this American. I am looking forward to surprising her."

Like he thought: troll.

"Landing in Moscow will undoubtedly be her first surprise," Ox said. "But we may have a complication. A storm is brewing in the East China Sea. NOAA has projected the typhoon will change directions and head toward Keelung."

"Most unfortunate. Is Decha monitoring the situation?"

"Of course. But the schedule has not been altered. He will visit the port tomorrow. To tie-up…loose-ends in the city."

"Will you accompany Decha?"

"Negative." Ox rolled his eyes, a benefit not available with videofacing—where the person on the other end saw physical reactions. But seriously: what did Vladimir think? Ox could wander the island without accountability or notice? He was a highly-decorated Lieutenant Colonel in the U.S. Marines, for fuck's sake. Now, he *could*, of course, if he had to—Ox commanded a willing team who'd cover for him, but he wanted to save that level of maneuvering for Ruby Never-Dies (or whatever-the-hell she was called) and her detoured flight to Moscow. "Decha doesn't need my help; he is *the brains* of this operation, remember?"

"Or so the man says!" Vladimir laughed until he choked.

"By the way, the President assigned two Marines from the consulate to keep the girl safe during her visit. From an undetectable distance."

The troll stopped laughing. Silence passed between them, which was good. Ox wanted to remind his partner that he—Quinton Oxford—was the one indispensable.

"Most unfortunate," Vladimir said.

"My bad. Did I forget to mention the Marines are *my* men?"

Ox heard the Russian release a stream of air. "Amusing then!" he chuckled. "I believe you Americans call that…ironic. Yes?"

Partners in crime were always peculiar. Usually they were alphas, playing-nice to get the job done. And when the mission was completed and the need for camaraderie exhausted itself, they turned on each other. The last-man-standing syndrome. Which Ox had mastered. And he had no plans of changing his record. *Oorah.*

"One more question," Vladimir said. "Will the weather change the flight itinerary for the girl?"

"Storm or no storm, the consulate is responsible for transporting the Spencers to the airport—that won't change. The word came from Ava Newton herself. If the when changes, I'll contact you. But our plan will happen either way."

"Прощай, my friend"

"*Prosh-chay* to you, Vladimir."

5

Sunday, July 11, 2032
Mandarin Oriental Hotel: Taipei, Taiwan

AT SUNRISE, WITH an empty glass of water by her nightstand, Ruby woke from a restful sleep on the plush bed in their hotel suite, serenaded by the rhythmic hum of air conditioning. During the night, she remembered rising to use the bathroom. She probably could've waited—her bladder was accustomed to being full until morning, but she couldn't resist taking advantage of her ability to flush at will. Amazing how much appreciation she'd acquired for flushing, something she'd never take for granted again.

Rolling onto her side, toward the window overlooking the city and mountains beyond, she frowned; it was gray and raining outside. And Clay was no longer in bed. But light twinkled behind the frosted glass doors of the bathroom, one that included a rainforest shower and a separate deep-soaking tub. Before they checked out tomorrow, they needed to indulge in both.

Tossing off the silky bedsheets, she walked across the room and slid the glass pocket-door along its track.

Her husband stood in front of the mirror, shaving.

"Good morning, sunshine," he cooed.

"Sunshine? It's dreary outside."

"Umm…you brighten my world?" He winked, before putting down his razor.

Reaching for her, he placed his hands on her waist and pulled her against him. She looked up, inviting his lips to meet hers. When they did, he gently pulled on her top lip, then her bottom. She opened her mouth and they explored each other with their tongues. It never got old.

When their heat almost took them back to bed, despite being on a tight schedule, he placed his hands on her shoulders and slightly pulled back. "Did you sleep well?"

"I woke up occasionally. Didn't want to miss hearing and feeling the AC or seeing the light in the hallway from under our bedroom door. Weird, right?" She grabbed her hairbrush. "Hey, would you mind if we called Margo and Tomas again? I want to check on Gabby. See how she's doing."

"I'm all in. I bet she's gained at least a pound since yesterday."

"I left strict instructions."

He smiled. "And Margo knows to explicitly follow them."

"No doubt." She winked. "So how'd you sleep?"

"Not great. I kept seeing Huo's face, imagining what he will look like as a *mature* zombie. Suffice it to say, the vision was horrific."

"He's a nightmare, alright. But like you've been telling me: we'll get through this together." She pulled her hair into a ponytail and secured it with a band.

"Are you looking forward to meeting with the scientific team?"

"I'm curious about their organic data. About how their findings might help us destroy this bizarre phenomenon." She dabbed gloss on her lips. "We can't forget...before we leave for the base, we have a morning conference with the President."

President Newton had scheduled a videoface session. Ruby was glad she had charged the laptop overnight, to be on the safe side. The government-issued device would connect them with the POTUS, via the Intelligent Service System Interface (ISSI) network: advanced, self-contained U.S. middleware that streamed real-time telecommunications from a stealth satellite, providing secure off-the-grid connections. Only problem was that the system took about ten minutes for signal acquisition. In addition, access required retinal scans and two separate security codes. But she wouldn't complain. ISSI, which was one-hundred percent American-made, was a key player in defeating Huo and his ruthless regime during the war.

After the virtual conference, they had an afternoon appointment at the temporary U.S. Naval Base in the port-city of Keelung. The compound was located on the outskirts of the harbor, hidden in the woods of Yizheng Park, where the undead Huo was celled, along with a CDC-worker turned zombie.

For the day's itinerary, she dressed in shorts and a sleeveless blouse—both black. The color would mask moisture from the humidity and rain, which would greet them the second they left the hotel. After lacing her hiking boots, she grabbed her money clip which secured cash, her ID, their keycard for the suite, and firearm permits. She stuffed the clip into her front pocket, beside a bandana.

Clay dressed into shorts and a golf shirt. "I was thinking," he said, pulling on his boots. "If the zombie phenomenon proliferates, the undead won't be a formidable enemy, right? You saw that zombie yesterday. He didn't have sufficient brain java to open the closet door. Which was unlocked."

"If brains were everything, I'd agree."

"They're not?"

"We're smarter than scorpions by a long shot, but would you want to face an angry horde of them? More importantly, would you survive?"

"Ouch."

"There's more. Once humans die from the ZOM-B infection, they reanimate. In three. Short. Minutes. What enemy multiplies at that rate? And once the undead are walking, seems they only drop when shot in the head. Think about an approaching swarm of zombies. What are the odds of shooting each one in the head before the group closes in?"

"Now I'm worried."

"And…the minute they smell blood, they morph out of their stupors and become bloodlust killers."

"We'd better stay ahead of the curve or we're in deep trouble."

"Exactly."

"Remind me why I encouraged you to accept this assignment?" He ran his fingers through his hair. Creases formed on his forehead.

"Because you understand there are two ways to protect Gabby. One is to avoid the world by being a shut-in; I've mastered that strategy lately. The other is to aggressively pursue the problem. Find the root cause and then annihilate it. I mean, how long will our home truly be safe if the crisis globally persists and multiplies? Hiding is no protection. Safety requires *action*. And you helped open my eyes."

"My plan all along!" He smiled. "Smart of me, right?"

"Don't get me wrong: I can't wait to board the plane tomorrow. I miss Gabby so much—a piece of me is missing. It's just that now, I appreciate how important this trip is. The need to come here was larger than ourselves."

"Agreed."

"Unfortunately," she said, "I still can't shake this nagging feeling that something's going to interfere with getting home. Maybe wanting something so badly increases the fear of not getting it."

"Let's face it: exposure to zombies is unsettling, especially since the U.S. won't be spared for long. So fear is screwing with us. But we'll rise above it. Gabby will be in our arms soon. Come hell or high water."

The bathroom lights flickered.

"Seriously?" She trotted from the bathroom and bedroom, down the hallway, heading toward the expansive Art Deco living-room which boasted ceiling-to-floor windows overlooking the city. Her eyes widened when she looked outside. *Come hell or high water?* Clearly the high water had arrived. Blowing sideways, the rain beaded on the glass. Below on the streets, pooled water swelled with each gust of wind, like rolling waves over asphalt.

"What happened to the weather?" she shouted to Clay, over her shoulder toward the bathroom, more like a statement than question.

Her heart jolted as a flash of lightning lit the living room.

6

PRESIDENT NEWTON WAS tired of fielding calls from anxious Special Warfare Council members. They'd seen international weather-forecasts and were whining, once again, about Ruby's safety. If World War III could be won in seven days, storms should be considered a minor complication.

Apparently, Luther Pennington, her National Security Advisor, saw things differently. Fifteen minutes ago, at 8:45 p.m., he insisted the record reflect that as SWC chair, he had repeatedly discouraged sending the girl to Taiwan. Most annoyingly, his tone resonated paternal concern, like he was motivated by something noble, rather than strategic.

She almost laughed out loud. Luther, noble?

Maybe "the record" should reflect that the SWC had hatched its offensive against ZOM-B in secret—intentionally excluding the Spencers. Announcing that fact would expose his phony fatherly-theatrics. The SWC was obsessed with a singular objective: restore America's rightful place as the leading superpower. And the rising threat of the undead could not be ignored if their objective was to reach fruition. Therefore, any strategy or tactic advancing the cause—legal or illegal, moral or immoral, transparent or covert—was fair game. War was war, people!

If she did say so herself, sending Ruby and her sidekick husband to Taiwan was ingenious. The Council had to be blind not to notice

34

the girl's waning interest in the SWC. Sitting around a table, talking to Washington's finest and watching zombie videos, submitted by the WHO and CDC, was hardly competing with motherhood and marriage. The signs of disengagement were blinking fluorescent-yellow. Over the last three months, the girl had participated in SWC meetings via videofacing. Couldn't tear herself away from "the child" to brainstorm with the President of the United States, for God's sake! Even skipped several meetings altogether. And when she finally blessed the Council with her presence at the last meeting, she barely paid attention.

Unlike the naysayers in the SWC—the ones who wanted to insulate and coddle the girl, which would surely end with her Council resignation—the President understood her. Not the having-a-child part: her ovaries had dried to raisins five-years ago, having never found acceptable sperm with which to produce offspring. No, she understood what *motivated* Ruby. Before she was appointed to the SWC, the girl had thrived in the field, thrived trying to save humankind from itself. Most certainly, the Taiwan experience would bring the girl back into the fold. Right where they needed her. Accessible.

Because the new Extinction Level Infection was far worse than its F8 predecessor. This ELI would not only end humanity, it would *replace* humanity. And even though the girl's blood was susceptible to ZOM-B like everyone else's, the SWC was focusing outside the box. Through their eyes, the girl stood—once again, as the singular beacon of hope.

Unbeknownst to the Spencers, Ruby was their blood supply for an innovative project. A project so classified that only the SWC members had clearance, excluding the girl and her husband. That meant nine individuals knew in the entire government. In the world, for that matter.

Despite the scolding from Council members for sending Ruby halfway around the globe—granted a slight uptick in risk, the President had taken precautions, about which the SWC had been briefed. First, she had personally contacted two ambitious Marines at the consulate in Taipei: Corporal Wyatt and Lance Corporal Insley. She might have overstepped, but as their Commander in Chief, she promised them fast-track promotions if they kept a watchful eye on the Spencers during their visit on the island. Of course, the Spencers would never catch wind of it.

Secondly, when Ruby and Clayton received immunizations for travel abroad, microscopic locator-chips were injected with the serum—and only ISSI detected them. Activating the chips, however, would be a last resort. The SWC didn't want to leave a scent for the underling hounds of the NSA, CIA, and FBI—those G-men who needed to prove themselves by sniffing down every trail. Their critical project had to remain airlocked. Not even the Spencers were aware they carried ISSI chips. And she planned to keep it that way.

The intercom system in the Oval Office beeped once. Her secretary's voice announced that Dr. Emory Bradshaw requested a word. *A word?* This time of night? The Seymour tall-case mahogany clock was chiming; it was already nine o'clock.

"Send him in."

Emory strolled into her office, confident and charming, wearing his white scrubs and starched lab coat. Every time she saw him, which was frequently these days since she had moved his high-tech lab into the West Wing—near the Situation Room, she affirmed her peculiar attraction. Why she lusted after him, in the first place, was beyond understanding. He was younger, half her age. Moreover, he was gay. How was it that his sexual appeal was transmitting to the opposite gender?

She supposed her attraction was boosted by his brains and demeanor. Admiring others was rare, yet he impressed her. His look contributed: his eyes were like wheat-fields at harvest; his skin, a silky chocolate-brown. But the cherry on top, the crème de la crème, was that Emory was a radical innovator. A rebel at heart. Someone who didn't shy from dark science.

"Take a seat, Emory," she said, pointing to the chair next to the Resolute desk.

"Thank you, Madam President."

"It's late and we're alone. Call me Ava and I'll call you Em. What's on your mind?"

He cleared his throat. "I need more hemoglobin."

"Excuse me?" Her face instantly flushed. "No. *You* gave me the green light to send the girl to Taiwan, to rekindle her interest in the Council while preventing her from snooping around. This project is earmarked for completion while she's away. A timeline *you* set, I might add. And now…now that she's halfway around the world, you're telling me you need more blood? Are you kidding me?"

"No, Ava. There's nothing funny or humorous about my statement. It's simply a fact."

"Then explain yourself."

He shifted in the chair, not nervously as she'd hoped, but to get closer, as if to show he wasn't intimidated.

"I wasn't successful in my first attempts," he stated flatly. "Consequently, I used more blood than anticipated. And since I'm doing something that has never been done, not in all of humankind, I'm hoping you'll spend more time collaborating about a solution than wasting time placing blame."

Should she stomp on his arrogant insubordination or deal with the problem?

"I assume you have a suggestion to initiate this…*collaboration*?" she asked.

"Bring her back a day early. It makes sense anyway. The weather is worrisome."

"So I've been told." She rolled her eyes. "It's a storm for Christ's sake."

"As per the latest update from NOAA: the *typhoon* has turned toward Keelung. Landfall is slated for Sunday evening, their time. Sounds more like a valid concern. Am I right?"

"Okay. Okay. I'll bring them back early. Then what? You were using her leftover blood, stored in modified-atmosphere packaging, from when you and Ruby developed an F8 cure. How do you plan on drawing fresh blood now, without getting her suspicious? Without her asking questions?"

"After they arrive at the White House, before they debrief with you about their trip," he answered, "have them receive a comprehensive physical."

"By comprehensive, you mean requiring blood being drawn?"

"Now we're…*collaborating*." He smiled, quite irresistibly. "Isn't this fun?"

"Such a smartass." She couldn't decide if he was flirting. "So what if they protest?"

"Tell Ruby I've recommended a thorough blood analysis. After all, going to Shifen and the Naval base means they've been exposed to ZOM-B. They wouldn't want to risk their baby's health by not taking every precaution. Believe me: she won't argue."

"Done." She glanced at the clock again. "I'm scheduled to videoface with Ruby and Clayton in under an hour, which is Sunday morning, China Standard Time. I'll advise them of the change in plans. First, I need to speak with my Chief of Staff, to arrange for their transport back to the States." She stood.

He followed suit and rose from the chair. "Thank you, Ava." The crystal in his nose-piercing caught the light from her desk lamp. Why was she always attracted to the impossible? Because years ago, she would have considered *his* sperm for offspring.

After Emory left her office, she summoned Christian, tasking her Chief of Staff with securing a flight for the Spencers, a day early, from Taiwan's Taoyuan International Airport. In addition, she moved her video conference with the couple, up by a half-hour.

Christian assured her all would be handled. He was forty, available, and good looking. Figures her Chief of Staff was of no interest to her. Easy meat, she called him in the privacy of her thoughts. Of course, workplace relationships were frowned upon— she had lectured the staff incessantly. Kudos to her that she wasn't attracted to him. Besides, she couldn't risk losing him after she got bored, no matter how promising he was in the sack. The man was invaluable.

At 9:29 p.m., the digital clock on the President's laptop showed one minute and counting. She fiddled with papers before sipping water to clear her voice. The laptop's royal-blue screen faded to a live image.

"Good morning—your time, Ruby and Clayton," the President said. "Hope my schedule-change didn't inconvenience you."

"Not at all," Ruby replied. "We're glad you could still make time for us."

"Actually, *time* precipitated the earlier debriefing. Seems we're running out of it. Low pressure in the East China Sea developed into a significant storm and the prevailing winds have shifted. Keelung is now in the typhoon's path. I'd like to move your appointment to visit the Naval base to eleven o'clock this morning, to be on the safe side. It's time to wrap-up the Huo project ahead of the storm's landfall. Then we can fly you back this evening—your time."

The couple looked at each other and smiled.

"I can see by your expressions," the President added, "that returning home ahead-of-schedule is not a problem. I'm sure Gabriella will appreciate your shortened assignment. Okay then, please debrief me on your visit to Shifen."

Ruby explained that she and Clay had found a zombie in the village. They learned that shooting the undead corpse in the head had effectively destroyed it. After detailing the science behind the tactic's success, the young scientist mentioned *their* theory—though the President doubted Clayton's analytical savvy was on-par with his wife's—that zombies had diminished frontal-brain activity and were unable to problem-solve the simplest challenges, like turning a doorknob. In addition, noise stimulated the undead.

The girl relayed information, most of which was already known. As Ruby spoke, her eyes were alive; her expressions, energized. She was engaged alright. Sending her out into the field had been wise. Storm or no storm.

As the girl concluded her report, she mentioned she and Clayton would be bringing home two artifacts: a journal and lantern-sock.

"Three. You'll be bringing back three artifacts," President Newton corrected.

"Three?"

"Yes. We need to investigate your theory that the ZOM-B pathogen only preserves the motor and sensory cortexes, so you need to bring a zombie's head home. I'm sure Emory would appreciate a close inspection. The head will still be…still be *functioning* if we remove the rest of the body, correct?"

"If the brain remains intact, it'll adapt," Ruby answered.

"Curious: why wouldn't the brain cavity bleed-out?"

"The only zombies that bleed-out are those whose brains have been destroyed. In that scenario, the goo seeks a new host. Otherwise, to ensure the 'live' zombie retains its life-force (its ZOM-

B), the black tar hardens to a crust-like lava, sealing wounds and keeping the active part of the brain *alive*. So the detached zombie-head should survive, without stress."

"Good. It's settled then," the President said. "I'll speak to my medical attaché at the base. He'll have the zombie head—from the undead CDC-scientist, God rest his soul—transported to the consulate to be returned to the States on your flight back. Will the head need to be iced?"

In any other conversation, at any point in time preceding September 2031, the question would've been absurd. But the zombie phenomenon was changing everything. *Normal* no longer existed. And the President had no intentions of falling behind, of becoming obsolete. No, she'd stay ahead of the curve. And to do so, she had procured the right team to drive the engines of innovation—the only strategy which gave humankind a fighting chance.

Ruby answered her question by explaining that if a zombie could survive scorching heat inside a closet, she was certain a head could survive within a room-temperature cooler.

President Newton couldn't help glancing at Clayton while his wife spoke. Sweet Mother of Jesus, he was gorgeous—olive skin, black hair, blue eyes. But how much of Clayton Spencer was limited to eye-candy? After all, he yielded to his wife more times than not, letting her do most of the talking.

Christian entered the room, sauntered across the Oval Office, and leaned over to whisper in her ear. The President smiled. "Perfect," she said, returning her focus to the laptop screen. "I've received confirmation that a helicopter will pick you up at five o'clock this evening (your time), near the consulate in Zhuchang Park. That's where you'll pick up the zombie...*package*. You'll be airlifted to TPE Airport, to board a government jet home. My Chief of Staff, Christian, will contact you if deteriorating weather warrants another change in plans."

"What will happen to Huo?" Ruby asked.

"The base has numerous tests planned for him today. In fact, during your visit—before you meet with our scientists, why don't you observe his reactions? And when testing is complete, Clayton can shoot him in the head. Let's test your theory one more time."

"I'll be happy to comply with that order, Madam President," Clayton said, smiling.

The Greek god speaks.

"Thought you'd like that." The President moved closer to the laptop's video lens. "No need to alarm you, but be cautious if you encounter Lieutenant Colonel Quinton Oxford; he's been known to drop-in at the base. Or you might see him at the consulate. Limit your interactions with him. Ambassador Jeffries has informed me that our military attaché, who's known as Ox, is under investigation, though he is unaware. Stay alert around the man. I no longer trust him, at least, not until suspicions about his…connections…have been discredited."

The military attaché was the President's only legitimate concern. Ox could throw a monkey wrench into her plans and priorities, if the Ambassador's warnings of suspected espionage were accurate. Of course, exaggeration was probably at play. The Ambassador had a flair for it. At least she had managed to keep the investigation a secret from the SWC, or she'd have to dish out Valium to Council members, just to calm their Ruby's-in-danger jitters.

"Thank you for the warning," the girl said. "Before we disconnect, have any ZOM-B outbreaks been reported in the Lower Forty-eight?"

"It's a fluid situation and we've had a few scares. Nothing more. Right now, we're stressing education—training hospitals, law enforcement, and schools about prevention and symptom identification. We're also establishing multiple fortified-camps across the nation, should a pandemic erupt. Our citizens are getting nervous. Your cellular analysis and behavioral observations are more important than you might think." She glanced at her smartwatch. "So good luck…and God bless you, our military, and our Country."

The laptop screen blinked to royal blue.

7

Sunday, July 11, 2032
Keelung, Taiwan

AT THE KEELUNG train station, sitting inside a base-issued van, Seaman Frank Davis waited for the Spencers. Painted nondescript white, the vehicle's windshield wipers worked like pendulums at hyper-speed. His mind kept pace. What station would he be assigned to after the ZOM-B experiments concluded? Which according to his intel, would be today, ahead of the typhoon.

Ever since he'd enlisted in the Navy after high school graduation, he'd been on land. Maybe it was time to deploy on a destroyer, aircraft carrier, or amphibious assault ship. Something with guns and missile launchers—a BGB: Big Gray Boat. All those years of video gaming, simulating war games at sea, could finally pay off.

Then again, he'd have trouble leaving his twin. She worked at the consulate in Taipei, as secretary to the Ambassador. Whatever station he sought next, he needed to keep Patti in mind.

Frank heard a knock on the van's window and waved for the couple to enter. To his surprise, they looked his age: mid-twenties. The girl was typical Yankee: chestnut-blonde hair—pulled into a ponytail, smooth skin without gobs of makeup, a few freckles, a smile that made you want to know her, and green eyes—okay, so they weren't typical. Back at the base, he had asked questions about her and learned she was "East Coast," with a fancy degree in microbiology, and like, she graduated second in her class from some highfalutin university. Impressive, but intimidating: smarts and beauty made him feel inadequate. Of course, science was also his jam, though he had nothing to show for it, no degree or anything like that. Maybe when he discharged from the Navy, he'd use the GI Bill to pay for some schooling.

Her husband looked Greek-*ish*, the model-type, but having enough brawn to notice. With blinding white teeth and blue eyes that looked like the Arizona sky, the guy made it hard for Sailors like Frank to compete. At least Clay Spencer was off the market.

The couple had to be movers and shakers. Who else got a personal invitation to a classified base by none-other-than President Newton herself? Or piqued the interest of the all-powerful Ox—who held the monopoly on asswipe-ed-ness?

After introductions, Frank pulled onto Zhongzheng Road, located at the base of Keelung Harbor, at its most inland point. Several minutes later, he turned off the main roadway toward Yizheng Park, a park that showcased decommissioned weaponry from multiple branches of the Chinese military. Surrounded by tropical woods, it was the perfect cover for a top-secret Naval compound. Totally cool.

"I wonder why the Taiwanese government allowed the U.S. to establish a base in this historical park?" Ruby asked him.

"They want to learn more about the undead, too, while having us foot the bill. You know?" Frank looked at her in the rearview mirror. "Besides, they hated Huo as much as everyone else did. And it can't hurt that we're in a military park. They probably want to remind us whose country we're in."

"Does the public know about the base?" her husband asked.

"Nah. Apparently, questioning isn't part of the Taiwanese or Chinese cultures. But we've taken precautions anyway. Aircraft are diverted around the area: a no-fly zone. And to the amateur visitor, the park looks like it always has. You'll see."

"Any updates on the typhoon?" she asked.

"We're used to rain around here, so no one's worried," he answered. "They're talking about landfall in the middle of the night. Flooding and losing electricity are our main concerns. But we've got pumps on-hand if there's flooding, as well as generator backup. You can't screw around when zombies are in the house. If you catch my drift."

"Any worry about the winds?" she followed-up.

"Nah. It's early in the typhoon season; the winds should be manageable. No worries, Ma'am."

On park grounds, Frank pulled the van over on the shoulder. "In position," he vexted into his smartwatch. "Ready for the underpass."

He watched as the couple's eyes grew wide with curiosity. All they could see, on both sides of the road, were thick woods. So they were probably thinking…*Underpass? What underpass?* Made him chuckle.

"Coast is clear," a voice responded. "Stand by."

To the right of the van, a rectangular parcel of land, about the size of a neighborhood American driveway, began to rise on thick pylons, trees and tropical shrubs included, creating an underpass.

"Are you kidding me?" Clay said, staring out the window.

"I know, right? Good old American know-how." He smiled. "The vegetation is artificial, of course, with shorter trees, but it looks real to drivers passing by. Technology: got to love it!" He drove under the raised platform and onto a driveway concealed with Cycas leaves.

He eyed the rearview mirror. Ruby turned, looking behind her as the parcel of land lowered back into place.

"If electricity goes out, can the generators operate that entrance?" she asked him. "Can vehicles still get out?"

"Oh yeah. The United States Navy does not like to be trapped, Ma'am."

It always felt stealth, driving down the long, narrow driveway which led to the camouflaged facility with a flat roof. On the ground, raised satellite dishes, a dozen or more, all painted in camo, reminded him of oversized mushrooms with inside-out caps.

He parked the van and shutoff the engine.

"Follow me inside, please," Frank said, exiting the vehicle. He opened Ruby Spencer's passenger door and darted for the entrance in a downpour. The winds were picking up.

After buzzing the three of them inside, Seaman Summer Getz, standing behind the lobby desk, saluted them. "Welcome to our temporary Keelung Naval Base," she said, sounding formal and chipper, as if she worked at a hotel's front desk. "We've been expecting you, Mr. and Mrs. Spencer. I'll need your handguns and smartwatches before Seaman Davis escorts you to the observation room." She pushed a plastic basket toward them, sliding it across the desktop.

Frank caught Ruby flashing her husband a look, like she was questioning the request.

"Standard protocol," Getz snapped, with iciness in her tone. The Getz that *he* knew.

Getz, in fact, was classic ate-up, never cutting anyone slack. By-the-books to the letter. Everything was about this regulation or that. Which annoyed, like...absolutely everybody.

"But why our smartwatches?" Ruby questioned, fingering her watch.

"No photographs or audio...of or in...our facility—most definitely not of the test subjects. Your handguns and watches will be returned after your visit." She nudged the plastic basket even closer. Her way of saying time's up.

Still looking reluctant, Ruby removed the nine-millimeter from its holster, unclipping the loaded magazine and placing both in the basket. She unlatched her smartwatch as well. Her husband followed her lead.

Getz exhaled into a breathalyzer device to the right of the interior door—probably the only action she ever got. He cracked himself up!

The deadbolt retracted, and the door electronically opened toward the lobby. He walked into the hallway first, asking the Spencers to follow.

They headed down the long hallway.

The overhead fluorescent lights blinked twice.

Before shutting off completely.

8

RUBY HADN'T NOTICED the steady hum of air-conditioning units or the electrical buzz of overhead fluorescent lights, until they shut down. Within the windowless hallway of the Naval compound, she, Clay, and the Seaman were insulated in darkness. Besides rain pelting the roof, the only other sound was her heartbeat pounding in her ears. Uneasy, she reached for Clay's arm. Touching him, feeling his warmth and strength, grounded her in the blackout.

The sudden thump and groan of backup generators traveled overhead like a wave. With the gradual surge of electricity, emergency sconces lit like candles, starting at the base of each bulb-stem and increasing their cast of yellow light.

"Like clockwork," Seaman Davis said, smiling. "Generators haven't failed us yet." He resumed walking. "Let's continue to the observation room."

At the end of the long hall was a security door equipped with a deadbolt, in addition to the standard doorknob with a spring-loaded lock. On the wall was a mobile scanning device mounted on vertical tracks, allowing the scanner to be moved up and down for proper positioning. The six-foot-*ish* Seaman raised the biometric device. When it was level with his right eye, he uttered "scan." A blue beam flashed, taking a photograph and presumably comparing the Seaman's unique retinal patterns against the ones in his electronic file. She was familiar with the scanning devices; the lab at Johns Hopkins had utilized them when she studied and worked there. Seconds later, the door's deadbolt retracted with a loud click. Seaman Davis turned the knob and opened the door.

Throughout the facility, interior doors were equipped with the same deadbolt system, requiring retinal scans. Except for the lobby door. "Just curious," she said to the Seaman. "Why is the lobby door secured with a breathalyzer instead of an eye scan?"

"It comes down to this: access into the facility requires an un-replicable form of identification. Because if there was an eye scan in the lobby and intruders wanted to gain access into the interior, they could still scan Getz's fresh eyeball—inside its socket...or out—if you see my point. But the breathalyzer can't be fooled. It detects the slightest chemical changes from the norm. *If there's stress, no access.*" He looked at her and shrugged. "What can I say? The Navy likes catchy phrases."

Down another windowless hall, the Sailor stopped by a door on the left. He unlocked it with another eye scan and turned the knob. "This is the observation room. We'll view the final exercises from here, before you meet with the scientific team." He held open the heavy steel door with his back, while waving her and Clay in.

She walked into the shadowy space, needing her eyes to adjust.

The room resembled a miniature movie theatre, with plush black-leather chairs arranged in a straight row behind a glass wall. Instead of a movie, the action happened in real-time, beyond the thick glass, in a large containment chamber that fed soft light into the observation room.

"Sorry I can't offer popcorn," Seaman Davis teased. He moved toward the chairs, barely looking beyond the glass, like he had seen the show a hundred times. "Let's get comfortable. The action will start soon."

She sat down between her husband and their escort. Her eyes widened. Gawking at the cell and its contents, she reminded herself to keep her mouth closed. Because next to the observation room. On the other side of thick glass. Was the former Chinese tyrant: Huo Zhu Zheng. He, or *it*, stood frozen several inches from the glass, facing them.

Her body temperature elevated like a struck match.

Even though glass separated them from the monster, being so close to a zombie as vile as Huo caused her neurons to ignite in quick-fire fashion. The rush of impulse-activity accelerated her heart, making her mouth dry and palms clammy. Maybe Seaman Davis wouldn't notice her white-knuckled clutch of the chair's armrests.

She looked at the Seaman. "May I get closer? Have a better look?" She hoped her voice didn't sound as shaky as she felt.

"Go ahead. Grays can't see you through the one-way glass." He pointed to Huo. "More importantly, they can't hear or *smell* you. So have at it."

"Grays?" Clay asked.

"Yep. When we get bored, we come up with stuff, like calling them Grays. See their skin? The ZOM-B goo makes their skin look gray. And the longer they go without food, the grayer they get. Huo's a hungry bastard right now. We call hunger...*motivation*."

"Their food is oxygen-rich blood, right?" she asked.

"You got it. And they aren't picky. *If it bleeds, Grays feed.* Good one, right?"

She answered with a weak smile. Standing, she inched toward the glass. Clay joined her.

"Look at his leathery skin," she whispered to her husband. "It's dried-up since we reviewed the transformation video with the Special Warfare Council. Besides dark gray, his skin is flaky and rough. Looks more like the Shifen zombie, like his skin oils are nonexistent. Without moisture and elasticity, his skin has shrunk on its skeletal frame."

"No need to whisper, Ma'am," Seaman Davis's voice boomed.

She jumped, heart spiking.

"This room is soundproofed," he continued. "We can hear a pin drop from inside Huo's cell, but if a grenade detonated inside *this* room, our Grays wouldn't know it. See, we like to control when and how they get motivated."

"So you've noticed they react to sound?" she said, not really asking a question, more like verifying that they were drawing the same conclusions based on independent observations.

"Affirmative. First is smell. They put Bloodhounds to shame. But after smell is sound. I think they can hear a heartbeat. Combine the smells and sounds of life coursing through veins, and you've got yourself an amped killer with snapping jaws. Some prefer to call them Clickers over Grays. You know, the sound their teeth make." The Seaman imitated the sound by chattering his teeth together in rapid succession.

Ruby had heard the distinctive clicking in Shifen, as well as when she'd reviewed footage of WHO and CDC videos. The sound sent shivers down her spine. Made her feel vulnerable.

Clay must have sensed her angst. He placed his hand on her back and gently rubbed, settling her nerves.

Zombie Huo remained stationary—a dark-gray molting rock of a corpse. With his head tilted forward, chin resting on his chest and tattered blue shirt, his black eyeballs remained open, unblinking. His lips had dried and shrunk, exposing his teeth and jaws. All were dark gray. It looked as though Huo had been forced to wear the skin of a child.

His chest didn't expand and contract from breathing. She hadn't noticed this before.

"They don't breathe?" she asked the Seaman, keeping her focus on Huo.

"Nah. Lungs are useless. The oxygen they need comes from absorbed fresh-blood. They're like sponges. And when they're not stimulated, they turn to stone, preserving their undead lives." The young Seaman threw back his head and chuckled. "That's a kicker, isn't it? Undead *lives*? The whole world's turning into a fucking paradox—my sister told me that one, minus the f-bomb." He snapped his head toward her, making eye contact. "Oops. Sorry for the foul language, Ma'am. Lost my manners. Being around the undead does it to me. No disrespect intended."

"None taken."

"Word has it you guys have figured out how to kill the undead." He smiled, looking eager to get firsthand confirmation.

"A bullet to the head," she said.

"We should've tried that. But we were more interested in finding what didn't kill the freaks. Process of elimination, you know? Anyway, we wanted to continue to study them."

"Clay gets the honor of finishing Huo when your experiments

have concluded. At least, that's what the President promised."

He nodded and eyed her husband. "You must rank, man! Since when does a civilian get to fire a shot on a Naval base? Anyway, we've got bets on how many shots it'll take you to hit the target. I'm in for one, so make it count. I could use a case of *Gold Medal* lager right about now. Ever had *Taiwan Beer?*"

Clay smiled. "You can give me a bottle when you collect your winnings."

"Confidence." The Seaman nodded. "I like it."

She scanned the cell. "Where's the other zombie? The CDC scientist with half a body?"

"Huo's sidekick lost his head!" He winked at her. "By now, he's in transit to the consulate. You're supposed to take the poor bloke stateside this evening, right?"

"Correct."

"You know…okay, maybe you don't," the Seaman said. "The base *acquired* another zombie two days ago."

"What?"

"Yep. Our flag's been at half-staff. See, one of our petty officers got too comfortable when he was feeding Mr. CDC. Got bitten and turned. I didn't know him well, but we're pretty torn-up about it." He lowered his head. After a moment, he locked eyes with her again. "Come to think of it, when our scientists meet with you, you might see Zorn—who's now called Z. They're pulling tissue samples from him today. Warning: be careful of Z. He's a hungry one."

A screeching horn blared in the detention cell, equally assaulting the observation room. Ruby jerked back from the glass, her heart hammering in her chest as if pounding to break through. She placed her hands over her ears and stumbled backwards. If Clay hadn't caught her, she would've crashed into a chair.

The horn had been discharged at the opposite end of the chamber, behind a barred barrier. With the sound blast, Huo lifted his chin from his chest. His black eyes grew wider, exposing his skull's gray sockets. His jaws rapidly snapped open and shut, over and over, filling the observation room with the hair-raising chatter of teeth. *Click, click, click.*

"You should issue a warning," she said to the Seaman, breathing hard and trying to collect herself. She and Clay returned to their seats.

"Sorry, Ma'am. They drill into us that sometimes life's little mishaps—like weapons-of-mass-destruction—don't give any warnings. Shit happens when you least expect it. Keeps us on our toes."

The truth of the Seaman's words lingered in the air as Huo turned from the glass and walked briskly, with purpose. Heading toward the ceiling-high barred barrier, Huo walked with his knees barely bending and arms dangling by his sides, slightly swinging with his jerky-stride.

The celled area reminded her of Shifen's elementary-school entrance. "What's on the other side of that barred wall?"

"A protected open-area where we can fire rounds and launch knives at the test subjects. Fun stuff like that. We can even use flamethrowers to torch the suckers. Notice Huo's burnt legs? But none of our tactics stopped the freaks." He leaned forward to look at Clay. "You'll be shooting this one from The Pit; that's what we call the open staging area, behind the bars: The Pit."

"Works for me," Clay said. "What experiments come first?"

Seaman Davis pointed beyond the glass to a Skycam system, a cable-suspended remote-controlled camera that filmed the activities below, from multiple angles. Ruby had seen similar camera setups at sports games.

"See that camera across the cell?" He paused, as if waiting for them to get a good look. "Yesterday, we rigged a device beside it that can release blood drops on demand: where and when we want, and how much. Technology: got to love it!" He smiled. "Apparently, President Newton wants to confirm that Grays can be herded like sheep, you know, if they start multiplying. Crowd control zombie-style."

Huo reached the bars of The Pit. He slammed his body against the celled divider, perhaps "thinking" sheer-force could topple it. When efforts failed, he tried to squeeze his arms through the thick metal bars, but they were too close together. He violently twisted his head from side to side, gnashing his teeth and moaning, as if frustrated.

Humans were in The Pit, and he undoubtedly smelled them.

Suspended several feet below the ceiling, well above Huo, the camera jolted into action, whizzing across the room on its cable, heading toward the observation room. The camera contraption stopped several feet in front of the glass wall. Beside the camera, a green light above a plastic-canister blinked once. One hardy drop of blood dripped, in what seemed like slow motion. The blood hit the white tiled-floor, leaving a crimson splat mark.

Before the large droplet even touched the ground, Huo had turned his body and headed toward the smell of blood. The horn sounded again behind the barred divider, but this time, the zombie continued in the direction of the splatter.

She looked at the Seaman. "So when a zombie has a choice between sound stimulus and the smell of food, it'll choose food. Do they have the same reaction to blood from a newly infected?"

"Negative, Ma'am." He pointed at Huo making his way toward them, toward the blood droplet. "After Mr. CDC turned, this one could care less about him. The labbers concluded that once victims turn, zombies ignore them. Grays don't attack their kind."

Interesting contrast to humans. Because humans attacked *their* *kind* all the time. Being on the cusp of dystopia proved it.

Huo reached his destination. Dropping to his knees, he bent at the waist and leaned over, placing his hands on the floor and bending his elbows. Like a knee pushup.

Within the observation room, a television monitor mounted on the side wall flickered to life. A floor-level camera, probably embedded inside one of the cell walls, activated to live-stream Huo's responses. The television provided in-your-face magnified footage.

The former dictator's black tongue, speckled with what looked like barnacles, lapped the splatter, lightning-quick like a lizard. His tongue was clearly rotting. She recalled the foul stench that the Shifen zombie had excreted, smelling like rotten eggs and spoiled sardines swimming in a slurry of rancid milk. Gag city.

Suddenly, in concert with an engine cranking loudly, the four-by-four section of tile around Huo began to descend below the flooring, until the zombie disappeared completely.

"What's happening?" she asked.

9

Sunday, July 11, 2032
U.S. Naval Base: Keelung, Taiwan

FROM HIS VANTAGE point, Clay saw a square void of darkness, where the zombie and tiled-floor used to be. "Yeah, where did zombie Huo go?"

"Oh, he's still there," Seaman Davis replied. "We've conducted this experiment before, but our commanding officer thought you might get a kick out of it. After all, you've come all this way. Might as well get a show worth remembering."

Minutes later, a mechanized gear-shift thumped into action, coupled with sounds of rushing water. As the zombie rose into sight, a glass tank encased him. Water rushed into the tank from jets that had replaced several floor tiles. Huo was nearly immersed in water, standing on the bottom of the tank, instead of floating toward the surface.

"Why isn't he floating?" he asked, looking at his wife.

"Without buoyancy from oxygen in his lungs, it makes sense that zombies are dead weight, especially after ten months of decay. The methane, carbon dioxide, and hydrogen sulfide gases produced during tissue breakdown—which initially would've made his body float—have dissipated by now. Initially though, I'm thinking that fresh zombies might float for a while, like a loaf of bread."

When the rising tank locked into place, flush with the floor, the emergency lights blacked out. The television in the observation room blipped—the screen fading to invisible. Darkness engulfed them.

"What the?" Seaman Davis said, sounding less cavalier than during the first outage.

The generators attempted to kickstart, releasing a strained roar. Clay knew motors, and these didn't sound good. His yacht's auxiliary engines—those used for navigating canals or busy inlets before sails on *The Gem* were unfurled on the open water, had challenged him on occasion.

Ruby grabbed his arm. "What is it with Taiwan and lights?"

"Seaman," he said calmly, in the inky blackness, getting more annoyed by the second. "Tell me you're armed with a loaded handgun."

"I am, sir."

With a drawn-out moan, the generators reanimated. Emergency lighting strobed to life.

"Doesn't this experiment require a lot of power, Seaman?" he asked. "Maybe it's too much for the generators."

"I leave those dilemmas to our electrical engineers." The guy pointed beyond the glass to the lit chamber. "Anyway, problem solved."

Glad the Sailor was so confident. But in his mind, it was too soon to celebrate.

The barred door between The Pit and the containment chamber opened and two people in white hazmat suits, wearing head units and oxygen packs, entered the cell. One carried a bucket and ladder, and the other, a high-powered rifle—like an M4 or M27. Both figures shuffled across the floor, toward the tank, like deep-sea divers on the ocean floor.

"Why full body suits?" he asked. "Are zombies that sensitive to blood-oxygen, even when they're submerged in a water tank?"

"They're *acutely sensitive*—that's the expression the labbers use. Acutely sensitive to respiration and a functioning circulatory system, no matter what we subject them to. Truth is: if Huo was motivated enough, he could kick to the top of the tank and throw himself over the sides. Trust me; we have footage to prove it. So we try to avoid stimulating them beyond the scope of an experiment." He nodded toward the tank. "Watch this."

The hazmat sharp-shooter stood at-the-ready, aiming the rifle at the top of the tank, while the other worker positioned the eight-foot ladder parallel to the glass. While carrying the bucket and awkwardly climbing the steps in the bulky suit, the person dumped the contents of the bucket into the tank. Two silvery fish—maybe pompano, began to swim around the tank, as the worker stepped down from the ladder and began to walk toward the barred door, carrying the empty bucket and ladder. Keeping aim on the tank, the armed guard followed, walking backwards toward the divider wall—keeping eyes on the tank.

Kicking his feet, Huo moved in the water and snatched a pompano, bringing it to his mouth and tearing a large chunk of the fish's dorsal away with his teeth. Placing his jaws on either side of the bite wound, Huo sucked the fluid from the fish like juice from an orange wedge. In less than thirty-seconds, the lifeless carcasses of both fish sank to the bottom of the tank.

Clay had always thought that if he, Ruby, and Gabby took to the open water on their sailing yacht, to escape chaos and carnage if all hell broke-loose, they'd be safe. But he was witnessing the truth. In the water, Huo regained his once-human agility.

"Will the dead fish reanimate?" he asked the Seaman.

"Nah. Although ZOM-B transfers from dead animals to humans, and from zombies to humans, there is no anthroponosis—no *reverse* zoonosis. The undead, or even corpses and carcasses oozing ZOM-B, can't infect animals with the zombie phenomena. Sure, the infected kill animals; they just don't *turn* them. Not yet, anyway."

His wife smiled. "Sure you're not a scientist?"

"A good listener, Ma'am."

The machine that had raised the tank emitted a loud screech before cranking back to life. The tank began to lower until it sank below the flooring. He heard the rush of water draining from the tank.

The emergency lights blinked again, which pissed him off. He and Ruby didn't need any complications. Impatience flushed through his system. "What's next? Is it my turn?"

"One more experiment," he answered.

Seaman Davis explained that an armadillo would be released into the containment chamber. The labbers predicted that when the animal balled-up and reduced its breathing and blood circulation, zombie Huo wouldn't be able to detect it. Depending on results, the information might lead to specialized body armor.

But the idea was shot to hell. Huo drank the balled-critter dry.

The retracting deadbolt-lock on the observation door clicked. His wife flinched.

A Sailor entered the room. "Seaman Davis, we're ready for Mr. Spencer in The Pit. Reporting to escort him. And Ma'am," he said, "someone will take you to Conference Room B in the lab area, when they're ready."

The emergency lights blinked.

"A quick minute with my wife, please," he said. Reaching for Ruby's elbow, he guided her to the far corner of the room, away from the two Sailors. "Listen: don't overthink this. But if the generators fail, the sound systems will shut down. We won't be able to communicate. If that happens, let's meet outside at the van. We'll wait for each other for ten minutes—oh, and the clock starts when the lights go out. After ten minutes, leave for the train station—no matter what. I'm not joking. Get back to the hotel and we'll reunite there. Understood?"

"Should I be worried?"

"The plan is precautionary. It'll narrow our focus, should the unlikely happen."

"Yes, but…"

"No buts, Ruby. You heard Seaman Davis earlier: shit happens. So no harm planning for a blackout." He put his hands on her waist and drew her near, placing his lips over hers for a second. "Don't let your fears immobilize you," he whispered. "Because by the end of the day, our ruby slippers will get us home." He walked toward the Seaman, haunted by an uneasy feeling.

"Wait!" Ruby said, looking at his escort. "May I accompany my husband to The Pit?"

"No, Ma'am," Seaman Davis responded. "Only have clearance for your husband. You'll be back together soon. No worries, Ma'am."

Before walking out the door, Clay nodded to his wife, hoping to convey that everything would be okay.

No lie, he had doubts.

10

Sunday, July 11, 2032
U.S. Naval Base: Keelung, Taiwan

WAITING IN SILENCE, Frank remained with Ruby in the observation room. He noticed she combed her bottom lip with her teeth, repeatedly, like she was nervous. It reminded him of his sister; that's what Patti did when their parents would argue. The memory tugged at his heartstrings and he wished he could console the lady microbiologist, make her understand there was nothing to worry about. Sure, the generators were acting up. Sure, his parents fought. Worse-case scenario, the compound blacked-out. His parents divorced—which they had. No big deal. Seaman Davis was on duty to protect. *Hooyah.*

Odds were always at play, like in poker or video gaming with the guys. And right now, odds were clearly in their favor. Case in point: Ruby and her husband were surrounded by armed Sailors and Marines. Two Grays against forty? Hardly something to get the jitters over. She was probably unsettled because she was separated from her husband. As Clay left for The Pit, Frank saw the unease in her face—the tiny trenches marking her forehead, the narrowing of her eyes, tightening of her lips. A love like that was hard to find. His parents never came close.

A gust rocked the compound, causing the building to shudder and emergency lights to blink. Generator units on the roof responded with a loud grumble and roar. Those suckers were beasts, refusing to back down. Take that, Typhoon Matilda.

He eyed the activity behind the barred divider, though details were hard to make out. He'd give anything to watch the look on London and Ulrich's faces, when Clay dropped the Gray in one shot. Bring on the beer, bitches!

The sound system crackled. "We will be activating the shooting window and blood dispenser. Observation room: the glass is bulletproofed, but remain alert."

Huo had been standing in the middle of the chamber, a statue of stone, with shredded armadillo by his feet. When the broadcast blared, the zombie jolted to life. Turning his rotting gray head toward The Pit, he clicked his teeth. Frank would be happy never hearing that sound again.

Rising from her chair, Ruby approached the glass. She placed her hands flat against the glass as if the touch was her husband's chest. Turning her face, she locked eyes with Frank, concern still creasing her forehead.

"How many Sailors are with my husband in The Pit?" she asked.

"Seven were issued the order. Why?"

"The more firepower, the better. That's all."

"Doubting your husband's mad skills?" He was trying to lighten the moment. Humor always helped his sister, so why not throw a little into the mix?

"Never," she snapped, like out of the blue. "Your generators are unreliable. Not my husband."

He was about to apologize when the Skycam system zoomed away from the glass, whizzing toward the barred divider. The device stopped about fifteen-feet from The Pit.

With a loud buzz, the shooting window embedded in the barred wall moved inward, toward The Pit, before mechanically shifting to the left, leaving a three-foot square-opening in the wall. Ruby's husband was already taking his place behind the window, wearing ear protection. Raising the M4, the guy began the process of becoming-one with the rifle. A ritual Frank always liked, especially with the magazine-fed carbine. It was sweet.

Overhead, the green light blinked on the suspended canister, releasing a droplet of blood. Huo headed toward the liquid food, moving in his I-want-to-drain-something swagger.

Get her done, Frank chanted in his head, waiting to hear the rippled echo of a rifle blast.

Instead, he heard a sharp, momentary *blip*.

Darkness blanketed the facility.

Fucking-A.

The audio system cut-off and the only sounds Frank heard, besides the effects of good old Matilda, were his and Ruby's amped breathing. Keeping his position near the door, he knew to stay-the-course when temporarily blinded, like when passing an eighteen-wheeler in the rain and suddenly loosing visuals as road-spray covered the windshield. Steady and calm: that's what he told himself. He hoped Ruby would stay calm, too. Panic always complicated things. And the way her nerves were showing, she'd probably be a screamer.

"Seaman?" she asked. "Has this happened before? Have the generators ever quit for good?"

He paused, hoping to hear a reboot. None came. "No, Ma'am."

"What can we expect? In terms of security systems."

"In our ten months here, we've never lost electric *and* generator power," he answered. "Good news is that the doors should remain locked. No eye scans to open them."

"No battery backup on the deadbolts? And that's *good*? We're trapped, Seaman!"

"If we can't get out, Ma'am, neither can the zombies. That's very good news all-the-way-around, if you ask me."

"But what if there's a fire? Security systems aren't designed to entomb you! Or are we collateral damage?"

He hadn't considered either scenario. Why hadn't he? Contemplating all the possibilities and formulating multiple solutions were regiments drilled into each Sailor, beginning in boot camp. Disciplined thought-processes, followed step-by-step, were the key to staying alive. To survival.

The hard snap of the observation room's retracting deadbolt jumped his heartrate, skipping gears. Damn it. He hated when his body reacted like that.

"So battery backup *does* exist," she said. "Which means all the deadbolts in the facility are likely on the same battery-operated safety-release system."

"Probably. Yeah, makes sense. But is there a particular reason you're mentioning it?"

"Does the door between The Pit and the containment chamber have a doorknob?"

"No, Ma'am. The door requires the highest security, like the lobby. The deadbolt is connected to a breathalyzer. Only a few have clearance to activate the system and if analysis warrants a green light, then with electricity, the door automatically swings open."

"Does the door swing *in* toward The Pit? Or *out* toward the detention cell?"

"In toward The Pit. Why?"

"If battery backup releases all the deadbolts, then think about it."

He was trying to mentally keep pace. It was obvious her questioning wasn't about some freakish obsession with door mechanics. First, not having battery backup was *bad*, then having it was *good*, which suddenly became *bad* again. Talk about whiplash.

But no doubt she was drawing a conclusion…about something.

Her first question was about doorknobs. Having them was good. He got that: Grays couldn't generate enough brain-fuel to turn a doorknob. Which meant *not* having a doorknob was bad. Zombies were able to push, push hard in fact, which meant the door opening *in* toward The Pit could be breached. The problem clicked like the sound of a trigger: zombie Huo could get inside The Pit.

"Seaman Davis, do you have access to a flashlight?"

"Yes, Ma'am. One's mounted on the wall next to the fire extinguisher and I'm inching toward it." Frank felt along the wall until his hand bumped against the flashlight. Snatching it from its mount, he pressed the button on the shaft. A white beam lit the room.

"Can you shine the light through?" she asked, peering through the glass wall. "Maybe we can see what's going on."

"Sorry. Light can seep into this room from the chamber, but not vice versa. More good news, though. If there was gunfire, we'd see the flames from each discharge. But it's dark."

She walked toward him by the door. "Nevertheless, I'd better find a way out of this building. Clay warned me that if there was a blackout, we needed to meet by the van. I have less than ten minutes to rendezvous before he assumes I've already left. Can I count on you to take me to an exit? Or do I go this alone?"

By herself? Was she serious?

"Seaman: do I need to go this alone?" she repeated.

"You can't roam this facility without an escort, Ma'am," Frank replied, with some authority in his voice. "I'd be disciplined; hell, court-martialed. So no way; no how. I'll lead you to an exit. Besides, engineers are working on the generators this minute. I wager the lights will turn on before we get there."

She reached for the flashlight. "I'll light the way. You can lead, with your pistol. Please."

"Sure you're not military?" He chuckled. "You remind me of Petty Officer Jones—always barking orders." Handing her the flashlight, he bent over, pulling his pistol from the concealed holster on his calf. At moments like this, he was thankful the military had finally allowed service personnel to be armed on bases. He cocked the nine-millimeter's action. Locked and loaded.

"Barking orders isn't my only talent," she joked. "I also bite. Does Petty Officer Jones do *that*?"

"Definitely want to avoid bites altogether. I've witnessed three-biters-too-many in my lifetime, if you catch my drift."

He slowly turned the knob and opened the observation-room door, pausing to listen. Quiet was good. Most personnel had duty in the front of the compound. Turning left, he took a few steps down the hallway.

"Shouldn't we head right?" she asked, holding the door open and shining the light beam in the opposite direction from him.

He exhaled a puff of air. "You want to be in charge, too?"

"I'm sorry. There's probably more than one exit."

He rolled his eyes.

As they walked down the hall, two gunshot blasts from the front of the building echoed off the walls. Fucking A: this good-to-bad cycle was getting on his nerves. And gunfire was bad. Worse than bad. Because everyone knew: there was no reason to shoot, until there was *a reason* to shoot.

"I've got to get you out of here," Frank said, hankering to defend his crew. The urgency had already risen to his tonsils. "Got to help secure this facility."

Reaching the door at the end of the hallway, he turned the knob and pushed it open. He waited, frozen in place, listening. Without hearing or sensing danger, he walked through, holding the door open. But a distant barrage of rapid-fire discharges signaled the situation was worsening up-front.

"Ma'am, I'm thinking your meeting with our scientists has officially been cancelled."

"No arguments from me," she said, which was a first.

He quickened his pace. After jogging the length of the back hall, he came to the next door and opened it. But the hallway—known as section D—wasn't quiet. He heard thumping to his left, up the hallway, coming from one of the rooms on the right.

"I need to investigate that sound, then help my fellow Sailors. So this is where we part." He pointed to his right. "The exit is through that door at the end of the corridor. It opens to the outside, to the back of the building. The parking lot will be to your left. Take the flashlight."

"No. I still have several minutes before I have to meet Clay," she argued. "And you need light more than I do. Besides, your hands should be free to protect yourself."

"The only rooms down this hallway are labs."

"*Labs?*" she asked, sounding sarcastic. "Like the kind of *lab* being used to extract tissue samples from the very hungry—your words—Z?"

The thumping grew louder.

He eyed her. She was right. "Yep. Like one of those."

Okay, so maybe he could use her help. Things were going to hell-in-a-handbasket...quickly.

"How many Sailors are stationed here?" she whispered, as they advanced.

"About seventy-five. But we have shifts and rotations, so only forty muster at a time."

They stopped near a door that rattled every time something—on the other side—pushed hard against it.

"This is déjà vu," she said softly.

"Déjà vu? Why?"

"Yesterday, Clay and I heard thumping behind a door in Shifen. When we opened it, a zombie attacked us."

He turned to look her squarely in the eyes. She was starting to sound wacko. Paranoid city. Like maybe the stress of the situation was finally sinking in. Newsflash: not every thumping sound in the world was a zombie.

"Ma'am? No disrespect, but you're letting your imagination take over. Let me handle this. Please. That's an order. Not one. More. Word."

"Yes, sir."

He rolled his eyes again. She had already disregarded his directive.

Standing in front of the door, he placed a hand on the knob. "Petty Officer Andrews? Are you in there, sir?"

No answer.

"Seaman Patterson?" he asked.

Nothing.

Something slammed against the door with force, making it rattle in its frame. He stepped back. His stomach tried to escape through his throat. Then something else, maybe a chair, screeched across the lab floor.

"What the?" Frank looked at her. "Stand back and run like hell if you have to. Understood?"

"Yes, sir."

The flashlight's beam danced on the ceiling which meant Ruby was probably losing it. She wasn't alone. Even he was feeling spooked. He'd grown accustomed to seeing the zombies from behind thick barriers. But what if something unexpected had happened in the dark? Was he ready to encounter one of the freaks up-close-and-personal? While protecting a civilian at the same time?

Inhaling a lungful of air into his chest cavity, he hoped the oxygen-boost would complement the adrenaline tingling his muscles. As he placed his hand on the doorknob, red lights activated overhead, up and down the hallway. In drills, the lights had reminded him of an ambulance: red beams rapidly circling within each tinted dome. But now, now they looked less like ambulance lights and more like a bloody doomsday.

"What do those lights mean?" she asked.

"Code Red," he answered, attempting to sound calm. "Someone had to press the button. It means compound-security has been compromised. It's the highest alert."

Another thud against the door.

"Ready or not, here we come," he warned. He slowly turned the doorknob, before raising his right leg and kicking in the door. Whoever—whatever—had been banging against the door was knocked down on impact. But someone else stood in the middle of the room, swaying. "That you Patterson?"

Ruby shined the flashlight on the figure. And then Frank saw. What was once Patterson…was no more. He was undead. Fuck, fuck, fucking-A. Significant chunks of flesh were missing from Patterson's neck, wounds so deep that white sections of his brain stem and spinal cord were exposed. Blood had spurted onto the front-and-back of his NWU—the saturated stain masking the shirt's speckled-pattern. Behind Patterson, on a gurney with a strap around his waist, was the son-of-a-bitch Z, his arms flailing—like *look what I did during the blackout.*

Patterson's skin was a deathly grayish-white, like all the blood had drained from his circulatory system. Leaving Patterson…hungry like a newborn.

"Stop," Frank said. "That's an order!"

Clicking his teeth together, Patterson released a gargled moan.

"He can't understand you!" Ruby screamed, backing up. "Hurry! Shoot him in the head!"

Patterson turned his head toward the lady microbiologist like an owl. She kept shining the flashlight on the ghoul, instead of running. And that's when the freak started walking toward her.

Frank raised his firearm, his finger pulling the trigger. But as the pistol discharged, he slipped on the blood-soaked floor. He pictured the bullet embedding somewhere in the cinderblock wall, missing the zombie-freak entirely.

Something grabbed his leg.

11

Sunday, July 11, 2032
The American Consulate: Taipei, Taiwan

OX WAS FUMING, sitting at his desk. Even his ears throbbed. Jonny Ambassador, as he liked to call the skate under his breath to ensure he never lost the utter disrespect he harbored for the needle-dick, didn't have the professional decency to inform him—the consulate's military attaché for fuck's sake—that Ruby Spencer's chopper pick-up at Zhuchang Park had been adjusted to…today. *Today* at 1700 hours. Instead, Ox's people had dug up the intel. Moles who were so underground that not even a weasel knew their tunnels led to him.

The cock-sucking Ambassador clearly suspected something.

Always flexible, he reminded himself: Semper Gumby, bro.

A knock tapped on Ox's office door.

"Enter," he said, tasting the irritation in his mouth. The interruption better be good.

"Lance Corporal Eugene Insley, sir."

The red-haired twenty-something boot—well, anyone was a boot compared to his own service—opened the door and then scanned up and down the hallway, as if making sure the coast was clear. Not *too* obvious. And who would name their fucking kid Eugene anyway?

"I can see who you are, Insley. Enter and cop a seat. Close the door."

The kid barely fit in between the door and his desk. Ox wouldn't be in the shoebox for much longer. That was for damn sure.

"Permission to speak freely, sir," the kid said.

Ox rubbed his flat-top, trying to dispel the aggravation like dust. He didn't want to say something he'd regret. Right now, he needed to pander to his team. Keep them sucking from the tit like babies. But still…

"No one says that for real, Insley. Only in the movies. Now what's on that impressive mind of yours? Speak."

"Pick-up for the girl has been moved to 1700 hours. Today, sir."

"Knew it."

"I flipped off the breaker for the AC. As ordered."

"Well done. Anything else?"

"The Russian vessel came to port in Keelung, sir. Received confirmation from our mole."

"Good intel."

Ox's smartwatch buzzed from inside his desk drawer. He had placed the watch on vibrate and obviously had neglected to return the device to his wrist. Maybe he was slipping. Or maybe he was distracted because he had to work with pinheads. Yeah, that was more likely.

He opened the drawer. The damn watch was flashing red with a notification. And now sweet-honeysuckle Patti Davis was calling him. He glared at Insley with a compact expression, which meant keep your mouth shut. Or else.

After adhering his watch to his wrist, he answered the videoface request. "Ox here," he said, out of habit. She obviously saw him on the watch screen.

"Sir, Ambassador Jeffries wants to verify that you're aware of the Code Red at the Keelung Naval Base. The base has lost power and no one at the compound is responding to inquiries. He is confident you are addressing the situation. May I confirm this with him?"

Code Red? Why hadn't his moles at the base contacted him?

"You may confirm," Ox answered her. "And while we are on the subject, I would like to brief him on our military response. Can he make time for me…say, in fifteen minutes? My office?"

"I'll ask the Ambassador and then confirm the meeting with you, Lieutenant Colonel. Thank you."

"Pleasure's all mine, Ma'am." He hoped the words tickled her tender spots.

Disconnecting, he glowered at Insley. "Instruct Corporal Wyatt to muster the response team—minus our men. Have him deploy the team to the compound immediately. In ten, send everyone else home from the consulate. Only our men will remain on campus, waiting for orders from me. I'll personally tell Patti Davis to head home; she needs to call me back anyway. Then find out from the response team why in-the-hell the base is in a Code fucking Red. But listen closely, Lance Corporal Insley: I am about to impart the most critical order, so don't be a Schmuck-a-telli, got it?"

"Got it, sir."

"Dispatch a chopper to apprehend the Spencers. They may still be at the base or in transit to their hotel: the Mandarin Oriental in Taipei. Have them extracted and brought here. To the consulate: now. Top priority. Are we good to go?"

"Sir. Yes, sir."

"Excellent. Let's get this party started."

After Insley left his office, he contacted his mole in charge of communications. All he said to the mole was: *CIS*. Which meant, *Complete the plan, Issue the order, and Supervise*. Everything was a go. No turning back.

Patti hot-pants contacted him to confirm the Ambassador was en route to his office. Of course, Ox never told her to head home. She was directed to remain at her station. He had other plans for the honeysuckle.

A knock on the door: meeting on.

"Enter," Ox said, as the door swung open.

Jonny Ambassador wore his typical navy suit, white shirt, and red tie—a walking American flag. As much as it killed Ox to stand as a sign of respect, he did, though it tasted like bile after a heavy night of drinking.

"Please," the Ambassador said. "Stay seated." And then the prick sat down, before being invited, sweat beading on the man's forehead.

"Thanks for coming," Ox said, hoping to sound congenial.

The Ambassador loosened his tie. "Have you noticed how humid and hot it's getting in this building?"

"Why don't I brief you about the Code Red and our response, as we check out the breaker for the AC?"

"Isn't that in the basement?"

"Is there a problem? I was thinking efficiency—two birds with one stone. Especially given the circumstances."

"Oh sure. That makes sense."

Like taking candy from a baby.

12

RUBY DROPPED THE flashlight and ran toward the exit door. She had no choice. Everything fell apart when Seaman Davis kicked in the door. And now a zombie pursued her.

The hallway tiles had become slippery with condensation, caused by humidity in the once air-conditioned facility. Except for the emergency lights, the darkened hallway reminded her of a recurring nightmare. While floating in the abyss of space, she tried to reach a sphere of glowing light—probably a spacecraft. But the lack of gravity, of friction, prevented her from getting any traction or forward motion. In every dream rerun, she drifted into nothingness.

Running on the slippery tile seemed equally futile.

With determination, she sought the sweet-spot for each running stride, somewhere between careful and forceful. Like running on ice. When she reached the door, an ear-piercing shriek assaulted her ears. Seaman Davis! Her heart quickened. Tears pooled in her eyes. She desperately wanted to help him. But looking over her shoulder, the only *thing* she saw was a grotesque zombie hell-bent on devouring her for lunch. And she had no weapon with which to defend Seaman Davis or herself.

"Shoot him in the head!" she shouted again, assuming Seaman Davis was encountering the other undead attacker.

Fumbling with the slippery doorknob, her hands were shellacked with perspiration. In her first attempt, her hand moved, but not the knob. Seaman Patterson was dangerously close. Her nostrils burned from his stench.

At the last minute, she turned the knob. The door flung open. Aggressive winds yanked it from her grip, banging the door against the building's exterior.

Closing the distance, the zombie was almost on top of her. Almost free—outdoors, where he could attack her. And multiply the infection.

She pulled the heavy door toward her, fighting against the wind. When the door was halfway closed, she moved in front, pushing it shut with her back. Patterson slammed his body into the door, just as the spring-loaded lock clicked into place.

Maybe their luck was turning. She prayed to God that Seaman Davis was successfully defending himself. That he hadn't been bitten. That her husband was waiting for her in the parking lot. That they'd make it back to their hotel...alive.

Outside, the weather was furious. Several of the mushroom-like satellites had toppled over in the swirling wind and rain. Holding her forearm like a visor, she ran toward the parking lot, trying to protect her eyes from the liquid assault. She had to find the white van.

When she stopped to scan the asphalted area, she observed three-dozen-or-more identical vans, parked throughout the expansive lot. Clay wasn't standing by any of them. Nor was anyone else. Where *was* everybody?

She was racked with a bolt of anxiety. Standing in the middle of the lot, with horizontal rain stinging like jellyfish tentacles on her exposed skin, she hollered Clay's name...twice.

Only the howl of the wind answered.

Maybe Seaman Getz was secure in the lobby, still manning the front desk. Code Red or not, Ruby needed to explain that Seaman Davis was in serious trouble. He needed help. And then Getz could tell her if Clay had exited the compound, since Ruby had taken longer than ten minutes. And with so many vans, maybe transportation could be arranged back to the hotel. Not to mention Seaman Getz could return her smartwatch and handgun, if Clay hadn't collected them already.

She raced toward the entrance where she and Clay had entered the facility. Jiggling the door handle, she felt a stab of disappointment, remembering they had been buzzed-in on arrival.

The windows surrounding the entrance were foggy from condensation, resembling frosted glass. Finding a clear patch, she knelt to gaze into the lobby. At least the natural light would brighten the room. Holding her hands like horse blinkers, she peered through.

Her stomach lurched, threatening to splatter acidy-chum on the window-panel.

Seaman Getz was writhing on the floor in a pool of her own blood. Her injuries consisted of multiple bite-wounds to her inner thigh. Wounds that looked like a shark had ripped away flesh and fabric, bite after bite. The spilled blood, which no doubt made the floor-tile slippery, was hampering the zombie's efforts to stand.

The interior door, which led to the main hallway, was stuck in the open position. In the darkened hallway, red emergency-lights were still pulsating.

The zombie eyed her. The former human stopped thrashing on the floor and stared with tar-black eyes. She clicked her teeth together. With intent.

An agonizing croak escaped from Ruby's windpipe.

Before abandoning her position on the rain-soaked ground, she glanced at the glass door leading from the lobby to the outside. Her inner voice released a bloodcurdling scream. The lobby exit was equipped with a panic bar: a horizontal spring-loaded handle that opened the door with a simple downward push. No brainpower required. Not even for a zombie.

Run: that's the order her brain gave every impulse firing within her head. Turning, she darted toward a van, the one parked closest to the driveway. Picking up several stones from the rock-bed edging the asphalt, she quickly constructed an arrow on the van's hood, pointing northwest, toward the harbor. Her stoned arrow would give Clay an indication that she'd left, in case he hadn't fled the building yet.

She resisted the urge to consider his whereabouts. Precious time would be lost. She had to follow the plan—the only thing keeping her sane and moving. Clay was right: the plan narrowed her focus. Kept her on track. Kept her from falling apart.

Looking behind her, her heart sputtered. The female Sailor—

Getz—was staggering toward her in the wind-whipped rain. She had freed herself from the lobby. And now the zombie freak was hunting her.

Movement on the side of the building caught her attention. It was Seaman Davis; he had escaped his attackers in the hallway! Advancing on zombie Getz from the side, he aimed his handgun at the walking-dead Sailor.

"Run!" he hollered to Ruby, before the wind stole his voice.

13

PATTI DAVIS, ADMINISTRATIVE assistant to Ambassador Jeffries—a generous and thoughtful boss, had failed to reach her brother, Seaman Frank Davis. Once Code Red had been activated at the base, she sent several vexts and videoface requests. Why wasn't he answering? What was going on over there? Her upper teeth combed over her bottom lip. Worried, there was no denying it. She needed her brother, needed to know he was safe. Frank was her rock.

Maybe if Code Red had happened five months ago, she'd be glad that Lieutenant Colonel Oxford was at the helm for a military response. After all, he wore the bars and medals which proved he was no coward. But recently, the *lifer*—a term she contrived to designate someone who was never going to retire from the military—made her nervous, uneasy. His eyes undressed her. His remarks flirted with inappropriate, but cleverly close-enough to acceptable that he could plead "misunderstanding." A real snake in the grass.

When Ambassador Jeffries asked her to track how many times Lieutenant Colonel left the consulate without signing out, she wasn't surprised. The military attaché was leaving for long periods of time, without his smartwatch. A protocol infraction.

She had confidentially told her brother about the situation and he wasn't pleased. Not at all. According to Frank, most of the Sailors felt negatively about the "all powerful Ox," as he called him. Only the Marines defended the man, but that was the whole Semper Fidelis thing—always faithful, even to a jerk.

Deep in thought, she startled when Lieutenant Colonel placed his hand on her bare shoulder. He curled his index finger and glided it over her skin. She got chills, but not the good kind. Creeps, that's what this guy gave her. Besides, she had her first real boyfriend. And anyway, even if she didn't, Lieutenant Colonel would be the last man on Earth she'd ever be interested in. He was a pervert and clearly up to no good. Plus, he was old enough to be her father. Yuck.

"May I help you, sir?" she asked.

"Thank you, Patti. Always so accommodating. Something—when I lay my head down on my bed at night, caressing the thoughts of my day, I acknowledge as an admirable trait. Yes, I've been meaning to tell you, Patti, your accommodating demeanor rises above the rest. It's quite hard…to ignore."

She squirmed in her chair. "Thank you, Lieutenant Colonel."

"Ox. I've asked you to call me Ox," he said, with sternness.

"Yes, sir. Ox…sir."

"There. See? Accommodating. You really are something." He winked.

She swallowed hard and looked around. The halls were empty.

"Oh, we're alone," he said, like he was reading her mind. "Enlisted are responding to the Code Red. Staffers were sent home. Wyatt and Insley are running errands for me."

"Is the base operational again, sir? I mean, Ox?"

His lips curled to a smile. "That's classified, Patti. I'd have to kill you if I told you."

She stared, not knowing how to respond. The hairs on the nape of her neck stood at attention. Her heart pounded. Fear, that's what was coursing through her.

He slapped the desktop. She jolted. He laughed.

"You really need to lighten up, honeysuckle!"

"I prefer Patti."

He tilted his head. Was his expression surprise? Didn't matter. Because if she was forced to call him Ox, then she could insist on being called Patti. Fair was fair. Besides, *honeysuckle* was never going to cut it. Like never, ever.

"Okay, *Patti*." He clasped his hands together like he was about to have fun. "Where's your boss?"

"He's not with you, sir?"

He arched his eyebrows.

"I apologize, Ox. If he was with you, I'd see him. And you wouldn't be asking." De-escalation, she was trained in it. Get the creeper to think she was on his side.

"Accommodating, like I said! Now the last time I spoke to your boss, he was heading to the basement to flip the AC breaker. It's been *moist* in here. Do you know where the breaker-box is in the basement, honeysuckle? I mean, Patti?"

"Yes, Ox, I do. The box is..."

He raised his hand and she stopped mid-sentence.

"I've got to return to managing this crisis," he said. "And I need the Ambassador's advice. Can you impress me some more by taking me to him?"

"Yes, sir."

She left her desk, heading toward the basement door. Lieutenant Colonel was at her heels, probably checking out her backside. Gross.

She opened the cellar door, flipped the light switch, and started down the poorly lit staircase. At the bottom of the stairs, she turned right. Her breath was sucked from her lungs. Ambassador Jeffries was lying face-down on the concrete! Her temples ached with alarm as she raced to his side. Grabbing her boss's shoulder, she turned him on his back. His eyes were still open. Blank. A dark purple-ring marked his neck.

She looked up at the Lieutenant Colonel, horrified. "He's been strangled!"

"Accommodating *and* observant. Nothing gets over on you, honeysuckle."

The chain in his hands wrapped around her neck so quickly, she didn't have time to gulp any air. Filling her lungs would have been crucial if by some miracle, someone happened to be nearby to rescue her. Which wasn't likely. The consulate had been emptied. And her rock, her precious gem—her brother Frank, was somewhere at the base. In who knows what condition.

Her body was lifted off the ground, feet dangling, and she kicked her legs...a little. Not much, certainly not enough to affect a hulk like the Lieutenant Colonel.

Her oxygen was thinning. With pressure compressing her windpipe, her eyes were about to launch from their sockets.

Velvety darkness started to envelop her, pushing out the light, like when the last bit of sunset yielded to the night. She pictured the colors—pink and orange and purple—before they faded to gray, and then black.

A single light shone in the distance, like a beam of sunlight in a storm. At that precise moment, she understood: the light was meant for her.

14

Sunday, July 11, 2032
Keelung, Taiwan

RUBY DIDN'T HESITATE to follow Seaman Davis's orders. She ran. Northwest. The main road was northwest. But without GPS, she'd have to rely on hunting strategies to guide her in the right direction. Like during the grouse season, in the field with her bird-dog, she'd pick visual markers every ten-yards. If she was mindful of the landmark behind her and of the marker ahead in the distance, she could travel in a straight line.

Today, that line needed to lead to Zhongzheng Road and the harbor.

Two gunshots sliced through the thick, saturated air. She pictured the female zombie getting shot in the head, falling to the ground and violently twitching.

The blasts—in their finality—triggered a reaction. She stopped running and dropped to her knees, consumed with grief. Everything she feared was happening. A crisis was unfolding. And she was alone, separated from Clay in a foreign country that she knew little about. All she wanted was to fly back home with her husband. Back home to protect their daughter. Was that too much to ask? Sobs racked her body, taking her breath away.

Two more gunshots echoed below the storm clouds.

She raised her head, abruptly suppressing her sobs. Had Seaman Davis missed with his first two shots? Or were there *more* zombies on the loose?

Rapidly blinking, adrenaline reminded her she still needed to *survive*. And she was a long way from the hotel. Picking herself off the ground, she wiped her tears and took off running, quickening her pace and finding a rhythm. No more stopping.

As she tired and began doubting her navigational skills in the tropical labyrinth, she intersected Lane 182. A road never looked so good. Because one always led to another.

She ran harder, faster.

Relief swelled again when the lane dead-ended onto Zhongzheng Road. She turned left, planning to run the perimeter of the harbor until she reached the train station. Almost immediately, she spotted a bus-stop. Good thing since angry waves crashed over the inlet embankments, sending spray and foam whipping across the sidewalk and street. A black-haired teenager, dressed in shorts and a drenched Sponge Bob T-shirt, stood by the bus-stop pole, clasping it and trying to shield herself from the rain that was driving across the Keelung Harbor.

Ruby looked to see if the girl wore a smartwatch, but her wrists were bare. "Excuse me!" she shouted, trying to sound non-threatening while projecting her voice over the elements. "Do you speak English?"

The girl looked up, keeping her right hand anchored on the pole and using her left as a visor. She nodded. "Some English. Yes."

"Do you have a smartwatch?" she asked, raising her left forearm and tapping her wrist with her index finger. She desperately needed to contact Clay and the consulate. Maybe the watch was in the girl's pocket.

"No. No watch," the girl said. "Broken."

A gust pushed Ruby, moving her several feet closer to the girl. She pointed at the bus-stop banner violently flapping in the wind. "Does the bus go to Keelung Station? To the train station?"

The girl looked at the banner. "Yes. To train." She pointed down the street. A bus was heading toward the stop, going in the opposite direction of the station.

"Does *this* bus go to Keelung Station?" Ruby asked again, hoping to minimize the language barrier by keeping her word-selection simple, without offending the girl.

"Yes. Bus turn around," she answered, drawing a circle in the air with her index finger.

With wet brakes squealing, the bus stopped beside the curb in front of them. The accordion-door opened, folding tightly against its frame. The girl grabbed the bus's handrail and climbed the steps before paying the fare to the bus driver. Ruby did the same, only her hands shook.

Most seats accommodated three people. And with the windows closed due to the storm, it felt like one-hundred-degrees inside. The air was pungent with body-odor, smelling of wet dog and a hint of onion.

Halfway down the aisle, a man waved before pointing to two vacant seats. They walked toward him, and the girl sat across the aisle from the man. Ruby sat next to him. He was dressed in a dark business suit and tie. A smartwatch peeked out from the end of the man's sleeve. Asking a stranger to borrow a personal item was considered rude. But as with the girl, breaking cultural etiquette was necessary under the circumstances.

As the bus moved forward, she was about to ask the man, but then the noise-level escalated to a roar. She scanned the interior. A dozen passengers stood in the aisle or in front of their seats, making exaggerated hand movements. Talking rapidly, their voices were elevated and animated. Some were shouting. The behavior was odd, bizarre really. Emotional outbursts were atypical in the Taiwanese culture. She'd read numerous articles that the Taiwan people were private and stoic in public.

In fact, a few passengers were crying. Crying, *in public?*

Perhaps the storm had gotten stronger. Dangerous, even. Not what she and Clay needed.

Ruby leaned across the aisle to the girl. "People…upset? Scared about typhoon?"

The teenager nodded. "Typhoon coming. Yes." She pointed out the window toward the harbor, toward the ominously dark skyline.

The bus abruptly stopped at a traffic light. Ruby jerked forward in her seat. Unlike the Naval base, electricity was still supplying the city. Which improved the odds that trains were continuing to operate.

The Taiwanese man beside her, wearing the smartwatch, tapped her shoulder as the bus made an awkward U-turn. Scooting back in the seat, she pressed on the floor with her boots to prevent being pushed against the man. She made eye contact. The man looked fifty-*ish*, with a round face. Shades of gray peppered the black hair above his ears.

"I apologize for my rudeness," he said in perfect English. "I overheard your question." He glanced at the passengers standing. "People are not speaking about the typhoon. They are talking about a Russian container ship. The ship came into port this morning, to dock ahead of the storm. Apparently, the crew is afflicted with a plague."

"Plague? What kind of plague?"

The bus rounded a curve and the passengers swayed right before leaning left.

"I am not sure," he answered. "They are squawking about gray people who look dead and snap their jaws together." He gave a crooked smile. "Storms have strange effects on people. Plenty of babies will be born tonight!"

Ruby couldn't return a smile. Blood drained from her face. *Gray people?* Her temples throbbed. "Sir? I'm sorry for *my* rudeness, but would you mind if I videofaced my husband and the American Consulate? Using your smartwatch? It's extremely urgent or I would never ask."

The man continued to smile, seeming to ignore the stress in her voice. "Sure. But my device will only activate on my wrist." He looked at her and shrugged. "Security, I am afraid."

After Ruby gave Clay's number to the man, he uttered a verbal command in Mandarin and the request was forwarded through his watch. Five rings later, her husband's video-recording played. Smiling, his image urged the caller to leave a message. Her heart sank. Clay obviously hadn't retrieved their smartwatches. Or if he had, something was wrong.

She closed her eyes and tried to regroup. But doubts about Clay's safety invaded her thoughts like black fog, constricting her lungs. What if he had needed help and she'd abandoned him at the base?

"Do you wish to call the American Consulate now?" the man asked, snapping her back into the present.

A loud crack of thunder ripped across the greenish clouds. Torrential rains blurred the outside world.

"Yes. Yes, please," she said, her bottom lip quivering. She needed to call while there was still a signal.

The man secured a successful connection with the consulate. He lifted his wrist so the device's screen was at her eye level.

"This is Ruby Spencer," she said, staring at the image of a red-haired Marine on the other end of the video stream. "With whom am I speaking?"

"Lance Corporal Eugene Insley, Ma'am."

"I need your help, sir. My husband and I are on assignment for President Newton. The compound is in Code Red." She briefly glanced at the man beside her, realizing she should choose her words carefully, although in her desperation, she had already said too much. "There was some *undesirable* activity on the grounds before I…before I vacated the premises. I'm still in Keelung but am attempting to return to Taipei."

"We are aware of the situation, Mrs. Spencer, and have disbursed response units. Tell me your location and I'll dispatch a chopper to extract you."

"I'll arrive at the Keelung Station momentarily. Can I be picked up there? Maybe from the parking lot?"

"Affirmative," he answered. "Help is on the way, Ma'am."

"Wait!" She had unintentionally raised her voice, turning several faces toward her. "Have you heard from my husband?" she asked with more control. "From Clay Spencer?"

"Negative. Focus on the rendezvous. Godspeed."

The smartwatch screen blipped to black.

"Are you *the* Ruby Spencer from the U.S.?" the man next to her asked.

"I am." She inhaled, turning her face toward him. "Do we know one another?"

"I am a fellow microbiologist. And you are famous in the scientific community. Your blood saved humankind from Huo Zhu Zheng's reign of terror."

Across the aisle, the teenager's eyes grew wide with mention of Huo's name. The microbiologist leaned across Ruby to speak directly to the girl, in Mandarin. She nodded after he addressed her. Her shoulders relaxed.

"I did not intend to eavesdrop," the man confessed, "but I heard that a helicopter will be arriving for you at the station. With *undesirable* activities plaguing the city, perhaps your friend should stay with you until the helicopter arrives."

"My friend?" Ruby glanced at the young Taiwanese she had met at the bus-stop. "Oh, we only just met." Turning back to the man, she added, "I don't even know her name."

Once again, the man spoke in Mandarin to the girl and she answered his questions without hesitation. He handed her a wad of yuan.

"My name is…Yu Kang," the girl said to Ruby, while smiling and nodding. "I stay with you. No problem."

Ruby glared at the microbiologist, retorting with her eyes, feeling uncomfortable by his assertiveness. Though on second thought, if for some reason the chopper didn't come, Yu *would* be helpful. The girl spoke the language and was probably familiar with Keelung and Taipei.

"I hope my forwardness is not offensive, Mrs. Spencer," he said. "However, if I was cavalier about your wellbeing, my colleagues and countrymen would disapprove, especially with someone of your stature. In fact, I would be honored to wait with you, if you would prefer."

"That's not necessary, Mister…" she said, drawling out the word, hoping he'd drop his name.

"Dr. Lin."

"Thank you, Dr. Lin. Yu will wait with me."

After the bus emptied at Keelung Station, Ruby and Yu stood outside in an open space in the parking lot. Their bodies were drenched, overwhelmed by the rain. They listened, waiting for the thrum of a chopper's rotating blades.

The rains temporarily abated, but the winds howled on.

Ten minutes passed. Then five more.

The rain resumed.

People gathered in the distance. There looked to be a commotion. Were people fighting? Did she hear screaming? A gravitational pull beckoned Ruby to head toward the station. Her inner voice warned her to move. Now.

"Come," she said to Yu. "Follow me."

Inside the station, she and Yu stood in line at the ticket booth for the Taipei Railway Station. Tapping her boot on the floor, Ruby's impatience grew. The train's departure time was minutes away and the ticket line was moving at sloth-speed. Finally, it was their turn to approach the counter. Several drops of fresh blood were splattered on the tiled floor. In public, blood droplets were ignored. At the Naval base, much less had attracted zombie Huo.

"Two tickets to Taipei, please," Ruby said.

The salesperson shook her head. "No tickets."

Ruby turned to Yu, shrugging to demonstrate her confusion. "Can you ask...what is the problem? Because I must return to my hotel."

Yu engaged the salesperson and exchanged words. She looked at Ruby. "She said: train leaving now. Last train to Taipei before typhoon. No tickets left."

Panic rose from Ruby's toes and concentrated in her lungs—the same sensation she had gotten as a child, every time her cousin tackled her underwater, thinking it was funny to act like he might drown her. She had always fought back.

Darting from the ticket counter, Ruby raced down the hallway to the roofed terminal. She slammed into shoulders and briefcases as she ran. No time for apologies. Her only focus was getting to the gate. Like getting to the water's surface for a breath.

The platform for the last train to Taipei, located in the far-right corner of the terminal, was speckled with a few people, waving. Not a good sign. She raced to the platform's edge. The train's rear observation-car crept down the tracks, nearing the end of the domed structure. About to be pounded by wind and rain.

Commotion erupted at the opposite end of the terminal and the three armed-policemen nearest Ruby fled toward the disruption. Her body reacted like the start of a regatta, like a horn had blared. No thinking involved, just reflexed reactions. Her body took over, knowing what needed to be done. Jumping off the platform, she landed on the graveled ground near the tracks and started running, fists pumping.

In full survivor mode, she wasn't about to change her mind. Catching the train was the only switch that had been flipped. Good thing the commotion in the terminal was still distracting security enforcers at the station. Gunshots reverberated within the building. And when the bullets didn't embed into her back or skull, she felt thankful.

With each stride, the observation car got nearer and nearer, though she recognized that the window of opportunity to catch the departing train was waning. Soon, acceleration would render the train out of reach.

Rain and wind violently greeted her as she ran free of the terminal.

By now, the railing around the observation car's outside deck was in reach. Ruby stretched her arms to narrow the distance. Even her fingers extended from their knuckles in the effort. The rain pelted her body, stinging her face as her legs feverishly pedaled. With a final push, she grabbed for the black rail. But moisture made the painted-surface slippery and her fingers slid across the top, failing to curl around the tubed metal-bar. A frustrated groan escaped from her body, warning that her energy was nearly depleted.

One. Last. Chance.

With strength reserved for desperate moments, she reached again. This time, she clasped the rail. First with her right hand, then with her left. Bending her elbows while pushing off with her feet, she lifted herself off the ground, pulling her body against the fencing that enclosed the railcar's deck. When her feet landed on aluminum steps, she inhaled.

"Ruby Spencer! Help me!" a voice pleaded behind her.

She turned her head. Yu was running several feet behind the observation car. The train accelerated.

"Quick! You can do this!" Ruby released her right hand from the rail and stretched her torso over the tracks toward the runner. "Grab my hand. Grab it now!"

Yu's body elongated like a rubber band and Ruby clenched the girl's extended hand. With a forceful yank, she lifted the teenager, slamming her against the rail. Yu clutched the hitched gate and planted her feet on the steps.

When had Ruby ever considered train hopping? In a foreign

country no less, and with a minor in tow. It was dangerous and illegal.

"I hope I didn't hurt you," she said to Yu, still breathing heavy from exertion.

Yu smiled, her jet-black hair drenched and stringy, flapping behind her. "Not hurt. Okay," she said, nodding. She touched each lobe, like she was confirming her pearl teardrop-earrings had remained in place.

"Maybe the door to the observation car is unlocked," Ruby said, speaking quickly. When the gap between Yu's eyebrows narrowed, she pointed to the door and added, "Inside. We go inside."

"Yes! Inside. Please."

After climbing over the fencing and stepping onto the deck, Ruby pulled on the door handle. The door opened. To her surprise, the cabin was empty, except for a lone passenger who was sprawled across several seats that were facing toward the aisle. Why wasn't the cabin stuffed with passengers, packed like the bus, given it was the last train to Taipei ahead of the storm? Especially since the ticket counter declared there were no more tickets.

She and Yu approached the passenger who was laying on his back, his face covered by a cap. Ruby recognized the blue-speckled Navy uniform. Maybe she had seen the Seaman at the base. Maybe he would know something about Clay.

As she reached the Sailor, hope fizzled. The Seaman's right thigh and calf were soaked with blood. The pantleg was shredded and a belt served as a tourniquet above the wounds which were oozing blackish blood.

No wonder the passenger car was empty.

15

AT THE TIME, Frank thought catching the MRT to Taipei was a good idea. The train often reached the city faster than navigating the bumper-to-bumper Sun Yat-sen Freeway. So he'd driven a van from the base to Keelung Station. And when he had purchased one of the last available train tickets, his plan seemed like a big winner. A trifecta.

Besides, he had done all he could at the base. With his own clock ticking down, Frank had changed priorities. He needed to get to the consulate to warn his twin sister that all-hell was breaking loose. He was Patti's guardian angel, and she was his. But he couldn't reach her by watch; she wasn't answering. And no way was he leaving the world without saying goodbye.

He and Patti did everything together, including coming into the world at the same time. Truth was, Patti meant everything to him. Their parents: they'd split long ago. Not only from each other, but from him and his sister. That's why he and Patti had enlisted in the Navy together. Forever faithful—to Country and each other.

His tourniquet wasn't holding back the breach in his femoral artery. It was leaking like the kitchen faucet in his and Patti's childhood home. Fucking-A, he was dying.

Did you hear that Arlene?

Arlene was his mother, and yeah, his favorite expression was all about her: the mother who gave no-never-mind to dumping him and

Patti at an orphanage—like no one in the small rural-town knew who their deadbeat parents were. Orphans *with* parents—living nearby? That's a good one. When it came down to it, everything bad in his childhood had something to do with Arlene. He hated to say it, but fucking-A, it was true.

The plan to see Patti one more time? No denying it: that was *his* mistake, plain and simple. He would die before the train ever arrived in Taipei, and if he didn't take care of business, he'd reanimate in three minutes—into an undead squid. *Hooyah.*

He fingered the cool metal of his nine-millimeter, which he'd tucked by his side for easy access. The time was nearing.

"Sir?" A familiar voice interrupted his mental wanderings.

The voice belonged to Ruby Spencer. Frank reached up to remove his cap, every joint feeling in need of oil.

When she recognized his face, she gasped, like she was staring down the eyes of a ghost.

"Yep, yours truly," he croaked, given his throat was so dry. "Minus a few pieces."

"Seaman Davis! Tell me what happened. Are you okay? Have you seen my husband?"

He smiled, hoping his lips moved. "There you go, Ma'am. Barking orders like a petty officer. Sure you're not military?"

A Taiwanese girl in a Sponge Bob T-shirt stood next to her. He would've asked who the girl was, but he wasn't feeling up to introductions. Ruby sat on the edge of a seat, sharing space with his waist. She pulled a bandana from her pocket, gently gliding it across his forehead, removing beads of moisture. He could tell she was a mother. A nice one.

"Talk to me, Seaman," she said. "And that *is* an order."

"First off, I killed the zombie bitch who was chasing you." A wave of coughing consumed him. He covered his mouth. When he lowered his hand, it was splattered in dark blood.

"When were you bitten?" she asked.

"In the lab. By Petty Officer Andrews. Bastard got me, Ma'am. I'm dying and we all know what that means."

"Why the...why the train?"

He deserved the question. "Not my best decision." He coughed again, tasting more blood. "I thought I could make it to my sister. She works at the consulate. Wanted to say goodbye before my appointment. To tell her I love her. You know, Patti and I are twins and we've never been apart. She's my guardian angel."

"Appointment?"

He revealed the pistol. "We know how this has to end, Ma'am."

"How long do you think you have, Sailor?"

"Death's about to kick in the door." He grimaced.

"Tell me about yourself," she said, stuffing the bandana back into her pocket before taking hold of his left hand.

Coughing again, his whole chest rattled. He took a shallow, gargled breath when the coughing fit passed. Fucking-A, death was no picnic.

"My first name is Frank, Ma'am. Frank Davis. I'm twenty-three. Dreamt of serving our country for as long as I can remember. Same with Patti. Not much else to tell." He attempted a smile and handed the pistol over. "You're going to have to shoot me in the head before I turn. Can you do that, Ma'am? Can you follow an order for once?"

"I can, Frank," she said, taking the pistol. She squeezed his hand again while she placed the handgun on her lap. "You saved my life, Sailor. I'll be forever-grateful for your bravery and heroics. In the short time I've known you, you've served our country honorably, without fear. I'm so proud of you."

"My pleasure," he whispered. "And you'll find your husband. I know you will." He squeezed her hand, like he was gripping the edge of a cliff to avoid freefalling into a bottomless pit. "Tell Patti…"

He usually sensed what his sister was feeling. But he felt nothing. No connection. His body was clearly failing. He was drifting now, floating. A feather. Like maybe his soul was lifting from his body.

"You've got my word," a female voice whispered.

Was that Patti talking? Ruby? An angel?

The pain was easing, maybe his body was numb.

A light shone in the distance, like a beam of sunlight in a storm. At that precise moment, he understood: the light was meant for him.

16

AFTER THE GUNBLAST and bullet-strike to Seaman Davis's forehead, Ruby understood the girl's confusion. Yu stared at her, face firm with tension, while she walked backwards across the aisle, hands extended in front of her, as if pleading not to be next.

"No, Yu. No!" Ruby shouted. "He died *first*. I had to shoot him. *After* he died. Or he would turn Gray." She pointed at the Sailor's wounds. "Gray people."

The teenager's brown eyes widened when she heard the word Gray. "Dead *now*?"

"Yes. Dead." She nodded. "For good."

With hands still shaking, Ruby heard commotion in the next passenger car. She asked Yu to look through the window, the one located on the door leading to the passageway between the two railcars. The teenager approached the glass, then stumbled backwards as if struck squarely in the chest.

"Trouble!" Yu said, her voice shaking. "Trouble is coming."

Trouble had to be security enforcers like the Taiwanese police or military. Ruby had, after all, fired a nine-millimeter bullet, close range, into an American Sailor's forehead. Between the eyes. No one would know the Sailor had died before she shot him. And holding the smoking pistol would be all the empirical evidence needed to lock her up at Qincheng Prison. Angst percolated in her stomach. Swallowing hard, she tried to keep her breakfast from erupting like fruit lava.

Acid burned her throat.

Could the day get any worse?

Shrieks and screams bellowed from the adjacent passenger car. The ruckus grew louder, more aggressive. Yet no security enforcers stormed through the railcar door with guns drawn.

Yu stepped further away from the door's window, color draining from her face, lips quivering. Unable to speak.

Ruby had to look for herself. Shoving the pistol into the back pocket of her shorts, she jogged to the window and gazed through the glass. Her brain froze. On the other side of the passageway, in the next railcar, were zombies: the undead. They were in a ravenous frenzy, brutally inflicting wounds before draining passengers of liquid-life. Dead victims were already reanimating and joining the feeding mania. The horror was multiplying in the overcrowded railcar. Blood seeped from wounded passengers, smearing on the floor, seats, and windows—its sickly-sweet smell wafting across the passageway and penetrating the loose seams of the door-jam into the observation car.

Her stomach churned.

A group of the infected slammed against the door and glass window of the adjoining railcar. The door bowed. With a loud ripping-sound emanating from its frame and hinges, the door gave way, toppling to the floor and dumping several zombies into the passageway between the cars.

Only. One. Door. Away.

"Gray people?" Yu asked, standing behind her.

"Yes. Grays."

She and Yu needed a plan. She canvassed options. All the seats in the railcar were mounted to the floor. There was nothing to barricade the door, except...

"Help me," she ordered Yu, while pointing to Seaman Davis and running toward his body. Grabbing the Sailor's shoulders, she nodded for the girl to hold his feet. They lifted him together and Ruby directed the placement of his body, pushing it snug with the base of the door.

Pounding startled her. She looked up to find the face of a male zombie glaring through the window with tar-black eyes, clicking his teeth. The undead, perhaps in his mid-thirties, rattled the door as if announcing that she and Yu were the next course on the menu.

Ruby took several steps in reverse. The door shook, threatening to break away from its hinges. No doubt the zombies would burst through the only barrier separating life and the walking dead. Grabbing the pistol from her pocket, she unclipped the magazine and counted six rounds. Two would be reserved for her and Yu, in case survival was unattainable, which the odds were favoring. Using the palm of her hand, she snapped the magazine back into place.

Violent thumping against the door grew louder.

Jogging toward the rear of the observation car, she stopped in front of the door leading to the outside deck. Figures it was equipped with a panic bar, making the door useless as a barrier—she had learned that from the Naval base. If she and Yu had any hope for survival, they'd need to find security. But where?

When Ruby opened the door, rain and wind caused their clothes to flutter and flap like luffed sails in a gale. The girl's hair twisted and twirled in the wind; her pearl earrings did donuts in front of her ears. Strands of Ruby's hair pulled loose from her ponytail and whipped wildly around her face.

Without options inside the railcar, she walked onto the observation deck, motioned for the girl to follow, and closed the door behind them. The landscape swooshed by in a blur of rain and wind.

"We jump?" Yu asked, eyebrows raised, holding onto the fencing that enclosed the deck.

Adrenaline pulsed through Ruby while she searched for a hiding place. "No." She pointed to a ladder on the left side of the train, mounted onto the exterior, beyond the seam where the railcar and decking met. The ladder led to the roof. "There!"

Yu walked toward the ladder. After lifting herself onto the fencing's rail and balancing, the teenager leapt onto the rungs, before climbing and stopping. Ruby was next. She eyed the stone ballast and railroad tracks beneath her. Heights made her queasy. She climbed onto the rail, wobbling. Jumping onto the ladder, she found her spot, lower on the rungs than Yu—which was fine with her. She scooted to the left, so her arms wouldn't tangle with the girl's legs. Rain pelted her back, stinging like hail.

Out of nowhere, the teenager swung down the ladder like a monkey, vaulting over the rail and jumping back onto the deck. Was she out of her mind?

"What are you doing?" Ruby screamed.

Yu bent over and retrieved a pearl earring from a puddle. It must have fallen from her ear in the fierce conditions. Smiling, the girl held out the recovered earring. "Grandmother's," she said, looking like an innocent child.

Maybe Yu's careless move had distracted Ruby. Or maybe the wind and rain had muffled the sound of their railcar's interior door crashing down, like the other one had. Whatever the case, a lone zombie, wearing a shredded white shirt stained with a bib of blood, pushed-open the door and emerged onto the deck.

Ruby's heart pounded like a piston. The girl was in danger. Leaning over the ladder and railing, she stretched her body toward Yu in another déjà vu moment. "My hand. Grab it. Now!"

Dropping the earring, Yu reached and clutched her hand. Ruby yanked her toward the ladder, but the zombie clasped the girl's leg and violently tugged on the limb in the opposite direction.

Yu's wet hand was slipping from hers.

The teenager released a harrowing scream. Whether from panic or pain, the shrill penetrated Ruby's soul. With a surge of adrenaline, she heaved Yu toward her, pulling her up toward the ladder, hoping the girl could grab a rung. It didn't matter that she had only met the teenager an hour ago. She wasn't going to lose her. Period.

Yu clasped the ladder and thrashed at the zombie with her legs, successfully pushing him away. She swung her feet over the deck's fencing and landed on the rungs.

Now the girl's body blocked Ruby's firing lane. She had to climb to get a clear shot. Reaching for the rung above her, she gripped it with her left hand. She stepped up. But her right foot slipped, jolting her body and causing her right hand—the one clutching the handgun, to fall away from the ladder. Flailing.

Hanging by a few fingers, her body swung over the tracks, before slamming back against the ladder, hard. Her foot caught a rung. And thank God she hadn't dropped the gun.

With stable footing, she climbed. Good thing, because the zombie was now clenching Yu's T-shirt, pulling the girl toward him as she resisted.

"Hey!" Ruby screamed, with pistol cocked and pointed.

The zombie raised his head to meet the sound. She fired, and the bullet embedded between the undead's eye sockets. The gunblast assaulted her eardrums, making them ring.

The freak released Yu's T-shirt, dropping onto the deck and twitching before its permanent death.

Five rounds remained in the magazine.

A ghoulish cluster of subhumans funneled out from the railcar onto the deck, in a never-ending stream. Pushing forward like an impatient crowd at a rock concert, the horde compressed each other, sending some hurtling off the back of the train. Undead bodies landed on the tracks—bouncing across the stones, with arms twisting and snapping. Legs bending in joint-less places.

The train lurched.

The piercing whine of metal-on-metal screeched so loudly that Ruby wanted to cover her ears. Only she couldn't move without the risk of falling. Sparks flew from the locomotive's wheels which glowed, like they'd been heated in a steel furnace. As the train shuddered and jolted to a stop, the zombie cluster swayed, toppling over into a mangled heap.

The moment the train stopped, Ruby jumped from the ladder, landing on stones. Yu followed, but when the girl hit the ground, she yelped. Her right calf revealed a deep ragged-edged wound in the shape of an eight. A zombie bite. Ruby's heart sank. But grieving had to wait. The first priorities were to stop the bleeding and get far away from the infested train.

Snatching the red bandana, she tied a makeshift tourniquet around Yu's wound. The girl winced as the cloth ends were manipulated into a taut knot.

Ruby pointed back and forth between them. "We run to Sun Yat-sen Freeway. Okay?"

Yu nodded.

Behind a curtain of darkening skies and pummeling rains, Taipei's skyline looked miles away. Sun Yat-sen Freeway ran north of Dunhua

North Road—the road that passed in front of the Mandarin Oriental Hotel. Maybe on the freeway, they could hitch a ride to their destinations.

A female zombie grunted and clicked her teeth behind the rail of the observation deck. Reaching, she extended her bloodied arm toward them. The zombie's waist stretched across the rail until the undead fell over it, landing on the gravel by the train.

"Go!" Ruby ordered. "I'll follow!"

The teenager ran as best she could on one good leg, dragging her injured limb behind her and pumping her arms to compensate, thrusting her body forward in jerky hops. They headed toward the lead railcar, keeping the train on their right.

At last they came to the first railcar—the locomotive cabin where the engineer and conductor operated the train. Ruby lifted her chin, glancing at the train's windows, hoping to see someone in authority.

Her heart sputtered.

Blood. Crimson blood was smeared on the side window so thick, she couldn't see inside. The onboard zombie attack had undoubtedly forced the team to abruptly stop the train. Sadly, their human existence had probably stopped at the same time.

Yu looked at her, eyebrows raised, as if looking for direction.

Ruby waved her hand forward. "Go! To the freeway!"

The teenager hobbled in front of the stopped train and navigated rows of tracks until she entered a wooded parcel of land. Ruby followed closely behind, shielding her eyes from the rain.

Amid the trees, Yu slowed to a limp. She pointed. A man was walking fifteen yards ahead, his back toward them. He was outfitted in a gray business-suit that was saturated, but intact. No shredded fabric. No blood stains. The opposite of Yu. With eggplant-colored stains on the bandana and streams of dark blood escaping under the cloth and running down her calf, discoloring her sock, Yu looked like a victim. But not this man.

When the distance between the man and Yu narrowed, the girl called to him in Mandarin. The man stopped. And turned. Unnaturally slow.

Ruby's hand trembled behind her, hovering over the pistol stuffed barrel-down into her back pocket.

As the man turned, a moist gurgle escaped from his lipless mouth. Although still wearing his office-best, he had been a main entrée. Because now he was faceless. No eyes, no ears, no nose—wearing the raw evidence of where flesh had been torn away to extract blood. A gruesome inductee into the immortal fraternity of the walking dead.

Grabbing the pistol, she cocked the action and extended both arms in front of her, pointing the barrel at the zombie and lining-up the sights.

"Down!" Ruby hollered to Yu, while nodding toward the ground.

The girl squatted while the zombie stepped toward them. Ruby pulled the trigger and shot him in the forehead. The undead dropped, twitching on the ground until ZOM-B's internal fight was lost.

Four rounds remained.

The teenager didn't blink or shudder.

"Freeway there." Yu pointed ahead.

17

Sunday, July 11, 2032
The American Consulate: Taipei, Taiwan

TO BE CLEAR as black ice, Ox videofaced the helicopter pilot tasked with extracting the Spencers from the Naval base. He warned the moron again, that he'd better find the girl *this* time. Unless the idiot wanted his balls shoved down his throat like oysters. Cocktail sauce included.

After ending the conversation, Ox pounded his fist on the mahogany desk, rattling the picture frames and splashing steaming French Roast onto the desktop. Did everything have to turn into a soup sandwich when he trusted his men to carry-out assignments?

When he gave the order to retrieve the Spencers from Keelung, he had anticipated the couple would be together. Okay, so he'd miscalculated. His bad. But could his team be such mental FUBARs that they did not comprehend, at this juncture in the game, that Ruby—and Ruby alone—was *the* prize? The only one that mattered?

At least Insley had redeemed himself. He'd give the young man that. When the girl contacted the consulate, Insley had kept his cool and arranged for a chopper pick-up at the Keelung Station, in the parking lot. Everything should have been textbook.

But no! The cheesedick pilot, who decided to follow flight-safety protocol, checking off each meticulous step one-by-one, took forty…LONG…minutes to arrive at the train station where he was supposed to rendezvous with the girl. And he missed her, for fuck's sake. Big surprise. Instead, he scoped the husband standing in the same parking lot and without seeking confirmation, landed the bird, picked up half-the-package—the *wrong* half, and returned to Zhuchang Park.

After delivering Mr. Spencer—which was followed by an ass-ripping, ball-pinching, face-spitting verbal assault from none-other than Ox himself, the pilot limped his pathetic butt-hole back into the chopper and lifted off, returning to the not-so-friendly skies to find the real prize: Ruby the fuck Spencer.

The only reason the husband retained *any* value, whatsoever, was as collateral, able to motivate his wife to do exactly what was asked of her.

Without the girl, there was no mission.

FUBARs: his entire team was fucked up beyond all repair.

18

Sunday, July 11, 2032
Taipei, Taiwan

CARS SPED BY on the freeway, spraying accumulated rainwater as they passed. Thunder roared over the steady rumble of engines.

Standing on the shoulder facing oncoming traffic, Ruby moved Yu behind her to prevent drivers from seeing the girl's festering injury. As the rain and wind swirled around them, Ruby waved her arms like a marooned Sailor. Maybe it was the raging storm or maybe she looked like the desperate American she was, but a vehicle pulled over to give them a ride.

She opened the rear passenger-door for her injured friend. She wanted to avoid having the girl sit in the front seat where the driver could gawk at her calf-wound before forcing them back out onto the freeway.

As Yu entered the sedan, Ruby eyed the teenager's injury. Black veins were already showing like squiggly, bulging black worms beneath the skin, boring up and down from the bite. The ZOM-B infection was spreading, invading her young friend's body. Yu's human life was ticking down to zero and would stop in less than four hours—momentarily.

At least Seaman Davis had died from his wounds *first*. Yu's bite, however, clearly wasn't going to kill her. Her death would be executed slowly, by the nefarious bacterial-mutation blackening her veins and organs, rotting her body while it was still warm.

As Ruby lowered herself into the front passenger seat, a chopper's rotating thrum was carried overhead with the wind. Maybe the chopper was the one dispatched from the consulate. Regardless, she was long-gone from the station in Keelung. Taipei and her hotel were now in her grasp. She'd stay the course.

After closing the car door, she looked at the driver and thanked him. She pointed through the front windshield, down the freeway, and said the name of her hotel. The man dipped his head forward and smiled politely, as if familiar with the hotel's location in the city.

The man drove into thickening traffic. From the backseat, Yu conversed with him in Mandarin. After a few minutes, she tapped Ruby's shoulder. "Man says Gray people—zombies—now in Taipei. Very bad," the girl translated.

All Ruby wanted was to reach her hotel, take the elevator to the sixth floor, swing open her suite door, and run into her husband's arms. After they contacted President Newton, they'd make their way to the consulate for a 5:00 p.m. departure in a helicopter bound for the nearby Taoyuan International Airport. She and Clay could not miss their flight home to Gabby.

The driver stopped curbside by the Mandarin Oriental. Ruby released the stale air she'd been storing in her lungs, waiting for the moment she was able to purge her building stress. Hopefully the driver wouldn't mind taking Yu to her home. The teenager's family, not Ruby, needed to decide what to do about their daughter's infection, about her countdown to *un*death.

Ruby exited the vehicle and bent over, looking at the driver. "Thank you so much." She did a body nod and the man returned the gesture. "Please take Yu home. Yes?"

But the girl opened the car door, raised herself out, and hopped on her good leg to Ruby's side. "No. Coming with you," Yu countered.

"Go to your family. This man: he will take you home."

"No. Stay here."

Ruby thanked the driver again and closed both doors. With pouring rain, high winds, and a zombie outbreak, it wasn't the time-or-place to detain the kind man who had so generously given them a ride. Nor was it appropriate to argue with the teenager who had helped her return to the Mandarin Oriental during utter chaos.

The man drove away.

"Come," Yu said, hopping toward the right side of the hotel, toward a narrow abandoned-alley between the building and the side of a bank.

"Wait, Yu! My husband. I have to see if my husband is here."

The girl stopped. Turning, she looked at Ruby with eyes of a wise elder. Like she understood the weight of the moment.

Tears streamed down Yu's cheeks. "Please," she cried.

"Okay. But only for a moment. Show me what's so important."

Ruby had no idea why Yu was leading her to the secluded alcove. The girl finally sat down on a drenched patch of grass, at the mouth of the alleyway. She removed the bandana. The wound was black. A lava-like crust sealed the bite.

The teenager locked eyes with her, then pointed to herself. "Me. Gray."

"Not yet. You still have time to say goodbye to your family—to your Mom and Dad. To your friends. Make the most of your last hours."

The girl scrunched her eyebrows. "Parents in Beijing. No gun." She touched her index finger to her forehead, in between her eyes. "Shoot. Please. No zombie. Not *me*."

Ruby couldn't fathom the girl's request. She couldn't shoot her: *alive*!

"Please," Yu whimpered before her body was racked with sobs. "Shoot, please."

But Ruby couldn't. She squatted and rubbed the teenager's back. "Come inside with me," she pleaded, pointing to the hotel. "We'll talk to my husband. Figure things out."

The girl shook her head. Determined. Stubborn. Like she knew the time and way she wanted to sign out. Death on *her* terms. And Ruby understood; she'd want the same.

"Shoot. Please," Yu said calmly. She peered into Ruby's eyes. "Ready *now*."

Behind them in the alley, the swooshing of a disturbed puddle caught their attention. A zombie was sloshing toward them, dressed in a blood-stained floral sundress, with one foot in a pump and the other barefoot, walking cockeyed and clicking her teeth. *Click, click,*

click.

Ruby stood and withdrew the pistol, taking aim at the zombie.

"No!" Yu yelled, sounding desperate. "Shoot me. Me first. *Pleeease!*"

Ruby swung her sights between Yu's eyes. Pausing. Trying to muster courage. Her trigger finger, trembling. But she still couldn't do it. And now the undead was only twenty-feet away. She pivoted and sighted the zombie's forehead once again. Her hand, shaking.

"Please!" the teenager begged.

Ruby's heart slammed against her ribcage.

"Now!" Yu screamed, pounding her chest. "Now!"

The pistol pointed back to her young friend. Ruby's heart was about to combust. Explode into a thousand pieces.

The zombie inched closer.

The wind subsided. The air thickened like molasses.

Everything froze. A hitch in time.

A loud siren suddenly wailed over the city streets. The sound was so piercingly shrill, that Ruby couldn't help but cover her ears with her hands. Her eardrums might burst.

Yu toppled over.

The zombie dropped to her knees before falling forward like felled timber.

Disorientated, Ruby blinked. The bone-jarring shriek rattled her brain. As the siren abated, it was replaced with screeching tires and twisting metal. Horns blew—relentlessly, like the drivers were protesting. And then there was quiet. Only the sounds of ruptured, hissing car-engines remained, in concert with the howls of whipping wind and rain.

Thumbing the de-cocking lever, Ruby returned the pistol to her pocket. She bent over next to the teenager who had fallen on her side. Gently placing her trembling hand under Yu's chin, she lifted her face. Darkened blood oozed from the girl's eyes, nose, ears, and mouth. Her lifeless bloodshot-eyes were open.

A crashing wave of sadness knocked Ruby to her knees. She recognized the weapon: Remote Electronic Detonators, Huo's nanorobotic WMD of choice. REDs were the size of pinheads packed with uber technology—the same devices embedded in the tainted Chinese-manufactured meat supplement which killed a billion innocents. The Taiwanese people had obviously consumed the microscopic devices after all, like the rest of the world. But unlike the World War III detonation, this attack had been delayed somehow. Who could have authorized *this* mass killing? Huo's government had been dismantled and Huo was a zombie.

Standing, Ruby ran toward the street, scanning the landscape. The dead were everywhere—humans and zombies alike. Dead people were in crashed cars. Were sprawled on sidewalks, their escaped umbrellas racing and bouncing down the street, carried by the wind. Dead people were on doorsteps. In the parking lot.

The city was lifeless.

Death once again had spared her, leaving her alive among the dead.

Destiny, her mother would have said. But whatever the reason, one thing was clear: she was changing. She no longer feared that death was chasing her, biting at her heels, threatening to make her face life alone. She was no longer a bystander, someone who happened to survive for reasons unknown.

And she'd no longer recoil. Or retreat.

She was emerging as a fighter, in the face of death. And for the first time, she'd claim *her* life, *her* time, no matter how much or how little she had left. So despite the undead or the typhoon or the pulseless city, Ruby would persevere. Survival wouldn't just happen; she'd *make* it happen.

She'd reunite with Clay, find the consulate, and return home to Gabby.

Let anything or anyone try to stop her.

19

Sunday, July 11, 2032
Mandarin Oriental Hotel: Taipei, Taiwan

RUBY PULLED OPEN the heavy, arched glass-door to the hotel lobby at the same time the electricity shut down. The hum of systems powering-off faded to silence. She glanced over her shoulder toward the street. Power had also been cut to the city.

Taipei had flatlined.

Stepping inside the lobby, the smells of normal life lingered. The massive room, boasting twenty-foot ceilings, still smelled fresh and clean. Scents of recently brewed teas and coffees and freshly cut roses wafted in the air. Death hadn't staled the surroundings. Yet.

The aromas contrasted the scene. About two-dozen people had fallen to the floor when time abruptly stopped. A man and woman, dressed in couture, lay next to each other—face up—on the white marble floor. Their bodies interrupted the symmetry of the swirling, decorative tiles that embellished the marble with patterns of black ribbons. The woman's pearl necklace, probably Akoya, had broken, scattering the cream beads. Blood dripped from opened eyes, ears, noses, and mouths.

Ruby raced to the entrance of the sitting lounge. "Is anyone here?" she shouted, her voice echoing off the walls.

Several ladies who had been sitting on the lounge's velvet couches—backed with silvery silk, had toppled over, spilling their Wuyi oolong tea. Spring-rolls and sushi once artfully decorating handheld dishes were sloppily disassembled on the floor. The dishes, broken. Violence hadn't spared even the most delicate of comforts.

And where there was previously polite chatter, no one spoke. Or giggled. Or whimpered. Or breathed.

Jogging back to the lobby, she glanced to the right of the reception counter. An elevator door was flush against a man sprawled across its track. Blood oozed from his mouth, forming a small pool on the marble.

Anxiety gripped her lungs like octopus-tentacles squeezing prey. Her heart pressed against her chest. Her breathing hitched. What if something had happened to Clay? Maybe he was injured when the brains of those around him exploded to mush. Or maybe he had never escaped from the Naval base. Maybe he'd been accidentally shot. Worse, bitten.

Now was not the time to fall apart.

She clenched her fists to regain control. Inhaling, she searched for the positive. Clay might be waiting for her in their suite.

Racing toward the hotel's stairwell, she stumbled across a security officer. He was lying near the door, face down. She eyed his utility belt which carried a pistol. Another firearm couldn't hurt. Anyway, she was low on ammo. Unsnapping the handgun from its holster, she grabbed the nine-millimeter and removed the magazine, eyeballing the clip. It was full: fifteen rounds. She snapped the magazine back into place.

"Positive thinking," she whispered, jamming the new pistol into her left back-pocket, leaving Seaman Davis's in her right.

She entered the stairwell. Windows allowed charcoal skies to brighten the spiraled shaft. She climbed the steps, two at a time. When she reached the sixth-floor landing, she was winded, but unstoppable. Opening the exit door, she glanced both ways down the shadowy hallway, dimly lit by emergency lights on battery-backup. To the right, two housekeepers lay lifeless on the patterned carpet, next to their cleaning cart.

She darted left, reaching into her front pocket for the keycard attached to her money clip. Battery-backup had its benefits.

After swiping her card, she threw open the suite's door and raced inside. "Clay?"

20

Sunday, July 11, 2032
The White House Oval Office: Washington, D.C.

JUST PAST MIDNIGHT, exhausted from an already strenuous day, President Newton was losing patience. She grabbed her laptop and left the Situation Room, flanked by Secret Service operatives, bound for the Oval Office. A break was in order. And if there were any changes, the assembled team would contact her.

Could the situation get any worse?

Code Red had been activated at the Naval base in Keelung. *Code Red*...while the Spencers were observing the freak show! If Ruby was killed, Emory's work would come to a screeching halt. The girl was key to everything. All would be lost. They'd have to reset at zero.

Also unsavory, the Special Warfare Council would have every right to blame her. Luther Pennington already did; he had been staunchly against the Taiwan assignment from the beginning. Perhaps against the classified project itself. But the President had insisted on sending the girl despite the Council's warnings. And why not? Emory had convinced her—promised even—that he had enough of Ruby's blood in storage to finish the job. Everything would go smoothly, he had assured her.

Smoothly? More like spike strips on a highway.

Sweet Mother of Jesus. She had hit a new low. When had she become so trusting?

If she didn't hear from Ruby soon, she'd activate the embedded locator-chips via ISSI, to find out where in the hell the couple was.

Of course, ISSI was operating at full capacity, given Taiwan's outbreak. And there was still the issue of not wanting to needlessly raise eyebrows about the girl's importance. Locator chips were typically reserved for high-level operatives and required mounds of paperwork. Which obviously hadn't been submitted for the Spencers.

No breadcrumbs could lead back to Project Voodu. None. At. All.

One fact was crystal clear: she should have ended the zombie study weeks ago. Should've incinerated the bastards, reducing them to ashes. Because one walking dead, just one, spread the infection like bindweed. The Naval base fiasco proved that. In less than an hour, the damn infection went viral, consuming two cities. Taipei and Keelung were war zones!

As forty-seven Presidents had done before her, she walked down the grand hallways of the White House. She rubbed her temple to slough off frustration. Or was it anxiety?

To compound the matter, SEALs on the ground reported another massive RED detonation. Who in the hell had orchestrated *that*? And why hadn't intel verified that the Taiwanese had RED implants in the first place? She had been assured—given a ninety-eight percent probability, in fact—that the opposite was true. The opposite!

Sharpen the blade. Someone's neck was going on the chopping block. And it wasn't going to be hers.

Next up in the pile of blunders and miscalculations: Ambassador Jeffries. He wasn't answering calls. Calls to find out where the girl was. But at least Lance Corporal Insley, one of the Marines she had covertly placed on "Spencer duty," had contacted her to report that he had heard from the girl and a chopper had been dispatched to extract her. Sounded great, except he promised to confirm when she arrived at the consulate…safe. As yet, he hadn't initiated another contact via ISSI—the only way to communicate since all other systems were now offline on the island.

At least Insley had confirmed the consulate was secure. Praise the Lord: no infections. No security breaches. And her Marine—whom she'd have to decorate and promote—had mentioned that Ambassador Jeffries was personally assessing conditions at the Naval base, onsite, to offer assurances and comfort to the handful of survivors. So "Jon." A do-gooder through and through. Mr. Eagle

Scout himself. Still, the man had to learn to *communicate*. With *her*.

The President entered the Oval Office, shed her security detail, and closed the door. Setting the laptop on her desk, she plugged in the power cord as a safeguard. She was anxious to hear the device's alarm: notification that someone with clearance was initiating ISSI for a live-stream communication. She stared at the laptop's screen; the Presidential seal rotated in 3D against a royal-blue background. No connections were in progress.

She'd give the girl five more minutes. After that, she'd activate the GPS locator chips.

While the clocked ticked on, her blood began to boil. Throughout the unfolding crisis, the consulate's military attaché was AWOL again. No more. His ass was getting court martialed. Quinton Oxford would be exposed. And she'd hammer the last nail into his dishonorable discharge. He'd be stripped of his precious bars and medals, if she had anything to do with it. Denied his pension— including the stipend for the MOH. She was done with Ox. Finished.

Her heart jolted when the laptop's alarm sounded: *beep, beep, beep*. The digital timer on her screen showed seven minutes for signal acquisition. She prayed the caller would be Ruby, or at least Insley.

Seven minutes passed, painstakingly slow, like getting a cavity filled. At last, the clock displayed thirty-seconds. The President sat at her desk as the live image came into focus.

"Ruby! Thank God!" President Newton said. "I've been anxious to hear from you. So much has happened. Are you safe?"

"My husband. Have you heard from him? Know where he is?"

"Clayton's not with you?"

The girl shook her head.

"SEALs have retaken the base. They'll conduct an inventory as soon as they can. I'm sorry, Ruby. At this point, I'm not sure if your husband is in the facility or not."

The girl lowered her head and covered her eyes with her hands. "Where could he be?"

"I'm sure he's on his way back to the hotel. Keep in mind: with the RED attack, the city is at a standstill. The only way to move is by military helicopter or on-foot, in a strengthening storm no less." She massaged her temples again, willing a solution to rise. Lifting her face seconds later, she stared into the laptop screen. "I've got it. While we talk, I'll have video footage of the base's exits reviewed, to determine if Clayton left the building. If he did, we should be able to ascertain his condition."

President Newton held up an index finger, signaling she needed a moment. Using her smartwatch, she contacted the Situation Room, gave the order to her VP, and ended the call.

"Thank you so much," Ruby said.

"Listen: I'd send a team to retrieve you, but all assets are fully engaged in the crisis. Even if I could deploy a squad, the streets are impassable, clogged with vehicles; it would take forever and there's no time to spare. So I'll need you to hoof-it to the consulate, which is secure by the way. Do you have a firearm with ammunition?"

"I have two pistols. In one, I have fifteen rounds. Four in the other. But respectfully, Madam President, I'm not leaving this hotel without Clay. We agreed to meet here."

"You don't appreciate the danger you're in. You need the security of the consulate and more than anything, you need to be evacuated and brought home."

"Security? Why? Most people and zombies are dead."

"Not everyone. Think this through…military personnel are RED-free, which means those infected weren't killed by the siren. Add to that the Russian container ship which limped into Keelung this morning (your time), delivering a shipload of infected. We haven't been able to determine if the aberrations were destroyed in the RED attack. And some Taiwanese undoubtedly resisted consuming the RED-tainted meat. Which leaves an undetermined number of zombies roaming the hotzone, looking for sustenance. And I need the odds in your favor, Ruby. *Gabriella* needs the odds in your favor."

President Newton mentally acknowledged that mentioning the child was a low-blow. But she had to play hardball. She couldn't risk having the girl physically vulnerable, more than she already was.

"Who's responsible for the RED attack anyway? Do you know?"

The girl was clever, shifting the conversation to buy time, while she weighed the options. The President couldn't let down her guard or she'd lose control. Ruby could be beyond stubborn.

"That is *the* question of the day," the President answered. "The one worrying me, my Cabinet, and Ambassador Jeffries at our Taipei consulate. The entire Federation, actually. But we're digging deep."

A knock on the Oval Office door, the one leading to Christian's office, interrupted her conversation. A staffer entered and handed her a piece of paper. After dismissing him, President Newton read the penned note to herself, written by Fletcher Baldwin, her VP.

Smiling, she locked eyes with Ruby on the laptop screen. "Good news. Clayton exited the compound at 1300 hours, or one o'clock. Fifteen minutes after you left. And he was running, visibly human, and appeared uninjured."

The girl exhaled deeply. Her shoulders lowered.

"It's settled then," Ruby announced. "I'll hunker down here and wait for him."

"Negative," the President snapped, perhaps too quickly. Too aggressively. "The situation is dire." She took a breath, trying to regain composure. "Let me suggest this: I'll order our responding units to be on the look-out for Clayton. We're already canvassing the entire area between Keelung and Taipei, so we'll find him. Meanwhile, as a backup, leave a note for your husband in the suite; let him know where you've gone. And then head to the consulate."

The President didn't feel particularly good about lying. But she certainly couldn't task boots, on-the-ground or with-wings, to search for a man who wasn't an asset in the first place. All was fair and *un*fair in war. Sweet Mother of Jesus: everybody knew that.

Over the speakers, a boom vibrated her laptop, sending it humming along the surface of her desk. The streaming image of the girl blurred for a second. Maybe the blast was caused from large-caliber artillery or an explosion?

"What was that?" the President asked, her blood pressure rising a notch. "Is your suite secure? Your hotel?"

Ruby scanned her surroundings and pulled a pistol from her back pocket. "Not sure. But my door is locked." She cocked the action and placed the handgun on the table.

"You need to follow my advisement," the President continued. "Go to the consulate for evac. Let me worry about finding your husband—I have the resources. As your President and Commander in Chief, I am giving you an order, Ruby Spencer."

Another boom rattled the room.

"I'm not sure how to get to the consulate," the girl admitted. "I have no smartwatch. No GPS."

"It's easy. Run due west from the back of your hotel. You'll pass through three small parks, the last being Zhuchang Park. The consulate is west of the park, on Lane 36. It should take you fifteen to twenty minutes—at most."

"What then? What happens when I get there?"

"Ask for the Ambassador. He's currently at the Naval base assessing damages. When he returns, he will personally see to it that you and Clayton are airlifted by chopper to TPE Airport where you'll board a military plane, non-stop to Dulles. When you arrive at the airport, you'll be met at the gate and transported to the White House. Before meeting with me, you'll be given a health evaluation—Emory suggested it. Then we'll debrief before you head to Annapolis. You are almost home, Ruby."

The girl paused. Her eyes shimmered with moisture.

"President Newton...why us? Why the personal attention? I mean, I'm grateful; please don't misunderstand. But I'm also curious. It's not like my blood makes a difference anymore. I know it saved the world from the F8 bacteria not too long ago. But now? Now, I'm like everybody else: defenseless against ZOM-B. Why work so hard to save us?"

"You and Clayton are key members of *my* Special Warfare think-tank. Besides, no one is expendable in my book. And let's be honest: you've been on my mission—one that pulled you away from your child. I hardly want Gabriella to grow up knowing the President of the United States didn't do everything possible to rescue her parents."

Tears streamed from the girl's eyes.

"One more thing before we disconnect," the President continued. "Like I warned you before, steer clear of Ox. Only work with the Ambassador. Understood?"

"Yes. And thank you, President Newton. Thank you so much. I'll head to the consulate after writing a note to Clay. And please, please find my husband."

"Count on it."

21

Sunday, July 11, 2032
Taipei, Taiwan

RUBY WROTE CLAY, leaving the note on the nightstand. Pulling six bullets from the loaded magazine once belonging to the hotel security guard, she added them to Seaman Davis's handgun and placed the pistol on top of the stationary. She slid the laptop into her backpack, beside the lantern-sock and journal. After zipping her hooded jacket and hoisting the backpack onto her shoulders, she raced from the suite, down the stairwell, and into the lobby.

At the front entrance, she pushed against the main door of the Mandarin Oriental, but the wind tried to force her back inside. She forged forward, gritting her teeth and squeezing through the opening before the heavy door slammed behind her. Pelting her jacket and legs, rain carried debris that stuck to her body like Velcro. On the concrete walkway in front of the hotel, she searched up and down Dunhua North Road, willing herself to see Clay. But he wasn't in sight.

The road was littered with crashed vehicles—some with engines still running, steam rising off hoods, with wheels planted against a tree or lamp-post or car, wipers swiping, and radios emitting pre-recorded programming. Other vehicles were crushed and mangled, metal smashed against a building or wall, billowing radiator steam. In the distance, a large plume of smoke mushroomed, the wind and rain hampering a full bloom.

Despite the mechanical world's resistance to die, nothing else moved. Except for her. She raced around the left side of the hotel, intentionally avoiding the other side. The place where Yu lay. She couldn't endure seeing the girl's lifeless body. Or watch ZOM-B goo being carried in breakaway streams of rain, searching for new hosts.

Thankfully, it would be easy to run west using buildings and streets as city-markers. The parks would be manageable, too. A lot less complicated than the dense woods near the Naval base in Keelung, in Yizheng Park where trees and bushes looked similar.

The intersection between Qingcheng and Xing'an streets resembled an overcrowded demolition derby, with vehicle survival at zero. Already drenched, Ruby climbed over the warm hood of a Camry, its driver slumped against the steering wheel. She eyed the jumbled vehicles around her. They were different makes, models, and colors. Some were full of passengers, seat-belted in place. Others were empty, except for the driver.

Each person had departed life with a story. Some might've been heading to the vegetable market, library, or university. Others had picked up their kids from school. A few were probably rushing to their last business-meeting of the afternoon. Or making a delivery, trying to beat the clock. Regardless, they had all stopped unexpectedly. With no time for last thoughts.

The hair on her arms stood-on-end and she shivered.

A mid-sized commercial truck had crashed into a tree, a branch piercing the windshield of the driver's side. As she neared, a zombie shuffled out from behind the vehicle. His nose was raised toward the sky like an animal registering prey.

She startled and the undead clicked his teeth, jaws snapping. Bloodied arms reaching.

Her heart leapt into double-time. Raising the pistol, she pulled the trigger. No hesitation. A bullet to the head.

The President had been right. Not all zombies were killed by the RED attack.

Where would she and Clay be without President Newton? Maybe dead. Most definitely stranded and forgotten. She shuddered thinking about it.

Fast paced and never looking back, she ran until she exited the last park: Zhuchang. She turned full circle to scan her surroundings. No one—alive or undead—was following her.

With the park behind her, she saw Lane 36 and tucked the handgun in her back pocket. She slowed as she approached the consulate which was sandwiched between two buildings, both with boarded windows. Two Humvees were parked in front of the property and a tall, barbed-wire fence enclosed all three buildings.

Two Marines stood inside the gate, in the rain, clutching military assault-rifles. As she neared, she recognized one of them: the Marine who had accepted her videoface from the bus in Keelung. Stubs of fiery-red hair peeked out from his hat and freckles dappled his cheeks and nose. INSLEY was embroidered on his military-issued raincoat.

"ID, please," Insley ordered, reaching for her passport through the chain links. "You are Ruby Spencer, correct?"

"Yes, sir," she said, pushing her identification through the fencing. "Thank you for taking my call earlier."

Insley didn't respond. He reviewed her passport, glancing back and forth between the photo and her rain-drenched face. "We've been expecting you." He returned the booklet.

The other guard, named WYATT, unlocked the gate and motioned with his rifle to enter. "We've got to frisk you, Mrs. Spencer. Strict Protocol."

"Here." Ruby pulled the pistol from her pocket and handed it to Wyatt. "This is all I've got. Believe me: I wish I had more."

He sniffed the barrel. "Have you shot this recently?"

"About ten minutes ago. Had to take down a zombie en route."

Wyatt ran his hands over her arms, patted her wet jacket and shirt on all sides, and smoothed over each leg, even though she was wearing shorts.

"Your backpack?" he asked.

She handed him the pouch. "Inside is a special laptop that connects me to President Newton. I'll need that back. I also have important artifacts in there, that I'll be submitting to the Special Warfare Council."

"Talk to Ox," Wyatt said, sounding unimpressed. "Orders come from him."

With Ox's name spoken, adrenaline shot through her veins, instantly raising her body temperature. Her lips quivered. Ox: the military attaché she was warned to avoid.

"Okay," she said, trying to maintain an even timbre. "Just so you know, the President has directed me to ask for Ambassador Jeffries."

"Then you've fulfilled your mission," the frisker said, smiling. "*Just so you know.*"

Ruby couldn't tell if the Marine was teasing or being aggressive. She smiled, hoping he was attempting humor, though it was an odd time to be joking.

"This way, Mrs. Spencer," Wyatt said, sweeping his hand toward the front door of the consulate, as if inviting her onto a dance floor. "Let's get this party started."

The Marine named Insley remained at the gate while she and her escort entered the building. Wyatt led her to a stately office on the first floor, appointed with wood floors and an oriental rug. Sitting behind the leather-topped desk was a chiseled man, maybe in his mid-forties, with straight posture and a flat-top hairstyle. Muscles bulged under his blue-speckled uniform, as if he needed a larger size but had refused. Probably preferred to flex his muscles as a warning.

Standing when she walked in, the hulk-*ish* Marine officer sauntered in front of the desk, with his right hand extended. "Mrs. Spencer, I've heard so much about you. We meet in-person at last. You may call me Ox; everybody does. Any trouble getting here?"

She shook his large hand. And he squeezed more firmly than expected. Almost to the point of being painful.

"Not anything I couldn't handle," she answered, hoping her words projected strength, without offering a challenge.

22

Sunday, July 11, 2032
The American Consulate: Taipei, Taiwan

OX WAS ANNOYED. The first thing Ruby Spencer did, after removing her windbreaker, was to ask for Ambassador Jeffries. That rubbed him the wrong way.

Little miss blood-bank had a thing or two to learn about hierarchy. *She* was the plucked ripe-peach and *he* was the sharp knife hankering for some warm peach pie. Which meant the only inquiries should be posed from his lips.

The GOFO truth, as in grasp-of-the-fucking-obvious, was this: if he didn't need her, if his plan didn't rest on her ability to bleed her precious oil into blood bags, then he'd certainly honor her request in a hot second. Of course, Jonny Ambassador wouldn't be speaking back, but she wouldn't live long enough to wonder why.

With his mood turning for the worse, Ox pressed his lips together and contemplated biting his tongue. Pain sometimes helped him overcome anger. Got his brain thinking about alternatives. And alternatives were always based on priorities, not desires. He knew this. Discipline 101.

There'd be plenty of opportunities for dessert.

No mistaking she was finger-licking sweet. Now that her jacket was off, he drooled over her defined muscles. He hated delicate wallflowers. What kind of challenge were they? They screamed too easily. But there was one thing he wished about this babe-of-a-peach standing in front of him, only two feet apart. He wished she was wearing a white blouse, instead of black. He would have liked to have seen her breasts, especially rubbing against wet fabric. Were her nipples dark? Would they be standing at attention, teasing him? Wanting to be licked and bitten? He was getting a hard-on. He almost looked down to admire it.

"Lieutenant Colonel?" she asked.

He retreated behind the desk. There was one disadvantage to wearing a tight uniform: his emotions stuck out.

"Take a seat, Mrs. Spencer," he said, pointing to the chair in front of the desk, before nodding to Wyatt who quickly retreated from the room. "President Newton insisted I brief you, the moment you arrived. When—"

"She *did?*"

"Mrs. Spencer, let me school you on military etiquette. When a superior is talking, you do not interrupt. It is insubordinate. Am I clear?"

"Yes, sir."

"Ahh, a quick learner." He smiled, flashing his chiclets. "We might get along real swell. Now as I was saying: when President Newton and I spoke minutes ago, I informed her that Ambassador Jeffries was a casualty during the siren. The damn fool, if you'll forgive me for speaking ill of the dead, must have eaten the RED-tainted dogmeat, despite being warned."

"Ambassador Jeffries is...*dead?* But I thought..."

"He was at the Naval base? That intel didn't pan out."

The girl looked like she was processing the sequence of events. Determining whether the information was credible. Ox stared at her, hoping to disrupt her with intimidation.

"I'm sorry. Did I interrupt again?" She lowered her eyes.

"Let's not dwell on bad news, shall we? Because your husband was found."

She gasped and pursed her lips, like she might speak. But then she stopped herself. She *was* a quick learner! And he liked people who took direction, especially reluctantly. He liked how their internal struggle, which they always thought was hidden, made him feel powerful.

"Mr. Spencer was taken to TPE International and is en route to

Geneva, where he'll wait for you. The President insisted you travel together, back to the States. But with deteriorating conditions and a few pressing matters—which I won't bore you with, a Geneva rendezvous was the best alternative."

He noted her reaction: her eyes grew wide; lips trembled. She clutched the armrests.

"Is there a question, Mrs. Spencer?"

"Yes, please. Is my husband okay? Is he hurt? Where was he found?"

"You have difficulty accepting literal orders, don't you? You've asked three questions, instead of one." He sighed, rubbing his flat-top in rapid succession, trying to slough off frustration. She was an oxygen thief, stealing his fresh air and time. "Yes, Mrs. Spencer, your husband is okay, unharmed. He was commandeered by our chopper in Keelung and temporarily brought here. You missed him by a half hour—tops."

The girl exhaled slowly before smiling.

"Knew you would appreciate the news." He rose from the desk and approached her, clasping the handle of a small cooler.

Why not have some fun? He was curious how she'd play it. Would she get squeamish?

"At 1700 hours—in twenty minutes," he continued, "you are going to board a chopper in Zhuchang Park. It will transport you to Songshan Airport, where you'll board a Yak-40 to Geneva." He placed the cooler on the floor next to her chair. "Know what this is?"

"The zombie head of the CDC scientist, I assume," she answered, wearing an expression he couldn't peg.

"Marines never assume. Open and see."

The girl leaned over and raised the cooler's insulated lid. The moment the lid lifted, he heard the Gray clicking his teeth. The cooler smelled like shorts, baked in day-old shit during hell-week—in August.

Closing the lid, she locked eyes with him. "The zombie head, like I thought. Thank you."

A quick learner *and* composed. A bonus.

His damn smartwatch chimed. Who was calling him *now*, for fuck's sake?

"If you will excuse me for one moment, Mrs. Spencer. Please remain seated."

Like a general, he strutted from the office, hoping she'd notice his tight ass.

23

RUBY ROLLED HER eyes as Ox paraded from his office. She was surprised he hadn't told her when to inhale and exhale. No doubt Lieutenant Colonel Quinton Oxford was the epitome of an ego-trip, his luggage overstuffed with testosterone and arrogance.

She glanced around the room, wondering if security cameras were recording her. Although she couldn't spot any, she remained in her chair, figuring she could obey the order while satisfying her curiosity. Lifting a frame displayed on his desk, she eyed the photograph. A classy woman—older than Ox—stood in the middle of four young-adult children: three boys and a girl. Their smiles, their eyes told her they loved, and were loved.

As she returned the frame, she eyed a pewter envelope opener, designed with a sharp metal-blade resembling a knife.

The heavy tread of military boots reentered the room. Her heart jolted.

"Where were we?" Ox said, swiftly returning to the leather chair behind his desk. "Looks like we have a few minutes before the chopper arrives. Any questions for me?"

She willed her heartbeat to slow. "May we speak freely, Lieutenant Colonel Oxford?"

"I prefer Ox. And yes, you have my permission to speak without limitations."

"Does Patti Davis work here, Ox? I was hoping to talk with her. I knew her brother."

"Did."

"Did?"

"Patti Davis *did* work here." He tapped his fingers on the desktop. "In case you haven't noticed, Mrs. Spencer, we're not in normal-operations mode around here. Patti's not in the staff kitchen microwaving a cup of green tea, chatting about how island humidity makes her panties get all moist in the crotch."

Ruby was horrified and must have shown it on her face.

"Now it's my turn to apologize," Ox said. "How rude of me. See, I'm surrounded by Marines and Sailors who haven't been home with their wives and girlfriends since World War III. We get a little…expressive, sometimes. I apologize."

"I understand," she said, lying. "So where *is* Patti? Do you know?"

"Stacked next to Ambassador Jeffries in the walk-in refrigerator, down in the basement," he answered, matter of fact. Sans emotion. "I can show you, if you would like." His eyebrows arched.

"No thank you." She urged herself to breathe steady.

"It is baffling why some Americans, especially government employees, ignore simple directives: *Do Not Eat the Meat.* For God's sake: if you can't resist childish curiosity, after a third of the U.S. has been killed, then you get what you deserve."

"Perhaps Patti and the Ambassador didn't know they'd ingested the tainted meat. Regardless, they didn't *deserve* to die. Patti was somebody's sister. Somebody's friend."

"You're soft, aren't you? I've read your file. You're a people-hugger. A patriot, sure. But you'll do anything to save others. Makes you a prime candidate for coercion, Mrs. Spencer. A prized-catch for an enemy. I'd be careful if I were you."

He winked and clicked his tongue like he was riding a horse.

Soft? She was *soft?* He obviously wasn't familiar with venomous box jellyfish. Soft should not be underestimated.

"We're both patriots," she said. "Take you, for instance. You could be at home with your family; but instead, you're here, like me. Trying to save the world."

"The only family that matters are my fellow warriors—my brothers in arms."

"And sisters."

"Yeah, whatever." He stood. "Now let's get this party started."

He stopped by the cooler near her feet. "May I? Or are you two personally attached?"

"I cut it off." She smirked. "He was headstrong anyway." She nodded at the cooler. "Regardless, there's no-*body* holding you back from assisting me."

"I like your humor." He licked his top lip. "A whole lot."

Ox grabbed the cooler and turned his back, walking toward the door. Ruby didn't hesitate. She lifted the envelope opener from the desk—a desk that clearly wasn't his.

Things didn't add up.

Walking behind him, she carefully stuffed the metal blade next to her skin, on the side of her right hip, using her underwear to secure it in place. She covered the handle with her blouse before putting on her rain jacket.

Ox looked over his shoulder. "Do your best to keep up, Mrs. Spencer."

"Haven't missed a beat, sir."

24

Sunday, July 11, 2032
Zhuchang Park: Taipei, Taiwan

CORPORAL BEAU WYATT was a southern boy with attitude. While his Mama and Daddy were working the farm outside of Sewanee, Tennessee, he made a killing. Literally. He shot his Henry lever-action rifle in the back fields, until he never missed. Coyotes and varmint, even crows, never had a chance. Two-hundred yards to ten-feet, made no difference, except close-range got messy. Folks wondered why he didn't use a shotgun for the smaller stuff, in the thirty-yard range, but with pellet spray, how hard was that? Besides, deadeye snipers didn't use shotguns.

Growing up, Beau was sick of being treated like a minnow in a fishing pond. Town folk didn't believe sharks were in watering-holes. Surprise, surprise. He was a Great White.

The last straw, the thing that sent him swimming for deeper water, was when his Mama pawned pigweed and lamb's quarter on him, calling the greens "southern spinach." She pretended that serving them was a delicacy and had nothing to do with hard times. Farm-life had come to that. Lies. Standing in shit and acting like you smelled lavender.

So when high school graduation rolled around, Beau Rufus Earl Wyatt—nicknamed Brew—enlisted in the Marines. *Could always would* was his motto (instead of *can't never could*). Success was attitude sweetened like tea, with hard-knocks and determination. And yes sir, he sipped on both ever since he was knee-high to a grasshopper.

Every now and then, his Mama would try to contact him, but he never answered. What was the point? Ox said family connections messed with the mind. Conflicted the heart. Made warriors vulnerable. And anyway, Ox was all the parent a country shark like Beau needed.

The rain in Zhuchang Park was coming down in buckets as he waited at the LZ (landing zone) for the Huey, and for the girl. He was thrilled as a wet chicken—meaning not at all—to be assigned to Ruby Spencer during the flight to Moscow. Twelve hours babysitting; well, ain't that something. But at least he'd be free from his shadow Insley. He liked him enough, but somehow Red Top managed to suck-up all the praise from Ox. Maybe his fiery locks were a natural beacon like a red-hot pepper in fried okra, yelling *look at me, look at me!*

Beau had a mind to dye Insley's hair brown in the middle of the night. Level the playing field some. He chuckled as he imagined Insley's expression in a mirror.

Two helicopters approached the clearing, marked with a waterproof spray-painted X. While one helo circled overhead, his Huey began its descent until the landing skids touched the ground. The chopper's main rotor thrummed loudly as the blades rotated around the hub.

He never tired of the sound. The power. The blades were like shark teeth.

Driving up in a side-by-side utility vehicle, Ox and the girl arrived at the park like clockwork, despite the deteriorating weather conditions. Typhoon Matilda was pissed at somebody, but that wouldn't stop his boss who exited the UTV like it was a sunny evening in rural America. Where nothing happened except for a few mosquito bites.

Beau saluted Ox and then approached the helicopter's main cabin. Bent forward, he ran under the blades. He opened the cabin door by sliding it to the side.

Ox followed, carrying a cooler. Leaning into the cabin, his boss placed the zombie "package" on the green-canvas bench, opposite the door.

"Are we good, Corporal?" Ox shouted, above the rhythmic hum.

"Yes, sir. We are good, sir."

After nodding his approval, Ox directed Ruby to climb into the chopper, offering her a hand up. "Corporal Wyatt will escort you to Songshan Airport, to your connecting flight," Ox said to the girl. "He'll see you through to Geneva. Think of him as your personal flight attendant." His boss smiled. "You can thank me later."

"Wait!" Ruby hollered. "What about my backpack? My laptop?"

This girl had a brain like a weevil. No one barked orders at Ox. No one. Maybe that's why weevils were easy roadkill—too stupid to realize they were no match for a tank.

"Happy reunion, Mrs. Spencer," Ox said in full-smile mode, looking like he hadn't heard her.

His commanding officer slid the cabin door shut.

Beau learned from this man. Every. Single. Day.

Jumping into the passenger side of the cockpit, Beau hoped the rotorhead pilot wouldn't be a chatty-patty. He slammed his door shut and saluted Ox, who was backing up as he returned the gesture. The helicopter lifted off, seesawing from side to side with the turbulent winds. Ox got smaller and smaller as the bird rose.

The pilot lowered the chopper's nose and pushed the cyclic stick forward. "This is going to be a rough ride," he said. "No blowing chow."

Conditions were fierce. In the shifting winds, the chopper sounded like it might rip apart. The vibration engulfed his body. Beau turned to the girl, to see if she was green. Beads of sweat formed on her forehead, but otherwise, she looked like she'd found her sea legs.

Did zombie-heads get motion sickness? He had no interest lifting the cooler-lid to get a look-see. None at all.

As the helicopter approached the regional airport, workers dressed in neon vests lined a runway and waved marshalling-wands that resembled oversized glow sticks. With the loss of electricity, the airport had turned Sewanee-style: universal hand-signals. Only here, it was called adaptability. At least the skies were still light, although the storm was ushering in darkness ahead of schedule.

Thanks to the RED detonation, the terminal was lifeless. Taiwan was clearly Fugazi—fucked-up, whacked, and screwy. Other than the vested military-workers, nothing else moved on the tarmac. Except for them. Except for the wind and rain whipping from yonder, which in this case, was northeast.

The chopper landed. He drew his nine-millimeter and cocked the action. He didn't give a hill of beans what Ruby Spencer thought. For all she knew, a zombie horde was right around the corner, behind China's slick jetliner, the Comac C919, grounded like all the other planes. The only thing he cared about was getting her on the Yak-40, as ordered.

He turned to the girl. "When I tell you, run straight to the jet, Mrs. Spencer. It's a few klicks ahead. Can't miss it. I've got your back." He exited the chopper, slid open the door, and glanced at the pilot. "The party has started."

The pilot turned his head in his bone-dome and smiled behind his microphone. "A piece of cake. Happy trails."

When the girl exited the Huey, he handed her the cooler. No way was he going to carry that freak for her. "Run," he ordered.

She listened. So far so good.

Ten feet from the aircraft, the girl stopped and looked up, like she was examining the make and model. The jet almost looked American. Its belly was painted royal blue, which rose like a wave, covering the tail and fin where a ribbon of white, blue, and red appeared to ripple in the wind. If he hadn't pegged her as dense-and-dumb, he might have worried that she would notice the word "Aeroflot" branded on the jet—clearly not a Swiss or American airliner. But she didn't turn and ask any questions. Like his Mama used to say: pretty as a peach, without a damn pit.

He pushed on her shoulder. "Keep moving."

They climbed the portable stairway leading to the fuselage. The cabin featured three seats abreast, two on the left, one on the right, with maybe eight or nine rows deep. No flight attendants waited to greet them.

Wind rattled the fuselage and the girl grabbed onto a seat for balance. She seemed nervous about the weather, but clueless about anything else.

"Go back midway," he ordered, closing the passenger door and locking the latch in place.

"Can't I sit where I want?"

"Sure, but sit on the left, midway back."

After placing the cooler by the window, the girl sat down beside it, in the aisle seat.

He walked to her. "Hand over the cooler."

She handed it to him, without an argument, and he placed it on the opposite side, on the seat. He turned back and glared. "Now move over."

"What? Why? We've got the whole plane and it's a long flight."

He was starting to lose his patience. "Ox warned me you resist orders. And ask a lot of questions. Move over to the window seat. Now."

Good thing she obeyed.

After sitting, he clicked together his seatbelt buckle. The cabin lights flickered.

"Welcome aboard," a male said, with a thick Russian accent, speaking over a crackling sound system. "This is your copilot. We anticipate turbulent conditions until we reach our cruising altitude. Seatbelts should remain fastened until then. We expect to arrive at our destination at 0500 hours."

The turbofan-powered engines ignited, and the aircraft shuddered. A few seconds later, the plane lurched forward and began creeping toward the runway.

"What time is it now?" she asked.

"1700 hours."

"English?"

He rolled his eyes. "Five o'clock."

"When is 0500?"

"Five in the morning."

The girl peered out the window, before looking back at him. "How can we make Geneva in twelve hours? At the least, the flight should take sixteen hours."

"Tail wind. How the fuck should I know?"

Surprise, surprise. Ruby Never-Dies was a mathematician.

His back pushed against the seat as the plane accelerated down the runway. Eying beyond the window across the aisle, the saturated landscape whizzed by. The wheels of the plane lifted from the ground, giving that momentary feeling of floating. Suddenly, the engines thrusted the aircraft forward, as the angle of acceleration steepened with a rapid ascent. The aircraft, wrapped in angry clouds, shook and shivered, causing seams to flex and the overhead compartment to rattle. The landing gear retracted, moaning as it lifted into the aircraft's belly and locked in place with a thud. The girl clutched the armrests, making her knuckles white.

About ten minutes into the flight, the clouds separated into horizontal layers, with clear space in between. The last layer became wispy, like the cotton candy he would devour at the Sewanee fair. The waning sunlight shone through the window. Bright orange.

All he wanted was a quiet trip. Deliver the girl and make Ox proud.

"Ox is your boss?" she asked, interrupting the steady hum of engines.

"You're smart as a whip, Mrs. Spencer."

"And you're crusty as stale bread, Corporal Wyatt."

He pressed his head against the headrest, closing his eyes. Hopefully she'd get the hint.

"Ox is impressive. You remind me of him. You're both prickly; I won't deny it. But it's obvious, to me anyway, that you were both born leaders. You take command of every situation."

He displayed no reaction. His eyes remained shut. Maybe, though, she was a tad smarter than he'd given her credit for.

"Well, ignore me or not, I appreciate your service. It can't be easy. Being a newbie Sailor, that is. I mean, you're stationed in Taipei, far from home. Your parents must miss you. Worry about you."

He lifted his head from the chair. Anger tightened his face. She'd already slipped back to dense-and-dumb. "With all your vast wisdom, Mrs. Spencer, you've managed to be mistaken on all counts—imagine that. First, I'm no newbie. Second, I sure as hell am no squid. Don't you know the Navy stands for *Never Actually Ventures Yonder?* I'm a bonafide Marine, Ma'am. And the only family I have are my brothers and sisters in the Corps."

"My mistake."

"Your cup runneth over." He cocked his head. "And just to clear your brain fog: I'm a ten-year veteran of the only military branch that matters. Semper Fi."

"Sorry. It's just that you look so youthful. Which is a good thing."

"Ever heard: looks can be deceiving?"

"Good point."

He rolled his eyes. "Whatever."

"Please. I'd really like to learn about your service. You can be cordial for two minutes, can't you? Then I'll leave you alone."

He took a deep breath. Maybe if he played along, she'd shut that trap of hers. "Joined the Corps the same day as high school graduation. Went to boot camp at Parris Island. Joined Force Recon, stationed in Okinawa. Met Lieutenant Colonel at a bar. Requested volunteer assignment at the consulate for security operations. Which means I do everything and anything Ox orders me to do. End of story."

"Impressive. How about Ox? What's his story?"

"Career."

"Like what's that supposed to mean: *career*?"

"Served practically his whole life as a Marine. He was a decorated attack pilot turned Naval Flight Officer, with a doctorate, who lives and breathes honor, courage, and commitment. And he believes in unconventional warfare, like me. Everything worth knowing, I've learned from him. Satisfied?"

"Almost," she said. "So where's the Marine Corps taken you 'yonder,' besides Taiwan and Okinawa?"

He gave her a half smile, his mood lightening. "I'd have to kill you if I told you, Mrs. Spencer. But I will say this: I've never been to Moscow. Come morning, I look forward to checking it off my bucket list."

"Wait. *Moscow?* But we're heading to Geneva. To connect with my husband! Aren't we?"

25

AS RUBY WATCHED the color drain from Corporal Wyatt's face, time lapsed frame-by-frame. Her escort's eyes shifted left, barely detectable. His jaw twitched.

She had suspected something big was off-kilter, especially when he sat next to her, boxing her in. And her whole conversation starter—*Ox is impressive, a born leader*—was a flat-out lie, intended to get Wyatt talking. Which it did. And now there was no denying it: she was a prisoner. Being kidnapped to Moscow.

What she didn't know was *why*. Or if she'd ever see Clay again. Or Gabby. Or if Ambassador Jeffries and Patti Davis had been murdered, which now seemed likely. And why Russia? She had no clue about any of it.

Her internal voice screamed, *this can't be happening; this can't be happening; this can't be happening.*

She wanted to fall apart. Curl in a ball. Rock herself to sleep. Escape the cruelness. Deny the reality. But she couldn't.

She had to fight.

Confidence over fear, she told herself.

Wyatt stared at her, his ice-cold eyes locking with hers. No doubt he could and would kill her, some thirty-thousand-feet above the ground. A bullet to her skull. A snap of her neck. A blade in her lung. *End of story*, as he liked to say.

Her brain was on overload. Nerve endings ignited uncontrollably like lit sparklers. She was on the cusp of losing everything important to her.

With reality rolling in accelerated-time, rather than the slow-motion playing inside her head, she simultaneously released her seatbelt, grabbed the envelope-opener from its hiding place, and stood from her seat, pivoting. She rammed the blade against the Marine's jugular notch. The sharp tip nearly pierced the soft skin at the base of his neck. While pressing the tip deeper, she reached with her left hand for the pistol tucked in his holster. She fumbled to free the firearm. Something was in the way. A strap? The seatbelt?

Out of nowhere, the heel of the Marine's left hand connected with the base of her nose like a sledge hammer, snapping her neck back. Her brain flashed white and her eyes instantly stung and wept. Sharp pain, searing pain, raced across her cheeks. The force of the blow knocked her against the seatback in front of the Corporal. She tangled with his legs.

In another move she didn't see coming, he twisted her wrist—the one holding the opener—and delivered a violent karate-chop at the crevice in her elbow, causing her right arm to buckle. She groaned in agony. The envelope-opener flew from her hand.

The Corporal shoved her across the aisle like a rag doll. She slammed against the seat where the cooler rested.

Blood streamed from her nose like a gushing river. No doubt the Corporal had broken it. She tasted sweet saltiness in her mouth. Throbbing had already started.

She backed up to the window and spat a mouthful of blood on the floor. "Stay away from me. I mean it!"

"Stupid bitch." He drew his pistol. "I'm a fucking Marine. Special Ops. You think you can take *me* on?"

"Why are you taking me to Moscow? Why? Are you *kidnapping* me? Does President Newton know I'm here?"

"Sit. The fuck. Down."

"Where's my husband?"

"Now!" He wielded his pistol.

"I'll sit if you tell me where Clay is."

"Now." He cocked the action.

"Okay, I'll sit." She lifted the cooler slowly. The zombie head was rapidly clicking its teeth, triggered by her spilled blood. The sound reminded her of a timer, ticking down.

Her brain pulsated. Pressure was building. She was trapped. Desperate to escape. A bleeding, panicked animal.

As she started to lower herself in the seat, she glanced at her nemesis, detecting a slight retreat in his extended arm. He was buying it—accepting she was about to sit. So she ignored her injuries. With all her strength, she hurled the container at the Marine standing in the aisle.

Corporal Wyatt's face reacted: a slight widening of the eyes, rapid blinking, a parting of his lips. Was he afraid? Shocked? Clearly, he didn't expect to have the cooler thrown at him. Let alone one containing a zombie head. Because maybe the lid would fly open. And then what?

When the cooler struck his chest, she hoped he'd drop the pistol. No such luck. But thankfully, her throw had carried force with it. He stepped back toward his seat to absorb the energy. Now he was off-balance.

Without planning or contemplating the consequences, Ruby stepped forward and raised her right leg, kicking the cooler which was pressed against the Corporal's lower torso. He fell back, over his seat's armrest. In an attempt to keep the cooler upright, he dropped the pistol. The nine-millimeter bounced, landing under the seat in front of him.

The cooler lid opened, and the Corporal screamed.

She squatted, snatching the firearm from the floor. "Piece of cake."

Her cheeks and nose were already swelling. Soon her vision would be impaired.

Racing to the cockpit, brandishing the pistol and turning back several times to make sure the Corporal wasn't following her, she stopped at the door. Taking a deep breath, she clasped the handle and turned it. To her surprise, the cockpit door opened.

The pilot turned, scowling. "I told you..." His eyes widened when he saw her. "What the fuck?" Ox shouted.

"You!" she screamed, aiming the pistol at him. "Why are you taking me to Moscow? Where's my husband? Answer me, damn it!

Or I'll shoot. We'll crash-and-burn together."

Ox didn't answer.

Instead, he flipped a switch and jerked the control wheel to the left. The aircraft banked sharply, slamming Ruby against the doorframe, knocking the pistol from her hand.

Before she could hold on to anything, the airplane's nose ascended. She took several wobbly steps backwards before falling. Seconds later, the plane dove, hard, and she heard the piercing whine of the engines screaming. She rolled toward the passenger door, on the side of the fuselage cabin. A loud bang, almost like thunder, assaulted her ears. As she felt the onset of a headache and nausea, her eardrums threatened to burst. Her wounds throbbed.

The cabin was losing pressure. She couldn't move.

Oxygen masks had dropped, but she was never going to reach them. The G-forces had her pinned by the passenger door like an elephant was sitting on her chest.

The world went black.

26

Monday, July 12, 2032
Moscow, Russia

RUBY WASN'T SURE which discomfort was gnawing at her to wake. Lying on cold, damp concrete was certainly a contender. Her body was stiff and shivering. The grumbles of hunger didn't help. Nor did her headache, throbbing nose, or swollen eyes. But she pinpointed the only discomfort that made wakefulness preferable to a pain-free, dreamland escape: her separation from Clay and Gabby. Awake was the only way she could fight for survival. The only way she had a chance to return to the ones she loved. And there was no hiding from that reality.

As consciousness rose to skin level, her eyes quivered. She opened them and blinked to focus. She couldn't be sure, but it felt like she'd been drugged. She was sluggish. Heavy. Like a dense fog that refused to dissipate.

A streak of late afternoon sun shone through a small window positioned high on the far wall, as if the floor where she lay was below ground. Several layers of vertical bars were between her and the window.

Her adrenal glands released a healthy dose of adrenaline, probably knowing she couldn't muster the energy to rise without a boost. She used the rush to lift herself into a sitting position. Her head pounded in tempo with her heart. Leaning against a cinderblock wall, she confirmed what she suspected. She was jailed in a prison cell.

"I have been worrying about you," a male voice said, coming from her left. "You look very…different. I imagine you are in pain."

Without peripheral vision due to swelling, Ruby hadn't detected anyone's presence. But the man's voice sounded vaguely familiar. She tried to turn her neck, but it was stiff from Corporal Wyatt's blow. Whiplash, no doubt. She pivoted her body instead.

A man twice-her-age was leaning against the same wall, in the cell adjacent hers. Even though he was wearing a business suit, he looked disheveled. And as if circumstances couldn't get any more bizarre, she recognized him: Dr. Lin—the microbiologist from the bus in Keelung. The man who loaned her use of his smartwatch.

"Please tell me you know why we're here," she said, her throat feeling dry and scratchy. "And where *here* is, exactly."

"*Here* is a prison in Moscow, but not one known by the public. I am not sure of its name or precise location. However, I can assure you, with confidence, that we are not here for ethical purposes. Our captors have a nefarious plan for me, and for you and your husband."

Her heartrate accelerated. "My husband? Clay is here?" She quickly scanned the cells, ignoring the pain in her neck.

The other cells were empty.

"I believe our abductors are interviewing your husband now," Dr. Lin explained. "They came for him before your arrival. I would not expect him to return soon. I believe *thorough* is the word that best describes their interview style. Yes, thorough."

While she was thrilled that her husband was near, that they'd be reunited—at least her mind refused to consider any other outcome, she worried about an "interview." Foreign prisons conjured images of interrogations and tortures, not interviews. And she couldn't imagine what the topic might be. Maybe their connection to President Newton? To the Special Warfare Council?

"Sounds like you've already endured the experience," she said. "Do you know what they want? And why us?"

He looked around, as though he wanted to make sure they were alone. "If I tell you, you must keep the information between us, for my sake. My hands and eyes are of utmost importance to me." His voice cracked. "They have threatened to remove them. Without my work in vaccine development, life would not be worth living."

She swallowed the bile that bubbled in her throat. "I won't

mention it. I promise. But please…please give me an idea why we're here. Help me mentally prepare."

"In one word: bioweapon."

"Bioweapon? You mean the last one didn't do enough damage? F8 practically annihilated the animal kingdom and then mutated into ZOM-B!"

"You and I understand the horror," Dr. Lin said. "But apparently, they see an opportunity associated with the bioweapon mutation."

"Who is *they*? I mean, besides Quinton Oxford? And what vile opportunity could possibly emerge from the existence of the walking dead?"

"*They* are Ox and Vladimir Volkov."

"The Russian President?" she asked.

"Yes. They have joined forces to fill the void left by Huo Zhu Zheng and his defunct regime. The opportunity, as they explained it to me, is to turn zombies—or Grays, as we call them—into weapons: soldiers who ensure their interests are met."

"Zombies are already *weapons*. Weapons that will bring humankind to extinction, without body-bags!"

"A gun is not a weapon unless someone fires it with intention. Likewise, zombies are not weapons unless someone *controls* them with purpose. And that is where the opportunity exists."

She was confused. "How can you control the undead when they don't have the capacity to process information? An organism that's alive, but really isn't?"

"A cure."

Think deeper, she told herself. At the surface, logic was absent from his answer and he was too analytical for irrational thought. A cure would transition the infected back to humanity, the opposite of an undead soldier. So why would the shift from undead-to-human be desirable, in terms of bioweaponry?

"The *control*," she concluded aloud, "is the ability to reuse the soldier. A cure would allow our captors to repeat the cycle, as needed, between undead soldier and human—over and over again. Am I right?"

He nodded, smiling. "My jovial expression should not be misinterpreted. The insanity of their suggestion is not humorous.

Rather, I can appreciate why they have abducted you."

She barely heard him. Her mind was processing. "You mentioned zombie soldiers would be used to ensure their interests. What are they?"

"What are the interests of every aspiring dictator?"

"Power…and more power."

"On a global scale," he added.

"I'm sure you pointed out the obvious pitfalls in their zombie-cure theory, from a scientific standpoint."

"For our first encounter," he said, "staying silent and listening felt like the wisest course of action. I believe the sharpened cleaver helped motivate me."

Ruby feared for Clay's safety. She prayed he would remain silent.

"However, in my private deliberations," Dr. Lin continued, "the concept has viability."

"Viability?" She hoped he detected the sarcasm in her tone. "A cure won't reconstruct the frontal cortex once bacteria have destroyed it. Consequently, a *cured* zombie would have no cognitive abilities. So what's the point?"

"Think of a closing door."

"Please. Let's move beyond riddles, Dr. Lin. But I'll play this once: the operative word is clos-*ing*, referring to a process over time. Are you suggesting humanity—intellectually and physically—can be restored to zombies within a certain span of time? Before the door closes on their humanness?"

"Precisely. Ox and Vladimir Volkov explained to me, as they will likely to you, that they have been working on a theory. Once infected, it takes humans four hours to die, three minutes to reanimate after death, and eight hours, they told me, to reach the point of…how do you say…no-return."

"Wait. How do they know that? Have they developed a cure already?"

"Oh no. Not yet. However, they claim they've accurately identified the duration cycle—the window of time in which the body can recover from infection."

"And how do they know for sure?" she asked.

"Experimentation, of course. They've infected humans with

ZOM-B. Once the human-subject turned, they destroyed each Gray at different hourly intervals. With brain autopsies, they discovered that after the eighth hour, the frontal cortex is unsalvageable. In addition, at this time marker, decomposition increases exponentially. The lungs become useless and…"

"I get the picture." Beads of moisture formed on her forehead and she wiped them with the heel of her hand. "Then why can't zombies *think* within their first eight-hours of turning?"

"Their initial behavior is more like insanity, induced by several conditions: severe pain from the invasion of ZOM-B, a breakdown of normal cerebral impulses, overactive nerve endings, and an insatiable thirst to restore oxygen depletion—symptoms much like animals suffering from F8. Outwardly mimicking full-blown rabies."

"You understand that using humans for this type of 'experimenting' is terroristic *murder*, right Dr. Lin? It's not 'science' to use humans as test subjects."

"I do believe the United States government used the former Chinese President for such an experiment. Did they not? Perhaps the idea was birthed at that moment."

She took a deep breath. Dr. Lin was partially right. Worse, she'd agreed with Em and the SWC to use the tyrant as a test-subject for his own bioterrorism. At the time, an eye-for-an-eye felt like justice.

"It was a proportional response," she countered, citing the government's talking point. "Because Huo was not an innocent man. He'd lost the right to make decisions ensuring his own wellbeing. A right that should've been preserved for Ox and Vladimir Volkov's human test-subjects. And let's be honest: I can't imagine their test-subjects *willingly* agreed to the brain study, especially when survivability was never an option. Furthermore, if a cure is developed, who'd volunteer for the freakish army? Who'd want someone else to choose when they'd be an enslaved human and when they'd be a psycho-zombie bent on killing and draining someone's blood? Their sick plan is terroristic slavery, Dr. Lin."

"Forgive me, Mrs. Spencer, for I may have given you the impression that my opinion on the viability of their diabolical plan reflects my acceptance of it. On the contrary. The wrong impression may have been conveyed due to my culture, which expects me to remain stoic. My emotions are well hidden. However, as you Americans say: you are talking to the symphony."

"You mean choir. You're preaching to the *choir.*"

"Yes, Mrs. Spencer. Preaching. To the choir."

"Please. Call me Ruby." She stared at him for a moment. "I understand why they've kidnapped you. I assume to develop a cure. But why *me?* Do they think I will help you? And why Clay?"

"I can only repeat what they have told me. They mentioned your close friend—the renowned microbiologist, Emory Bradshaw, has himself been working on a cure. You might say, using another American expression, it is a race-against-time to be the first to develop such a cure."

"He's working on a ZOM-B cure?" She paused, confused by the suggestion. "Well, I wouldn't know. Em is working under the auspices of government research, and I haven't been briefed on the specific nature of his projects."

Her heart raced. She wasn't being one-hundred-percent honest. If Em was working on a cure, she'd know about it. As a Council member, she had security clearance. So why would a U.S. military turncoat like Ox and the Russian President think Em was working on a cure?

"Unfortunately," Dr. Lin said, "our captors believe Dr. Bradshaw's work involves you."

"*Me?* In what possible way?"

"According to their sources, he is using your blood."

"Now that is ridiculous! I've donated blood, back when we formulated an F8 cure. I was the only elite-controller for the infection. But I haven't donated since."

"But it explains why they have captured you and brought you here, does it not? They want to investigate if your blood holds the key to a ZOM-B cure, since F8 is the mutation's genesis. Otherwise, why would Dr. Bradshaw be using it?"

"Please! Stop saying that. Em is *not* using my blood to develop anything. If he was, I would know about it." The truth was spilling out of her like a burst pipe. "Besides, my blood is like everyone else's now—useless against ZOM-B. I even analyzed my own bloodwork." She took a deep breath, frustrated. "Ox and the Russian President are wasting their time. Most importantly, mine and Clay's. We have a daughter who needs us!" Her nose throbbed. And she was exhausted again. Tears welled in her eyes. "What time is it anyway?"

"I've been trying to gauge time, based on when they abducted me and on the angle of the sun. I believe it is around four o'clock in the afternoon, Moscow time. Which means it would be nine at night in Taiwan."

"Thank you." She rubbed her neck, trying to loosen the tight muscles. "Dr. Lin: you don't plan on helping them, do you?"

"That depends."

"On what?"

"On the leverage they use."

"You mean like threatening to remove body parts?"

"Yes."

"I'm frightened to think of what leverage they'll use on me," she said.

"I believe they are speaking to that leverage this very minute—to your husband."

She stopped breathing. Panic pulsed through her circulatory system. Her back slid down the wall and she slumped into the fetal position, instantly sobbing. This couldn't be happening to them. Clay was the love of her life. He and Gabby were the reason *her* life was worth living.

Her body convulsed with each sob. And even though crying made her wounded body feel so much worse, she couldn't stop.

A hand stretched through the bars and touched her shoulder.

"Please. It will be alright." He withdrew his hand. When it returned, he draped his business blazer over her. "Here. Take my jacket."

The warmth helped calm her. Dr. Lin was a kind man, in the same predicament as she and Clay. They needed each other.

"Ruby, I almost forgot," he said. "Your husband handed me this when he arrived. He asked me to give it to you, if I could."

She looked up and took a torn piece of paper from his hand. Opening the small strip, she read the words in Clay's handwriting: "Be strong. We'll find our ruby slippers."

27

Tuesday, July 13, 2032
Moscow, Russia

RUBY WAS SUPPOSED to be home by now. Home with Clay and Gabby. Home, starting her new life. Instead, daybreak peeked through the cellblock window. Footsteps—pairs of them—marched down the center aisle.

Lying on the moist concrete, she scanned the other cells without raising her head. No Clay. No Dr. Lin. All the cells were empty, which meant the prison guards were coming for her.

Dr. Lin's blazer had kept her warm through the night. Hopefully, she'd get the chance to thank him for the jacket. And for Clay's note which she'd tucked into her short's pocket.

Pushing with hands pressed flat on the floor, she raised her torso. Her arms ached, especially her right. Corporal Wyatt's karate-chop had left a distended, eggplant-sized bruise that needed to be drained. She gave herself credit, though. Albeit not her wisest decision, at least the blitz on the Special Ops Marine qualified as gutsy. As confidence, not fear. More importantly, she survived.

The soldiers approached, wearing green-camo uniforms and matching caps.

The guard sporting a military rifle barked a command at her in Russian. She didn't flinch. He thrust his hand up in the air and spat the order again. She knew exactly what the guard wanted, yet anger and defiance prevented her from standing. Already feeling like a pressure cooker, she needed to vent. And why hold back? Wasn't likely the guards would kill her before the "interview."

The second guard unlocked the cell. "Up," he ordered, with Russian *umph*.

"Sure!" She stood and attempted to smile, but the expression hurt her swollen cheeks and nose. "Why didn't you *say* so?"

She hoped the guards detected her needling. Her sarcasm.

The first-guard walked into the cell. With his rifle strapped over his shoulder, he moved behind her, grabbing her wrists and cuffing them behind her back. The handcuffs were small. The metal dug into her skin. He nodded and smiled with his yellow teeth, as if saying, *take that*. But she disregarded him, as if he were invisible.

"Walk," the second guard said, nodding toward the left.

Ruby walked from the cell and down the long aisle, with empty cells on either side. Every muscle in her body hurt. With the guards behind her, she exited through the door marking the end of the cellblock area. They immediately came to a stairwell with steps leading in both directions—up and down. The first guard poked her with the rifle's barrel in between her shoulder blades. When she didn't move, he poked her again, harder.

"Up?" she asked the guard brandishing the firearm, as if attempting to teach him English.

He narrowed his eyes, clenched his jaws, and answered with an even stronger barrel-jab.

"Yes," the second Russian guard said. "Up."

After a flight of stairs, they came to a landing. A glass door connected the stairwell to the floor level. People dressed in lab coats were scurrying in and out of doors along the hallway. Some were pushing carts that appeared to carry vials and medical tools, while others read from clipboards as they walked and conversed with colleagues. It reminded her of a hospital or research facility, except this one had armed guards.

The barrel pushed against her back, urging her to continue up the next flight of stairs. She turned to face the first guard, staring at him blankly, her feet planted firmly on the floor. He met her resistance by jabbing her on collarbone. He finally said, "Up."

Ruby smiled despite the pain, hoping to taunt. "I knew you could say it. Kiss your brain!" She turned and ascended the stairs, as the guard growled behind her.

At the next level, a guard opened the glass door and nodded toward the hallway, intending for her to enter. Three doors later, on the left, they stopped in front of a door equipped with a Samsung box—the size of an old cellphone, located above the handle. The second guard pressed a silver bar on the device, activating a touchpad similar to her smartwatch. He entered a numeric combination and then turned the handle. The three of them crossed the threshold into an expansive office. When the door closed behind them, the deadbolt snapped back into place.

Two men stood by an empty fireplace, their backs toward Ruby. Continuing to chat quietly, the men made no effort to greet her. Or acknowledge her.

The first guard removed the cuffs. He pointed to her hiking boots before swinging his finger toward a floormat where other shoes had been neatly positioned. After unlacing, she placed her boots by the others. The second guard handed her a pair of red slippers, which she took and stepped into. They fit. Not like the cuffs which had pinched her skin. While she rubbed her wrists, both of her Russian escorts assimilated into the background, like flies on a wall.

The smell of freshly-baked bread teased her, stimulating her salivary glands. She eyed a table, draped in red and topped with serving bowls of kasha porridge, black bread, potatoes, fresh fruit, and juice. She was ravenous.

Ox turned toward her and paused. "Can't say I'm sold on the new look, Mrs. Spencer." No doubt he was referring to her bruised and swollen face. "Hope my flying didn't contribute. Guess I'm a bit rusty." He winked.

She glowered at him. He had the nerve to wear his Service Dress Blues, showcasing rows-upon-rows of colorful bars, signifying his Marine heroics. Ironic, since he was a turncoat.

Vladimir Volkov approached her. His white hair was tied in a ponytail and his abdomen stretched the buttons on his dress shirt. With a frosted lowball-glass of clear liquid in his left hand, he extended his right for a handshake. "Such a pleasure to meet you."

Ruby detected garlic on his breath, and vodka. Refusing to clasp his hand, she said nothing. Her lips would stay sealed like Dr. Lin's, until she assessed the tone of the encounter.

After eyeing her wounds, the Russian President turned to Ox, lowering his hand. "How did Corporal Wyatt fare in this altercation thirty-five-thousand-feet above the Earth?" He chuckled, as though he already knew.

"I imagine he has a splitting headache."

The Russian grinned, looking back at her. "We admire tenacity, Mrs. Spencer. You have the qualities of a valued team member."

She inhaled before pursing her lips to protest, poised to lay into him.

He raised his hand to stop her. "Not now. Eat first. I invite you. And call me Vladimir. I insist."

"No, thank you...Vladimir. Just tell me where my husband is."

"And she is loyal, too," he said to Ox. "Yes, those qualities are most desirable. Your assessment was accurate, Ox. Well done."

She crossed her arms, hating when people spoke about her like she wasn't standing beside them. At arm's length, no less.

"My dear," Vladimir said to her, like father to daughter. "Your husband is cleaning up and will join us shortly. Do not fret: Ox and I wish you no harm. You are honored guests."

"I'd hate to see sleeping arrangements for your enemies," she snapped.

Vladimir laughed. "And a sense of humor as well. I like this American woman!" He pulled out a chair for her at the banquet table. "Sit and eat, dear. Replenish your strength."

"Is the food laced with ZOM-B?"

He grabbed a bread slice and stuffed the whole thing into his mouth. "If infecting you was our intention," he said, pushing the bread around with his tongue to make room for words, "we would have injected you when you arrived. Now, eat. Please."

Ruby had expected a hostile interrogation. Truth be told, a hospitable approach to questioning was hard to refuse, especially when it involved food. Starved, her hands shook with anticipation as she loaded her plate. Instead of bringing the food to her mouth in manageable forkfuls, she lowered her face to the dish, shoveling in the goodness. Equally rude, she guzzled two glasses of apple juice, not the tiniest bit sorry for making gulping sounds. Her mother would've had a conniption.

She scanned the table as she gorged on seconds. No knives to slip into her pocket.

When she finished her meal, two plump and wrinkled women entered the office, pushing a kitchen cart. They exchanged the bowls and dishes with a delicate teapot, a self-boiling samovar, teacups, lemons, and jam. Vladimir joined her at the table. One woman poured a tea compote into their cups, about a third full, while the other diluted the dark tea with hot water.

The women were about to push their cart into the hallway. "Wait," the Russian President demanded. "How many forks?"

The woman with teeth, who obviously understood English, answered in Russian.

"Good. Very Good," he said. "Continue."

Vladimir Volkov had undoubtedly heard of Ruby's attraction for utensils, especially those with sharp points, like forks and letter openers that doubled as knives.

The women waddled from the room, closing the door behind them.

28

Tuesday, July 13, 2032
Moscow, Russia

VLADIMIR VOLKOV DID not choose to interrogate with time restraints. One had to find rhythm before the dance. KGB and impatient Marines had their tactics, but he had his: Russian tea. The perfect instrument to ease into artful questioning. What was the rush?

He had warned Ox to let him take the lead, to set the tone. Perhaps being in Vladimir's beloved Russia, in his private prison, helped convince his churlish partner to yield. That, or Ox's knowledge that the Russian President would slice his throat and feed him to the zombies locked in his underground cells if he didn't. He smiled at the mental image.

"Here," Vladimir said to Ruby, sliding a teacup closer to her. "Let me show you how to enjoy Russian tea." He scooped a spoonful of jam and placed it in his mouth, on his tongue, and then sipped the warm tea. After he swallowed, he cherished the lingering sweetness coating his throat, like the taste of a delicate woman. "Try it. You may never want to leave Russia again."

The girl scooped jam with her spoon and delivered it on her tongue, wrapping her lips around the utensil before slowly extracting it.

"Quickly. The tea," he urged, feeling the seductiveness of the ritual, the importance of the timing.

She brought the teacup to her mouth and sipped. He caught himself holding his breath, waiting for her reaction. And then she smiled at him, contented.

"Delicious, Vladimir. Such a wonderful Russian tradition! And I appreciate your hospitality and generosity. Thank you."

He was pleased and satisfied. This American girl liked to dance!

Keeping his focus on her, he made every effort to ignore Ox who paced in the background.

"My pleasure," he said, slightly nodding his head. "Now, while we enjoy, let me explain why you and your husband are our guests."

"And Dr. Lin."

"Yes, and Dr. Lin."

"Did I mention she likes to interrupt?" Ox jeered.

Vladimir raised his hand slightly, to quiet his partner, before explaining the reasons why the girl was kidnapped. He described how they planned to turn zombies into weapons. How a cure would help them manage their undead warriors, turning them from zombie-to-human and back, a looping infection-and-cure cycle, as needed. Most importantly, he told the girl how her blood was key to it all.

While he spoke, she displayed no reactions, although he had to admit her facial bruises and swelling made subtle expressions more difficult to decipher. Although she wore what Americans called *a poker face*, her eyes reacted when her husband was mentioned. They widened slightly, revealing concern. And that was good. Very good. After all, it was Vladimir's suggestion to include Clay Spencer in the kidnapping. Knowing someone's motivation was as important as picking the right dancing shoes.

And Ruby's motivation was clearly her husband.

"Do you have any questions, my dear?" Vladimir asked, trying to keep his voice soft and kind.

"This ought to be good," Ox piped in, dripping with American sarcasm.

She sneered at his partner, unmasking her face and showing contempt in her mouth and narrowing eyes. "I always have questions," she answered, looking at Vladimir as if she needed to qualify Ox's comment.

"Take your time, my dear. And do not let Ox affect you."

"I've been curious: at the consulate, did Ambassador Jeffries and Patti Davis really die from REDs? Or did your partner kill them?"

Vladimir lowered his shoulders and tilted his head forward. He was disappointed. He had just explained how a zombie cure was feasible and how the cure could be used to recycle zombie soldiers. The world would be at their fingertips for the taking. And she was a microbiologist, an expert scientist for the SWC, whose blood was superhuman, or at least, the prospect piqued his curiosity. And her first question was in search of *justice?* For inconsequential humans? Most disappointing, indeed.

Perhaps the dance had ended before it began.

"Such simple questions, with most-obvious answers," he replied. "Anything more challenging, Mrs. Spencer? Before I become bored?"

The girl glared at him, with force and stubbornness and defiance. And for one second, she seemed like an equal match. But challengers never endured. He had never found a worthy rival who lived to claim superiority over him. What did Ox call him? A troll? Yes, a troll. With Siberian blood.

"Were you responsible for the RED attack in Keelung and Taipei?"

"Again: obvious. But I see no harm admitting it…yes."

"Was the infected Russian container ship part of your experiment?"

Ox neared the table and was about to speak, but Vladimir raised his hand to stop him. The Russian President placed his palms together, as if praying, and touched the tips of his index fingers against his lips. He locked eyes with her now, hoping she understood that she was being initiated into the inner circle. That the shared knowledge would precipitate her death, if she resisted their offer. She did not look away, which meant she was strong and unafraid. He liked that. Very much.

Finally, he lowered his hands to the table and fiddled with a spoon. "Yes. We implanted REDs in the crew of the *Askold* and infected them with ZOM-B, by spicing their first meal. The only crew-member privy to our mission was the captain. We fortified the bridge. It was impenetrable, ensuring the vessel would reach Keelung.

"Once the undead invaded the port city," Vladimir continued, "we gauged the infection rate of ZOM-B. Then we determined how effectively the undead could be stopped—on a large scale—by activating the nanobots: REDs." He pointed at her casually. "I am sure a scientist, such as yourself, can appreciate the need for data. But imagine our surprise when a horde of zombies escaped from your Naval base—zombies without RED implants!"

"Expect the unexpected," Ox said, using his lecturing voice, which annoyed Vladimir to the point of nausea.

"Was spreading the infection to Taipei part of the plan?" she asked.

"No, my dear. With public transportation, the infection spread faster and farther than predicted. And RED detonations only work if humans (infected or healthy) carry the implant. We confirmed through our experiment that the best solution to zombiism is a cure. A cure, over any other strategy, will provide the greatest control and opportunities. Surely you find this logical."

"So you knew the *Askold* crew carried the implants, but how did you know the Taiwanese people had been doctored with REDs? The world thought Huo had spared his people."

"Ahh," Vladimir said, thankful the questions were getting more interesting. "Huo's people *were* spared initially, but not from implantation. They were spared from *detonation*. You see, my dear, REDs can be programmed to explode at different decibels. It allows targeted detonations."

"You avoided my question," she said. "How did you *know* the Taiwanese had REDs embedded in their brains?"

29

Tuesday, July 13, 2032
Moscow, Russia

FINALLY, IT WAS Ox's turn to speak. As if passing an imaginary baton, Vladimir looked at him to answer Ruby's question. He'd be taking the lead at the great reveal. Hell yeah.

"Huo was…our front-man in *The Cause*," Ox said, savoring the taste of each word as it left his lips. "That's how we knew people in the Chinese territories carried REDs." He smirked. "Vladimir and I? We were silent partners." Ruby Never-Dies was clearly surprised. "What?" He tried to sound innocent. "You didn't think one man could conquer the world alone, did you?"

The girl balled her fists on the table and groped her bottom lip with her teeth.

"I know. I know," he continued. "You're probably sore about the assassination of my former Commander in Chief. Or about the casualties of FIN leaders. Or…" He looked at Vladimir for effect, even though he knew the answer. "How many deaths were there in the non-allied populace?"

"Nine-hundred and eighty-five million, three-hundred and forty-two thousand, and seventy-three souls. Or was it seventy-four?"

Ox whistled. "Who's counting, right?"

The girl dug her index finger into the skin of her thumb. Maybe he and Ruby weren't that different. Maybe pain calmed her, too.

"To our chagrin," he admitted, "FIN Special Operatives tainted our partner's food—our own idea used against us." He rubbed his flat-top. "As luck would have it, Huo's death—or *un*death—expedited our contingency plan. A plan that involves none-other than you, Mrs. Never-Dies."

"It shouldn't, of course," she barked, "since I can't help you with a cure. And even if I could, which I *can't*, creating an army of slaves who are forced to morph at your will, in a looping cycle of zombie-to-human, is utterly barbaric. Inhumane. I will never help you."

"Your reluctance to join our partnership is another matter entirely, my dear," Vladimir said. "Ox assures me he can motivate you. However, you underestimate your own ability to generate a cure."

"Enlighten me then."

Ox pulled a chair from the table and turned it toward him. He straddled the seat, facing the chair back. Placing his elbows and forearms on the top rail, he leaned toward her.

The girl was a withered rose between two thorns. A part of him hoped she had more fight left.

"We're not the only leaders racing-against-time to develop a reusable zombie-soldier," he whispered. "Partnered with your genius friend Emory, President Newton has a head-start in this war game. Our counterattack was to bring their prized blood-bank here, as collateral, ahead of tactical negotiation."

"Who's giving you this intel?" she asked. "To cure F8, I *volunteered* my blood. There'd be no reason not to help with a ZOM-B cure, especially with *this* ELI. And no reason, whatsoever, for Em and the President to hide their need for my blood. What you're saying is simply hogwash."

"Call it hogwash; call it pig shit," Ox said, rising from his chair. "But they've probably figured out that people-hugging Ruby Never-Dies would object to the whole zombie-human recycling initiative. Do-gooders usually don't embrace that sort of thing. But kudos to Ava Newton. To think: I had reduced her talents to having a prime set of tits and butt cheeks."

Ox walked to the desk near the fireplace, against the back wall of the room. An intentional move, like their offer was drifting out of reach. Which would place her and her family on the fast-track to death.

Would she reel him back?

"What do you need from me for this tactical negotiation?" she asked Vladimir at the table. "My blood?"

"Not quite yet," his partner answered. "First, we seek to persuade Dr. Bradshaw to join us in *The Cause,* to become a *have* in our growing kingdom of *have-nots.* A lab has been prepared for him here—cutting edge, I might add."

"That's how you plan to lure Em…with a lab? He already has the finest in the U.S.!"

"No, my dear. *You* are the lure," Vladimir said. "By the way: how is Gabriella doing with the Gonzalez family, while you are away? She must miss you. Annapolis is such a lovely town. My friends tell me the view of Whitehall Creek from Sharps Point is spectacular. Indeed!"

Ox heard Ruby gasp from across the room. He couldn't have written a better script. Maybe he and the troll made a better team than he thought.

"Let me cut to the chase," Ox said, returning to the table with a laptop. "We expect you to videoface with Dr. Biology and insist he join you here. We have a statement for you to read. If you refuse, we'll shift to another contingency plan: we'll drain your blood right now and keep it refrigerated. Of course, we'll regret losing your service as a blood bank, able to regenerate blood, but sacrifices are inherent in every mission." He frowned, just for show. "Then, we'll terminate your husband, daughter, dog, and Tomas and Margo Gonzalez. Your parents, too. You know, your inner circle. Operatives are already in position, waiting for the word."

His dick hardened. The only thing better than stripping clothes off a woman was stripping her of everything she loved. The power was intoxicating. "Curious: which option are you leaning toward?"

"Let me see the statement," she whispered, sounding defeated.

Ox handed her the paper, smiling. Watching her hand shake as she took the note was icing on the cake. He looked over her shoulder as she read the note.

Em, please listen carefully. You are not the only one working on a ZOM-B cure. My captors plan to use me as a blood donor. They insist you join us, or Clay and I will be terminated, along with Gabby. They know where she is. I'm so frightened. Please, Em, my baby's life depends on you getting here.

On July 14th, take Flight 1643 from Dulles. You'll receive directions when you land. Multiple, independent layers are in place to camouflage my captors and their location. And you will be scanned for identity, weapons, chips, and bugs. Of course, you'll be rewarded significantly for your efforts. Don't let us down, Em. Please. Clay, Gabby, and I are defending on you.

Ruby glared at Ox. "Are you forcing me to read the typo, too?" She pointed to the mistake. "*Defending* instead of depending? A premonition perhaps?"

Vladimir slapped the table, nearly launching his germ-infested spoon from the jam jar. "This American woman: I really like her!"

Ignoring the troll, Ox placed the opened laptop in front of the girl. Time for the rubber to meet the road. He keyboarded Emory Bradshaw's personal number and enjoyed detecting surprise on the girl's mangled face. She must have really pissed off country-boy Wyatt.

Ruby's microbiologist-bff accepted the videofacing request.

"Where have you been? We've been worried sick," he whined. Then he paused, his eyebrows tightening, probably registering her facial wounds. "What in the hell...what happened?"

Ox, standing behind the girl, determined from the screen-image that Dr. Biology was in a lab. The girl raised the note to reveal the paper within the video frame. Amateur hour.

"Em. Please. Listen carefully..." she started, without intonation.

Dr. Biology's eyes grew wide. Ox hoped the guy wouldn't be a prick to work with.

"You..." She paused, sounding like she was choking up. "You... SAVE GABBY. DON'T GIVE INTO DEMANDS," she screamed.

Couldn't anyone follow a simple fucking directive?

Heat overwhelmed him, like he was drowning in fire. And when he felt like that, when it happened on a mission, he only had one thing on his mind: survival. *His.*

When that switch was flipped, he became a killing machine.

Ox slammed the laptop closed, crushing the girl's fingers. When she looked up at him, still looking defiant like she didn't care if he killed her, his rage deepened. He crashed his head into her forehead, so hard he practically heard her skull crack. The green in her eyes hid in their sockets.

She was out cold, slumping off the chair and onto the floor, taking the laptop with her.

If the blow ended up killing her, so be it.

He was Lieutenant Colonel Quinton Oxford, recipient of the Medal of Honor.

And he would not be bested by an errant bitch. *Oorah.*

30

Tuesday, July 13, 2032
Moscow, Russia

SALIVA OVERWHELMED RUBY'S mouth and she spat on the floor of her cell. Ribbons of blood swam in the spit. When Ox rammed his brow into her forehead, she must've bitten her tongue. Swollen, it was the least of her ailments. Because the inside of her skull was raw—like her cranium was sandpaper, scraping against her brain. Cognitive brush-burn.

Both Ox and Wyatt had taken aim at her head. The military manual on hand-to-hand combat must read: blunt force to the head renders the enemy useless—a muddled mass of human stupor in slippers. Slippers? She was still wearing the red slip-ons.

Squinting from the midday sun which now crept into her cell, she swooned from a wave of nausea. A concussion, no doubt. But when she tallied her physical pain, adding her nose and arm injuries, the torment was still bearable compared to her heart. Grief was corroding her pericardial lining, burning through it like acid. Her heart literally felt like it was dissolving.

For forty-eight excruciating hours, she'd been separated from Clay. From her anchor.

And now she was drifting, unsure of her next move.

At least she hadn't played Ox and Vladimir's extortion game. Resisting was her only chance to save Gabby. She remembered what the Platoon Commander of SEAL Team 86 had told her after he'd collected the F8 cure-serum from her and Em, years back during martial law. He'd warned that compliance or negotiation with terrorists, from a lone wolf to a regime madman, yielded certain defeat. Irrevocable loss. What were the chances, he had asked rhetorically, that an enemy like Huo—who'd massacred a billion people and practically the entire animal kingdom—would keep a promise? Any promise?

None. Zero. Nil. Nada.

Ox and Vladimir were Huo's partners. Ruthless terrorists through and through.

Resisting was the right decision.

Gabby's life was now in Em and President Newton's hands: two people she trusted unequivocally. Two people who had enormous influence and assets at their disposal. They'd protect Gabby. And Margo and Tomas.

Defying Ox and Vladimir had probably saved Dr. Lin's life, for that matter. Without Em coming to Russia to genetically engineer a zombie-to-human serum, the need for a substitute microbiologist, one who could facilitate the molecular side of the scheme, had skyrocketed to critical. Pretty much ensuring job security.

The only life expectancy at serious risk was Clay's.

Tragically, her latest act of defiance had heightened his expendability because hurting her husband was one of the demented-duo's bargaining chips. And during her *interview*, she'd thrown the cards in their faces, unwilling to play, as if there'd be no consequences.

Her stomach acid churned. She gagged and spit again.

Oddly, her life was the most secure. If Ox and Vladimir didn't need her as a living, breathing blood-bank, they would've killed her by now. After draining her blood, of course.

Slowly pushing with her arms, she lifted her chest off the damp concrete. Her head throbbed. Blood dripped from her nose and splattered on the floor. Breaking free from her barred cage was paramount. She had to help Clay before it was too late.

Images flashed in her mind.

The word *cage* reminded her of birds. Birds, of infected animals. Infected animals, of eyes like blood blisters.

And that's when she derived her plan and began preparing. Until she was ready.

Then she screamed. Not a high-pitched, a bat's-in-my-hair shrill. No, hers was epic. Visceral. She wailed as if wounded beyond the pain barrier. Which was close, given her brain pounded in her skull, flashing white before her eyes.

Ruby listened. No footsteps.

After gagging from what she'd done, she screamed again.

Adrenaline pulsed through her. Sweat beaded on her forehead and delivered a burst of coolness as evaporation lowered her body temperature. The flush in her cheeks drained, probably turning her skin a grayish ash.

Footsteps—a single pair, thank God, approached the closed door at the end of the cellblock aisle. She screamed again. The door opened and the "second" guard, as she'd referred to him earlier that same morning—the one who spoke a speck of English, raced down the walkway to her cell, his pistol at the ready.

His eyes grew wide, mouth popping open.

She could only imagine what he saw: a blood-drenched mouth, with crimson filling each crevasse between her teeth, on a face already bruised and swollen. She hoped blood had crept passed her lips and was dripping from her chin. Her hands were in view. They were painted in blood, as if she'd inserted them into a deep wound.

"Help me!" she pleaded. "I need a doctor. Doctor!"

The guard placed his pistol in its holster and fumbled with a keyring. Although the camo cap hid his eyes, his hands were shaking. He was probably imagining his fate. Imagining what would happen to him if the girl suspected of having unique blood died on his watch.

Nausea rocked her as if she were a boat listing on rough surf.

She vomited on the floor. Blood, more purple than red, tinted the remains of her ingested porridge and bread.

The guard entered the cell and squatted beside her.

"Doctor?" he asked, almost sounding like he cared.

"Yes," she whispered, nodding.

He reached with his right hand, attempting to place it under her left elbow, to help her stand. She shook her head, indicating she could do it herself. She started to rise.

As the guard stepped back to give her room, she stomped her left-foot forward while raising her bent right-arm—her forearm, parallel to the floor. Pushing with her right-foot, she twisted her body to the left, driving the ulna bone—the long bone extending from wrist to elbow—into the guard's trachea. She didn't jab like a boxer. The key was to drive *through* him, never retracting from her forward assault, picturing her forearm cutting through his neck like a sword.

The guard fell onto his back and her forearm followed him. Thrusting. Pressing. He choked and gasped for air.

This was life or death, she reminded herself. No second thoughts.

Ruby leapt onto the guard's chest in a sitting position, straddling him. Using the socks she'd removed minutes before, she stuffed them into the guard's mouth, pushing them to the back of his throat, hoping to weaken him further by depleting his oxygen. His mouth was so full, he couldn't bite her.

His fingers frantically tried to clutch an edge, a tip, a pinch of sock-material. But his throat and mouth were tightly packed. His eyes grew wide. He was suffocating.

The guard abandoned his efforts to remove the socks. Instead, he grappled for her throat.

She clutched his ears. Raising his head off the floor, she smashed his skull against the concrete. His pupils got lost behind opened eyelids and his hands fell from her neck. Blood oozed onto the concrete from his head wound.

Dismounting, she grabbed his pistol. A nine-millimeter, equipped with a full fifteen-round magazine. No bells or whistles like thumb identification. Good.

Unconscious, the guard began to convulse. She yanked a sock from his mouth, before pulling out the other from deep in his throat. His lungs involuntarily gasped. His chest inflated. Thankfully, he was alive, though she didn't know if his head trauma would be fatal. She hoped not. Her goal was to save Clay, not kill Russians. Unless they gave her no choice.

The guard had a water bottle strapped onto his utility belt and she grabbed it. Twisting the lid, she swished water in her mouth before spitting, repeating the regiment until her discharge was blood free. Taking a cupped-handful of water, she splashed her face, wiping away blood, being careful around her eyes and nose.

She smiled. Clay would be impressed with her tactical trickery. The image of birds and blood-blistered eyes had reminded her of the ballooning-bruise inflicted by Corporal Wyatt on her inner right-arm. The massive blood-pustule needed to be drained. So she had held the bend of her elbow to her mouth and broke the skin with her teeth, sucking and drinking her stale blood. She made sure she smeared blood on her lips and chin in the process.

During her exchange with the guard, she'd planned on sticking her finger down her throat, making herself heave. Hoping her puke would resemble internal bleeding.

Turns out, she vomited on her own—well, not really. Truth was, after drinking old blood from her bruise, she grossed out. So much so, that retching came without physical prompting. Adding to her good fortune, the guard bought into her act.

She searched his utility belt, relieved that the Russian soldier was a walking artillery depot. Quickly familiarizing herself with his security gadgets, including a Taser, two switchblades, rope, and a flashlight, she removed the holster and began to wrap it around her waist. She stopped. Her black shorts and blouse were beacons for capture.

After undressing the guard, she buttoned his utility shirt over her blouse. She stepped into his camo pants, zipping them over her shorts. The guard was thin, but taller than she was. She rolled the pantlegs and shirt-sleeves under, hiding the misfit. The finishing touch was his camo cap. She curled her ponytail on top of her head and secured her hair under the cap.

Before leaving and locking the cell behind her, she checked the guard's pulse. It was weak but ticking.

Ruby guessed Clay was being detained on the next level up: the floor where she'd seen lab workers. At least, that's where she'd start her search.

Walking toward the stairwell, voices lingered in the distance, but thankfully, she didn't encounter anyone. She climbed the steps, stopping periodically to listen for company. On the next level's landing, she stood to the side of the door, keeping her body hidden, and eased her head forward, glancing through the glass. The hall was empty. Maybe it was lunchtime—the main meal of the day for Russians, which usually occurred between one and three o'clock in the afternoon.

Opening the glass door, she stepped over the threshold, holding the handle and easing the door back slowly, until the latch clicked. She headed down the hall, one quiet step at a time.

A door opened and a man in a lab coat walked into the hallway.

Her heart raced, pounding in her ears.

She looked down, hoping he would avoid seeing her mangled face.

"Добрый день," he uttered.

She had no clue what the man had said, or even how the words had sounded. So she kept her head lowered and continued to walk.

His footsteps stopped. "Добрый день," he snapped loudly, with that Russian *umph*.

This time she heard him, heard his enunciation loud and clear. Hopefully, he had uttered a greeting, not a question.

She stopped, turning her head sideways, just a bit, keeping her back toward him. "Dōbriy den," she *umphed*.

Apparently satisfied, he continued walking away from her, down the hall and through the glass door. But that's where her luck changed. The Russian greeted someone else.

Her breathing stopped.

Continuing to walk at an even pace, she opened the next door on her left, marked number-103. She closed the door behind her, quietly rotating the lock on the doorknob. She inhaled, filling her lungs as she turned to inspect the lab.

The room was brightly lit, minus technicians. However, she was not alone. Not exactly. There were two bodies—both dead, she suspected. One on each gurney. Sheets were draped over the corpses, faces included.

Her world was about to shatter.

31

Tuesday, July 13, 2032
Moscow, Russia

OX LEFT VLADIMIR'S office fuming about the girl's lack of cooperation. And his partner couldn't talk him down. Not even vodka shots chilled his fire. In fact, the burn grew hotter.

The troll had reminded him to be *patient*, but that was like asking an eagle to walk instead of fly. Wasn't happening.

To lift his spirits, Ox headed downstairs to the next level, to the lab where Clay Spencer was being interrogated KGB-style. Maybe Ox's order to snuff the prisoner after questioning had already been executed. One could only hope. He needed a turbo-boost to quell the feeling that their plan was stalling.

As he walked, he couldn't decide who raised his combustion more: Ruby Never-Dies, whom hours ago he'd headbutted like an eighteen-wheeler to a bicycle, or himself, who caved to violence over restraint. Fuck patience. But personal restraint? That was a bitch.

Even though the threat had been articulated, he and Vladimir never intended to drain the girl to death. If she didn't cooperate— voluntarily joining their little powwow, they planned on sedating her into a coma. They'd extract her blood as needed, keeping her alive so her body could replenish itself, like a bottomless keg of hemoglobin. Because in what universe would they ever destroy their ticket to world dominance?

So a lethal headbutt would have seriously compromised their mission. He fisted his hands at his lack of control.

Complicating matters were his conflicted emotions. While he regretted his lack of restraint, he also felt disappointment. After an act of violence, he looked forward to the endorphin rush, savoring the euphoric high—his self-generated drug of choice.

This time, he had to deny himself that pleasure. This time, he was forced to feel regret immediately after the act. Zero satisfaction in that. Which deepened his anger.

As he opened the glass door to the hallway housing the labs, a Ruskie lab coat passed him. "Добрый день," the guy said, smiling like a pathetic kiss-ass.

"Yeah. Whatever." He wasn't in the mood for niceties.

His mood, in fact, wasn't going to help Mr. Pretty Face if he was still alive. He dug the nail of his index finger into his thumb.

Ruby Never-Dies would be his next visit. He needed to assess her physical and mental fortitude. Or lack thereof.

He stopped in front of lab 103 and reached for the doorknob. Light fanned out from under the doorway. Had Vladimir said Clay Spencer's interrogation was in number-103 or 105?

The vodka fogged his memory.

32

Tuesday, July 13, 2032
Moscow, Russia

FOOTSTEPS STOPPED OUTSIDE the lab door. Ruby's hand hovered over the pistol on her confiscated utility belt. Her eyes stopped blinking, her lungs froze. Only her heart ignored the pause.

The heavy stride of military boots resumed.

She closed her eyes, relieved.

The door opened to the adjacent lab, or at least it sounded close. Inhaling, she filled her lungs, before cleansing with an exhale.

Shifting her attention to the corpses, she walked toward a gurney. A stainless-steel lab cart was in her path, topped with medical instruments and a syringe and needle—its barrel filled with clear liquid. She rolled the cart to the side.

Dread overtook her. What if one of the corpses was Clay? Her knees grew weak.

She peeled the sheet back from the first, revealing the dead man's face. Her knees buckled. Bile raced upwards from the dredges of her stomach. With lids petrified open, milky eyes stared at nothing. Ruby grabbed the edge of the gurney for support. Her legs shook. The ashen face belonged to Corporal Wyatt.

Obviously, there was no love-lost between her and the Marine. Her face and arm were living proof. What buckled her knees was the bullet-penetration marking his forehead. It told a story; one that terrified her. Since his eyes weren't black as tar, he must have avoided being bitten by the zombie-head during the plane scuffle. Which meant the only reason he was lying lifeless on the gurney was that Ox and Vladimir no longer needed him. They were eliminating bread-crumbs to cover their tracks.

A spherical rise protruded from the sheet, beside the Corporal's chest. Wondering what caused the bulge, she raised the sheet further, revealing more of the Marine's body. Tucked under his lifeless arm, as if protecting a child from danger, was the zombie head she'd been transporting, intended for Washington, D.C. The freak show which was once Mr. CDC was no more. A bullet hole bored into his forehead, too. Black goo seeped from the wound.

Turning, she gazed at the other gurney. Tears welled. Was she too late for Clay?

She had no choice but to look at the remaining corpse. Moving to the gurney, she fingered the edge of the sheet, near the victim's head. With a shaking hand, she lifted the sheet, staring at the corpse's deadpan expression.

"Thank God!" she whispered.

The dead body belonged to the Russian co-pilot of the Aeroflot airplane, the one used to hijack her from Taipei to Moscow. His neck revealed deep, purple rings, some with crimson trenches, like he'd been strangled using strands of wire.

Relief fortified her knees.

Maybe she still had time to save her husband. Perhaps even Dr. Lin, who had been so kind. Unfortunately, she'd be stuck in the lab until she heard the adjacent door open and shut, hopefully indicating the person whose footsteps she'd heard was leaving the floor.

Even though she was temporarily trapped, she no longer felt like a victim. Overtaking the guard in her cell had boosted her confidence. And with the arsenal she had acquired, she resembled a warrior on a mission. Of course, if the guard was found in her cell, she'd quickly become a hunted animal. Her sense of security was temporary.

Scanning the lab, she searched for anything that might help avoid capture. A sink cabinet was in the far corner; above it, a mirror. She hadn't seen herself in days, since before her injuries, so she headed for the wash basin.

When she stood in front of the mirror, her jaw dropped. She raised her hand to cover her gaping mouth. Under her eyes and coloring her swollen cheeks and nose were shades of plum, grape, raisin, and boysenberry. At least her nose wasn't crooked, but that was of little consolation. On the right side of her forehead was a bulbous lump; the skin was cracked at the point of impact, where Ox's head had slammed into hers.

She was grotesque.

A wave of tears crashed through her ducts and careened down her cheeks. She desperately needed ruby slippers. If she could, she'd click her heels together and wake up at home with Clay and Gabby. And their dog Lollie. Instead of being in this Moscow hellhole, fighting for Clay's life and her own.

One thing was clear as she stared at herself: the camo cap wasn't hiding her facial injuries. She needed a better disguise. Hurrying to the closet, she opened it and found white scrubs and lab coats. The best find was a facemask dispenser mounted on the wall.

Without hesitation, she exchanged her camo outfit with the lab attire, wearing her holster beneath the lab coat. After changing, she removed a switchblade from its sheath, dropping it into her outer pocket.

In front of the mirror, she re-formed her ponytail and secured the facemask. Only a sliver of purple peeked out below her bottom lashes. The discoloration could pass as a lack of sleep.

As she turned to move closer to the door, she stopped in her tracks. The journal she and Clay had found in Shifen was laying on a desk, open, in front of a computer monitor. The screen displayed word processing.

Approaching the desk, she noticed the text was in Russian. But as the words *damn it* were about to roll off her tongue, she saw "language" on the screen's upper taskbar. She sat in the desk's chair and moved the cursor over the menu option and clicked. Twenty or more languages appeared in the dropdown menu. She clicked English. The translation was instantaneous. Her eyes widened. The transcription of the journal was before her, representing the man-in-the-closet's final hours.

She scrolled to the beginning of the document and began to read:

I am Ian Mă. I must write quickly because I am infected. Time is counting down.

Born to generations of coal miners, I live in the mountain village of Shifen, a tourist attraction for sky lanterns, souvenir shops, and a nearby waterfall. My wife Huang and son Chen sew lantern socks to support tourism in our town. My wife and I are thirty-six years old. Although she still walks, she died nearly an hour ago. I do not know the whereabouts or condition of our son, who is eighteen.

This is my first and last entry, as I sit in a fire-resistant closet, in the school which once was Chen's. I am alone; the only human left in our village. On the other side of the closet door is chaos. Un-death.

In my last hour, I wish to document the truth. The year is 2031; the day, the fourteenth of September. A Sunday.

Five Hours Ago: In the afternoon, I took the Pingxi Branch Line from Shifen to Keelung. From the train station, a bus transported me to Kanziding Fish Market. There was nothing unusual in my routine. The market and alleys were crowded, as they normally are. People were talking and laughing. There was much life in the port city.

I purchased cuttlefish and oysters at Huang's request, and bought a bottle of goryangju, a distilled liquor of fermented sorghum. A surprise, and one of her favorites.

When a bus transported me back to the train station, I found the Pingxi line was closed. The ticket booth was dark, and the wire gate had been rolled down and locked over the counter. This was odd, since no one standing about the booth had been warned of its closing. Some held tickets in their hands, sold minutes before the abrupt shutdown.

I was fortunate, or at least I thought so at the time, to acquire a taxi back home. The driver turned onto the 106 County Road. The winding road is always busy with tour buses, every day of the week, transporting visitors to and from the attractions. On the way home, however, the road was empty, except for a few taxis behind us, heading south like we were.

About five kilometers from Shifen, the driver slowed. A massive fence had been erected, perhaps twelve-feet high, with rows of barbed wire on top. A military guard, dressed in fatigues and heavily armed, ordered my driver to stop.

The driver asked what the problem was. Why there was a fence. The guard answered that the roadblock was a checkpoint for gangs, which had been hauling drugs using the mountainous throughway. The guard said President Huo would not tolerate drug running.

Then the guard looked at me suspiciously, asking me why I was on the road.

Asking me if I was a local. So I showed him my bag of seafood and told him my home was in Shifen. Born and raised. And I had been shopping at the Keelung market for our dinner meal.

The guard was not satisfied. He asked me what was inside my other bag. And I told him it contained liquor, goryangju for my wife.

He mentioned goryangju was his favorite. If I wanted to pass the checkpoint with my driver, then I would have to hand over the bottle. Laughing, he said it was a fair deal—that goryangju should not be wasted.

More than anything, I was annoyed. The guards were acting like days of old. My father had told me stories. Frightening stories of an abusive military.

I did not hesitate to relinquish the liquor. Being home with Huang and Chen was my only consideration. A bottle of liquor was a small price to pay, or so I thought.

As we drove past the rising fence, I looked back, out of the rear window. The fence extended into the forest, on both sides of the road, and I wondered how I could have missed its installation. I traveled the road or train tracks almost every day. Certainly the fence could not have been raised in one day.

When we arrived in town, there were military vehicles everywhere. My heart pounded in my chest. Something unprecedented was happening. I suspected the Chinese President. The military answered to him, and him alone.

Except for camo Humvees and Jeeps, and armed guards milling about, there were no town's people. The streets were empty. No tourists either.

After paying my fare, I raced from the vehicle to my townhome. When I opened the door, Huang and Chen were not home. A note on the kitchen countertop explained that President Huo was treating the town to dinner in the elementary school cafeteria, for the inconvenience of placing two checkpoints on the 106. She wrote that she had thanked the guards which had entered our flat (uninvited), grateful for the President's generosity. But she explained that I was bringing home cuttlefish for geng, so we would not attend.

The guards told her it would be a dishonor to refuse the meal. They allowed her to write the note. In the last written line, she urged me to meet her and Chen at the school. Through her written words, I sensed her unease.

Huang always included the time on her notes. This note was marked five o'clock. It was already six.

After I read Huang's note, a guard entered our flat, rifle pointed. I raised my hands slightly, unsure of his dispute with me. He demanded that I go to the school for dinner. I was anxious. My hands shook, and it was difficult to swallow.

Danger polluted the air.

I left the purchased seafood on the counter, knowing it would spoil and somehow understanding that it no longer mattered.

The guard followed behind me to the school. I glanced at the sky. Blue with puffy clouds. Birds flying here and there. Free. Without worry.

The barred entrance to the school was locked and five guards stood on the outside, smoking cigarettes and talking in hushed voices. They seemed surprised to see me, but opened the gate and directed me toward the cafeteria.

Almost every chair was taken. Somehow in the crowd, I spotted my taxi driver.

When I found my wife, I sat next to her and asked where Chen was. She whispered that he had escaped midway through the meal. He had been nervous, she said, because the guards carried guns, making him suspicious. He promised to return, if he could. Chen had told a guard he needed the restroom. As he was escorted, Huang said he turned back to glance at her. She had not seen him since.

I looked around. Everyone had eaten. I told her it was time to go. But Huang said that was impossible. The guards explained that no one could leave until they heard closing remarks from an American.

This surprised me. An American? In Shifen with the Chinese military?

A guard plopped down a plate of warm meat, swimming in brown gravy. Some of the gravy splashed on my shirt. I am not a beef eater, so I politely shook my head and told him no thank you.

The guard rammed the rifle barrel into my back and hollered for me to eat. The chatter at nearby tables ceased when they heard the raised voice. Huang nudged my leg underneath the table, as if urging me to comply.

The entire room watched as I ate.

On the elevated stage, a brawny man with buzzed hair and American features appeared. Beside him was a translator. He explained that a convoy of drug runners had already been apprehended, but a few of the criminals had averted arrest, escaping into the nearby woods. He feared the lawbreakers might have sought refuge in our homes. After they conducted a thorough sweep, we would be allowed to return to the village. But for a few hours, we were to stay shielded within the protective walls of the school. Piece of cake, he had said.

A few beads of sweat formed on Huang's forehead. She complained that she had the beginnings of a headache. When we overheard whispers of those around us, we learned they were experiencing the same symptoms. Everyone was thirsty. We asked for water and were denied. We asked to use the restroom. Forbidden.

My wife had eaten the meal an hour before me, like everybody else. If the meat was foul, I would experience the same symptoms in time.

Our mayor, sitting at a table near a glass sliding-door, stood. He was usually reserved and stoic. Which is why I was surprised when he hollered to our citizens. With words racing from his mouth, he warned that things were suspicious. He had never been informed about the checkpoint or dinner. He shouted that our best chance for survival was to escape.

Those were his last words.

He was shot in the chest, rapid fire, and his body crashed into the glass door, shattering it, creating a breach in the building. A few people rushed for the opening and were shot and killed. Their bodies piled near the mayor.

The room hushed. People were in shock. Like Huang and me, all turned to prayer.

Huang's headache was worsening. The muscles in her jaw occasionally twitched, involuntarily. Sweat beaded across her forehead.

My body temperature was slightly elevated. I began to sweat, maybe from the humidity in the room. Like my wife an hour earlier, I felt a headache emerging. Perhaps from the stress.

Huang rested her head on my shoulder and we quietly reminisced about our son, remembering the day he was born and recalling milestones as he grew into a man. A man who made us deeply proud.

Time elapsed slowly. Each breath, memorable.

Huang had a fever and mentioned her heart was racing. She coughed a bit of blood. The headache was excruciating now, and she was having difficulty thinking clearly. Wheezing had begun. Her eyes were bloodshot. Her blouse drenched in sweat. In a non-stop spasm, her jaw muscles rapidly twitched, causing her teeth to chatter together, as if she were cold and shivering.

Looking at me, tears raced down her cheeks. I cried as well. I was losing her. My wife. My friend. The mother of our son. The only woman I had ever loved, was fading.

Something else was taking her place. Something evil. Something the guards had inflicted on us.

I must have dozed off, holding my wife in my arms. When I woke, the military had left. Smoke filled the air like poisonous fog, both inside and outside the school. I coughed, and blood stained my hand. The noise jolted Huang. She raised her chin to gaze at me. Her eyes were black. Her skin had shrunken. Teeth clicked. And as she pressed closer, with such strength, I knew she was not my wife. She smelled like death, only she was not dead.

Suddenly, Huang lunged at me and I pushed her away. The commotion caused all the faces in the cafeteria to look at me. Their eyes: all were black. The clicking of their teeth was haunting. They rose. And I ran.

Ran from the cafeteria and down the hallway. I remembered where the library was—in the back of the building. Before I raced under the arched entranceway, I looked over my shoulder. A horde of dead villagers, somehow walking, shuffled toward me. I could not tell if they were pursuing me or simply reacting to the disturbance.

In the library, I found a closet with an internal light switch. Inside were two filing cabinets and I pulled them out. I grabbed a journal, pen, and a student chair and placed them inside the closet. I turned on the light.

As I shut the door, the horde entered the library. I believed it would be the end. That they would open the door and drag me out, biting me to death.

The door, however, has remained closed.
Even now, they are scratching at it. Screeching. Hissing. Moaning.
Huang among them.

Eventually, the sounds stop. My skin feels like it is burning. I wonder if the school is on fire.
The door remains shut and I am writing. Feverishly. Almost done.
Deteriorating quickly. Lungs cry. For air. Thirsty. Skin shrinking.

Death. Nears.
Love. Huang. Chen.

It was the end of the transcription. Ian Mǎ had no doubt morphed into a zombie. The zombie she had shot in the head in Shifen.

With hands balled into fists, she clenched her teeth. Ox was at the center of everything evil.

A gargled scream interrupted her thoughts. Was it Clay's?

Another scream curdled her blood. She was sure now: the voice was her husband's. And by all accounts, he was fighting for his life.

Adrenaline supercharged her muscles. Darting from the desk, she neared the lab door, hearing another open in the hallway. A few footsteps later, Ox laughed. She recognized his demonic voice.

"He's breaking," he announced, as if wanting the entire floor to hear. "He'll be spitting up that laptop combination like a baby. Keep him burping for a little while longer!"

Footsteps faded down the hall.

Slowly, Ruby unlocked and turned the knob, pulling the door toward her, just slightly. The coast was clear to her left. Poking her head out to glance right would look suspicious. Instead, she boldly walked into the hallway, embracing her disguise as a technician. Thankfully, the hall was empty so she inched toward the adjacent lab. Ox had left the door open a crack. She strolled by number-105 before flattening her back against the wall, near the door frame. She listened.

"You heard the man," an American voice said. "We ain't got all day. Ox wants those security codes. As in, yesterday. No more fucking around."

"Fucking around?" another voice questioned. "We've been working on this guy since he arrived. And he still hasn't broken."

"Let's hold him in the drink longer, 'til his legs quiver," the first voice taunted. "If that doesn't work, we'll add electricity to this party. We get to kill him anyway. We've got fifteen more minutes before Mr. Pretty Face's time is up."

Then and there, she vowed to kill that son-of-a-bitch turncoat: Ox. And his accomplices. Every last one of them.

But for now, she had to focus. She hoped there were only two of his goons in the lab. Any more, and her chances of recovering her husband would plummet. In crash-and-burn territory.

She pulled the pistol from its holster and readied it. As she inched in front of the door, an alarm sounded. A piercing, non-stop *beep, beep, beep.*

Lights activated in the hallway, red beams swirling around and around.

No doubt Ox and Vladimir had learned of her escape.

33

CLAY WAS BEYOND exhaustion. He had endured being hung in shackles by his ankles, naked. His assailants centered a sticky-surfaced tarp, resembling fly paper, underneath him. And then they released fire ants on his body. Initially, he had stayed calm and motionless, controlling his breathing. His strategy was working. Until the bastards whipped him with a belt.

The ants gripped his skin with their mandibles and stung him with venom. Each sting burned. He pictured his body covered in welts, like chicken pox on steroids. All the while his torturers, who were clearly American, asked for the combination to Ruby's government laptop. Bite after bite, with blood collecting in his head, he didn't answer. The codes meant nothing without eye scans. And once Ox and Vladimir obtained the codes, they would no longer care if his eyes remained in their sockets. They hardly cared as it was.

The options were straightforward. Withholding codes meant more pain. Sharing codes meant death. Torture was the clear winner.

Sensory overload followed the fire ants. The menu included strobe lights and loud music, preventing sleep. Then came more hanging upside down, more whipping.

Thankfully, he had mentally transported himself; he was sailing *The Gem* with Ruby and Gabriella. For some reason, Gabby was five-years-old in his vision. Her sun-kissed hair was wispy, dancing wildly with the wind. Standing on the quarter deck as a family, they were laughing, tasting the salt on their lips. Lollie wagged her tail, mouth open, tongue curled at the tip. The yacht was racing over the water. They were free. Together.

But when water became the enemy, when his captors turned to waterboarding, his resolve began drowning with his lungs. The chance to save himself never materialized. Which meant he couldn't save Ruby either, if she had even made it to the prison. And if he couldn't save Ruby or his daughter back home, what was the point in prolonging a losing battle?

His heart was crushed as if Ox had penetrated his chest cavity, fisted his hand around Clay's heart, and then squeezed like hell.

Death was inevitable. He'd heard it with his own ears. Ox had stepped into the lab and instructed his goons to kill Clay after fifteen minutes. The reality struck like stabbing a balloon with a knife.

The goons joked about how they'd do it: hold him under longer, add electrical current. So as they tilted his head downward by lowering the seesaw-styled plank, he barely inflated his lungs. He wanted to control his own death. To be less of a victim.

When his head submerged, he let his mind drift back to his schooner. He placed his hands on Ruby's waist and drew her to him, their bodies touching. Placing his mouth on hers, he kissed her. Deeply. Their love for each other would transcend time, a constant anchor. In this life, as in the eternal life that awaited him in Heaven.

He felt weightless as a feather. Floating. Free. At peace.

A ray of light shone brightly.

A tug on his shirt. *Daddy, what's that sound?*

Though his oxygen was nearly depleted, he fought to regain consciousness. He had to answer his daughter, his beloved Gabriella.

He heard a blaring alarm, even with his head submerged in water. And then he remembered. He wasn't on *The Gem* at all. He was in a Moscow prison, in a lab being tortured.

Not knowing where his wife was.

Did the alarm signal hope?

Could he hold-on long enough to find out?

34

RUBY STOOD IN the hallway beside lab 105. The alarm assaulted her ears. She moved in front of the door, the pistol in her right hand. Footsteps approached from inside the lab, and she raised her right leg and held it. Ready, waiting.

As one of Ox's goons reached the door, she drove her leg into the wood panel with all the strength she could muster. The door, nearly ripping from its hinges, slammed the unsuspecting Sailor to the ground.

Quickly scanning the lab, she registered two of Ox's men: the one dazed on the floor beside her and the other who stood diagonally, near the back corner, to the right of a seesaw-style apparatus raised in the up position. The downed thug hadn't drawn his pistol, which bought her a millisecond. She aimed instead at the Sailor by the seesaw, who was pulling a handgun from his holster. She fired twice. He sagged to the floor.

She shifted her attention to the Sailor near her. He was fumbling for his firearm, having difficulty maneuvering around the strap securing his handgun. But when he landed in her pistol's sights, he moved his hands near his ears, palms up, trembling like a white flag in the breeze.

"We can talk this thing out," he said. "I'm a victim, too."

"No deals with turncoats." She pulled the trigger, not believing the scum.

But the firing pin clicked, and the gun powder failed to ignite.

She tried to cock the pistol to eject the faulty bullet, but the action was stuck.

The Sailor smiled wide, eyes blinking rapidly. Maybe mimicking a flirt?

Sharp pain stabbed her Achilles tendon.

The strike from the Sailor forced her legs out from under her.

"Come join me," he cooed, as her body came crashing down. "Let's get better acquainted."

When her body slammed into the floor, the pistol jolted from her hand. Luckily, she landed on the Sailor's right arm, preventing him from freeing his handgun. It was enough time, just enough, for her to dip into her lab-coat pocket and retrieve the knife. Releasing the blade, she jammed the point into the Sailor's left eyeball, driving it to the back of his skull. His body convulsed before it surrendered to death.

"Guess your party's over, asshole." Standing, she jogged to the lab door, closing it and locking the knob.

Racing back to the seesaw, her eyes grew wide. From her vantage point by the door, she had no way of knowing that Clay's head had been submerged in a deep sink filled with water. *Water!* The entire time! And her husband wasn't moving. At all. His eyes were open underwater, unblinking. His lips, slightly parted.

"No, Clay! No!"

Reaching above her head, she pulled the raised side of the seesaw into a down position. Clay's head lifted through the water and his body jolted as the end of the seesaw's plank struck the floor. He was strapped to the wood slab by three belts, one around his shins; another, his thighs; the last, his chest. She had to free him from the slab. Get him onto the floor.

Holding the end of the seesaw down with her foot, she fumbled with the belt over his shins. With shaking hands, it was hard to manipulate the strap through the buckle. She could barely think. Her brain screamed for her to *hurry, hurry, hurry.* Seconds were ticking. Clay's life was in jeopardy. On the brink, if not already out-of-reach.

Managing to keep the seesaw down, she freed both the shin and thigh straps. But that was where progress stopped. Clay's chest was too elevated, too far away on the seesaw to reach the belt around his chest, unless she released her foot and let his head lower back into the water—which wasn't an option. She needed weight on the bottom of the slab to enable her to move to the side of the seesaw, to unstrap the belt where she could reach it.

She glanced around. The shot Sailor was stone-cold in a pool of his blood. She squatted. Placing her hand on the end of the seesaw to hold down the plank, she scooted toward the dead man. Sitting and stretching her legs to reach him, she hooked her slippers around his leg and slid him toward her, in brief bursts of energy. When his torso was in reach, she clasped his shirt and drug his body, one handed, to rest over the edge of the slab, over Clay's feet.

It seemed like hours had passed. Every second, unfolding in slow motion. She was sweating and breathing heavy.

Darting to Clay's side, she unbuckled the belt and yanked his limp body from the waterboarding apparatus. His feet were stuck under the Sailor's body and she yanked him free.

Lowering Clay on his back, she straddled his waist. No need for a pulse check. It was clear he didn't have one. Instead, she started CPR compressions, pushing down hard.

After fifteen pumps, there was no change. Only water trickled from his mouth.

"Don't leave me, Clay! I can't do this alone!"

More compressions.

She moved to his side and pulled down her facemask, intending to deliver two breaths into his lungs.

His mouth was full of water.

Turning him on his side, she pounded his back. The blunt force caused water to slosh onto the floor. Lowering him on his back again, she pushed two breaths into his lungs, as far as the air would go. Which wasn't far. Clearly, his lungs were inflated with water.

"Breathe, damn it! Gabby and I need you."

Straddling him again, she turned his head to the side and administered more compressions. "Try, Clay. Please! Get back into your body and help me!"

She was crying now.

When it was time to deliver oxygen, his mouth was no longer full of water. She forced two breaths into his airway.

Her exhale traveled farther.

"Breathe! There's no other option. Fight through it."

On the third chest compression, his body convulsed.

35

Tuesday, July 13, 2032
Moscow, Russia

CLAY SAW HIS naked body stretched on the lab floor. His wife straddled him, administering CPR and crying. Yelling at him. But he struggled to understand the reality of the scene. Was he dreaming again? Had his brain cruelly transitioned the peaceful vision of his family on *The Gem*…into a nightmare?

From his elevated view, he heard Ruby beg him not to die.

He had to get closer to figure out what was going on. To stop from drifting higher. He struggled, like swimming against the current.

Now inches from his own face, which was blue and expressionless, he watched her administer three more compressions. He felt the pressure of the last compression on his chest, at the same time his aerial view faded.

Then his body tensed, as if every muscle was coordinating to perform one simple task: a cough. The release of which, ejected water trapped deep within his lungs. He gasped for air as she pushed him on his side. He vomited water and gasped again, inflating his lungs with air. Precious *air!*

With arms draped around him, his wife cried: "Oh my God, Clay! You're alive! Alive!"

He coughed again. She knelt over him and touched his cheek. The touch of an angel. His angel.

His mind wrapped around the reality. Ruby was at the prison and it wasn't a dream. She had rescued him. Saved him.

Rolling onto his back, he focused on her face. His eyes narrowed with confusion. Her nose and cheeks were swollen and bruised. His heart thumped in his chest. "What…" He coughed, his words still painfully waterlogged. "What…happened…to you?"

"This from a man who was just dead?" She kissed his lips softly. "The only thing that matters is that you came back to me!"

"I love you." He gently brushed his thumb along her jawbone, careful not to touch her swelling. "I love you so much." Raising his head, he glanced at the two dead Sailors and smiled. "Still my superhero, I see." The alarm continued to blare in the hallway. "Sounds like we don't have much time. What's going on?"

"I'm guessing they've discovered the body in my prison cell. So the facility's probably in lock-down, with guards going room-to-room to find me. Which means we need to escape from this hellhole. As in, right now."

Clay sat up slowly. "Whoa. My equilibrium's off. Guess that happens when you're hung upside down. Then strapped to a plank, tilted head-first."

"Hold tight and get acclimated for a second." She left his side and collected pistols from both assailants.

"Anything we can use?"

"The handguns are nine-millimeters, with full magazines and laser grips." She dropped them into her lab pockets.

He watched her jog to the closet. She returned holding scrubs, a lab coat, and facemask.

"Here's the plan." She handed the clothes to him. "When you're dressed, we'll head left out the door, away from the stairwell that leads to the cellblock. Maybe we can find a back exit."

He chuckled, looking at her feet.

"What's so funny?"

"You managed to get ruby slippers."

She glanced at her footwear. "I guess I did! Let's hope they get us home."

"Wish I had a pair." he said, slipping into his scrubs as he sat.

"Boots will have to do." She squatted by the dead turncoat near the seesaw. Unlacing his boots, she pulled them off, including the socks, and handed them to him.

"I'm feeling weak," he admitted, pulling on the socks and boots. His hands wouldn't stop shaking. "I haven't eaten in days. I hope I can do this."

"You came back from the dead, didn't you? You're much stronger than you give yourself credit for."

"I know someone just like that." He winked. Attempting to stand, his legs wobbled and shook. He took a few steps to steady himself.

"Here." She handed him a pistol.

"I'm worried. Worried I'm going to slow us down. Put us at risk."

"We've got each other; that's all that matters. And we will escape. One way or another. Confidence over fear, remember?"

Nodding, he was uplifted by her attitude. He couldn't let her down. He had to keep going.

"Facemasks on," she said, positioning hers.

After securing his facemask, he took a few shaky steps before she stood beside him and placed her left arm around his waist for support. He willed for his body to recover, so he wasn't a burden, wasn't risking their lives.

She unlocked the lab door and they exited into the empty hallway. Red lights swirled. And the alarm repeated its rhythmic warning. She re-locked the lab door and closed it, probably figuring the barrier might buy them a few seconds. They turned left and walked down the hall. It dead-ended at a perpendicular hallway.

"Left," she whispered.

Clay felt nauseous from being full of water. And empty of food. They needed to find an exit soon.

Walking through several darkened hallways, they turned right, then left, then left again. Arriving at the entrance to a long and dark corridor, he saw a few doors located on either side of the hallway. More importantly, a door was at the other end. And the door had a window. A window that basked in natural light. From the *outside!*

When they entered the corridor, overhead fluorescent tubes lit as they walked toward each fixture. Clearly motion sensitive. The concert of hums grew louder as each lighting-track illuminated.

His heart upshifted. Adrenaline helped steady him.

"We're getting there," she whispered. "Freedom is beyond that door."

36

Tuesday, July 13, 2032
Moscow, Russia

RUBY'S HEART SANK as she and Clay approached the end of the corridor. Several feet in front of the door, invisible from the hall's entrance, was a wire-mesh screen with threads the thickness of guitar strings. The screen barrier stretched from floor-to-ceiling and from wall-to-wall and included a thin doorframe with a metal handle.

"Bet it's charged," Clay whispered. "They like electricity around here."

She leaned her husband against the cinderblock wall for support. Pulling the rope from her utility belt, she tossed it at the mesh barrier. On contact, the rope crackled and hissed, before dropping to the floor ablaze. She stomped on the lingering flames with her red slippers, singeing some of the fabric. She closed her eyes in disbelief.

A door opened behind them, from down the hallway. Out walked four figures, silhouetted in the fluorescent lighting.

"Two M4s and one forty-five are pointed at your dearly beloved," Ox shouted to her as he approached, leading the pack. "Only one of us needs to be a good shot. Now both of you drop your weapons. Then lower your facemasks and raise your hands. Do it now."

The wind had been knocked from her lungs.

"Do as they say," Clay whispered, placing his pistol on the floor and kicking it down the hall. "We need another chance to fight. We need a tomorrow." He lowered his facemask and raised his hands.

She followed his lead.

"The utility holster, my dear," Vladimir said. "Remove my comrade's belt and kick it toward me."

Unbuckling the belt, she complied, finishing the order by lowering her facemask and raising her hands.

As the figures closed in, she discerned two guards—one Russian, one American—walking alongside Ox and Vladimir. The turncoat Lieutenant Colonel was now dressed in fatigues, aiming his forty-five at Clay. The Russian President was the only one not brandishing a weapon.

"My, my, my." Ox whistled like he had witnessed something pleasing. "You could've had a bright future in the military, Mrs. Spencer. Blood of a savior; fight of the devil."

"You and Vladimir have the monopoly on evil," she countered. "We're on God's side. Remember?"

"Every good savior must sacrifice." Ox focused on Clay. "Apart from your wife's cell, which lacks cameras if one can fathom the ineptitude of that, Vladimir and I have been watching you both on camera. Her attempts to resuscitate you in the lab were damn right touching."

"Brought tears to my eyes!" Vladimir bellowed. "Almost made us reconsider your fate, Mr. Spencer."

"*Almost* is as satisfying as blue balls," Ox said, turning his attention back to her. "But since your beau isn't willing to share the laptop's security codes, we no longer have use for him."

"The codes don't matter," she snapped, rolling her eyes. "If you want to speak with Ava Newton, just contact the White House. It's a no-brainer that you'll get through. You have two people she wants. And she doesn't need a secured communications-system—which is the sole purpose of the laptop, by the way—to negotiate for our return."

"Well, ain't that something," Ox said. "All that torture for nothing. Which means your better-half is now one-hundred-percent expendable. Because it's you, Ruby, who the President wants. You, and you alone."

"Not so fast," she spat. "I won't play in your *little party* unless Clay's alive. And since you tend to overlook the obvious, let *me* be clear: if I can kill your thugs right under your noses while you're watching, I can drain my own blood and ruin your hopes for a living blood-bank. And don't doubt that I'll find a way. I'll kill myself if Clay's harmed."

Deep down, she had no intentions of killing herself. That's why she was fighting so hard *to live*. Fighting for a life with her daughter and husband. But if her kidnapping was indeed part of an elaborate war game between superpowers—one where the players mistakenly considered her *the prize*, she needed to negotiate. Using her life as a bargaining chip seemed worth a try.

"Ruby," her husband said. "Don't say that. Don't even think it."

Vladimir snapped his hand downward as a gesture and released a puff of air. "Nonsense! That is what you Americans call…an empty threat."

"Excuse me?" She'd have to be more convincing. The Russian President wasn't easily persuaded.

"If you killed yourself," he explained, "you would leave your child, your precious Gabriella, unprotected. And that, my dear, would never happen. Your words are groundless."

She clenched her fists and gritted her teeth. "Try me."

"I'll say it again," Ox said. "Your Achilles heel, not to bring up recent wounds, is that you're soft. Your obsessive concern for others makes you a prime candidate for coercion. Pliable as clay." He glanced at her husband. "Pun intended."

She sneered at her captors. "Here's what I say: *your* disregard for human life makes you prime candidates for death. And when I kill you both, you won't be pliable at all. You'll be stiff."

Vladimir shook his head and made a *tisk, tisk, tisk* sound. "So much talk of death."

Seeming bored with the exchange, Ox turned to the American guard. "Frisk Mr. Spencer and then escort him to his cell. I'll deal with him personally, after I've chatted with his witty wife." He eyed her face. "I would've said beautiful, but you're far from that these days." He stomped his boot, glaring at the Russian guard. "And have someone turn-off that fucking alarm!"

Her brain felt like exploding when the guard began frisking Clay. Her husband was so weak from being tortured. "Don't touch him!"

"I'll be fine," he whispered. "Trust me."

The alarm and emergency lights deactivated.

After frisking, the American guard poked the barrel of his rifle into Clay's back and jabbed him repeatedly down the hallway. She watched them walk to the end of the corridor, until they became small silhouettes. Then they turned left, out of sight.

She and Clay were separated again. Exhaling slowly, she felt beaten. Game over.

With weapons still drawn, Ox, the Russian guard who'd returned, and Vladimir tightened their half-circle around her. She had no place to run. The electric barrier was behind her, by only five feet.

"You know this is going to end badly, don't you?" she asked Ox. "President Newton is going to rescue Clay and me. And Dr. Lin."

"Dear child," Vladimir cooed. "What makes you think Dr. Lin needs rescuing?"

"He isn't dead, is he? Please tell me you haven't killed him!"

"Of course not," he answered. "If we killed Dr. Lin, who would work with your blood, now that you've sabotaged our recruitment efforts with your friend Emory Bradshaw?"

"You can't make Dr. Lin do anything he doesn't want to."

Vladimir shifted his eyes toward Ox, frowning. Like he was disappointed.

Ox shook his head. "You've bragged incessantly that she's smart beyond her years...blah, blah, blah. *You've pegged her wrong,* I argued. And now, without any interference from me, she has exposed what she really is: a stupid, fucking cunt. Just. Like. I. Said. And to think, Vladimir: you claim you're the true brain of this operation!"

Ruby drowned-out the noise—the hideous sound that was Ox. She needed to think clearly. What obvious puzzle-piece was she overlooking?

Another door opened. Dr. Lin entered the hallway, with an American Sailor walking tightly behind him. The microbiologist looked tired, but unharmed.

"Thank God you're okay, Dr. Lin," she said.

"Unrested, but well." He gazed at her. "I overheard what you said to these idiots. And you are indeed correct: I only do what I want. Any guesses on the operative word?"

Her heartrate spiked, her hands grew clammy. She detected

sarcasm. No doubt Dr. Lin was toying with her, like cat to a mouse. Presenting another riddle.

The answer was staring her in the face. "The operative word is *want*," she answered, lowering her head. Understanding at last. "Which means you're one of them."

Vladimir clapped his hands together. "Now who is right, Ox?"

The Taiwanese microbiologist glared at his accomplices. "And to be clear, my friends: *the* brain of this operation is neither of you. Say who is, Quinton Oxford. Say it. *Now.*"

"You, sir."

37

RUBY WAS IN shock. An American Sailor—rather, a turncoat—
frisked her to confirm she wasn't hiding any weapons. While
unfamiliar hands glided over her scrubs and lab coat, she felt nothing.
No panic, only numbness. Her mind reeled from Dr. Lin's betrayal.
How could she have been fooled?

The entourage escorted her at gunpoint, back to the hallway with
the lab rooms. As she walked, she contemplated escape options.
Problem was, none materialized. Moments ago, she and Clay had
been fueled by hope. Now she couldn't picture a future. The mental
image was blank.

With a rifle barrel poking her back, she was pushed past the room
where Clay had been waterboarded. Workers were mopping the
floors. The slain guards had already been removed.

Dr. Lin unlocked the door to lab 103 where the corpses of
Corporal Wyatt and the co-pilot, along with the zombie head, still lay
on gurneys. She hadn't noticed before, but the bodies smelled like a
landfill leaking methane gas. Perhaps her nose was healing.

Scowling at Vladimir and Ox, Dr. Lin asked, "Can you not smell
the decay? Surely you can grasp that laboratories must remain sterile."
He shifted his glare to the guards. "Remove these corpses
immediately. Take them to the incinerator."

Each guard grabbed a gurney, wheeling the bodies into the
hallway. The door closed behind them. Silence drew the lab walls

closer, like a powerful vacuum, pulling moisture from her body. She wiped beads of sweat from her forehead, careful not to aggravate her contusion.

Grabbing the desk chair, Dr. Lin rolled it to the center of the room, near the stainless-steel instrument cart. Her eyes caught the shimmer of an instrument. Her breath hitched, but not enough to be noticed as the chair's wheels rattled to a stop. Tucked next to oversized clamps, almost hidden, was the syringe she had seen earlier. The needle's barrel was full of clear liquid. A flash of optimism kickstarted her body. Her cheeks warmed.

"Please sit down, Ruby." Dr. Lin tapped the back of the desk chair.

She took a deep breath, trying to calm her jitters.

"I wish for you to understand our mission," he said, "since your services—offered or forced—are necessary. And I imagine you have more questions."

"Here we go again," Ox said, rolling his eyes, clearly impatient.

She was perplexed her three captors were more than willing to confess, in detail, their most heinous atrocities. They were like bank robbers who pulled off the heist of a lifetime, but couldn't avoid bragging about their ingenuity. Which inevitably led to capture. Because arrogance was evil's poison.

Of course, Ox, Vladimir, and Dr. Lin killed potential leakers. There was *that*.

"I do have a few questions, especially for you," she said, keeping her eyes fixed on the microbiologist. "Was our meeting on the bus in Keelung intentional? Planned?"

"Delightfully unexpected. As a scientist, I do not give much credence to fate, though I must admit, fateful coincidence, or *Yuanfen*, intrigues me. The unexpected can be quite remarkable. And please, call me Decha. All my friends do."

"What were you doing in Keelung?" she asked. "Relishing in the unraveling of a city? A city you destroyed?"

"You do not conduct an experiment without observation. Surely as a scientist, you concur. In addition, I needed to tie-up loose-ends, an expression I am sure you understand."

Vladimir chuckled. "How is Captain Yeltsin? Were his quarters on the *Askold* suitable? I am thinking of inviting him for tea."

"It better be iced," Ox said, smiling. "Last intel was that he was burning up."

"Enough," Dr. Lin barked.

"Since kidnapping me was your intention," she continued, "why not abduct me in Keelung? It would've been easy. We were sitting right next to each other on the bus."

"I confess: I am methodically minded. Once a plan is underway, similar to an experiment, it is best not to interfere. Many wheels are turning. Deviation is only when necessary. Besides, I had confidence you would return to Taipei and thereafter, to the consulate. And I knew you were not implanted with REDs." He shifted his glance to Ox and back. "While others underestimate you, I have confidence in the strength of your resolve. Your actions from Taiwan to here have affirmed my assertion."

"Why kidnap my husband? Why not leave him in Taipei? It's me you wanted."

"If Mr. Spencer was not here, especially if he had returned home to your daughter, your cooperation would be unlikely. In fact, now that you have refused our plan, I have no doubt you would have sacrificed yourself by now, if you thought your husband and daughter were safe. Love is the ultimate motivator."

"Perhaps you haven't considered the opposite end of the spectrum," she said. "If you kill him now, or hurt him, the result will be the same as if he and Gabby were safe: I'll destroy myself and my blood. Your aspirations will hemorrhage, right along with me."

"No need for spilled blood, my dear," Vladimir said.

"What *is* your plan?"

"More concerning than your refusal to join us," Dr. Lin said, "you have proven too savvy for captivity. The risk of your escape no longer falls within an acceptable range." He gently caressed her shoulder, as if attempting to be fatherly. "You have been a formidable adversary, Ruby, and now we have no choice. In the next few minutes, a technician will sedate you into a coma. You'll be sustained intravenously. Using your blood, I will work diligently to unmask its wonders and develop a ZOM-B cure. A zombie army, one that can be harnessed and recycled, will help us unify this planet around *The Cause:* one world, one superpower, one army, one supreme ruler."

A hard spasm racked her body. Panic gripped her, took away her breath. "Please," she gasped. "Please don't kill my husband. I beg you; let him go! We have a child!"

Dr. Lin turned away. None of them looked at her. It was as though she were already gone.

Anger rolled over her like a wave, converting a swell into crashing, frothing panic. Water turned to fire. Her throat burned with rage and she pictured herself as a dragon, exhaling a stream of flames. Her fingers curled into fists.

"Stay with her until the technician arrives," Dr. Lin ordered Ox. "Need I remind you of what she did to your Corporal? Restraining her would be wise."

Ruby's heart sputtered. Her head throbbed. If she didn't get a grip, panic would immobilize her. And she needed to use her internal fire to scorch her captors, not herself.

Dr. Lin and Vladimir walked toward the door. Ox followed like an attentive host escorting out his guests. For a few seconds, their backs were turned. They whispered.

Arrogance was evil's poison, she said to herself while carefully snatching the syringe from the instrument table. She flicked off the protective needle-cap before lowering the syringe into her lab pocket. Her heart felt zapped with a jolt of current. Her internal voice screamed that the time to save herself was now...or never.

And she prayed that an opportunity would present itself...*now.*

Ox's partners left. He chuckled and locked the lab door. Turning, he slithered toward her smiling, looking down at her seated in the chair.

"Stand up," he said.

"I'd rather sit."

"I'm sure we'll fit that in. But right now, stand. I want to see you."

"See me?"

38

Tuesday, July 13, 2032
Moscow, Russia

OX WATCHED AS Ruby reluctantly rose from her chair. His fingers trembled with anticipation.

Before Vladimir and Decha had left the lab, he ran his idea by them. He would have done it anyway, but why not let his partners think their approval was needed? Respected?

Sometimes Ox amazed himself. Okay, so *sometimes* was a colossal understatement.

No surprise they suggested he wait until she was sedated, but he disagreed. He wanted, maybe even needed, to watch her eyes as he touched and explored. As he made her powerless. He would carry her reactions, her expressions, with him like a shared secret. Not that he wouldn't boff her when she was comatose; after all, it was on his bucket list.

As good fortune would have it, his partners finally approved, as long as he didn't kill her.

He moved close to her, barely leaving an inch between their bodies. She tried to back up, but the chair was immediately behind her. He smiled.

"Do you prefer white or dark meat?" he asked, observing her eyes narrow. Creases formed on her forehead. "You know, when you eat chicken?"

She said nothing. Her expression returned to deadpan.

"Well, I'm a breast man. And when I met you the first time at the consulate, when you were drenched from the rain, you left quite an impression on me. I couldn't help fantasizing about your breasts. What they'd taste like."

The girl bumped into the chair, sending it rolling a few feet behind her. As a counterpunch, Ox thrust the instrument cart across the room and it crashed against the wall, causing the medical tools to clank and jangle on the stainless-steel surface.

He liked this new world. One where he satisfied his urges without fear of litigation, arrest, or a dishonorable discharge. Yes, joining his partners was the best decision he had ever made. And his reality was only getting better.

"I like it rough," he said, "and in case you were wondering, I'm no Corporal Wyatt. I won't be bested."

She retreated against the wall, like a frightened animal.

Her retreat would have been disappointing, except he knew she wouldn't go down without a fight. And it was resistance that fueled his libido. He advanced with purpose, pinning her body against the wall. His dick was hard and pulsing. He imagined her thrashing at him, fighting, and most of all, the sweetness of her come.

Grabbing both sides of her lab coat's collar, he yanked with force, unsnapping the front so he could see more of her. Soon, he'd rip the black blouse from her. Then her bra. But no reason to rush. The technician would have to wait. This was *his* rodeo.

With his right hand, he cupped her left breast and squeezed. Hard. She whimpered. Lowering his head so that his lips touched her right ear, he whispered. "Our fuck will be epic. Mind blowing. You'll dream of it. Promise."

He felt pressure on his cock, through his fatigues. His mind searched to make sense of it. He pulled back slightly and glanced at his crotch. The girl's left hand was gripping his junk. Like in what universe did he ever imagine *that* happening? Maybe her husband sucked in bed and she wanted a real piece. A thick piece. Especially before the lights went out. It was the opposite of resistance, but tossing Mr. Pretty Face to the sidelines for him ramped-up his drive. As if it could get any higher.

"Don't hold back." He placed his left hand flat against the wall while placing his right hand on top of hers—on top of the one pressing against his cock. He massaged her hand, showing her how he liked it. "I'll be rough with you, so be rough with me."

She moved, but women liked to squirm during foreplay. So what got his attention? It was *the type* of move that confused him. It was like a baseball pitcher and the sudden explosion of power during a pitch. Like from zero to one-hundred miles-per-hour.

A needle plunged into his left side. Through his shirt, he felt burning from an injection.

His brain finally registered the meaning behind her seduction.

He stepped back from the filth that was Ruby Spencer. "What the fuck did you inject me with?"

"Was that rough enough for you? Epic enough?"

"Bitch!" His tongue began to feel dry and thick. He reached to grab her, but she darted away. His feet were lead. His arms heavy. "A tranquilizer," he whispered.

"As Corporal Wyatt might say, before you shot a bullet into his skull: you're as smart as a whip."

He slumped onto the tiles.

After throwing her lab coat to the floor, the bitch grabbed his pistol and keyring. And he could do nothing.

More than anything, he wanted to put his hands around her neck and squeeze until her eyes popped out. Instead, he was spinning, falling through a tunnel, getting heavier and heavier. Falling faster and faster. The light got farther and farther away.

She pointed the pistol at his head.

Then his world faded.

To black.

39

Tuesday, July 13, 2032
Moscow, Russia

CLAY SAT ON the cell floor. Wrapping his arms around his bent legs, he placed his head between his knees, trying to quell the nausea. He was emotionally drained, as well as physically. How had his and Ruby's trip to Taiwan become a nightmare with no escape? What ever happened to the honeymoon getaway while accomplishing two simple tasks for the SWC?

Deep down, he knew the answers. He clenched his fists thinking about it. The blame fell on *him*.

At the Naval base in Keelung, he had given his wife strict instructions if the generators failed: rendezvous within ten minutes or leave for the hotel. And yet, he'd disregarded his own directive.

When the lights blacked out the final time, he'd been in The Pit, getting comfortable with the assault rifle he'd use to silence Huo forever. Even in darkness thick as tar, he remembered every detail.

He had stepped back from the firing window and hollered for someone to activate a flashlight. Sailors scrambled, bumping into each other as they searched, but the area remained inky black.

Movement stopped in The Pit when the deadbolt retracted on the door leading to the containment chamber. Battery backup had a major downside in a facility meant to contain the undead.

Shortly after, pounding reverberated off the barred wall. *Huo.* Huo was trying to enter The Pit. Sounded like he had started at the far end of the bars, crashing his body against the wall and slowly working his way up. No one moved in the dark, probably frozen from disbelief that the zombie was executing a plan. Methodically.

Like a warning, a boom of thunder rattled the building.

Sailors nervously chattered in search of a flashlight.

When Huo whammed against the barred door, Clay heard the low-sill slide over the concrete toward The Pit. The door had been pushed open. And then he heard scuffling. Followed by a scream: a Sailor's. Followed by another's. Sailors shouted their locations, attempting to paint a mental picture: a high-stakes game of Marco Polo where screams defined Huo's location.

Someone yelled for Clay to activate the spotlight on the M4 still clutched to his chest. No one had mentioned that the rifle came equipped with a spotlight, and he hadn't checked. He fingered the barrel, gliding his hand over the carbine until he reached the bottom-side of the rail. He found the small scope-like device, probably a laser and light combo. On the backside of the mount, closest to him, he clicked the switch. His fingers were shaking.

A beam of light illuminated zombie Huo who was suddenly standing in front of him, reaching for his body. Huo's clawed hands extended, his teeth clicked, and he stunk like bay-mud and dead fish. Clay's heart jolted. Adrenaline ripped through his body. He kicked the bastard in the chest, forcing the freak backwards. That's when his finger found the trigger. He shot, planting a bullet in zombie Huo's forehead. Dropping to the floor, the undead tyrant fell on a Sailor whose throat had been ripped out. Blood still spurted from the wound. Clay shot him, too.

He turned toward a Sailor who was gawking at the scene illuminated by the M4's spotlight, gawking with his mouth open as if watching a horror movie. Clay explained he was going to search for his wife. And since the Sailors needed light, he asked the twenty-something to exchange his pistol for the assault rifle. As he was handed a nine-millimeter, Clay instructed the Sailor to shoot anyone in the head, dead or alive, who'd been bitten.

In reflection, he should have fled the facility then and there. Waited by the van like he and Ruby had agreed. But he didn't. Instead, he ran into the building's interior holding the pistol, visualizing the layout and retracing his path to the observation room, feeling his way in the dark by sliding his free hand along the walls.

A burst of gunfire raged behind him, from The Pit or from the front of the building. He couldn't be sure. But all his senses detected danger, every nerve warned him. He had to find Ruby. Had to get her away from the spreading infection.

As if answering his prayer, red lights—swirling in their fixtures—illuminated the hallways in crimson. Seeing gave him hope that he'd find her. Now he could run. Racing down the hallway, he stopped in front of the observation room: empty. He called her name to be sure. No one answered.

Instead of backtracking, he headed in the opposite direction. The building was a large rectangle and he guessed Ruby had gone toward the back, maybe toward a rear exit; otherwise, they would have crossed paths on his way to the observation room. At the first door, he made another left and ran the length of the hallway. At the next, he had planned on turning right, hoping to find an exit. But to ensure an "all clear," he glanced left. Terror struck with a blow.

Could the person lying in the hallway be his wife?

He dashed to the body. Relief had swept over him. Death belonged to a Sailor, not his wife. Chunks of the guy's neck were missing. And a bullet was lodged into his forehead. The name PATTERSON was embroidered on his shirt. A violent battle had clearly taken place, and he had no way of knowing if Ruby had been involved. Or if she'd been bitten.

A raspy moan had sounded from within the lab. Walking inside the dark room, with red light-beams circling like lighthouse beacons from the hallway, Clay saw another body. This one was facedown. Hooking his boot under the Sailor's shoulder, he flipped the corpse onto his back, toward the door and out from the shadows. ANDREWS. Andrews also had a bullet between his open, black eyes.

Two blasts sounded from outside the building. Most likely a nine-millimeter. As he turned toward the lab door, something grabbed his shirt. He jerked away, twisting his body and raising his pistol.

From a gurney masked in the charcoal darkness, he saw a moving silhouette. His eyes adjusted to the low light. A zombie stretched toward him, breaking the strap securing his waist. The freak's jaws snapped like a piranha. Clay would've fired, but the zombie toppled off the gurney and he didn't want to waste ammo on a bad shot. As the undead Sailor began dragging himself along the floor, Clay nailed the bastard who had ZORN embroidered on his uniform. The bullet planted in the freak's rotting brain. He twitched to his final death.

Clay raced from the lab, down the hallway, and out the exit door.

In the rain and wind, he had shot two more zombies. As he ran across the parking lot, he found an arrow made from stones on the hood of a van. Ruby. She was showing him that she'd made it out, that she'd headed northwest toward the harbor and train station.

He had run through the thick tropical landscape in the same direction. When he arrived at the Ruifang Station, out of breath, he found himself in the middle of a tick hatching. Zombies clustered in packs around the parking lot. They raised their noses when they caught a whiff of him. His blood stirred them.

Miraculously, a helicopter topped the trees like a dragonfly. Standing on the pavement, he waved his arms at the chopper. With zombies advancing, if he didn't get a lift, he'd be screwed.

When the aircraft touched down, he darted under the blades and scrambled to open the door. The undead were chomping at his heels. As he leapt inside the cockpit, one clutched his pantleg, preventing him from closing the door. The pilot ordered Clay to duck, which he did. The discharge whizzed over his head, embedding into the zombie's head and dropping him onto the asphalt. Clay yanked the door shut as the chopper lifted.

Another undead clasped onto the landing skids. The rising chopper heeled to the passenger side and the pilot shouted for Clay to shoot the stowaway. So he opened his cockpit door. When the freak looked up at him with tar eyes, rasping and moaning, he shot the bastard in the head, sending the reeking aberration plunging thirty-feet to the blacktop.

Minutes later, the chopper landed at Zhuchang Park where he was met by a buff Marine dressed in tight fatigues, wielding plenty of pent-up testosterone. Ox, no doubt. The A-hole must have struck him in the head, rendering him unconscious before he exited the aircraft. Maybe he was even drugged. Because the next thing he knew, he was in a Moscow prison, nursing a headache and celled next to a Taiwanese microbiologist who claimed he had met Ruby.

As he rethought the events since Sunday, Clay affirmed his regrets. Ultimately, he was separated from his wife because he didn't follow...

His. Own. Plan.

Commotion beyond the cellblock snapped him back to the present. Raising his head slowly, he tried not to aggravate his queasiness. At the end of the cellblock aisle, on the other side of the opened door, soldiers escorted ordinary people—civilians, down the steps toward the lower basement. From his perspective, the group seemed jovial, unafraid. Some were laughing.

A man gaped through the doorway, stopping to stare at him in his cell. A guard responded in Russian and pulled the door shut.

None of it made sense.

He scooted against the wall, resting his back on the cool cinderblock. He let his mind drift in hopes that a plan would materialize. A plan that could free him, so he could search for Ruby.

An alarm system reactivated.

The looping *beep, beep, beep* assaulted his ears. Red beams swirled across the bars and walls. Had Ruby escaped again?

The door at the end of the cellblock aisle flung open. Thrust against the wall, the door hitched in an open position. The person who had stared earlier was shouting at him, with a thick accent. But without a reaction from Clay, he exchanged Russian for English. "Run! They are loose!"

Run? If he wasn't bound by bars and a locked cell door, he would have done *that* long ago. On second thought: if zombies were the *they*—the ones loose—then he had the safest seat in the house.

Fear percolated. What about Ruby? What about *her* safety?

More people raced up the stairs from the basement. Some screamed. A few soldiers were among the fleeing.

His tension reached boiling, on the verge of erupting.

Although it wasn't rational to warn his wife, given she was nowhere in sight, he *needed* to scream. He jumped to his feet and clutched the bars, ignoring his nausea. "Run, Ruby!" He yanked at the bars, as if he could move them. "Run!"

A gunblast popped. His heart jolted. What the hell was going on?

That's when he saw her. She was no longer wearing scrubs and a lab coat. He had to blink to make sure he wasn't hallucinating. Sure enough, Ruby—dressed in her black shorts and blouse, was racing down the cellblock aisle, brandishing a pistol.

And two zombies were in pursuit.

"Behind you!" he hollered.

She turned and fired at the closest undead, striking him in the head. Firing again, she missed the second.

"Take your time," he said.

She turned and dropped to one knee, extending her arms in front of her. Steadying her hands around the pistol's grip, she pulled the trigger. When the bullet penetrated the zombie's forehead, the female nearly fell on top of her. Ruby rolled before the zombie hit the concrete floor, twitching. Black goo spewed from the ruptured skull.

Running to the cell after the second zombie dropped, she stuffed the pistol in her back pocket and fumbled with a keyring. Jamming keys into the lock mechanism, she attempted to find its match.

"Thank God you're okay," he said. "What's happening?"

"I think guards were making new zombies and some got loose. The undead are overtaking the facility."

He heard a guttural moan. Another zombie was approaching, trudging across the concrete, arms straight and swinging with each jerky stride, almost toppling over the downed corpses. Almost.

"Not to pressure you, but hurry," he urged.

Another key didn't work. And another. Her hands were shaking.

"Damn it!" she cried.

"Hand me the pistol and keep trying."

She wedged the handgun between the bars. He held-off firing until he knew he wouldn't miss. While he aimed at the zombie, she located the next key and shoved it into the lock. It turned! Throwing open the cell door, she ran inside and pulled it shut. She reached through the bars with the key and relocked the door.

As the zombie reached for her, Clay shot him in the head.

Like he feared, the gun-blasts attracted more zombies. Within minutes, a horde of undead clustered around their cell, arms stretching between the bars and teeth chattering.

A blast boomed above them, rocking the building's foundation. The prison rattled and shook.

40

IF THE WORLD was sunny-side-up before the war, it was scrambled now. And high-profile kidnappings were as common as buttered toast.

Lieutenant Commander Dexter Marks would know. He was the go-to specialist when the President of the United States needed to extract high-valued assets from behind enemy lines. With the call-name *Eyes,* he was a former Platoon Commander of SEAL Team 6 (*the* elite counterterrorism unit) who had been elevated three-years-ago to Commanding Officer (CO) of an elusive Naval Special Warfare Evacuation Group (NSWEG), also known as EVACGRU or SEAL Team 86. But résumés never fueled his hunger.

Hostage rescue and asset evacuations were his jam.

A week ago, he had been on a non-eventful recon mission collecting intel on the supreme leader of North Korea. Seems the paranoid maggot was having trouble accepting that Huo Zhu Zheng had lost the war. Guess he wasn't thrilled about FIN oversight.

With a new assignment looming, Eyes was airlifted from Kaesong in the North Hwanghae Province and delivered to the Sixth Fleet's USS Simpson, a Naval wasp-class amphibious assault-ship which was idling in the Gulf of Finland—a thumb of the Baltic Sea, near Narva on the border of Estonia and Russia.

So much for getting leave to attend the annual Marks family reunion. His CHIT form would be withdrawn…again. His wife understood; she never made him feel guilty about putting country first. Elizabeth was a true patriot, a saint. He'd already videofaced her and like always, she took the news like a champ. She'd explain to the kids who already accepted that their Dad was securing a future...for them and the rest of humanity.

Four hours ago, while he was in Chow Hall eating slop the Navy pawned as chicken à la king, trying to pretend it was as good as grilled beef-franks from the reunion barbecue, he got the call. Eyes and two SEAL platoons, which equated to 32 specialists (some assault and some evac), were to be transported by a CH-53E Sea Stallion, a heavy-lift transport helicopter that held its own in battle. They'd be dropped at a ghost prison in Moscow, one operating covertly by none-other than Vladimir Volkov, the Russian President. The inbound flight would cover 600 kilometers and take about an hour-and-a-half. Scheduled to be refueled mid-flight by a KC-30 (keeping it on the safe-side), their transport chopper would be accompanied by four AH-1Z Viper Attack Helicopters, the most advanced in the Navy's arsenal. Sweet!

His platoons were stoked.

During transport, Eyes explained the raid to his SEALs. At the target, the Vipers would execute a four-leaf-clover formation, covering the prison on all four sides. The platoons would break into four squads of eight, each squad entering a side of the building, tactically referred to as "level-two" or the ground-level's first floor. The mission would be performed rapid-reaction style. Quick in: locate the Spencers; quick out: evac the Spencers to the USS Simpson.

After Eyes delivered orders, everyone sat back and chilled, mentally preparing for the mission. For him, it was time to rehash the risk assessment—review the positives and negatives.

The mission itself didn't worry him. Sure, there were zombies onsite. Intel warned that Volkov was building an undead army and kept the freaks locked in a containment chamber in the basement. The batshit Russian was a real Einstein—of the twisted variety. Dark science would, no doubt, bite him in the ass if it hadn't already. Despite the complication, zombies were the least of his worries. Every SEAL specialist on the mission was a sniper and knew to aim for the head. And in his mind, one SEAL was worth ten in uniform. This mission employed the power of three-hundred-and-twenty fighters. *Hooyah!*

What gave Eyes pause was the time of day. Instead of the stealth of darkness, his team would be exposed in broad daylight. Raids rarely took place between sunrise and sunset. But at least in the post-war landscape, Federation aircraft were cleared over all airspaces (because the U.S. was top-dog, since China and Russia weren't part of the FIN fraternity). His team would fly low over Lake Peipus, which he called Lake Pepsi to give it that fine American-fizz, and then take a rural flightpath to Moscow. Still. With another war brewing, who's to say some wacko combatant wouldn't launch an ABM—a stinking anti-ballistic missile? Ceasefires only lasted until someone's itchy finger pulled a trigger or pressed a button.

The thrum and vibration of the chopper was soothing like his wife's assurances. Eyes looked beyond the open door of the Sea Stallion's cabin, beyond the gunners scanning the landscape for hostiles. The sun, bright and cheery, masked the firestorm they'd be facing. Because the mission included the capture of three psychos— alive: Quinton Oxford, Vladimir Volkov, and Decha Lin. And terrorists generally pulled-out all the stops to avoid capture.

If Eyes was honest, he wouldn't mind accidentally discharging his Glock 19 into Oxford's sicko brains. Traitors and defectors were the cockroaches of the world. They were scum-of-the-scum. An accidental discharge? Sometimes casualties just happened. It was a thing. One that his brothers and sisters would keep between themselves, eternally.

On the good side, Eyes hoped Ruby and Clay Spencer were breathing. The GPS chips embedded in their bodies were still showing the pair was on location, represented by blinking lights on the prison schematics displaying on his AIME eyewear—the most high-tech Ambient Intelligence Mounted Eyewear he'd ever worn. AIMEs were powered by the U.S.'s ubiquitous computer called ISSI. The blinking dots on the grid revealed both had been on the move, which was positive. But now the couple was together and stationary on level-three, the floor below where the team would enter. Reality check: chips didn't stop working in dead bodies. Or in zombies.

Hopefully, the couple had a pulse. He'd met the Spencers during his first tour with SEAL Team 86, when his squad extracted the F8 vaccine-formulas from a remote hunting club in the homeland's Pocono Mountains, during the first martial law in 2030. A brainiac microbiologist discovered the girl had blood that could save the world from the original bacterial bioweapon; that is, before it mutated. Club members had constructed a makeshift lab, sophisticated enough to develop a cure onsite. Only in America, baby! Problem was, the group had also broadcasted their epic achievement and Huo was all ears. But ultimately, the madman was no match for American perseverance. The rest was history.

As the aircraft neared the prison, Eyes gave his team hand signals to be on-the-ready.

When the bird's skids touched down, his SEALs swarmed from the chopper like yellowjackets from a disturbed nest, before breaking into four organized squads. Eyes and Squad A would penetrate the rear of the prison.

A SEAL named Boomer took down the back door with explosives. An alarm inside the building, in concert with rotating emergency lights, suggested the combatants were aware they had visitors. In daylight, being on the radar was expected.

It was his good fortune that Hotwire was in Squad A. After entering the facility, they came to a juiced wire-mesh barrier, blocking them from a long corridor. Within thirty seconds, the electrical genius dismantled the charged screen-wall, and they were running down the hallway, guns drawn. Sounding like mice on carpet.

Squads A and B were to sweep level-two before heading down to where the Spencers were located. Squads C and D were assigned to level-one (or the second floor) where Volkov's private office was thought to be.

Squad A worked its way to the lab rooms in the hallway furthest north, toward the front of the building. The labs were clear—no hostiles, except for a room marked 103: it was locked. Knocking down the door, Eyes found Quinton Oxford, the traitor himself, lying on the deck unconscious but breathing. Eyes kicked him in the ribs, jolting the prick's limp body. Mostly out of frustration. Because without a struggle, shooting the turncoat in the head would be cowardly. And Eyes was no coward.

He commanded Hornet to secure the steroid-junkie and transfer him to the chopper. If Quinton Oxford gave Hornet any trouble, she'd sting him so hard he'd wish he was dead.

The remaining specialists of Squad A met with Squad B by a glass door leading to a stairwell landing. That's when his adrenaline experienced a slight uptick. Zombies had collected on the landing, as if waiting for someone to politely open the door, so the freaks could inflict their flavor of hell on anyone they encountered.

The prison had clearly been spiraling out-of-control before their arrival. Chaos was a tactical strategy and even though *his* team hadn't unleashed it themselves, bedlam was masking them. Because ten minutes in and there were no human defenders thwarting any squads' progress. And the undead didn't count.

The mission was unfolding better than expected.

After signaling to his team and pulling the safety pin on a grenade, Eyes opened the door a few inches and tossed the explosive into the stairwell. The team retreated and took cover for the timed detonation. No doubt the grenade would dismember the undead and give the squad ample time to pick them off, one by one.

The detonation rocked the prison's foundation and shattered the glass door. Emergency lights and the alarm hiccupped before continuing their rotations. His ears rang.

In an orchestrated barrage of gunfire, twenty-one zombies were given an instant death in less than a minute. Except for a few twitching freaks, the stairwell was now passable.

Eyes radioed C's squad-leader via his AIME glasses which included an inter-communications system. As soon as Squads A and B moved downstairs to levels three and four, Squad C would transition to level-two, keeping it secure.

Eyes gave the SEALs a fist pump before ordering them down the flight of stairs to level-three. Pointing to the corpses, he warned the SEALs to be careful while traversing over the rotting, smoldering bodies—many missing limbs from the blast.

At the next lower-level, the door leading to a cellblock area was open. Eyes scanned the cells. The Spencers were in one, backs against a cinderblock wall, with a horde of a dozen zombies clustered on the aisle-side of the cell, arms shoved between the bars. The undead were reaching and moaning. Making that trademark clicking sound.

Eyes ordered Squad B to continue to the dungeon (level-four).

After Squad A entered the cellblock area, Eyes, Hotwire, and Boomer knelt while the four remaining SEALs in the squad stood behind them. Pistols aimed.

"Don't move," Eyes hollered to the couple. "And cover your heads."

The sound of his voice attracted the zombies. Good. The mutant freaks turned and advanced on their firing line. All were shot in the head, dropping to the cement floor and twitching until real death claimed them for good.

Eyes led the squad to the cell. He tried not to react to their physical conditions. He had seen victims much worse, but they usually required body bags.

"Mr. and Mrs. Spencer," he said, "SEAL Team 86 is here for your exfiltration. The President of the United States will be pleased you are alive."

41

Tuesday, July 13, 2032
Moscow, Russia

RUBY FELT DISBELIEF. Like when an eight-year-old girl had wished and wished for a shiny blue bike—one with a basket and bell and pretty streamers on the handlebars. And at the crack of dawn one Christmas morning, she tiptoed from her bedroom, raced down the stairs and into the den, and stopped in her tracks. Before her, tucked next to the Douglas Fir sparkling with tinsel and colorful lights, was the very bike of her dreams. The feelings were so pure, so memorable. Amid relief that she no longer had to wish on bright stars or with pennies tossed into fountains, or pray extra-hard on her knees by the bedside each night, were doubts. Doubts that she deserved something so perfect.

When Ruby saw the SEAL team and Eyes—whom she remembered from handing over the original vaccines, her feelings mirrored that unforgettable Christmas memory.

"Eyes! You came for us!" she said.

"Yes, Ma'am." He nodded. "Damn glad to be of service. Now I'll have to ask you to stand back while Boomer, here, blasts this lock."

She extended her arm, dangling the keyring and clasping the lock's matching key in the fingers. "Good thing I've got the key." Smiling, she handed the ring through the bars.

Eyes raised his eyebrows above his clear-lensed glasses. "I'd be interested in hearing *that* story." He unlocked the cell door and swung it open. "I'm guessing possession of the keyring and pistol had something to do with the unconscious traitor in the upstairs lab."

"Your guess is right." She took Clay's hand and exited the cell. "Please tell me Ox is in custody. As a prisoner." Her knees were still shaking from adrenaline.

"Yes, Ma'am. Quinton Oxford is now the property of the United States government, facing treason charges."

The words were music to her ears.

Eyes announced they'd stay put until Squad B reported back.

"Out of curiosity," he said to her. "If you had the chance to kill the turncoat in the lab, why didn't you?"

"Two reasons really. First and foremost, I chose love over hate."

"You mean like…love your enemies?"

"No, I've never been good at that. What I mean is, when I had the pistol pointed at Ox, the alarm sounded. And my first thoughts were for my husband—finding and protecting *him*. I stopped thinking about the scum passed out at my feet."

"The other reason?" Eyes asked.

"I'm not a cold-blooded killer. And with Ox unconscious, somehow shooting him seemed…cowardly."

"I get what you're saying," he said. "Not the cold-blooded killer part. I am a SEAL, after all. But I get the cowardly part. That's why I didn't shoot the prick myself." Eyes touched the earpiece attached to his glasses like he was receiving information. "If you'll excuse me."

She turned to Clay and wrapped her arms around his neck, threading her fingers in his hair, still damp from the waterboarding. He delivered her favorite smile, wide and radiant, despite his being starved and nauseous, looking pale, and covered in red welts from ant bites.

"We're going home," she whispered to him. "We're going home to Gabby."

Eyes turned back to them. "We've captured Decha Lin, but unfortunately, Vladimir Volkov is no longer in the facility. So are you ready to blow this pop-stand?"

Was she ever.

"Wait," Clay said. "Dr. Lin is a…*bad guy?*"

She nodded. With all the commotion, she hadn't had time to tell him. "After the guard took you back to the cell, Dr. Lin appeared and boasted he's been their leader all along. He only pretended to be a prisoner to collect information from us."

"Narcissistic chameleons," Eyes said. "The only life they value is their own." He pointed down the aisle to the end of the cellblock. "Let's get you out of this death-hole. We've got a Naval ship in the Gulf of Finland waiting for your safe return. Bet a warm shower and some chow sound good."

"Amen to that," Clay said.

They left the cellblock and climbed the stairs, navigating over corpses and glass. Burnt flesh, infused with smells of dead fish and manure, assaulted her nostrils. She fought back a gag.

As the group approached the labs, she asked Eyes if she could retrieve the journal she and Clay had found in Shifen. He nodded. When she entered the lab, her body shuddered, remembering her encounter with Ox.

SEALs were everywhere, buzzing around rooms, performing final sweeps. Eventually, the entourage exited via the prison's rear door, beyond where the electrical barrier had once been.

Outside at last, the thrum of helicopters saturated the air. Her body hummed like a live wire. A slick attack-helicopter hovered over their heads, missiles pointed toward the rear of the building. She heard additional choppers but couldn't see them from her vantage point.

Two massive helicopters were parked in the prison's expansive grass-lot which was enclosed by fencing. The largest aircraft looked like an airplane, except a vertical rotor was attached at the end of each wing. The cargo door at the rear of the craft was closing and the rotors started to spin.

"Are we leaving in…in that airplane looking chopper?" Ruby asked Eyes.

"Negative. That's a V-22 Osprey. See those rotors? After liftoff, they tilt forward, turning that bad-boy into a plane. Oxford and Lin will be transported in the Osprey. The brig awaits them on the USS Simpson." He pointed to the other chopper. "Our ride is on the Sea Stallion. You'll be joined by SEALs. Hope you don't mind."

"We'd be honored," Clay answered.

"Yes, honored," she echoed.

"Great," Eyes said, raising his voice to compete with the thwacking-sound of the Osprey. "While we wrap this up, why don't you climb onboard the Stallion and take a seat."

As Ruby and Clay boarded their helicopter, the Osprey rose. A minute later, the thrum of its blades faded in the distance.

SEALs began to enter the aircraft, finding seats. After rollcall, the chopper lifted. Hovering above the jail, she studied the facility which had imprisoned her and Clay. Resembling a Russian church or cathedral, the building was made from fieldstone, painted terracotta, with narrow windows. Topped with three domes painted in gold-leaf, it blended with Russian architecture. To think, Vladimir had his own personal jailhouse under the noses of his people.

Closing her eyes for a second, she gave thanks that President Newton had sent SEALs to rescue them. If the POTUS hadn't, Ruby believed Clay would be dead and she'd be a comatose blood bank.

From their aerial view, she saw attack-helicopters positioned on each side of the prison.

"Ever see fireworks in Moscow?" Eyes asked her.

"Never."

"Hold tight."

All four attack-helicopters fired missiles into the prison, blasting the structure and causing the sides to cave, sending the bricks-and-mortar crashing to the ground. Fireballs mushroomed above the building. As the Stallion banked away from the explosion, the SEALs hooted and hollered, ending with a *Hooyah* chanted in unison.

Then the stories started.

A SEAL named Hotwire was sitting to Ruby's right. His squad praised him for dismantling the electrified barrier near where the SEALs entered the prison.

"It was in record time, dude," said a SEAL named Boomer. "Like how'd you do that?"

"Wires are like brassieres; you know, cleavage commandos," Hotwire answered, speaking over cackles and chuckles. "See: the snaps are all different, but after a while...snap, crackle, pop...and you're in!"

"No booby trap is gonna stop you, Hotwire!" a female SEAL called Blade added.

"Damn straight. I'd try yours, but you're too sharp for me, girl. And I sorta, kinda need my hands for the job." He winked.

When the ribbing settled down, Ruby added her voice to the conversation. Eyes raised his hand, silencing the team.

"Words can never fully-express our gratitude," she said. "You don't know us personally; you don't know that we have a three-month-old daughter back in the U.S. Truth is: we don't know you either. Each of you has a family, too—a mother, a father, a spouse or partner, children. And yet you risked *your* lives so we could have *ours* back. How could we possibly thank you enough?"

"I agree with my wife," Clay added. "We'll be heading home, and you'll still be going on missions. You are heroes, and Ruby and I will never take you for granted. Never forget you."

"There are two ways to do something," Eyes said, shifting his eyes to his men and women. "The right way…"

"…and *again,*" the SEALs on the chopper chanted.

"So Ruby," Eyes continued. "How *did* you incapacitate that traitor hulk-of-a-Marine?"

She explained how she'd hidden the syringe in her lab-coat pocket until she was able to stab Ox in the side, injecting him with serum. She skipped over details too painful to recall out-loud.

"Did you know what you were injecting him with?" Boomer asked.

"No, but I had no choice. Good thing it was a tranquilizer."

"Strike first. Die last." Boomer snapped his fingers to emphasize the point.

"That's *kill* first," someone else said, slapping Boomer's shoulder.

"I know, man! But she didn't kill him, so I had to improvise."

"I'm curious," Ruby said, gazing at Eyes. "How did you know where to find us?"

"Your GPS chips."

"Our what?"

"You have one-of-a-kind GPS tracking-chips embedded in your bodies," Eyes answered. "You knew that, right?"

She glanced at her husband, tensing her eyebrows. She knew nothing about having GPS chips. No one had ever asked her. Or even told her. Should she admit it or play along?

Clay gently squeezed her hand, indicating he'd take the lead. "You're referring to the government-issued chips, I assume?"

"Affirmative. ISSI is the only system that can detect their presence. No one else has tracking devices as sophisticated. Lucky for you, you were chipped by the good old U.S. of A."

"Yes," she said. "Lucky for us!"

She was genuinely thankful, but what confused her was why she and Clay had been kept in the dark about the chips. President Newton would know the answer, and she had every intention of asking when they got home.

Hotwire reached down and rubbed his calf. When he returned his hand to his lap, she saw blood on his fingers.

"Did you cut yourself?" she asked him.

"Excuse me, Ma'am?"

"Your fingers. They're bloody. Did you cut yourself?"

Hotwire stared at his fingers and his eyes grew wide, like the blood surprised him. He leaned over and raised his uniform's pantleg. A straight three-inch cut—clean, as far as cuts go—marked his calf. The wound was still bleeding.

"Well…I'll be," he said. "Must have gotten cut by a glass shard walking over the dead zombies in the stairwell. Damn!"

Eyes looked at Hotwire. "Once we land, head directly to the infirmary. Have it checked out."

"Aw, do I have to boss? It's just a scrape."

"That's an order, mister…snap, crackle, pop." Eyes smiled before compressing his face. "But ribbing aside, it *is* an order. Seriously."

"Looks like you might need stitches," Ruby said. "Does it hurt?"

Hotwire tilted his head. "Pain is weakness leaving the body, Mrs. Spencer. No worries."

42

Tuesday, July 13, 2032
Sochi National Park, Russia

VLADIMIR LOUNGED ON the deck of his mountain-top chalet, overlooking the Western Caucasus and sipping vodka at sunset. He smiled. Being well insulated was a good feeling. In addition to surface-to-air missiles (SAMs) on ground-mounted platforms stationed around the compound—reinforced by soldiers carrying portable SAMs, snipers were strategically positioned high in the canopy and on the chalet's roof. Armed guards, paired with dogs or ATVs, patrolled the perimeter. Yes, he was well insulated. Being President of his beloved Russia, and ruling with a heavy hand, meant all the protections and luxuries a powerful man could want were at his disposal. This pleased him. Very much.

At his fortified retreat in Sochi National Park, he was able to slow time. Inhaling fresh air, he admired the sky's painted tapestry and listened to a chorus of insects welcoming nightfall. He chuckled. He was alive and free because he had outwitted the U.S. Navy *and* his partners in crime.

The minute the U.S. helicopter squadron flew over Pskov, he had been notified. Their destination was obvious. He shook his head. Even though the Federation of Independent Nations had so-called "oversight" of his country, did the FIN parasites not understand that Russians were loyal to Russia? And *only* Russia?

Vladimir Volkov *was* Russia!

Always thinking ahead, he had devised an escape plan the moment he and his partners decided to abduct the Spencers and deliver them to his private prison in Moscow. His escape plan was limited to one person: himself. And he had decided that if escape was necessary, why not dispose of Decha Lin and Quinton Oxford at the same time? A clean separation. Because if either or both survived, Vladimir's hands would look clean. Who could blame him for fleeing during the carnage?

Carnage *he* would unleash! What had Ox called him again? A troll. Yes, he liked that metaphor very much. It suited him.

Sipping his Russo-Baltique, he let the aged chilled-vodka, thick as syrup, warm his throat.

Unbeknownst to his partners, he had concocted a remote switch to unlock the containment chamber in the lower basement. He smiled at his clever ways. At any time of his choosing, he could free the zombie detainees—his test-subjects. Release of the undead would hurl the prison into chaos, masking Vladimir's escape.

The underground tunnel was integral to his plan. After learning U.S. Navy SEALs were en route to rescue the American woman, he had filled his briefcase with essentials to *The Cause* and headed to the basement where the tunnel's entrance was located. The timing was perfect. He walked among civilians who giggled like school children, excited to see zombies up-close like animals at a zoo. They had paid significant rubles in the black-market for the chance. Had he confessed their visit was a one-way ticket, a petting zoo with no return, civilians might not have clamored for their spot. The irony would have been tragically lost.

Chuckling out loud, he took another sip of vodka, enjoying the mental recounting of his shrewd getaway.

His departure was not without complication. On the last flight of stairs before the basement, someone in the prison's control room had activated the alarm once again. Without his authorization! This was unexpected. Fortunately, it did not alter Vladimir's plan. He veered from the crowd toward his secret exit, located on the other side of a seemingly inconsequential-door that had always remained locked. Once he entered and relocked the door from the inside, he activated the remote to the containment chamber. As the final step, he initiated the combination to open the hatch leading to the tunnel.

Civilians screamed from the other side of his hidden escape-closet, near the stairwell, meaning the remote had worked. What was the American expression? Oh yes: sometimes you got what you paid for; sometimes you got much more. Capitalism in the making!

Carrying his briefcase, he had jogged the length of the tunnel, becoming winded. He really needed to cut back on brown bread.

The exterior mouth of the tunnel—camouflaged by overgrown shrubbery—was located beyond the fencing that enclosed his prison compound. In a nearby wooded field, a side-by-side all-terrain utility vehicle was waiting for him. He climbed in, clutching the metal case on his lap. The driver sped on a winding, bumpy trail for three kilometers to where a black limo was idling on a dirt road, ready to transport him to his private airfield and jet.

His legs and arms had gotten stiff after absorbing the jolts of the off-road vehicle. He had climbed out, briefcase in hand, and walked toward his limo. The driver opened the rear passenger door. As he had demanded, a small cooler containing ice was resting on the leather seat. The contents of his briefcase needed to be chilled. It pleased him when orders were followed. Pleased him very much.

At the time, Vladimir had been streaming security-footage on his smartwatch. So he watched as the attack helicopters destroyed невидимый, which he had named Invisible. His beloved prison was engulfed in plumes of fire. Such a pity. But he had many others.

He praised himself for knowing when to act and when to hide. Trolls were wise regarding these matters.

He'd chosen to hide at his mountain retreat in southern Russia for many reasons. The compound was naturally isolated. Beyond the city of Sochi and the ruins of the Olympic Park, two-thousand square-kilometers of forest were between the Black Sea and the Western Caucasus, with rivers like the Shepsi, Magri, and Psou providing geographic barriers. His chalet was remotely located within the topography. Few hikers had the courage to interfere with the protected habitat of the Persian leopard. The cats were thriving, thanks to Vladimir. And if hikers happened to stumble across his property, the leopards were all too pleased. He made sure of it.

"Vlad," Alyona cooed, strolling onto the chalet's deck, dressed in a sheer nightgown that rippled in the cool evening breeze. "Come to bed early, my pet. We have some catching up to do."

Alyona's nipples teased him through the gown. Her slender body would feel good under his experienced fingers. Twenty-year-olds were his favorite. And this one was particularly memorable.

"Ahh, you grow impatient for me?" he teased.

"Always."

This pleased him. "Fill my glass with more vodka and meet me in the bedroom, my dear. Bring some caviar as well."

She took the glass and sauntered toward the bar room.

He headed to the master bedroom.

Already in bed, naked, and working his cock to ensure it was ready, he smiled as Alyona walked into the bedroom, her gown open and flowing behind her. In her one hand was his glass of freezer-cold vodka, in the other was an opened can of Beluga Sturgeon caviar, not that she would know to appreciate its rareness.

"Vlad? I am curious about the items in your refrigerator," she said, eyebrows raised.

"The blood bags? Do not worry, my child; they do not concern you. Nor will you remember them."

"Remember...what?"

"Yes, we are a good match, you and me." He winked, throwing off the silk bedsheets, exposing his hard on. Despite his age, his cock had never failed him. "Now come to me."

43

Wednesday, July 14, 2032
USS Simpson: The Baltic Sea

THE FIRST THING Ruby did after boarding the USS Simpson was ask permission to contact Margo and Tomas, to find out how Gabby was doing. To make sure she was safe.

Prayers had been answered. Em had called the Gonzalez's about the kidnapping, about Gabby being at risk. And thankfully, the President was providing a Capitol Police deputy to surveil the house and property. The baby was thriving. Everyone was safe.

After eating; showering; being issued the standard blue jumpsuit and black boots (which meant saying goodbye to her red slippers); and getting treated in Medical, she and Clay were assigned to individual racks in the enlisted co-ed berth-area of the USS Simpson. They opted to sleep in one bunk, though they hadn't asked permission. None of their Marine or Sailor bunkmates complained.

To fit together in the tight space, she lay on her side, draping most of her body over her husband's. Her ear rested on his chest, which rose and fell with each rhythmic breath. His heart sounded like an angelic drum.

The wall-clock ticked past midnight, yet she couldn't sleep. And cramped quarters had nothing to do with it.

Her restlessness came from almost losing her husband at the prison. With flashing images, her mind wouldn't quiet. She relived the desperation she'd felt when Clay's body was lifeless. His blue-eyes had been frozen open, blank with death. Losing him, even for minutes, was unbearable. Heart-wrenching. Now, listening to each heartbeat was a precious gift. She would never, ever, *ever* take his life for granted.

Excitement also preoccupied her. The USS Simpson would go to port in Helsinki, Finland, where she and Clay would be transported to the city's airport. They'd board a plane for Dulles International. Were they finally heading home? Would Gabby be in her arms soon? Elation coursed through her veins, keeping her system working overtime. Home meant Ruby could begin her life as a fulltime mother, ensuring her daughter's health and safety. Internalizing a new motto of *less stress, more balance.*

So why was uneasiness still lurking in the hidden nooks of her brain? Something felt amiss.

She drew her husband more closely to her. "Are you awake?" she whispered, stretching her chin upwards, toward his face.

His breathing hitched. "What?" His eyes fluttered open. "Everything okay?"

Using her toes, she pushed her body along her husband's, inching closer to his ear. She didn't want to wake anyone else or share her conversation. "I wish Ox and Dr. Lin weren't on this ship. I want to believe we're heading home—believe it'll happen this time. But knowing they're here, in the brig, frightens me. We know what they're capable of."

"Don't worry," he said softly, rubbing her back. "They're locked behind bars. We've got three-thousand service men and women onboard, watching our backs. They can't hurt us now."

She squeezed him again. "Did I thank you for *not* dying?"

His lips curled. "Have I thanked *you* for bringing me back into the ranks of the living?"

Kissing his cheek, she told him how much she loved him.

"And you're the girl of *my* dreams, Ruby Pearl Spencer," he said. "Now try and close your eyes. Think happy thoughts."

"Okay, but Helsinki can't get here fast enough."

She must have dozed off. Because suddenly, an alarm was blaring. A loud bell, mounted on the wall by a clock, rang seven short times, followed by a longer ring. The cycle repeated itself while red lights blinked in the berth area. How many alarms would she be forced to endure on this trip from hell?

Marines and Sailors leapt from their bunks, throwing on their boots and racing down the passageway.

"What's happening?" Clay asked a Marine.

"All hands are being called to General Quarters, to Battle Stations," he said, securing his boot and running at the same time. "Wait here. You'll be safe."

By the time she and Clay lowered themselves from the bunk and stepped into their boots, the racks were empty. With the bell still ringing, they waited in the dim lighting for what seemed like an eternity. Finally, a silhouette of a man jogged toward them.

"Eyes!" Ruby said, as the flashing lights illuminated his face in crimson. "What's going on? Have Ox and Dr. Lin escaped?"

"Worse," he said. "Infection. The glass shard that cut Hotwire must have been laced with ZOM-B. He was resting in Medical when he turned. Everyone was sleeping, so he tore into several patients and nurses before Boomer arrived and ended him. But the infection is not contained. And I've been given strict orders from President Newton to get you off this ship."

"Off this ship? Why?" she asked, feeling Helsinki and home slipping away. "Aren't we safest here with you?"

"When the POTUS gives you an order, you do not ask why. You simply answer, *Yes, Ma'am.*"

"But where are we going?"

"I'm taking you to the waterline, to the well-deck at the stern of the ship. A life-raft is waiting."

"Why wouldn't we fly out on a chopper?" Clay asked. "Fly from the ship to Helsinki?"

"The flight and hangar decks are hotzones right now, so no one can man stations for flight operations. The only safe direction on this ship is down. So until the threat is neutralized, President Newton wants you off the USS Simpson. Pronto."

"We're just going to float around on the Baltic Sea?" she asked, anxiety creeping up her throat.

"It's only temporary," Eyes assured her. "Just until the infected have been killed and deep-sixed. Your GPS chips will lead us back to you. Promise. Now follow me and stay close. And here; take these."

He handed them each a nine-millimeter. "Both have full magazines with fifteen rounds. If you see a zombie on our way to the well-deck and have a head shot, take it."

She and Clay followed Eyes down a metal stairway to the waterline level. They encountered several Marines racing up the stairs, taking two steps at a time. Ruby's heart pounded in her chest.

At the stern, the ship's electronic hatch had been lowered, like a huge trailer ramp. Water was lapping-up the deck. Boomer and Hornet held a life-raft on the ramp, in shallow water. It was pitch black beyond the opened hatch.

"We're supposed to be in Condition Zebra: buttoned-up tight," Eyes said, giving them life-jackets, "but SEAL Team 86 takes directions from the President, not the ship's Commanding Officer." He placed a flare gun into her husband's palm. "In case we come for you before daybreak, the flare will make it easier."

She and Clay snapped their orange vests across their chests, climbed into the raft, and sat beside the oars.

About two-dozen Marines funneled into the well-deck area, brandishing firearms. "Just checking," a Marine hollered to Eyes. "Everything Jake?"

"Affirmative," he responded, pushing the raft toward the open water. "Following POTUS orders."

Ruby's eyes scanned the service men and women who had paused, frozen in their stance, as if a ship was leaving port for deployment. Even with dim lighting, she spotted flaming-red hair. Her eyes stopped on a Marine. A Marine she recognized.

"Insley!" she shouted, pointing. "That's Insley!" Her heartrate went ballistic.

"Who?" Eyes asked, his image fading, even after Clay had stopped paddling.

"One of Ox's men!" She searched the crowd again. Only she couldn't find him. Perhaps she was too far away to discern details. Perhaps she had imagined him.

Eyes turned around, his back facing them, as if trying to find who or what she had pointed to among the Marines. He faced toward her and Clay again, raising his hand to his ear.

But the ship's stern was already closing, like a mouth refusing to talk.

Surrounded by darkness, flares of fire marked the flight deck of the USS Simpson like a flickering nightlight. Gunfire was quickly swallowed by rough water splashing against the raft.

Before long, the ship was a diminishing dot of light.

Only the full moon kept a watchful eye.

44

Wednesday, July 14, 2032
The Baltic Sea

CLAY TASTED SALTY spray on his lips. With his arm around Ruby, he rested his back against the raft's tube wall. Their heads were tilted back, gazing at the night sky. The stars were brilliant, like a magical sparkling-blanket.

The USS Simpson was nowhere in sight. The full moon cast a glistening wake, starting at the horizon and growing wider to their raft, as if highlighting the Navy vessel's route. The seas had calmed. He listened to the water gurgle and slap at the raft as it gently rolled up and over each swell. He thought of *The Gem*. Despite the circumstances, being on the open water was good for his soul.

"What if I *did* see Insley?" Ruby asked.

"I trust your instincts. But here's the good news: one man can't take down an assault ship. Especially with zombies on the loose."

She turned her face toward him. Her eyes were dark with shadows, and he couldn't see her expression.

"Ox's men are fleas in carpet," she said. "There's never just one. That's what worries me."

"Then the minute we return, we'll warn Eyes."

"Something else." She took a deep breath and exhaled slowly.

He gently squeezed her shoulder. "Hey, don't hold back."

"Ever wonder why President Newton goes to such lengths to save us? I mean, is it strange or am I overthinking?"

"You're on point. When a Naval ship is being overrun by

zombies, why would the President focus on saving one civilian?"

"*One* civilian?"

"It's you they're protecting, Ruby. Not *us.*" He ran his fingers through his hair. "Do you think there's any validity to Ox's assertion that President Newton and Em are working on a zombie cure of their own? Using your blood?"

"Maybe. But why the secrecy? And why weren't we told we were chipped?"

"Which proves the President's willing to withhold information from us," he said.

"Then again, she *is* the President. She's bound to have classified information we can't know about. That the SWC isn't privy to. And anyway, maybe getting chipped is standard protocol. With international crises unfolding—human and undead, she probably forgot to mention it."

"Careful you're not explaining this away. If classified information involves your blood, you have a right to know." He recalled what Ruby had told him earlier. "Didn't Ox claim that the President and Em were keeping their plans from you because you'd probably refuse to support their project?"

"Ox is a bonafide liar!"

"Can't hurt to at least consider what he's suggesting, especially since the President is moving Heaven and Earth to protect you. The truth is usually in the middle."

"But is it believable that President Newton and Em would be planning something nefarious...with my blood? Em and I are college best-friends! I can't see him working on a project that I'd flat-out disapprove of."

"How about using your blood without telling you?"

"I don't think so. Em's loyal to me. Really," she said.

"Then we're back to the beginning, wondering why the President is so intentional in extracting you from harm's way." He kissed the top of her head. "Which by the way: I'm extremely thankful for!"

"You're right, though. We have a lot of unanswered questions." She twisted her waist and looked behind her. "Do you hear that?"

Clanking in the distance reminded him of rigging hitting a metal mast.

She rolled to her knees and pointed. "Is that a sailboat?"

He was dumbfounded. Inching out from the curtain of darkness, into the moon's spotlight, was a sloop-rigged yacht, the jib and mainsail luffing in the breeze. Forty-six-feet, by his estimation, of sleek beauty. He imagined the smell of teak and the feel of cool aluminum or carbon fiber on his fingers, as if gripping the wheel of the helm.

"A gift from the President?" he teased, smiling at their good fortune.

"Very funny. But seriously, there might be people sleeping onboard. We need to be cautious we're not mistaken for modern-day pirates. Let's avoid getting shot."

"Doubtful anyone's onboard. No one leaves sails rigged overnight without someone manning the bridge. Have we ever? It's dangerous. Flirting with disaster; therefore, unlikely. So let's row over. Check it out."

He placed the oars in the oarlocks and rowed to the sailboat. When they pulled abreast of the vessel, he immediately appreciated the craftsmanship. The hull was dark in color, with two white-pinstripes painted above the waterline. The name on the beam was *Elää Elämää*, Finnish for *Living Life*.

"This vessel is a Hylas," he said, running his hand over the smooth hull. "It's not *The Gem*, but we're looking at a finely-crafted sailing yacht."

"We're stranded on the Baltic Sea," she said, "in the middle of the night, with our ride to Helsinki...gone. Gone because it's involved in a zombie battle. Is this really the time to drool over a yacht? Please, Clay. Focus!"

"Sorry. You're right. Let's inch toward the bow. I think the most-forward window on the hull ventilates the stateroom. It's probably open in this heat. Maybe we'll get someone's attention."

Under the window on the port side of the yacht, he raised himself to a standing position. Balancing on what felt like an underinflated air-mattress, he gripped the window's inset-sill, while Ruby supported his calves. The glass panel was open, with the rectangular-window pushed in toward the stateroom. Through the screen, a rancid stench assaulted him.

The odor sent his heart thumping against his chest cavity like a boxer working a punching bag. He recognized death's stench, whether the corpse was walking or not.

"Is anybody there?" he asked, keeping some distance between him and the screen.

Nothing. Just the water slapping against the raft and sailboat.

"So you really think the yacht is abandoned?" she whispered.

He looked at her as she sat on the raft floor, holding his legs. "Now I'm not sure. I'm getting an eerie feeling. It doesn't smell right."

"I'm sure there's rotten food onboard. But try getting someone's attention, one more time. Just to be sure."

He swallowed hard.

Facing the window again, he placed his hands against the screen, trying to block the moonlight as he peered inside the stateroom.

"Hello?"

Nothing.

With his face still framed by his hands, and his nose touching the screen, he murmured, "Good news. I think it's aban..."

Before he finished his sentence, a freakish face appeared on the other side of the screen, so close to his own that panic exploded in his system. The ghoul stretched open its jaws—as if they weren't hinged—and hoarsely roared, spewing gag-worthy breath on him. Feeling like his stomach contents might erupt geyser-style, Clay fell backwards. His wife gripped his calves, making sure he didn't land in the water. On impact, the floor of the raft slightly folded inward, forcing water to splash out from under the sides.

"What the hell happened?" she asked.

"A freaking zombie," he said, fighting back the bile that burned his throat. "I think it's trapped in the stateroom."

"What do you want to do? Should we let the sailboat drift away?"

"But it's shelter. And if the USS Simpson doesn't return anytime soon, I'd hate to pass on a sure thing."

"Agreed. Besides, we might be able to sail to Helsinki ourselves."

"Deal. But first, we'll have to destroy any undead passengers."

They derived a plan before tying the raft to a cleat on the stern's waterline diving-platform. They climbed the steps onboard, with pistols drawn and cocked. Moonlight revealed that the upper deck of the sailboat was clear of humans…and zombies.

Quietly, they tiptoed down the steps to the lower deck.

The first order of business was finding or creating a light source. He flipped the light switch for the entire saloon and it still functioned. Basked in light from the kitchen to the closed door of the stateroom, the area was zombie-free. And since that was the case, he took a second to admire the warmth and clean lines of the teak interior. He'd be lying if he didn't admit to himself that the workmanship was magnificent.

The stateroom door rattled. The zombie knew they were onboard.

Since the door to the stateroom happened to open inwards toward the bed, Clay planned to turn the handle, push the door wide open, and then run back the length of the vessel. He'd climb the stairs to the bridge deck where Ruby would be waiting. Together, they'd fire down on the undead—how ever-many there were—before the freaks attempted the steps to the upper deck.

When he kicked in the stateroom door, it was go-time. And the plan worked flawlessly. The zombie, only one, dropped to his permanent death at the base of the stairway, after being shot in the head.

"Let's clean this mess," she said, staring at the felled ass-rot.

"Not so fast."

"What do you mean?"

"I've been thinking…solo sailing this Hylas is doable for a seasoned expert, but with a forty-six-foot vessel and two sails, hardly anyone does."

Tension tightened his wife's eyes and lips.

"You think more zombies are onboard?" she asked.

"There are two bathrooms on this vessel. Both doors to the head are closed. And zombies don't give second chances, so we'd better check them out. Better safe than sorry, right?"

45

IN THE OVAL Office, President Newton converted the time difference. Eight o'clock at night in Washington was three-in-the-morning on the Baltic Sea. She pounded her fist on the desk. Still no word from Henry Kilgore, her Secretary of Defense.

Sweet Mother of Jesus, if they'd pinpointed Ruby's location by activating her GPS chip, why in the hell couldn't the girl be picked up and airlifted to Helsinki?

Raising her smartwatch, she instructed her newly uploaded Digitally Enhanced Personal Ego, whom she'd named Justine, to connect her with Henry. No time like the present to test her DEPE's artificial intelligence. See what "she" was made of.

The President had been told Justine was cutting edge. That her capabilities weren't limited to linear one-dimensional commands. Apparently her DEPE accomplished multilayered tasks, determining the most logical and efficient strategies for successful completion, on a case-by-case basis. More mind-blowing, Justine infiltrated other electronics as needed—like nearby smartwatches, computers, televisions, and radios. So if Henry's smartwatch was deactivated, her "personal ego" would analyze his implanted GPS chip to activate telecommunication systems closest to his coordinates, such as the smartwatch of a person standing next to him. And if the Secretary of Defense was alone, Justine might interrupt electronics in his proximity, such as cutting into a television or radio broadcast.

The President admired that level of commitment, especially when it benefitted *her*. Figures it came from intelligence that was only virtually alive.

"Yes, Madam President," Henry said, scowling as he dried his body with a towel.

She was curious. "Are we speaking through your smartwatch?"

He looked down at himself, at his nakedness which he didn't bother to cover. "Negative, Madam President. I'm in my master-bath, having exited the shower. Your new DEPE has commandeered my television. Bravo."

"Well, cover-up, Henry. I have business to discuss."

The towel dropped to the floor. Henry folded his arms. She averted her eyes from his...

"With all due respect," he chided. "If you barge into my home uninvited, you get what you get."

Like most of her Cabinet, Henry didn't appreciate Justine's intrusiveness. News flash: Too. Damn. Bad. There were more pressing issues than personal privacy.

"Have it your way," she snapped. "So then help me understand why we haven't picked up Ruby Spencer by now. Before you get...cold."

"I need your patience, Ma'am. The USS Simpson is still offline, which means we cannot deploy a Huey to evac them from the life-raft. Not yet. But we're monitoring the situation."

"What about another ship in the fleet? Why not send a Sierra helicopter from our aircraft carrier?"

"You separated the USS Simpson from the Sixth Fleet for the Moscow prison rescue, remember? The rest of the fleet is in the English Channel." He moved his hands on his hips and she couldn't help but glance. Turns out, her Secretary of Defense likely excelled at more than war games. Impressive.

"Need I remind you," he continued, "that I did not concur with your directive to separate the vessel from its fleet? This, Madam President, is *why.*"

Her admiration quickly faded. "Spare me the lecture, Henry. Surely one of our FIN allies can assist in extracting them. I need the Spencers in Helsinki for evac."

"I'm well aware. However, is it wise to involve our allies? If Ruby is key to our project and if our project can elevate us as a superpower amid another brewing war, are the risks worth it? Especially with Vladimir Volkov on the loose? He may have more moles. And we don't want the girl kidnapped from under our noses again. Do we?"

She was sick of people disagreeing with her. Challenging her. Passing blame. Or applying pressure. Even Emory had joined the ranks of the complainers. He wanted his hemoglobin *now*.

She was surrounded by a bunch of whining, entitled babies.

Her frustration was building.

"Don't get condescending with me," she spat, feeling her face flush. "I expect you to find a way to get that girl back here. Be…*creative*. And if you're not making progress, I will work with my own international contacts—or any other assets who can assist me—and I will show you how to get the job done. Risk is part of the bloody fucking job! Understood?"

"Yes, Ma'am."

"Justine: end this pathetic connection."

46

STANDING BY THE bridge on the upper deck of the sailing yacht, Ruby looked down the stairs at the dead zombie which she and Clay had shot in the head. A gust of wind kicked-up, catching in the mainsail and jerking the vessel to the left. She sidestepped and squatted to keep her footing.

"Before we do anything else," Clay said, "I'm going to lower the mainsail and jib."

"Need help? Or should I look around below deck?"

"I've got the sails. But hey, don't open any doors until I join you. Okay? We'll check out the heads together." He must have seen the slight roll in her eyes. He added, "Seriously."

At the base of the steps, she carefully maneuvered over the undead corpse, making her way to the galley. Opening a few kitchen cabinets, she smiled that the vessel was well stocked with canned goods like peaches, green beans, and corn. Her stomach grumbled.

The refrigerator was a different story. Spoiled milk and fish reminded her of the fragrance-of-choice for the undead. She shuddered. If they were to spend any time on the *Elää Elämää*, they'd have some cleaning to do.

A thump caught her attention.

"Are you almost done?" she hollered above.

She heard the whirl of the mainsail lowering. Her husband clearly hadn't heard her and was still working with the sails.

Walking to the closed door in the galley, she placed her left hand on the teak slab, as if she could somehow feel if the bathroom was inhabited by something evil. Anyway, she held a loaded pistol in her right hand. And she'd already lost count over how many zombies she'd killed. So why was waiting for Clay necessary?

Grasping the door handle, she pushed down. As the door opened, she aimed her handgun inside the bathroom, scanning for movement. For a target.

She exhaled. The head was empty. And clean.

Another thump.

The stateroom head might be another story.

Trekking to the master bedroom with her heart accelerating, she felt like a pirate invading another person's space and belongings. But she reminded herself: once a human turned, the person they *had been* was dead. Gone. What survived in the body wasn't even a whisper of the former individual. So no one who had owned or sailed the *Elää Elämää* was "technically" onboard anymore.

She stood in front of the door to the master head and opened it slowly. But while she was visually sweeping the bathroom at eye level in the dark, a hand wrapped around her ankle. The grip was so forceful that she thought it might crush her bones. She screamed. With a yank from the zombie, Ruby crashed to the floor. Her head slammed against the tiles. The pistol flew from her hand.

Why had she been so careless? Why hadn't she waited for Clay?

The zombie, a female, clawed her way on top of her body. Ruby slapped and kicked. Each sharp, overgrown fingernail pricked against her jumper's fabric. The undead's strength was overwhelming. The rotting aberration—with gray flaking-skin, frizzy blonde hair, and dressed in a torn floral nightgown—lowered her face, with gray teeth snapping, advancing toward Ruby's pulsing neck.

"Please," she begged. "Please don't..."

Everything flashed before her eyes: Gabriella's tiny face, Clay's eyes and smile, the feel of her dog's fur around the ears, the sound of wind in the sails—her happy thoughts.

A whistle shrieked. The zombie raised its peeling face at the source.

"Don't move," Clay warned.

He fired his pistol, and the bullet penetrated the zombie's forehead. Black goo exploded from the skull like a piñata filled with tar. Her husband's hand grabbed hers, pulling her from the tacky splatter.

"Check me!" she cried. "Check that she didn't cut or scratch me. Remember Hotwire?"

She tore off her soiled blue jumpsuit. Clay inspected her skin. Other than finger-imprints forming a bruise around her ankle, he confirmed she had no new abrasions, scratches, or open wounds. Her pre-existing facial wounds were already healing and her arm injury had been covered by her jumpsuit. He gave her the all-clear.

"I'm sorry," she said. "Sorry I didn't wait."

He held her close, rubbing her back. "You're okay; that's all that matters." He raised her chin so they locked eyes. "I can't lose you."

"Thank God you walked in when you did. You saved me."

"Hey, I did, didn't I? At last I've returned the favor." He sniffed the air and twisted his face. "Not that I wouldn't find any fragrance on you appealing, but how does a shower sound? The other bathroom is clean. Promise I'll find you clothes and a fresh towel."

No arguments from her.

In the shower, she let the warm water wash-away any zombie goo that might have lingered on her body. She scrubbed her skin until it turned pink. When she exited the shower stall, she grabbed the towel he had left her. A turquoise tunic decorated with sailboats and a pair of white capris were draped across the sink. The clothes fit. The Top-Sider deck shoes were a tad small, but they'd work.

Clay was waiting for her outside of the bathroom, with extended arms. She walked into his embrace and soaked in his warmth. They were motionless for a moment, before their work began.

Getting the corpses off the vessel and sanitizing the living quarters were their next priorities. Finding Latex gloves in the galley, they protected their hands and carried the corpses above deck. But her energy was fading.

"Can't we toss the corpses and linens overboard and call it a night?" she asked.

"Would you be comfortable eating a fish that's nibbled on zombie flesh?"

She lowered her eyes, knowing she wouldn't.

Her husband had always considered himself a staunch steward of the ocean. She admired that. He explained that dumping dead zombies into the water would be careless. Would have consequences. So instead, he'd build a contraption on which to burn the infected bodies and contaminated linens.

He started his project by unhinging the stateroom's teak door and taking the slab above deck. While she disinfected and scrubbed below, and lugged linens and pillows to the top of the stairs, he drilled and hammered above deck.

An hour later, he entered the stateroom which was now pristine, with fresh bedsheets on the mattress.

"Looks and smells clean," he said. "Have a minute to come above deck? Daybreak is imminent, and I'm in the mood for a bonfire."

They walked to the upper deck which was fully lit. She glanced toward the bow. Clay had furled the mainsail to the boom, securing it with sail ties. The jib had also been lowered and secured. "Wow. You've been hard at work."

"Check this out," he said, sounding proud.

As he flipped a switch, a spotlight cast a beam of light toward the stern, on the port side. Hanging from a dinghy davit was a stack resembling a campfire s'more, sized for a giant. The door from the stateroom was the graham cracker, layered with white bedsheets and pillows, and topped with two zombies. Using ropes, he had secured the layers together and then tied a barrel hitch with a bowline knot on the end. Creative! The package—attached to the davit hook and extended over the gunnel—gently swayed with the breeze.

"I've already doused them with lighter-fluid I found in the galley." He held out a plastic utility lighter. "Would you accept the honors?"

"I'd be happy to." She clasped the lighter, walked to the stern, and leaned over the gunnel. Clicking the lighting mechanism, she ignited the undead couple's clothing and linens in as many places as she could reach.

When the zombie package was ablaze, they lowered it into the water and cut the rope. Clay turned off all the lights above deck as the door drifted with its fiery cargo. Embers took flight, blinking through the air like overgrown fireflies, landing on the water with a hiss. It reminded her of a Viking funeral.

Pinks and oranges peeked over the horizon. Dawn was arriving. They held each other in silence, watching the flaming door drift out of sight. After a while, the sun rose. Blue skies were speckled with puffy clouds and a steady breeze.

"What should we do today?" she asked, getting her second wind. "Contact someone on the radio? Sail to Helsinki?"

"I was thinking about our next move, too." He leaned against the rail and raised his chin toward the sky for a moment. "I'm exhausted, Ruby." In their embrace, she was pressed against his chest. "I could use a day of R&R. Just a day. And I trust Eyes. If anyone will keep his word, it's him. Am I being a wuss to need a day of recovery?"

"You were tortured. And you died. A little downtime is not too much to ask. And I need it, too."

"It's almost like being on *The Gem,* right? Only Gabby and Lollie are missing."

"Being in fresh air, on this boat, is giving me hope. I'm starting to feel like getting-home is possible. So yes, it's like being on *The Gem.*"

"Only, we're *Living Life,* baby." He winked.

His optimism always inspired her. Lifted her mood.

Using the fishing rods onboard, coupled with spoiled meat from the refrigerator as bait, they cast for most of the day, hooking two Baltic cod. Clay cleaned and filleted them. If the USS Simpson continued to be a no-show, they'd eat cod for dinner, with canned green beans and peaches. Accompanied by a bottle of white wine: Montrachet Grand Cru. She was looking forward to all of it.

Taking a break from fishing, they changed into bathing suits found in the drawers of a stateroom dresser. Jumping off the gunnel of the sailboat, they torpedoed into the brackish sea. They splashed each other, enjoying the coolness, until they remembered how well Huo had maneuvered in the water tank, during the experiment at the Naval base in Keelung. Quickly climbing the sailboat's steps on its sugar-scooped stern, they agreed the water was off limits.

In the late afternoon, they lay on the forecastle deck, sunning.

"I'm sort of hoping the USS Simpson doesn't retrieve us until tomorrow," she admitted.

"Me, too." He turned toward her and smiled. "I'm enjoying this alone-time. It's like the honeymoon we were promised, but never got."

"Let's pretend we're here by choice, drifting, and that the world is normal again." She smiled and moved a strand of hair from his face. "And if the Naval ship doesn't show by tomorrow morning, then we'll hoist the *Elää Elämää's* sails and head to Helsinki. Deal?"

"Deal."

For the rest of the day, time passed lazily. Like she'd hoped.

When she woke from a nap, next to her husband, the bottom tip of the sun touched the horizon, casting shadows. A fighter jet thundered overhead, tilting its wings as it roared past.

"They know we're here," Clay said.

"Except...fighter jets aren't carried by the USS Simpson. And since the ship's not here, and they haven't deployed a helicopter, I'm assuming normal operations haven't resumed."

"Which isn't good." He raised his eyebrows. "But on the upside, it means we still have downtime...together."

Not wanting to be rescued before enjoying a private evening, they prepped for dinner early, alternating between cooking and showering. The plan was to have dinner outside on the beam's deck, atop the circular table positioned behind the cockpit.

For their dinner date, her husband chose khaki shorts and a matching collared shirt—adorned with the same turquoise and sailboat pattern. They looked like tourists who wanted everyone to know they were a couple. Clay's eyes matched the color in his shirt.

Alone and safe, heat warmed her inner thighs.

Sitting across from him at the dinner table, she relaxed. The sun had dipped below the horizon, so they dined by candlelight.

The meal was exquisite. The fish was tender and flaky, and even though she typically resisted anything in a can, the beans and peaches melted in her mouth like they were gourmet. Fruity and smooth, the French wine warmed her throat and gave her a welcomed buzz.

"Here's to the love of my life," she said, raising her wine glass.

"Yamas," he answered, using the Greek equivalent of cheers and clinking his glass with hers.

Her heat grew into a yearning. The candle flickered, causing light to dance on her husband's face. She smiled.

"Would you consider dessert in a more private setting?" He reached for her hand.

"Thought you'd never ask!"

They left the dishes on the table and headed for the master suite.

Once in the stateroom, she lay down on the bed, fully clothed. He lay next to her, turning on his side to face her. He propped himself up with his elbow. Gazing into her eyes, he ran his thumb lightly along her cheek, across her lips, and down her chin. She loved when he touched her, like he cherished every part.

"You're my one and only, Ruby," he whispered. "My forever."

Reaching up, she grabbed his collar and pulled it toward her, bringing his lips to hers. She brushed against his mouth, teasing, before parting his lips and kissing him hard and deep.

Butterflies took flight.

While they kissed, he moved his hand from her neck to her chest, gliding over the blouse and onto her breast. He moved his thumb softly over her nipple, pressing a little, but not too much. A rush of warmth, of urgency, deepened in her thighs.

"I want to feel your skin with my fingers, with my lips," he said, slightly rising, placing several inches between their chests.

She craved his touch.

While keeping his eyes on hers, he unbuttoned the borrowed blouse and opened it. Placing his hand flat on her stomach, below her bellybutton, he caressed her skin as he moved toward her bra. Nerve endings danced in anticipation. Unsnapping the front clip, he slid her bra-cups to the side, exposing her breasts. Her breathing quickened.

"Have I reminded you how beautiful you are?" he asked.

"Even with bruises?"

"I know they're there, but I don't see them. I see *you.*" His lips reached her breast and he swirled his tongue around her areola before taking more into his mouth.

When the anticipation grew too strong, she clutched the back of his collar and tugged. His mouth lifted from her breast and he paused, waiting for direction.

"I want your skin next to mine." She began to unbutton his shirt and when she was done, she slid it behind his shoulders.

He sat upright and removed the shirt, flinging it to the floor. At the same time, she took off her tunic and bra, tossing them.

Before he lowered his chest on hers, she ran her fingers over his pecks and abs. She had seen his body—touched it, savored it—countless times; yet each time, her wonderment intensified. "Kiss me, Clay. Kiss me hard."

He hovered over her for a second, long enough to increase the excitement—the magnetic pull. When their lips and chests finally touched, the heat between them was scorching. While kissing, she ran her hands down his back until she felt the waistband of his shorts. Placing her hands on his bottom, she pressed him against her, feeling his hardness through the fabric. She was wet for him.

Rolling off her, he stood beside the bed, reaching for the button above the zipper on his shorts.

"Let me do it," she said, moving to the edge of the mattress and draping her legs over the side. He moved in front of her. Unbuttoning his shorts, she clasped the zipper and lowered it, lifting his clothing over his erection. She slid the shorts and briefs down his legs and he stepped out of them. He was beautiful; his penis, thick and long. Touching him, she ran her hands over his shaft, feeling him. Appreciating him.

Lifting her to her feet, he kissed her again, with more fervor.

With hands on her waist, he seamlessly turned her one-hundred-and-eighty-degrees and sat, exchanging places. Now he was on the bed and she stood in front of him. Unzipping her capris, he pulled them down, along with her lace underwear. She flicked them to the side with her foot.

Pulling her closer, in between his bent legs, he softly kissed each breast. She ran her hands through his hair.

As the moon rose, they continued to kiss and touch. And when they made love, they shared one another like their union might be their last.

Well-past midnight, they lay naked on the bed. Their skin was cooled by the sea breeze finding its way through the stateroom windows.

47

Thursday, July 15, 2032
The USS Simpson: The Baltic Sea

A SHIP'S HORN rattled the *Elää Elämää*. Clay startled from his sleep. He sat up, trying to find his bearings. The sun shone through the porthole above the bed.

"Quick!" he said to Ruby. "We'd better get dressed. I think our sea chariot has arrived!"

He threw on clothes from the night before. His wife did the same. Grabbing the pistols off the dresser, he handed one to her. "Stuff this in your back pocket."

She was ahead of him as they jogged the length of the saloon, toward the stairway. Before reaching the steps, he touched her arm. She slowed and turned. Bodies touching, he placed his palms on the sides of her face, tilting her chin upwards. "Yesterday was wonderful." He kissed her forehead. "And now we're going home."

She nodded, smiling. "Home to Gabby."

He led the way to the deck. The morning was mid-sixties with clear skies. A steady fifteen mile-per-hour northeast wind teased him. Perfect sailing conditions.

Port side, he watched as the massive hatch opened on the USS Simpson's stern. After the well-deck lowered, a hovercraft emerged and raced over the water, propelled by fan-like blowers. The craft bounced off swells, throwing sea-spray from its sides. Two Marines were onboard, outfitted in orange vests, with assault rifles slung across their chests. Protocol, no doubt.

He grabbed his life-vest and handed Ruby hers. After clipping the strap-ends to secure their vests, they walked down the stern's steps leading to the sailboat's waterline platform. When the hovercraft neared, the pilot shut down the blowers and drifted abreast the sailboat, perfectly aligning the craft with the Hylas.

They stepped onboard, but before they sat, a Marine approached him. "I've got to frisk you both, Mr. Spencer," he said. "Standard protocol."

"Sure. I have one weapon." He raised his hands slightly. "The pistol's in my back pocket. My wife has one, too."

The Marine confiscated the handguns, unclipping each magazine. After conducting clothing searches, he nodded to the pilot who ignited the blowers and turned the hovercraft toward the Navy vessel.

"Has the infection been contained?" Clay asked, more as a conversation starter since the answer was obvious.

"Yes, sir," the pilot answered. "The Simpson's back in order. A piece of cake, really."

Ruby, who was holding his arm, squeezed his bicep. Looking at her for an explanation, his heart sputtered. Her eyes were wide. She ran her front teeth over her bottom lip. He replayed the Marine's words in his mind, analyzing them for an implied threat. Nothing surfaced.

"How's Eyes? You know, SEAL Team 86's Commanding Officer?" he asked, taking a stab at who might be on his wife's mind.

"Oh, he's part of the greeting party," the pilot hollered over the blowers and wind. "You'll see for yourself in a minute."

"The prisoners," Ruby pressed, homing in on her concern, no doubt. "Are they still...*detained?*"

"Everything is Jake, Ma'am. Just as it should be."

When the hovercraft entered the ship's belly and travelled up the ramp onto the deck, the two Marines onboard stepped out, turning to help him and Ruby exit the craft.

Clay raised his hand to stop them. "Thank you, but I've got my wife," he said, trusting in her intuition that something was amiss.

"No sweat, brother." The Marine clutched his rifle, lowering it slightly from his chest.

"So where's Eyes?" he asked.

"For fuck's sake, show some patience!" Ox emerged from the shadows, holding a pistol against the SEAL's temple. "Looky here: I spotted your man. Is that what you call an eye for an eye?"

Some things hit like a brick. His knees buckled, and his wife slumped to the deck. Steadying himself, he pulled Ruby to her feet, placing his arm under hers for support.

"Sorry guys," Eyes said. "In the battle to contain the infection, moles let their rat out. And he's commandeered the ship."

Clay clenched his fists. Why the hell hadn't they sailed to Helsinki themselves? He'd had enough of this mayhem bullshit.

"Eyes, here," Ox said, "is one of my insurance policies—to motivate you, Ruby Never-Dies. Clay: you're still the primary."

Several Marines walked onto the well-deck, brandishing rifles.

"This *cannot* be about me again," she snapped. "You seriously did not overtake a Naval ship because of...*me!*"

"It's always been about *you*. From the beginning."

"I keep telling you my blood is like everybody else's. Regardless, I would *die* before I ever helped you."

"Guess we'll have to make sure that doesn't happen," Ox said.

With flaming red hair, longer than the standard military-buzz, a Marine stepped onto the deck. Must be the guy Ruby thought she saw. The jerk named Insley.

"Want me to take them to the brig?" the guy asked Ox.

"Affirmative. And have someone watch them around the clock. Remind the guards that I want the girl in my captain's quarters this evening. Join us as well, Insley."

Clay took several steps toward them, rage causing his fingers to shake. He wanting to tear the turncoats apart, limb by limb.

"Don't Clay," she warned.

"Now, now, Mr. Pretty Face," Ox said. "Listen to your wife and back the-fuck off. Unless you'd rather die now."

Clay stepped back.

"Thought so." He scanned the deck, looking at his men. "Now let's get this party started, team."

48

Thursday, July 15, 2032
The USS Simpson: The Baltic Sea

OX WASN'T EASILY impressed, but he had to admit that the captain's quarters on the USS Simpson, which became the admiral's lair when the Navy's top-dog graced the ship with a visit, were beyond sweet. To think, five days ago he was sitting in a closet-sized office, appointed with Walmart specials, taking orders from the Taipei consulate's needle-dick Eagle Scout, Jonny Ambassador. At last his surroundings reflected the level of respect he deserved. Hell, that he had earned. *Oorah!*

The cabin resembled a compact upscale-apartment, but on a ship where every inch was used and accounted for, it qualified as the Taj Ma-fucking-hal. The sitting room was appointed with two leather couches, a stately dining-room table, a kitchen efficiency, and a top-shelf bar. A private stateroom and personal head were also part of the real estate. Well, ain't that something. He was finally living large.

Insley brought the girl into his quarters at 1800 hours. Her facial injuries were healing. Who knows? Maybe their conversation wouldn't have to end with head-to-head or fist-to-face contact. But to minimize her tendency to trigger a physical response from him, one that might snuff his prized catch, Ox insisted the bitch be cuffed behind her back, to avoid provocation. He should've had her mouth taped shut as well, but he didn't want to deny himself *all* the fun.

He motioned for Ruby Never-Dies to sit at the dining room table. Insley knew his place, retreating next to the mounted flat-screened

238

television, like a spitball stuck to the wall.

"You're moving up in the world, *captain,*" she snarled, sounding belligerent as always.

"The ascension has only begun." He scanned the room. "Fitting, don't you think?"

"Like a bug to a torch."

"Now-now, Mrs. Spencer. Let's not butt heads again." He winked. "Let's keep our exchange cordial this time."

"Cordial? Is this why I'm not comatose on a gurney in the Medical ward, serving as a non-stop drip for your misdirected blood-bank stash? Because you've suddenly got an itch to be *cordial?*"

"Ahh, you know me well. Unfortunately, this ship's senior medical officer and her corpsmen were casualties. Not discounting the fact that the infection broke-out within their turf; nevertheless, their life-saving nature is a death sentence in the new world where a bullet-to-the-head is the only effective treatment during attack. Healers don't tend to go for that. Think they can save each precious life…blah, blah, blah. So not surprising that responders were the first to join the undead. With the ward swimming in sticky tar—searching for breathing hosts, Medical's no place for an asset like you."

"Why do you need Medical anyway? When you have Dr. Lin?"

"Turns out, *my* nature didn't serve the doc well. As Insley released us from our cells, several zombies approached the brig. In a split second, I had to choose. On the one hand, Insley is young, but also invaluable. He was stationed on the USS Simpson prior to his consulate assignment. He knows the real estate and some of the crew, in addition to my moles. On the other hand, microbiologists (even good ones) are a dime-a-dozen—no insult to your profession intended. Simply stating the facts." He shrugged. "So I tossed Decha like a bone and told the zombies to fetch."

"Wasn't he the brains of your operation?"

"If he was, he'd be sitting in this chair, calling the shots." Ox looked around the room for effect. "Like I thought: he's a no-show."

"What about Vladimir Volkov? Won't he object to your self-proclaimed ascension?"

"He's gone Elvis—flown the coop. To your point, though, when the troll emerges from under the bridge, he undoubtedly will object.

But I'm in possession of the bargaining chip. So who gives a troll's ass about his disapproval?"

"What makes you think President Newton isn't going to bomb this ship and end your pathetic, self-serving zombie-army scheme, once and for all?"

He shook his head. "You still don't get it. We're in a high-stakes war game here, and you're what everybody wants—the prize. Possession of you is the difference between a powerless title-holder and the absolute ruler of the world. You know…if you were smarter and more cunning than me, you'd find a way to win the game yourself. Thankfully, that's not in *your* nature."

"I wouldn't do a victory dance just yet. Going it alone is risky."

"You're lecturing *me* on risk assessment?" He huffed, halfway-between disgust for her stupidity and a laugh because the joke was on her. "Apparently, you haven't noticed the chest-candy decorating my Service Dress Blues. I'm a bonafide hero. A killing machine. The last man standing. So if I were you, I'd forget about *my* risks and start mentally preparing for the long rest that awaits you when we dock. You'll be the modern-day Sleeping Beauty, only your charming Prince Phillip is going to be pulverized. Tossed overboard as shark chum."

Her eyes widened slightly. She was beyond predictable when it came to Mr. Pretty Face. Almost boring except Ox enjoyed using her husband to toy with her.

"Get to your point," she snapped. "Why have you invited me here to these quarters?"

"Such impatience. Can't a man…"

His encrypted cellphone rang.

Although he was expecting a crucial call, did it have to come when the fun was about to begin? For fuck's sake.

49

Thursday, July 15, 2032
The USS Simpson: The Baltic Sea

THE CELLPHONE CONTINUED to ring. Ruby watched as Ox rose from his chair and nodded to Insley, his Marine puppet standing by the wall. Strutting across the room with his device pressed to his ear, the turncoat Lieutenant Colonel walked out the door, closing it behind him. Insley stepped forward, nearer to the dining room table, as if to remind her that she wasn't alone.

The Marine avoided eye contact. He stared across the room at nothing, like a military guard at the Tomb of the Unknown Soldier. Silence lingered.

"Relax, Insley," she said. "We don't have to be formal. It's not like you're actually *in* the U.S. Marine Corps anymore. I mean, you're a traitor, right? You've commandeered a Naval ship and answer to Ox, not the Corps."

His jaw-muscle twitched from clenching his teeth.

On second thought, she'd get nowhere by insulting him or his service. Instead, she had to find a way to tug at his heartstrings so he'd open-up, so she could win him over. Because her and Clay's survival depended on inside help. Of course, getting him to switch sides was a tall order. Maybe impossible. Bottom line: she didn't know much about him. Not to mention time was running out.

"Sorry," she said, using a softer tone. "I'm angry, that's all. I get there aren't any former or ex-Marines. *Once a Marine, always a Marine.* Even after death." His jaw relaxed. "Guess that gives you solace for your friend Corporal Wyatt. Such a shock to see a bullet lodged in his skull. Apparently, your boss no longer needed his service."

"Corporal Wyatt was bitten by the zombie head *you* threw at him," he seethed through his teeth. "A permanent death was required. And he accepted it with honor. Make no mistake: his death was your fault. Yours alone."

"You mean, *almost* my fault. No denying I threw the zombie head at him in defense. And I won't lie: I hoped it would kill him. No doubt Wyatt had wanted to kill *me*. Look at my nose and arm injuries! But I saw your friend—up close and personal—sprawled on a gurney in the Moscow prison. His eyes were frozen open. And they weren't tar black. Not at all. They were white, with a blue iris. Your sidekick wasn't shot because of infection. You have my word."

"Your *word* means squat," he snapped. "Lying is the only thing you're good at."

"Guess you won't believe me about the dead Russian co-pilot either—the one on the gurney next to Wyatt. He didn't have contact with the zombie head at all. But he was stone-cold dead. Strangled. I saw the purple rings around his neck and his bulging brown eyes. Aren't you the least bit concerned that Ox terminates his moles once they've exhausted their purpose? Look what he did to Dr. Lin! And *you* witnessed that."

Insley said nothing, resuming his detached stare.

"Not sure why you're surprised," she continued. "You already knew Ox murdered the Ambassador at the consulate. For a man like Ox, murdering is as easy as eating cake. That's one of his favorite expressions, right? A piece of cake? Ironic, since my Mom's a pastry chef. But now, cake is dead to me. Cupcakes, too."

Ruby detected a reaction. Had the Marine's breathing hitched? His knees buckled? Heartbeat quickened? She wasn't sure. But she sensed the energy had changed in the room. Anxiety had entered. Which meant the conversation was heading in the right direction. And she was pretty sure baked desserts had no relevance.

"When I met with Ox at the consulate," she resumed, "he told me Ambassador Jeffries had died from the RED attack and his body was being stored in the basement. But when I was imprisoned in Moscow and asked the Russian President about the Ambassador's death,

Vladimir practically admitted that Ox had killed him; at least, he didn't refute it. Neither did Ox. The murder happened the day I arrived at the consulate. The day Ox *occupied* the Ambassador's office. Right before I met you and Wyatt at the gate."

"Ambassador Jeffries was at the Naval base that afternoon, addressing the Code Red," he argued. "And Ox only borrowed the Ambassador's office to cover his phone extension, since our receptionist had been sent home as a precaution. Ox explained everything to me. No one was murdered."

"Wait. Ox told you Patti Davis had been sent *home?*"

Insley shifted his weight and swallowed hard. She was making progress and hoped Ox wouldn't suddenly barge through the door and prematurely end the conversation.

"You know Patti Davis?" he asked.

"I never met Patti in-person. But I shared a special friendship with her brother Frank. Over several hours, we experienced a lot together. In fact, he asked me to share a message with his twin—whom he called his guardian angel. But I arrived at the consulate too late."

"Message?"

"That he loved her. See…Seaman Davis saved me at the base. He was a hero, an honorable Sailor. But he'd been bitten. Made me promise to shoot him after he passed. Which I did. His death was tragic. A terrible loss."

Insley scrunched his reddish-blond eyebrows and blinked rapidly. "I know Patti Davis," he whispered. "When I can, I'll relay the message. Even if you're lying about her brother's death, she'd appreciate the message. Everyone knows how close she and her brother are."

"You mean *were.*"

He shook his head and smirked, like he wasn't going to fall for the trickery. Which, of course, was nothing more than the truth.

"Not trying to be argumentative, sir," she added, "but if you truly knew Patti and Ox well, you'd know she's gone and that he murdered her, along with the Ambassador."

"Lying again."

"Look at what we know: Ox told me the Ambassador and Patti were killed by the RED attack and were stacked in the basement. Ox told you that the Ambassador was at the base and Patti had been sent home. And when I asked Vladimir at the prison, while Ox was present, neither of them denied being responsible for their deaths. I asked them, Insley, point blank. Bottom line: the Ambassador and Patti are dead, and Ox had everything to do with it. Even if you can't handle the facts."

"Funny." He rolled his eyes and his face turned crimson. "Ox warned me you were a liar. Why don't you shut your mouth-trap before I force your words back down your throat and make you choke on them?"

"Disappointing. I've always respected the military, especially the Marines and SEALs. But Ox is his own contagious infection. And now you can't think for yourself. You're nothing more than a *human* zombie."

He said nothing.

"Anyway, the question I keep asking myself is: where *are* the few good men and women of the Marine Corps? Since this war game started, I haven't come across many."

The door opened. Ox strutted back into the captain's quarters, his nose in the air, rubbing his hand on his whiskered chin.

The turncoat smiled like a rat who'd found a chunk of cheese floating in the middle of the ocean.

50

Thursday, July 15, 2032
The USS Simpson: The Baltic Sea

OX SAT AT the head of the table, with Ruby Never-Dies on his left. Smiling, he admitted to himself that the phone call couldn't have gone better. Twists and turns in the game gave him a rush, gave him an opportunity to show off, since he always stayed ahead of the curve. Always positioned himself for the win. In fact, he'd nab the Dom Pérignon from the bar, stuff it in his duffel bag, and pop the cork later that night. His bedtime jack-off would be epic. Fuck the fat lady singing. When Quinton Oxford said it was over...It. Was. Over.

"Looks like your lucky night," he said to the girl.

"Oh? You'll be walking the plank?"

He chuckled. "I think one day, you and I are going to be friends. You know: we're more alike than different. We both go to great lengths to impact the world, to exert power over it."

"Please! I didn't release a bioweapon to wipe out the animal kingdom in hopes of starving the world. Or taint a meat product with nanobots to kill one-billion people. I'm not trying to engineer a ZOM-B cure to control an army that morphs from human to zombie and back again at your whim. You and I are *nothing* alike."

"When you chronicle my accomplishments like that, guess I'd have to agree. My successes are far more impactful than yours." He nodded. "Point well taken."

She acted as though she hadn't heard him. "What *happened* to you? Once a hero. Then to become *this*...this monster?"

No one had ever asked him that question. Maybe if they had, or if they'd seen and done what he had in combat, or even if someone had *cared* how his experiences haunted him—day and night, his loyalty might not have gone on-sale.

But rehashing what-ifs was a waste of energy.

He gazed into her eyes, giving his anger a brief remission. "Let's just say that when TRICARE repeatedly stalled my medical appointments for PTSD, calling my residual anger a *normal* scar that would heal over time, I decided to use my new "normal" as a personal advantage. If you can't define your sickness, why not rewrite the dictionary? Turn it into an asset? *Oorah.*"

"Is that why you murdered the Ambassador and Patti Davis? Because your twisted dictionary now says it's okay to kill innocents to elevate yourself?"

"Predictable." Looking at Insley, he tilted his head for emphasis. So the girl could see. "I warned you she'd make those accusations, didn't I?"

"Yes, sir," he answered. "She's a liar. Right as usual, sir."

"You're pathetic, Insley," she hissed like a snake. "You hear-no and see-no evil, yet you call him *sir* and do his bidding." Turning her eyes from Red Top, she glared at him with such vexation, his skin might have burned. "Now that we agree we're nothing alike," she added, "I'll bite. Why is this my lucky night?"

"Interested, are we? Turns out, Sleeping Beauty stays awake."

"Wait. What?"

He loved knowing that the girl needed information from him. That she was salivating over every word leaving his lips. That's why he wanted to go slowly, like a dripping faucet. She had to play his game whether she wanted to or not.

"Unless, of course," he continued, "you were hoping to be mounted in your sleep. Believe me: it's still on my bucket list. I mean, after you felt my junk in the Moscow lab, I imagine your dreams have left your bedsheets juicy. That's why you didn't kill me when you had the chance. But my ripe, fuzzy peach…think how much you'll remember if you're awake."

The bitch stood from her chair. "Don't play cat-and-mouse with me. If you have something to say, then say it."

She knew how to throw ice on scorching-hot balls.

"Sit. The fuck. Down," he ordered, turning sour. The playfulness he'd hoped for was…shrinking. He banged his fist on the table.

She didn't flinch. Or sit down.

"I'm getting your vibe," he said, running his hand over the polished wood surface. "You prefer that I keep my promise: to turn Mr. Pretty Face into shark chum. Have I interpreted correctly?"

She sat.

"Thought so."

"You won't harm him, right?"

"Again, predictable. We're different after all."

He expected that by now, helicopters were thrumming on the flight deck. Two Sea Stallions would transport his team off the ship, with three Vipers flanking for protection. Even though his men were surprised, they followed his orders. No questions asked.

"Insley," Ox said, "grab the bottle of champagne and my duffle bag. We're getting the hell out of Dodge."

"We are, sir?"

Ox flashed him a look that hopefully made Red Top stain his briefs. Shat city.

"I meant…champagne and duffle bag, sir. Coming right up."

"You're leaving? Just like that?" she asked.

"What did Corporal Wyatt say to you? Oh yes: you're as smart as a whip. Ha! I liked that Marine; I really did. He was good with words. Too bad we were forced to give him a permanent death."

He snatched a rope from the narrow closet in his quarters. Wrapping the rope around the girl and chair-stiles, he tied the ends out of reach. He wasn't overly worried about her breaking free. For one thing, she was still handcuffed. And she only needed to be restrained long enough for him and his team to abandon ship.

"This is good-bye then," she said, sneering. "Or should I say: good riddance? I never want to see you again. Either one of you."

"Oh, did I give you the wrong impression?" Ox asked. "Did I make you think our time together was over? My bad."

The girl looked confused.

Good. Let her chew on that one.

He and Insley left captain's quarters, heading for the flight deck.

51

Friday, July 16, 2032
The White House Situation Room: Washington, D.C.

PRESIDENT NEWTON RARELY felt anxious. But when spiraling situations abruptly leveled off, she suspected the ensuing relief was premature. Like when retreating soldiers—bloodied and exhausted—marched into an emerald valley, only to hear birds chirping playful melodies in the outlying trees, as wind danced with the leaves and carried fragrances of summer. Had the threat been left behind? Or was the enemy deceptively planted over the crest of the next hill, waiting to finish what they'd started?

She took a deep breath and headed toward the West Wing, toward the Situation Room where she'd meet with Ruby and Clayton in less than a half-hour. Her heartrate accelerated. Her hands were clammy.

As she walked, she recalled the threads of intel she'd received. Secretary of Defense Henry Kilgore was first to break the "official" news. Unable to reach her on his first try, Eyes, the CO for SEAL Team 86, had contacted Henry next. The CO reported that Ox's team of sixty Marines and Sailors—*sixty* defectors, for God's sake—had evacuated the USS Simpson. Sure, they had assassinated defenders of the ship and commandeered five helicopters—all a significant blow. But look who was gained: Ruby Spencer. She was alive and safe, back on domestic soil with her husband. Sweet Mother of Jesus, what a dramatic about-face.

Hopefully the turn of events wasn't too good to be true.

Maybe their project was still viable.

A security detail had met the Spencers at Dulles International, transporting the couple to the White House. In fact, they had arrived on campus an hour ago and were receiving comprehensive physicals. As planned, blood had been drawn in separate rooms. The President didn't want Clayton to start noticing details. Like his vile, to her pint.

With Ruby safely home, perhaps the President could be regarded with favor by the SWC once again. But did she truly care?

Raising her watch, she commanded her DEPE Justine to connect with Emory. Seconds later, she eyed her device's screen, gazing at her indispensable genius: the savant she was getting close to, especially over the course of Ruby's kidnapping. Surprisingly, she found it easier and easier to lower her guard around him. For brief moments, she could shed the emotional armor of the President of the United States, able to be Ava Marie Newton of Tallahassee, Florida.

"I'm nervous," she admitted.

"Don't be. Simply tell them, like we've discussed."

"And you'll be on-hand in case I need you to smooth things over? If I irritate them?"

"Who, *you?*" He chuckled. "I said I'd be available. And I will."

"Okay, good. I'm just concerned she'll throw up barriers. Make our project so much harder to execute."

"Remember what I said: appeal to her altruism. Besides that, own what you say. Ruby will be more apt to trust you. And *trust*—perceived or real—is everything in this game."

"Got it. I'll videoface if I need you." She disconnected.

The President waited in the Situation Room.

At last, the door opened and Ruby and Clayton entered. Holy hell: the girl looked terrible. Her nose and cheeks were purple, although her bruises were darkening to brown as the blood aged. A cracked circle like a stone hitting glass was engraved on her forehead. And a brownish-bruise marked the crevice of her right elbow, extending from her forearm and to her bicep like a massive birthmark. Clayton had seen better days, too. He was thinner; his turquoise eyes dimmer. Red welts marked his skin. The couple had clearly been through hell.

Although hugging wasn't a greeting she enjoyed, she reached her arms toward the girl and embraced her. "My God, Ruby. It's a miracle you survived. I'm so relieved you're both back home. Safe."

Clayton approached her, with his right arm extended. As Ruby stepped back, the President clasped his hand for a shake.

"Madam President," he said. "Thank you for all your efforts to keep us safe. And for getting us home. We're exhausted and can't wait to reunite with our daughter."

"Please, take a seat," the President said, pointing to the chairs on her right. "I've reviewed your assignment-debriefing and I must admit, few would've lived to tell about it. I've said it before: both of you are fighters and I'm proud of you. The SWC and my administration are proud of you. Let's talk so I can get you to the Gonzalez's home, so you can see Gabriella and begin to recoup from this hellacious ordeal."

As the couple took their seats, the President fisted her hands, trying to expend the adrenaline that was coursing through her body, making her fingers tremble. Mercy's sake: what the hell was wrong with her?

"Do you know why," Ruby asked, "the technician extracted an entire pint of my blood? Clay only had a vile, which seems more reasonable."

Figures. The couple had obviously compared notes. Instead of rolling her eyes, the President maintained a poker face, knowing she had to answer quickly and with conviction, if she was to retain credibility.

"Emory wants to run a battery of tests on your blood. Our understanding—from your own accounting—is that you, Ruby, came in close contact with a zombie, even feared being scratched. Wasn't the close encounter on the sailboat in the Baltic Sea?"

"Yes, but an entire pint?"

"You know…Emory." She stammered, shaking her head and fearing she sounded dubious. "He wants to be…thorough, and with your blood's history of being…complex, I didn't argue. I leave science to the scientist."

"In terms of our accounting," Clayton said, sounding impatient. "We submitted an electronic report during our flight home. And as mentioned, you've reviewed the document. So if you don't mind, Ruby and I would like to ask *you* a few questions."

He was more aggressive than she remembered.

"Please don't hesitate," she answered. "Ask me anything."

"Quinton Oxford, Vladimir Volkov, and Decha Lin," he started, "claimed you and Em were working on a ZOM-B cure, using Ruby's blood. They admitted they kidnapped her to beat you at your own war game. How is it they were so convinced, when we knew nothing about a cure?"

"You named *criminals*. Anything they claim should be suspect. Right? For starters, Ruby's blood isn't capable of curing ZOM-B. No one's blood is. You both know that. Your captors' efforts and the kidnapping were erroneous—flawed."

"Were you working with my blood for *any* reason?" Ruby asked. "Because maybe that's why they assumed, albeit incorrectly, that Em was attempting to develop a cure."

She stopped breathing. This was the moment, the precipice, where she'd either plunge to her figurative death or remain king of the hill.

"We've been exploring a matter of tactical defense," the President admitted. "Merely investigating a possibility. But we are seeking your approval to continue. Obviously."

"Obviously," Clayton mimicked.

Her heat level spiked.

"Precisely what does this *possibility* entail?" Ruby pressed.

"Emory believes he can propagate a hybrid—using ZOM-B and your blood—which will allow an infected to survive in human form, sparing cognitive damage. And what's even more remarkable," she continued, hoping her smile emoted confidence, "is the infected might be able to walk among the undead...undetected. In theory, of course."

Clayton pounded the table. "Of. Course."

"You're aware that ZOM-B is already a hybrid, right?" the girl asked. "Look at the devastation *that* fluke-of-nature is causing. And now you want to play God with my blood?"

"What are we to do, then?" the President snapped. "Nuke the entire planet? Or stand back and let the freak-bacteria destroy our world? Not much altruism in that! No, I choose to fight for a future, for humankind! I thought you'd choose the same. So unless you have a better idea, engineering a hybrid—one that saves lives and gives us a fighting chance—is the best solution we've got."

"And how do you propose to *test* this theory?" she asked. "Irreparable damage occurs to the infected's brain eight-hours after contraction. So the hybrid would be useless on most zombies."

The President let her eyes drift downward, hoping to convey the difficulty of what she was about to say, though the words wouldn't pain her. Not one bit. "Test subjects may be required, but I let Emory handle those particulars. Focus on the big picture, Ruby. The world can be saved!"

The girl narrowed her eyes. "Who gives *you* the right to use humans as test subjects? That's what my captors were doing—the criminals, as you called them. They were infecting people and autopsying their brains at different intervals, without hesitation. No, I won't agree to it. Every life has value. We'll have to fight for the future in another way."

"Does the SWC know about your plan?" Clayton asked. "And do they support it?"

"Yes. They are aware and hope you will give your blessing."

"How long has this project been in the works?" Ruby asked.

"Not very long. We didn't want to float the idea unless Emory felt confident a hybrid was achievable. And now, after his research, he finally believes that one can, indeed, be propagated."

"This is despicable," the girl said, scowling.

"Pardon me?"

"Our trust has been broken, Madam President. The Council masterminded this project which you all hid from us? Even more abhorrent, Em's been working with my blood...*my* blood, but we've been kept in the dark? For God's sake: we were kidnapped. Clay, tortured. And we had no clue *why*. But now...now we understand the reasons you went to such lengths to rescue us!"

Tensions were nearing combustion. Her temples throbbed.

"You also chipped us without consent," Clayton yapped, as if the comment had any relevance, whatsoever. He sounded like a yipping mutt.

Her face flushed. Mood shifted. She was the President of the United States and these peons were chastising *her*?

"Chipping is standard protocol for overseas operatives," she snapped. "Besides, the GPS chips saved your lives, so gratitude would be more appropriate."

Ruby stood. Her husband followed her lead.

"Here's a more *appropriate* response," she said. "I want my blood back. The pint you stole from me an hour ago? I want it back. *Now.*"

Oh dear God.

52

Friday, July 16, 2032
The White House Situation Room: Washington, D.C.

RUBY WAS STEAM-OUT-OF-EARS fuming. But President Newton convinced her and Clay to let Em join them in the Situation Room, touting he'd be able to resolve the misunderstanding. Even though Em had been her college best-friend and a confidant thereafter, she doubted he could resolve anything. Expectations were a lot higher for him, and he was vaulting way below the bar. At least the President confirmed that he'd bring her pint of blood with him. That was something worth waiting for.

The door opened and Em, dressed in his usual crisp lab-attire, sauntered up to the table: calm, cool, and collected. And smiling. No cares in the world.

"There's my girl!" he said, placing the blood bag on the tabletop in front of her. He extended his arms for a hug.

She remained seated, elbows on the table.

Undoubtedly recognizing her cold-shoulder treatment, he said nothing more. Not to her or Clay. Walking around the table, he pulled out a chair on the left side of the President and sat.

"Listen," Em said. "I can see you're both angry and I get it. But maybe I can help you understand the project and more importantly, explain *why* we were secretive."

Wiping moisture from her eyes, she glared at him. Hurt. How could a best friend keep a secret, especially one involving *her*? His actions, no less, had launched her and Clay into peril. Em knew...he knew that as new parents, Gabby was the only one who mattered. The job and "the project" were secondary. Yet he'd chosen silence. Chosen to withhold the truth. Chosen to betray them.

Gabby was almost orphaned because of it.

"Start talking," Clay said. "We've got our daughter to see. Who happens to be *your* Godchild."

"Right." Em clasped his hands together, resting them on the table. "I'll start at the beginning." He cleared his throat. "Prior to Gabby's birth, you both missed Council meetings, which is understandable. But at one meeting, we read a FIN report that projected the number of infected over time. And Ruby, projections are devastating. You know how you and Clay want to give Gabby—*my* precious Godchild—a normal life? Well, unless we find a way to stop the mutation from spreading, human life is nothing more than a fantasy.

"Three months from now," he continued, "ten-percent of the remaining American population—those who survived the F8 and RED attacks—will be infected with ZOM-B. Six months from now? Fifty percent, or one-hundred-thousand Americans. Similar statistics are projected for other countries. And stats exponentially worsen from there. The future is nonexistent.

"We decided back in February to withhold the report from you," he admitted. "The decision was wrong. But the intentions were good. New life, healthy life is vital to our survival as a species. And stressing you out wouldn't have altered the report, though it might have affected the baby's wellbeing."

"With an Extinction Level Infection, I was already stressed out, in case you hadn't noticed," she snapped. "Regardless, I never asked you to determine what I *can* and *cannot* handle. You've crossed the line on our friendship. You have no right, no right at all making decisions for me or Clay."

"I think we've acknowledged that our actions—*my* actions as a friend, Godfather, and professional—crossed several lines." He locked eyes with the President. "You've expressed the same, right?"

"If I didn't, I'm admitting it now. We were wrong."

"Until you hear the entire story though, we don't have a chance to earn your forgiveness," Em continued, seeming earnest, but clearly asking her to listen. "Can we agree on that?"

"Fine."

"The SWC is committed to aggressively tackling this crisis," he said, "and someone mentioned your blood. Luther Pennington, I think. I explained your blood had no effect on ZOM-B, that I'd already conducted an analysis…with your approval, remember?"

She nodded.

"The Council urged me to take another look, to see if your blood had any defensive value as far as the new pathogen was concerned. After all, ZOM-B mutated from F8 and your blood and immune system had a lifesaving response to F8. Made sense that I should turn over every stone. So I accommodated their request, using a leftover blood-supply preserved during our development of the F8 cure."

"Why didn't you tell us at that point?" she asked. "I would've encouraged it."

"Think of knitting. If you undo one stitch, the entire row can unravel. So we all agreed to wait until my analysis was complete, until I was sure about your blood, one way or another. Results affirmed your blood cannot *cure* ZOM-B. However, right before you left for Taiwan, I experimented beyond the findings and discovered that I might be able to propagate a hybrid, using your blood and the mutated bacteria. And that the hybrid, injected into an infected early on, might preserve brain functions and sustain human life. Not a cure, but close. My conjecture, however, was still just a hunch. Why ruin your assignment and honeymoon with a supposition?"

"Humankind is on the brink of extinction and you worried about our honeymoon?"

"Em's overstating the honeymoon part," said the President. "Your mission was vital. We needed to get an expert microbiologist to review the analytics collected by my scientists at the Keelung Naval Base. Regretfully, unforeseen circumstances prevented you from reviewing their work."

"Overstated or not," Em chided, raising his eyebrows at the President, "waiting to brief you after your return was logical. I needed to spend the week advancing my lab work to determine if a hybrid *could* be engineered. My work progressed until your blood unexpectedly ran out."

"But then your safe return became compromised," the President said, as if grabbing the baton at a rehearsed moment. "Compromised by the storm and the Code Red at the base."

"No one," Em said, "had any intel that you were at risk for kidnapping. The President assures me of this."

"Ox was already being investigated," Ruby countered. "I'd call that risk."

"Yes," the President admitted, "but we had no idea what the bastard was up to. We didn't know Huo had partners and that Ox was one of them. And I had warned you from the start to avoid him." She shook her head and pursed her lips, seeming like she might tear up. "I was sick, just sick when I learned you had been kidnapped. And I did everything to get you both back home. Everything."

"Why send us on the assignment in the first place?" her husband asked. "Especially if my wife's blood held such potential? I'm not getting that at all."

The President glanced at Em, before looking back at Clay. "The island is—or should I say *was*—the safest place on the planet. Even so, I made special arrangements to ensure your safety, like acquiring handgun permits for your visit, hiring a driver to take you to Shifen, and asking the consulate to keep a watchful eye on you. Back here, Emory anticipated he had enough of your blood, over the course of your assignment, to determine if he could propagate a hybrid. Our actions seemed reasonable, with your safety in mind." She rubbed her hand on the table. "And on a personal level, I hoped the trip might reinvigorate your interest in the Council." The President looked at her. "I worried that we were losing your interest. That you were about to resign. And regardless of whether your blood could be used for a hybrid, we *need* you on this Council. You are a top pandemic expert in the world, and we're facing an ELI."

Had her intent to resign been so obvious?

"Why wasn't the Council in agreement, then?" Ruby asked. "Many resisted us, *me* going."

"True," the President said. "If it were up to them, they might place you in a padded room and supply you with nutrients even before Em confirmed that a hybrid could be engineered! With no disrespect intended toward the Council, Em and I place so much more value on your professional work. You are scientists."

Ruby's body temperature was lowering to a simmer, but she still wasn't convinced that she and Clay should trust them. Lies rarely stood alone. In fact, lies—which included information deceptively withheld, usually kept plenty of company.

Thinking of *company,* she noticed the strange new bond between Em and the POTUS. At times, it seemed like he was in control.

"What's the status of this hybrid?" she asked Em. "I take it you withdrew a pint of my blood, without my consent, to further hybrid development."

He nodded. "That's correct. I'm extremely close to confirming a hybrid can be engineered. And if you'll allow me to use more of your blood, then as early as tomorrow, we'll be ready for a live trial."

"By live trial…do you mean using a *human* test-subject? Someone you'd intentionally infect with ZOM-B before injecting them with the hybrid?"

"Yes."

"Like I said to President Newton, we'll never agree to human trials. Not ever."

"Ruby: do you hear yourself?" Em challenged, slapping the tabletop. Turning from amenable to caustic. "You're saying you wouldn't risk the lives of three people—two death-row convicts and a homeless man—to save humankind? To save your daughter? Get it through your head! In one year, the planet won't be populated with humans. None. According to FIN, WHO, and the CDC? There'll be zero humans walking the Earth."

"And who gave *you* the right to play God?" she asked, soured by his arrogance. "Every action has an equal and opposite reaction. Every step leaves an imprint. You have no idea, for example, what effect the hybrid will have on gestation. We want humankind to survive and proliferate, don't we?"

"Of course, but the countdown on humankind is ticking away. We're running out of time. It's do, die, or turn, girlfriend."

She shook her head. "We have to find another way. I don't support dark science. Besides, you cannot manipulate humans, take them against their will, and use them as test-subjects. Or alter humankind without understanding the ramifications. No, I will never agree to this project. I forbid you to use my blood for this hybrid.

Forbid it!"

The air thickened in the room. So heavy no one breathed. She waited for Em's reaction. For the President's. Would they turn into her captors? Drain her blood anyway?

Clay placed his hand on her back. His touch meant he was with her. That he would support and defend her.

"Okay," Em whispered. "But I hope you don't blame us for trying. Hope you won't hold a grudge."

"Okay? Just like that?"

"What?" His eyes darted, looking defensive. "Now you're going to argue with me that I'm agreeing to drop the project...too quickly? What's going on? Has your level of trust in me sunk that low? That no matter what I say, it's suspect?"

"You withheld important information from me. From Clay."

"I did. But I also explained why. And I admitted, flat-out, that the President and I wanted your approval to finalize the project. We asked; you said no. We accept your answer."

"Sounds so harmless. Except we almost died because others knew something about your work. And we knew...nothing. This kind of breach in trust can't be easily repaired, Em."

Her longtime friend reached his hand across the table, inviting her to do the same. To meet him halfway.

"Just tell me," she said, keeping her hands clasped in front of her.

"This is *me* sitting across from you. The guy who studied with you at JHU, day and night. Your lab partner. Your college confidant. The guy who's been there for every milestone. Every scare. You *know* me, girlfriend."

Tears welled in her eyes.

"Please. Look at me," he said softly.

She did.

"I've always been on your side. And by your side." He wiped a tear from his cheek. "I screwed up here, but I believed—wrongly, that my intentions were bigger than you and me. I'm sorry. I recognize my mistake. Please forgive me."

"Maybe in time," she answered. "But not now." She wiped her cheeks dry. "So what's next then?"

"We have another option," Em said. "It'll take longer to develop than the hybrid, but holds promise nevertheless."

"What is it?" Clay asked.

"Think heat-seeking missiles. We're collaborating with NASA and the NRA on ammo that automatically targets brain activity in the frontal cortex. Fire a round—you don't even have to worry about accuracy, and the bullet finds the skull, permanently killing the zombie." He regained the twinkle in his eyes, the look he always got when innovating. "Picture this: you're faced with a horde of zombies and you fire an automatic—a machine gun. Rounds are released. And each zombie is destroyed before you can blink."

"What stops the rounds from striking the same zombie?"

"Technology, bro! The rounds are packed with networking capability to input data from the targets, share the info between bullets, and coordinate strikes. Artificial intelligence, ammo-style!"

"And the good guys?" Ruby asked. "What prevents the rounds from targeting them?"

"Good question," the President said. "The good guys—the shooters—will be wearing protective helmets so the weaponry can't detect their brain activity. Prototypes are being developed, though like Emory said, completion will take a while."

"Sounds promising." She glanced at her smartwatch for the time. "It's getting late and Clay and I want to see our daughter. Thank you both for accepting our refusal." Reaching for her husband's hand, she wrapped her fingers around his. Together, they stood.

"Anything else before we leave?" Clay asked.

"Actually, there is." The President sounded serious. "We have intel that Ox has returned to the States, to Maryland in fact."

"What? Why?" Ruby asked, feeling panic claw at her throat. "Does he still think my blood can be used for a cure?"

"We're not sure," she answered. "We're doing everything in our power to apprehend him. To put the traitor behind bars. With your permission, I'd like to deploy a security detail to surround the Gonzalez residence, as a precaution. That's where you're going, right? Where Gabriella is?"

"Yes, but we plan to pick her up and head home."

"Can I persuade you to stay overnight at the Gonzalez's? We've surveilled both premises. Since the Gonzalez residence is more isolated—located alongside the water, protecting their property and house will be easier, more effective, and less intrusive to the community. Is this acceptable?"

Ruby looked at her husband to confirm agreement. He nodded.

"Yes," she said to the President. "I'm sure Margo and Tomas will agree to let us stay the night. And we appreciate the protection. After the flight, we're going to crash hard. And knowing Gabby will be safe is a Godsend."

53

Friday, July 16, 2032
The Gonzalez Residence: Annapolis, Maryland

MARGO GONZALEZ WAS ecstatic that Ruby and Clay were finally safe, back in the States, and heading to their house to reunite with their baby. When Ruby asked if they could spend the night and bring a security team with them, Margo didn't hesitate. Anyway, the sun was dropping and casting its orangish glow over Whitehall Creek. Before long, the moon and fireflies would replace the sun and usher in Gabby's bedtime. Staying overnight at their house would cause the least disruption to the baby's schedule. Besides, her friends had to be exhausted. To boot, electricity was shut down every night at ten o'clock. By the time they arrived and collected Gabby's things, it would be close to nine. Why risk traveling and unpacking after the electricity grid had been switched off?

She and Tomas sat in rocking chairs on the rear stone-deck by the pool, overlooking the waterway. Gabby, dressed in a one-piece sleep-and-play made of white cotton and adorned with pink hearts, was cradled in her arms. An isolated thunderstorm rumbled in the distance as it headed toward the Chesapeake Bay. The day had been humid, but the storm left dryer, cooler air in its wake. Tonight, sleeping with the windows open would be welcomed. A pleasant contrast to the humidity which had plagued them most of the summer. A refreshing breeze would be like an icy smoothie after a sauna.

"Your Mommy and Daddy are coming home, Gabby!" she cooed,

causing the baby to smile. "I know you've missed them. We all have."

Sweet Lollipop, the Spencer's orange-and-white bird-dog, approached Tomas's rocker, tail wagging as leg feathers fluttered with the breeze. "Yes, Lollie," he said, "they're coming for you, too."

"I saw Ruby's facial injuries when we videofaced," she said, rocking the baby. "She's pretty banged up. Some honeymoon. Turned out to be the assignment from hell." She gazed at Gabby. "I'm sorry, sweetie. I need to watch my tongue. Anyway, I'm glad Ruby's getting out of the SWC. It's too dangerous and she's a mother now. Gabby needs her Mommy."

"Yeah, both need to get out," Tomas said. "When I pressed Clay, he admitted he was waterboarded to the point of death. Ruby brought him back to life! Don't think I could've survived. Gabby doesn't know how lucky she is that her parents are alive."

"Awful what they went through." She kissed the baby's forehead, realizing how much she was going to miss having the baby around, twenty-four seven. Gabby reminded her of both her friends. While having wisps of black hair and olive skin like her Daddy, the baby's eyes were starting to look green like Ruby's. And she was the happiest baby ever. Of course as her Godmother, Margo was a tad biased. "Any ideas what the security detail might involve?"

"Probably a few more policemen patrolling the property. Maybe from Capitol Police, like the deputy who's been watching our house."

"Does it make sense they'd pick our place to patrol over Ruby and Clay's? Their house is bigger, but ours sits on nine acres. They have less than half that."

"I guess it makes sense," he said. "I mean, they live in a neighborhood and neighbors won't appreciate armed policemen lurking in the bushes. Neighbors ask questions. Here, law enforcement will go unnoticed."

"Should we be concerned?"

"No. With a dog, four adults, a couple of firearms, and armed law enforcement, we've got nothing to worry about."

"Still, I wish we had electricity at night so we could activate our alarm system." The doorbell rang. "Here," she said, handing Tomas the baby. "It can't be Ruby and Clay; they're a half-hour away. Has to be security."

She walked inside the house toward the front door. Tomas, with the baby in his arms, followed. Lollie trotted beside them, barking.

"Sit and stay," she said, as she opened the door. Lollie obeyed.

"Ma'am, I'm Corporal Ross. Pleasure to meet you." He was dressed in military fatigues, not a police uniform. Extending his right hand, he shook hers, then Tomas's. "May I come in to discuss security?"

A truck was in the driveway. A camo canopy covered the extended trailer, located behind the engine and cabin, like the kind of truck which transported troops in the field.

"Please, come in." She moved to the side of the opened door.

"Let's talk in the library," Tomas suggested, turning toward the back of the house, with Lollie following.

As they walked, she had to know. "Are you a Marine?"

"Yes. MARSOC, Ma'am."

"MARSOC?"

"Marine Corps Forces, Special Operations Command. MARSOC represents Federal Internal Defense, specifically skilled in counter-insurgency."

"Wow," her husband said. "Sounds serious. How many Marines have you brought?" Tomas pointed to the couch in Margo's favorite room, inviting the Corporal to sit. Except for the fireplace and a large window, the library was appointed with shelves and books on every wall, from floor to ceiling. Could never have too many books.

"Fifteen are on this mission, but no worries, Mr. Gonzalez. We are simply taking an abundance of precaution. Quinton Oxford is no amateur. But rest assured, he will not penetrate this safe zone. I can promise you that."

A helicopter thrummed overhead. Lollie barked and the baby flinched. Margo raised her eyebrows at the Marine, hoping he'd interpret her question.

"Throughout the night, you'll hear some Vipers—helicopters—performing recon over your property. We may even use spotlights. Please don't be alarmed."

"How long will you be here?" she asked, starting to feel uneasy, like this was a bigger deal than she'd anticipated.

"Definitely throughout the night. Our other units should

apprehend Quinton Oxford before morning. But we'll keep you updated so you know what's going on."

"About our windows," she said. "With electricity shut down at the night, we usually leave them open. Is that a problem?"

He tilted his head forward and delivered a half-smile. "Ma'am, MARSOC is protecting your home. You're the safest you've ever been on this property. On Earth, for that matter." He stood. "Now, please show me where everyone will be sleeping. If we need to enter your home tonight, it'll be pitch black. We'll need to know where everyone is."

Tomas handed her the baby and led the way to the guest suite on the first floor. Guest quarters were on the left side of the house and included French doors that opened to the pool and deck areas. She waited in the hallway as her husband showed the Marine where Ruby and Clay would be sleeping. Adjacent to the room, with access from the hallway, was the nursery. The room was actually Margo's office, but she and Tomas had installed a crib and changing table after they had agreed to take care of Gabby during her parents' Taiwan assignment. Besides, they had plans to start a family of their own.

Their master suite was next on the house tour so they headed upstairs, leading the way.

"Any firearms in this home?" the Marine asked, standing in their bedroom.

"Why?" she asked. Quite frankly, it was none of the Corporal's business. *Some* backup protection should be allowed. They had rights.

"Again, if we need to enter your home and you're frightened or disoriented, we don't want you to take out the good guys. Simply precautionary. Promise we'll give them back." He smiled.

"We have one handgun in the nightstand," Tomas said, walking to the small table and pulling open the drawer. He made sure the safety was on before handing the forty-five to the Marine. She noted her husband did not mention the shotgun in the closet.

"Where is the dog sleeping?" he asked. "With you? Up here?"

"No, Lollie will be downstairs with the Spencers," she answered.

"Nice dog." He reached into his pocket and retrieved a treat, feeding it to Lollie.

"Do Marines always carry dog treats?" she asked, eyebrows raised.

"No, Ma'am. But on a mission, we attend to every detail. We knew a canine would be on the premises and it's important that the dog (Lollie, right?) doesn't consider us a threat." He patted Lollie's head, and she wagged her tail. He reinforced with another treat.

"Thorough," she said.

"Yes, Ma'am. We're that and more."

They walked down the stairs and to the front door.

"ETA for the Spencers is momentary," Corporal Ross said, as he opened the front door. "Come nightfall, we'll be positioned throughout your property, so best to stay indoors. You won't be able to see us, but with night vision, we'll be able to see you."

"Sounds good," Tomas said. "Thank you."

As Corporal Ross walked outside, the truck was no longer in the driveway. But a Marine in camo was positioned high in a tree, like a perched hawk. Undoubtedly a sniper.

"Your cooperation is most appreciated," the Marine said, as he glanced over his shoulder at them. "Semper Fi."

54

Friday to Saturday, July 16-17, 2032
The Gonzalez Residence: Annapolis, Maryland

IN THEIR HASTE to reach the Gonzalez's, Ruby realized midway to the house that she and Clay had forgotten to take the blood-bag with them. Both agreed that if Em had returned her blood once, he'd return it again. Rebuilding trust had to start somewhere. Besides, they had someone more important on their minds.

When they arrived at Margo and Tomas's, the reunion was hugs and tears. Elation beyond words.

Now, standing in the kitchen holding her baby, Ruby's eyes were glued on one little person: Gabriella Emily Spencer. She stared at her daughter who was beautiful and precious. Adorable. The adjectives couldn't keep pace. And her baby smelled wonderful—like cotton and flowers and sweet milk. A unique smell that was engrained in her memory, like a seal able to find its pup by scent alone.

When Ruby was kidnapped and struggling, thoughts of Gabby and Clay had pulled her through. Made her fight for survival. Their bond was powerful, like nothing she'd ever felt.

Clay wrapped his arms around her, as she held the baby. "My family," he said, sounding equally overwhelmed. "The two of you kept me going. I love you both so much. And Lollie, too."

Ruby nestled her forehead in the crook of her husband's neck, feeling the security of his arms. "I was thinking the same. You are both my rocks, my anchors." She started crying. "We're done with assignments from the SWC! We're staying home, together. A family."

Margo and Tomas joined the group-hug, adding tears to the soggy downpour.

After their embrace, Tomas popped the cork on a bottle of Krug Clos d'Ambonnay and poured the champagne into crystal flutes.

"You're bringing out the good stuff, amigo!" Clay raised his flute, smitten with admiration as the bubbles raced to the surface before popping.

"It's always bugged me," Tomas admitted, "that people purchase exquisite champagne and wine, never to open them. Why buy them? Just to say you did? Absurd! We purchase to enjoy with those whom we love." He raised his glass. "May I make a toast?"

"Please," she said, kissing her daughter on the cheek.

"To lifelong friends and a remarkable couple—shining beacons, showing one another the path home. Warming each other's hearts. Serving as anchors during a storm. And teaching each other the power of forever." He raised the flute higher. "To one and all. Yamas, friends!"

"Yamas!" she said, in concert with everyone.

As they sipped, they chatted about the security.

"So windows *can* be opened tonight?" Ruby asked. "Even with an increased risk?"

"Yes," Margo answered. "What did he say, Tomas? *You're the safest you've ever been on this property. On Earth, for that matter!*"

"Arrogant, right?" Tomas took a sip and smiled. "But guess that's better than wimpy Marines patrolling our property—which I guess is counterintuitive. Do wimpy Marines even exist? I don't think so."

"Tonight's breeze will feel like a ceiling fan, or even AC, so I'm thankful the windows can be left open," Margo added, obviously ignoring her husband's banter. "I can't wait until electricity restrictions are lifted."

Ruby caressed her daughter's tiny hand, enamored by the perfection of each finger. "I was thinking of bringing Gabby into bed with us."

"Are you sure? Why not recoup from jetlag?" Margo picked up the small video-monitor on the kitchen counter. "I also have a monitor in our bedroom."

"In practically *every* room!" Tomas piped in.

"Does the monitor still work without electricity?" Ruby asked.

"Sure. We leave units plugged in during the day to recharge the batteries. And when the electricity shuts off, the main monitor in the nursery automatically switches to camping/outdoor mode." She raised the video monitor as if it were proof-positive that she found the device reliable. "Why not give yourselves a night of deep slumber? You both need it. Let the baby sleep in the nursery."

Ruby looked at Clay. "She's right. We're dead tired." Left unspoken, it occurred to her that she might lose awareness of where the baby was in the bed, if she slept soundly enough. Catching up on sleep was a wiser idea. And it eased her mind that MARSOC was protecting them. "But let us have a monitor, too. We need to get back in the saddle again."

"Agreed," Clay said. "And thank you both so much for looking after our Gabby, with such love and nurture. You and Tomas are a Godsend. We owe you big."

"Remember that on the golf course, my friend!" Tomas said, laughing, collecting the empty flutes and placing them in the sink.

"We'd better head to bed," Margo said. "The lights go off in fifteen minutes."

Ruby and Clay took Gabby to her crib, laying her on her back. Her husband gently twirled the animal mobile, sending the horse, pig, duck, cow, and sheep around and around. If animal populations didn't recover soon from the devastation caused by the F8 bioweapon, their daughter might never know them as common farm animals.

"She's the most precious child…ever," she said.

"Our greatest accomplishment."

"Thank God she's safe, and we're home."

"Amen to that."

She opened the window. Cool breeze, smelling of salt water and sea grasses, accepted the invitation to enter through the screen. Crickets chirped in the distance. They each kissed their daughter. Before leaving the nursery, Ruby checked the monitor. The device's switch was "on."

In the guest suite, Clay raised the largest window. After she changed into her nightgown and he stripped into his snug boxers, they climbed into bed. Electricity blinked off at ten o'clock. She reached toward the night table to adjust the baby monitor's orientation, wanting to see the live-streaming footage from the bed.

The device worked. The baby was already asleep.

Turning to Clay, she settled next to his body, laying her head on his chest. With his arm wrapped around her, she fell asleep quickly. But although she had hoped deep-sleep would consume her, her rest was intermittent. Lollie was restless. The dog whined several times throughout the night, waking her for brief moments at a time. No doubt Lollie was unsettled because of the Marines positioned on the property. Occasionally, Ruby glanced at the monitor. At least Gabby continued to rest peacefully.

Sometime after two-in-the-morning, Ruby must have drifted into a dark void in time—a dreamless sleep. Too quickly, morning greeted them with sunshine, streaming through their window and French doors.

Ruby hoped Ox had been captured during the night, so they could put the nightmare behind them.

She was especially excited to return home and begin her life as a fulltime mother. She leapt from bed, tossing the discarded sheets onto her husband. Electricity was already on and she smelled the aroma of coffee wafting into their bedroom. Racing from their suite, she ran into the hallway and flung open the door to the nursery.

The curtains luffed with the breeze. But the crib was empty.

Her heart sputtered.

Margo. Margo had likely heard the baby and gotten her early, to let them sleep. That had to be it.

As she left the nursery for the kitchen, Clay entered the hallway, running his fingers through his disheveled hair. Did he detect her worry? Her building panic?

Unable to speak, she flew toward the kitchen, anxious to see her daughter.

"Good Morning, sleepyheads!" Margo cheered, pouring a cup of coffee by the kitchen island. "Did you move Gabby in with you after all? Is she still asleep?"

"What?" Time slowed. Ruby's brain began to misfire. She looked at Clay, panic starting to drown her. "No. And the baby's not in her crib," she gasped, turning to Margo. "She's with you, right?"

"What are you saying?" Margo looked confused. "We let you all sleep in. Tomas is upstairs showering."

Light-headed, Ruby fell to her knees. Her chest and throat tightened. She couldn't breathe.

Clay raced back to the nursery.

"What is it, Ruby?" Margo cried. "What's happening?"

Clay, ghostly white, returned to the kitchen carrying the monitor from the nursery.

The device had been turned off.

Gabby was gone.

55

Saturday, July 17, 2032
The Gonzalez Residence: Annapolis, Maryland

RUBY RACED OUTSIDE in her nightgown. Across the driveway was a Marine, dropped from a tree like a piñata, twisted and broken on the pavers. Lying in a pool of blood. She raced to him as though he might be alive, might be able to explain what had happened. The Marine, wearing a protective helmet and vest, had been shot in the neck, below his Adam's apple.

He was beyond speaking, or breathing, ever again.

Detecting movement in her peripheral vision, she turned to see Clay jogging toward her, winded. "I counted six dead, including Corporal Ross. No sign of Gabby. Which means nine Marines are missing. *They*—no doubt connected to Ox—must have kidnapped Gabby. Margo and Tomas are searching the house, just...just to make sure. We've got to call the President right away. We have to get our daughter back before it's too late."

She needed help getting back to the house. Her legs were shaking. Weak. A darkness overtook her like she was being sucked away from the present, from the now. Sucked into limbo, between life and death. A dark place where time ceased to move forward.

Clutching her husband's arm, she entered the house. Margo and Tomas stood in the foyer.

"I'm so sorry," Margo cried. "We couldn't find her in the house. She's gone. What should we do?"

Ruby dropped to her knees again, lost in a deepening sea of

despair. Her whole reason for existence had been stolen from her. And she had no idea if her baby was hurt, or killed, or crying for her Mommy. Sobs started in the depths of her core and spasmed in her body, forcing their way to the surface, like demons expelled during an exorcism.

"Please take her to our room," Clay said, sounding as though he was a thousand miles away. "I've got to call the President."

Margo lifted her from the floor, placing an arm around her waist for support. Ruby was unable to think, to process. Her body was living—her lungs expanded and contracted, her heart beat, eyes blinked—but her soul was stalled. If she could only turn back time, Gabby would've slept with them. Would've been wrapped in her arms. Secure. Safe. Protected.

"Here we are," Margo said, arriving at the bed in the guest suite. "Lie down and rest for a minute. I'll stay right here, by your side."

As Ruby was being helped into bed, she clutched her girlfriend's bathrobe. "I can't survive without Gabby. We've got to find her."

"I know. And we will. Just hang in there."

Margo sat on the bedside and smoothed Ruby's hair, as she whispered support. Ruby could say nothing. Think nothing. Feel nothing. She *was* nothing.

Clay finally returned to the room. "President Newton is deploying two SEAL squads. No Marines this time. Ox clearly has moles in that branch. And she ordered us to stay put. Not to leave. Help is on the way. SEALs should arrive in less than two hours."

"Two *hours?*" Margo asked. "That's a long time. I mean, what's their plan? They have one, right?"

Ruby's eyes were open but couldn't focus. Her ears listened, but she was on another plane of consciousness.

"One SEAL squad will come here. The other will head to the Annapolis City Docks," Clay answered. "Suspicious activity was reported at the Harbormaster's office and President Newton believes, based on intel received minutes ago, that Ox might be there. That maybe he kidnapped Gabby as a bargaining chip to get Ruby back. For her blood."

"But he already *had* her captive on the Naval ship," Margo said. "This doesn't make sense."

In her fog, Ruby saw her husband shake his head. "I don't get it either," he said. "I don't know why this is happening. Or how to start fighting for our daughter."

A muffled ring sounded from Ruby's purse.

Her brain clicked on, her heart jolted into overdrive. She sat up in bed. "My smartwatch. It's in my purse. Quick. Please give it to me. Hurry. Before the call's missed."

Clay grabbed her purse with shaking hands. Fumbling through the interior pockets, he located her watch and handed it to her.

She accepted the videoface request from an unknown caller, holding the screen in front of her face. Her heart pounded.

"Damn good morning to you, Ruby Never-Dies," Ox bellowed. "It promises to be a fine day in Annapolis. Sunny-side-up."

"Give me back my daughter. Now."

"So much attitude for someone who should be begging."

"Tell me what you want." She glanced at Clay who had sat down on the bed, hoping he'd catch details if Ox named an unknown address.

"Is that Mr. Pretty Face you're looking at? Tell him Gabby looks just like him, except for the eyes. They're all you."

"You want something in exchange for my daughter. Tell me."

"Okay, okay. Let's do this. It's still *you* I want."

"You had me. You let me go."

"I did, didn't I? Because I came to realize everything was premature. But now...now the timing is on-target. The mission is failproof. And I almost have everything I want. *You* will be the icing on the cake."

"Where do you want me to go? Where can I find you?"

"Come to the end of the docks, on Dock Street. I have a yacht in the last slip on the right. Obviously, I'm heavily protected. You have forty-five minutes. And do not bring Mr. Pretty Face or anyone else, for that matter. If you do, Gabriella will be tossed overboard with weights. Not a pretty picture for such a sweet tyke. With tiny lungs, I fear you wouldn't be able to revive her, like you did your husband. Am I clear?"

"Crystal." She tightened the grip on her watch, feeling the rage building, feeling like she might crush the device into dust.

"For fuck's sake, get here fast…and alone. These weights are heavy." He disconnected.

"We've got to call the President," Clay said. "To let her know."

"No. I'm going. And you're coming with me."

"But you heard him say…"

"I have an idea, and you're going to have to trust my instincts."

Several minutes after throwing on clothes, she and Clay fled out the kitchen's side door toward their vehicle.

Her husband drove on Sharps Point Road, heading to Route 179 South, toward the Severn River.

And beyond that, to the docks.

56

Saturday, July 17, 2032
The City Docks on Spa Creek: Annapolis, Maryland

WATCHING THROUGH BINOCULARS from the first-floor deck of the *Lady Sarah,* Ox followed the couple as they walked past the Harbormaster's office building toward him, toward the last slip. Never mind the Harbormaster was slumped over his desk, face down in a pool of blood, resting on paperwork that would never be signed.

Ox's team had sanitized the dock area, even the restaurants across the canal. Most people were removed; the uncooperative, killed. The mouth of the creek was patrolled as well, right under the nose of the Naval Academy. Whatever happened to "expect the unexpected?"

His operatives had informed him when the couple parked their car on Main Street, where the road intersected with the beginning of the city docks. From the roof of the Harbormaster's office building, a Marine radioed him, announcing the targets were visible, with an ETA of thirty seconds.

Targets—plural. In what universe did Ruby fucking Never-Dies think he'd spare Mr. Pretty Face, after he had ordered the bitch to come *alone?* Too bad she'd have to watch her husband drop.

On Ox's verbal order—which left nothing for the kid to interpret on his own, Insley leaned over the transom of the sixty-five-foot engine-powered catamaran and sighted his M27 Infantry Automatic Rifle (IAR) between Clay Spencer's eyebrows, set on single shot to ensure the girl was spared.

"Wait for my go-ahead," Ox said. "I want to see her squirm first."

The couple stopped on the decking in front of his slip. But before he could savor the moment, the girl whipped out a knife—touting a nine-inch blade—from under her shirt and pressed the tip against her carotid artery, on the right side of her neck. The blade glistened in the sun. Her husband gasped, like he was clueless she was going to pull the bonehead stunt.

"I want to negotiate," she said. "But if you kill my husband or my daughter, or hurt them in any way, I'll slice my throat. Here and now. You know I'll do it. And all my precious blood will spurt onto the dock and into the water. Lost forever."

"What the hell are you doing?" Clay asked, turning to his wife.

"Don't," she snapped, continuing to glare straight ahead at the *Lady Sarah*, at him and Insley. "What do you want to do, Ox? *Hmm?*"

"Such drama," he answered, rolling his eyes. "I'm all ears. But hurry. My patience for insubordination is running out. Like when a baby won't stop crying…"

Insley continued to aim the rifle at Mr. Pretty Face.

"If you hand over Gabby to Clay," she said, "and let them leave, unharmed, then I won't fight you. You can use my blood how you want. Put me in a coma. Drain me, for all I care. Build a freak army. Whatever you want, you can do it without resistance."

"Stop this, Ruby!" her husband pleaded. "This is your *plan?* The one I'm supposed to trust you with?" He reached for her arm.

She stepped away and pressed the blade harder against her throat.

"Wait! Talk to me," he begged his wife. "What's going on?"

"This should be interesting," Ox said, smiling. The drama was intriguing, so he'd let it play out a while longer. Maybe he'd slap her. On second thought, she wore the pants.

"I figured it out, Clay," she said, continuing to step back. "I figured out why I've always been a survivor, while others around me have perished. It was for *this* moment."

"I not following you, babe. You have to stop this."

The guy's hands were shaking; the color drained from his face.

"It's my turn to sacrifice. A *real* act of bravery, this time," she said.

"You're scaring me. Stop it. You're the bravest person I know! And you've already sacrificed. Already saved the world once."

"That was different. There was no pain, no sacrifice sharing my blood to develop a cure. My blood's uniqueness has nothing to do with *me*. It's from my transfusion in utero."

"Doesn't matter."

"But it does. Remember the apartment fire I survived? A lady had carried me out and then raced back inside the burning building to rescue others. I can still see her face. Her eyes. Everyone in my unit died but me. And the freak accident on the ferry? A man had handed me his life-jacket. He insisted he'd be fine. Yelled at me, even. But he wasn't. No one was fine. They all drowned or died of hypothermia. Every disaster I've survived, had nothing to do with me outrunning death. It had to do with *others*. Others sacrificed so I could be saved. Seaman Davis and you were the last to rescue me. And now? Now it's my turn to save you and Gabby. It's my fate. Confidence over fear, right?"

"I'm not leaving without you and Gabby."

"The deal sounds reasonable," Ox said, swooshing his hand in front of his neck like he was slicing, to indicate that Insley should lower the rifle.

"Fuck you," Clay snapped at him.

The baby cried from the galley.

Ox couldn't have asked for better timing.

57

Saturday, July 17, 2032
The City Docks on Spa Creek: Annapolis, Maryland

RUBY HEARD HER baby cry from inside the catamaran's galley. Her resolve strengthened. Sacrificing herself was the only option.

"Tell Mr. Pretty Face why he should listen to you," Ox said. "His whimpering is pathetic, and I'm getting bored."

Continuing to press the blade-tip against her artery, she pleaded with her husband. "There's only one way you and Gabby get to leave here alive, and that's with my deal. Otherwise, he'll kill you both, whether I slice my throat or not."

"But they're coming," he whispered. "And…"

"Are you mumbling about the SEALs?" Ox interrupted. "Because they're an hour out. We'll be long gone before they arrive."

"Get the baby," she shouted back. "Let's get this party started."

"Now that's an order I can follow." Ox winked, before waving his hand to summon someone from the galley.

Holding Gabby wrapped in a blanket, a teenager—maybe late teens, walked from the galley onto the boat deck. The girl's hair was fashioned with gothic streaks of black onyx and purple. A tattoo of octopus tentacles crept up her neck, and multiple piercings accented her nose, ears, and lips.

"We have a deal, right?" Ox asked Ruby. "You're not going to do something stupid and hurt yourself anyway, or make a run for it…"

"It's a deal. But no one comes near me until Clay gets into our car with Gabby, beeps, and drives off. I swear I'll slice my throat if you don't follow those orders. Am I understood?"

"As long as I get to see a juicy kiss goodbye, we're good to go."

She wanted to kiss Clay goodbye, but knowing Ox was hankering to see it, to get a perverse kick from their farewells, made her want to slice *his* throat instead. To watch the turncoat gasp for air as he choked on his blood. Somehow, someway, the man was going to die. And she was going to kill him.

The gothic girl walked down the portable bridge connecting the *Lady Sarah* to the dock. With Gabby still crying, the teen held the baby away from her body as if she was diseased and contagious.

"Quick. Get the baby," Ruby said to Clay.

He approached the girl and snatched Gabby from her. The teenager quickly turned around, retreated toward the boat, walked back onboard, and faded into the shadows of the galley.

Their daughter stopped crying in her father's arms. He kissed her, whispering her name.

Tears streamed down Ruby's face. Her heart was breaking apart.

"I can't leave you," her husband said, locking eyes. "I can't."

"You have to. Remember to beep and keep driving. Don't stop."

She used her left hand to touch her baby, to caress the soft skin on her cheeks and forehead. To run her fingers through her hair. Ruby wanted to remember the feel of her daughter. To never forget.

With her right hand, she continued to press the blade-tip against her neck. "Kiss me goodbye," she said.

He leaned in and kissed her lips. "I love you, Ruby Pearl Spencer. You're my one-and-only. My forever." He kissed her again. "My superhero." Tears cascaded down his cheeks.

"And you're mine. Take care of our daughter."

"How very sentimental." Ox clapped. "G-rated like a Disney movie, but at least the dagger to the throat adds a nice touch. Now get the fuck out of here Mr. Pretty Face. Before I change my mind and lodge a round into that blubbering mouth of yours. And don't think about calling the local police. Paybacks are a bitch."

Clay walked toward Main Street with Gabby in his arms, looking back at her on the dock. Desperate to find another way.

But she knew there wasn't one.

Keeping the knife-tip pressed to her skin, she watched the

distance between her and her husband grow. Watched until he was out-of-sight. The breeze slapped at the trees in the sitting area adjacent to the dock and slips. She held her breath waiting. Hoping. At last, their car horn blared and the wheels peeled-away on the asphalt. She took a deep breath, relieved.

Insley, with his red hair lengthening by the day, headed to retrieve her, gripping the IAR. He confiscated her knife and pushed her toward the vessel. They walked onboard to the boat deck.

"Let's go inside and get more comfortable," Ox said, holding open the door to the galley.

Two chairs were positioned in the middle of the cabin area, facing each other. The teen was sitting in a booth to the right of the chairs, working a video game on her electronic tablet.

"Time to go," Ox said to the teenager, handing her two one-hundred-dollar bills. "Not bad for a couple hours of work, right?"

"What do you want? Me to kiss your ass, old man?"

Ruby's heart burst into double-time. But not for herself.

Ox narrowed his eyes. "Be careful how you speak to me, Olive with the octopus on her neck. Who knows? Those tentacles might actually squeeze."

"Pain and death don't scare me."

As quick as a hornet's sting, Ox grabbed the teenager by the hair and dragged her from the booth to the carpeted floor, managing to keep her standing. With hair in fist, he wrenched her head back. The girl dropped the tablet and winced, bringing her hands to her head, trying to prevent Ox from plucking her hair by its roots.

Using his free hand, he yanked the nose ring—a silver loop, ripping it through her skin until the piercing was free. The girl screamed. Blood raced from the split on her nostril.

With her head still pinned back, Ox lowered his face to hers. He clicked his teeth together as if he might bite. Then he licked under her nose, collecting blood on his tongue. "Anything you want to say to me, sweet Olive?"

"I'm sorry, sir."

"Ahh. Much better." He released her hair. As she cried and cupped her nose, he stomped on her tablet, cracking the screen. "Now race back to Mommy and remember: the Ox-man knows where you live, honeysuckle."

The girl bent to retrieve her device from the floor. His boot remained on the screen.

"This is your last invitation to leave…breathing," he warned. "Now what's your decision, Olive with the octopus?"

The teen bolted from the *Lady Sarah*.

Ox stared at Ruby. "Teenagers aren't raised well these days. Coddled. Undisciplined. Entitled. Given everything except lessons on attitude, hard-work, and respect. Hope Mr. Pretty Face does a better job with your daughter."

Insley led Ruby to one of the wooden folding-chairs, to the one facing the bow. He nodded for her to sit. As she did, Ox lowered himself into the chair facing the stern. A metal briefcase was on the floor beside him. Insley took his place behind his boss, near the vessel's bar. In her full line of sight.

"You obviously don't do well with young ladies," she said. "Do you always want to strangle them? Is that how you killed Patti?"

Insley jerked his head at the mention of Frank's sister. Another reaction? She needed to build on what she'd started in the captain's quarters of the USS Simpson. Find out if she could work the connection—whatever it was—to her benefit.

"Not that it matters," Ox said, "but why are you obsessed with Patti Davis and the Ambassador? Even now, when you should be boohooing about being separated from your family again, you're thinking about inconsequential people."

"Inconsequential? They were people with purpose. With rights. People who had family and loved ones."

"Plan on running into them someday and boasting about your noble concern?"

"Pointless when they're *dead*. Truth is: I want closure. And your charade that they're alive isn't helping." She looked down. "Maybe you're too insecure to admit it…"

"Since you're giving me what I want, let's play crystal ball. You've got one question to ask me, about any topic. Word your question wisely. It's your only chance to learn the unfiltered truth. Only one restriction: the question can't be open ended."

The only reason he'd suggest playing a stupid game was because he probably thought she couldn't formulate an intelligent question, one forcing a confession from him. No doubt he fancied himself a genius, like every criminal did.

She concentrated. Asking flat-out if he had killed the consulate's administrative assistant might not work, especially if he had ordered one of his goons to do the job. No matter what, she had to show Insley that his boss was a liar; someone who could never be trusted. Maybe then he'd help her.

"Here goes," she started. "Pick the statement which best reflects the truth: A) Patti Davis is still alive, to your knowledge; B) Patti Davis died from the RED attack in Taipei; C) Patti Davis was killed by you, Ox; or D) you ordered one of your team to kill Patti Davis and to your knowledge, the order was obeyed. That's my question. And you didn't say it couldn't be multiple choice or that it had to end in a question mark."

"Damn! You're good, Ruby Never-Dies." Ox turned behind him, looking at his accomplice. "She got me on that one, didn't she?"

The young Marine looked as though he wasn't sure how he should answer. "She certainly milked the opportunity for all it's worth, sir."

"Good answer, Insley," he said. "You're learning how to navigate these waters without flipping the raft on yourself." He clapped his hands together. "So alrighty then. The crystal ball says the answer is...C. I killed the sniveling bitch who was so pathetically loyal to that needle-dick Eagle Scout, Jonny Ambassador. Strangled both, in fact. I admit: she wasn't expecting it. Didn't even get the chance to suck in that last bit of O_2. She kicked some, but I was hoping for a better struggle. There. Gave you more than you asked for. Can your brain rest now? Are you at peace?"

She quickly glanced at Insley, trying to seem like she was staring into space, thinking about the answer. The red-haired Marine looked pale. In shock even.

"I'm heartbroken," she said. "But what do they say? Oh yes, the truth shall set you free."

"Figuratively, of course. Because freedom is not yours to receive." He grabbed the briefcase and laid it on his lap. "Insley: get me a glass of whiskey. Make it rye. *Redemption* should be stocked in the bar. Pour it on the rocks."

Insley walked to the bar and stepped behind it.

Ox opened the briefcase. "Are you up for a surprise? See, I'm no longer interested in extracting blood from you." He pulled a syringe from its foam pocket within the case. "Instead, I'm going to inject something very special into your bloodstream. Think of it as payback. If I recall, you stabbed me with a needle not too long ago."

She had mentally prepared herself for becoming a comatose blood-bank. Or even for having her blood drained. But being injected with something? Like *what?*

"Wait a minute," she said, swallowing hard against the acid racing up her throat, burning the thin membranes. "The SWC wanted to use my blood to create a serum that...if injected into an infected, might stop a human from cognitive degradation. Is that the serum you think you've got? Did you steal a prototype from Emory Bradshaw?"

He prepped the needle for injection while he spoke, flicking the barrel with his finger to bring air bubbles to the surface of the fluorescent green liquid. "Crystal ball says you had one question. One. That was our agreement. I owe you nothing now."

"But I'm not infected! My blood was tested yesterday. And the ZOM-B pathogen is *not* in my bloodstream. Please! Testing a serum on me is pointless."

He placed the briefcase back on the floor, holding the prepped needle in his right hand. "I told Decha and Vladimir—especially the Russian troll, that you weren't as smart as they gave you credit for. I'm the one ahead of the curve, not you Ruby Never-Dies. Not. Fucking. You."

Insley approached his boss from behind.

Her eyes widened.

"Where is my bloody drink?" he snapped, twisting his neck in search of his Marine puppet.

58

Saturday, July 17, 2032
The City Docks on Spa Creek: Annapolis, Maryland

OX WAS PROUD he'd led a life where he never had to utter the words: *I never saw it coming.* Maybe his visual prowess was like a sixth sense, giving him three-hundred-and-sixty-degrees of sight. Not like an owl. Owls had to turn their heads to see behind them. Not him. He just *knew.* Except on the *Lady Sarah.* Perhaps the excitement of wanting to inject Ruby Never-Dies had distracted him. Or maybe his thirst for top-shelf rye whiskey had short-circuited his acute sharpness. Whatever the reason, for the first time in his forty-seven-years, his internal voice admitted he never saw *it* coming.

It was Insley.

When Ox turned to see what-in-the-fuck was keeping Insley from handing him his drink, his brain hiccupped at the visual input. Insley was holding a rope taunt between his hands. Not a drink.

He took a deep breath, prepared to verbally-whip the Lance Corporal—whose mother had had the audacity to name her bastard son Eugene—about deciding to tie-up the girl without his superior's approval. Restraining her with rope? Waste of time. Because the doofus had an IAR at his disposal, for fuck's sake. And anyway, Ox wasn't going to let her go anywhere. Duh-ville.

But when Insley wrapped the rope around *his* neck and tightened it, making the fibers twist and burn against his skin, he acknowledged he had slipped behind the curve. Had failed to use his God-given gift—his sixth sense—and now he found himself in a blind-spot.

More importantly, without evasive action, he was going to crash-and-burn. Regrettably, he had to drop the syringe to defend himself. Which royally pissed him off. At least he had gulped plenty of O₂. The Marine he liked to call Red Top was about to morph from boy to man. Dead man, that is.

Ox knew from combat that time would be wasted if he grabbed for the rope. People being strangled always fumbled with the damn rope or wire. All that did was expend oxygen without changing the inevitable. No, the key was attacking the *strangler*.

Just as he reached behind to grab Insley, the red-haired wonder tightened the rope and pulled. The chair fell backwards, dropping him to the floor. If Ox could have smiled, he would've. Falling on the floor gave him access to legs: Insley's legs.

Blind-spot number-two: the girl drove her foot into his crotch, creating a blinding flash of white. Then the bitch did it again. He wanted to curl into a ball to protect his nuts, to absorb the pain, but he couldn't. His brain screamed to stay on target. Reaching over his head, he clutched Insley's ankles and yanked them toward him. The boy toppled over, releasing the rope.

Game over.

In one fluid motion, Ox rolled, thrust Insley's legs underneath him, straddled the Marine's chest, and placed his hands around his neck. Gritting his teeth in the exertion of force, he squeezed so hard it looked like the boy's eyes were going to shoot out like balls in a pinball machine. Rage filled Ox's head with fire.

"Die you son-of-a-bitch," he said, seething. "No one takes-on Ox and lives."

"*I've* done it," the girl said, moving into his range of sight.

Ruby Never-Dies held the IAR, aimed at him.

He clenched his jaws. Why in-the-hell was he making so many mistakes? About now, retirement didn't seem so bad.

"Stand up," she ordered.

The bitch was a bluffer. And she probably had no clue how to operate the M27, so he kept strangling Insley. Anyway, the job was almost done. The kid was blue.

Blind-spot number-three: the girl fired the automatic at a window, shattering the glass. Maybe his Marines positioned around the dock area would storm the boat. Then again, they wouldn't guess *he* was the one in jeopardy.

"You have trouble following orders, don't you?" she chided. "Now stand up."

Reluctantly, he released Insley who immediately gasped and placed his hands around his neck. Rolling around on the floor, the kid coughed and hacked like a pussy.

Ox stood. Slowly.

"I know what we can do," she said, taunting him. "Let's play crystal ball. You get one question to ask either one of us, about any topic. Word your question wisely. It's your only chance to learn the unfiltered truth. No restrictions on question type. Go."

He was going to kill the cunt. But for now, her little game—which probably made her feel like she had grown some, like she was in charge—would buy him valuable time to assess his tactical defensive.

Insley was standing, still having trouble breathing.

"I'll play along," Ox said. "Red Top: why did you attack me?"

Insley neared. Purple already marked his neck. His eyes were bloodshot. "You're a liar, that's why." He coughed. "You told me you sent Patti home as a precaution, and I believed you. But you lied. You strangled her. Strangled an innocent person who only wanted to serve her country. And to think…I wanted to be like you."

"Why in the hell would you care so-damn-much about a sap like Patti Davis? This is me you're talking to Insley. Lieutenant Colonel Quinton Oxford of the United States Marine Corps. A Medal of Honor recipient. *Your* superior."

"You've asked a second question," she scolded, "but I'll bend the rules and allow it."

"I was in love with Patti," Insley said, looking all starry-eyed. "She was my girlfriend."

Well, ain't that something. Blind-spot number-four.

The girl raised the IAR. "Killing you will be a piece of cake."

And then the bitch fired.

If he'd had the time, he would've admitted that he never saw *that* coming either.

59

Saturday, July 17, 2032
The City Docks on Spa Creek: Annapolis, Maryland

INSLEY'S THOUGHTS WERE scattered like a finished puzzle tossed off a table. The only section still intact was his decision to overtake his commanding officer. Because when Ox admitted he'd strangled Patti—someone Insley knew to be kind, devoted, and patriotic, he realized he had mistakenly chosen the wrong side.

And there was no way out with Ox in the world.

Like his fellow Marines, he had joined *The Cause* to save his country. The country he'd die for. Without a second thought.

Ox's sales-pitch started with the FIN report showing that in 2033, there wouldn't be any humans left. As if that news wasn't bad enough, the U.S. government was moving like a turtle, not an eagle. So when Ox—the Godfather of the Corps, explained he had a fast-track plan to secure a future for the United States, returning the Red-White-and-Blue—in all her majestic glory—to a superpower status, the mission sounded like a no-brainer. His CO further sweetened the pot by explaining their boldness would launch the U.S. so far ahead their enemies wouldn't even spot the contrail.

Insley couldn't leap onboard fast enough. *First to Fight,* baby. *The Corps and Country.* Do, die, or turn. And he was all about the "do."

Then came the figurative IED that just exploded in his face, waking him from the madness. Ox was killing innocents. *Innocents!* Humans weren't the enemy; the infected were!

How could he have missed the signs? Because why would his

Lieutenant Colonel—the man he had admired more than his own mother—partner with the Russians and Chinese to elevate the United States? A monumental WTF. Brainwash city.

With Ox's confession, the truth splattered all over Insley's face as if he had committed the murders himself. No denying, anymore, that his CO had killed the love-of-his-life, as well as his buddy Wyatt. Probably scores of other Marines and patriots, too.

The reality nauseated him.

The Cause was nothing more than Ox's personal pipeline to power.

"Insley!" Ruby said. "Snap out of it. Ox's goons are planted all over this dock area. We need to get out of here."

Ox's radio crackled to life. "Heard gunfire, sir. Whiskey, Tango, Foxtrot…over?"

He bent down and detached the radio from his CO's belt. Ruby still held the IAR, as if she wasn't sure what his next move might be.

Holding the antiquated radio to his lips, he pressed the button. The frequencies were no longer monitored. "Red Top here. Confirmed: Charlie Foxtrot. Repeat: Charlie Foxtrot. Girl shot CO; I shot girl. Pop-smoke to Check Point one. BOLO for SEALs—their ETA is in eighteen mikes. I'll wipe evidence and meet you at tactical operations center. Repeat: fall back to TOC. Pass it on. Over."

"Fuck," the other Marine said. "Roger, Roger That. Over."

He looked at Ruby. "Do you want to wait here for the SEALs?"

"No. I want to get home to my husband and daughter. Any suggestions?"

"Ox and I stashed a vehicle. I'll drive you. But let's give the unit time to bug-out. Let's keep them thinking you're dead."

After placing the IAR on the bar, she reached down and grabbed the syringe and protective cap from the floor, snapping the cap over the needle. "I'll make sure this gets into proper hands. Do you know what it is? What the serum's supposed to do?" she asked, returning the syringe to the briefcase and clicking it closed.

"No Ma'am, I do not. But I'm sure we can agree…whatever it is, the injection's not in your best interests."

She locked eyes with him. "Thank you, Insley. I know you had other motivations, but thank you for saving me. And I'm so sorry about the killings, especially Patti's death."

"Me, too. I loved her. And Ma'am? I want to thank *you.* "

"Me? Why?"

"For reminding me: I need to be one of *The Few. The Proud.* I am a United States Marine. Semper Fi."

60

RUBY WAS LYING in the trunk, equipped with a flashlight, water bottle, and loaded pistol—in case something went wrong as Insley drove to Margo and Tomas's house. The briefcase was tucked beside her. Thank God the summer sun hadn't begun to bake. The trip was going smoothly, with the expected starts and stops of traffic.

On the road, she had time to reflect on her hellacious week and what it all meant. Her brain replayed the day she and Clay had arrived in Shifen, the day she'd climbed the flagpole and retrieved the fuchsia lantern-sock, painted with ghoulish faces. And the Mandarin glyphs denoted what she'd already believed in her heart: *The world is damned. Death is rising.*

When had she first accepted the world was irreparably cursed? She couldn't remember. The belief had taken root over time. But one thing she knew: the curse caused her to retreat in fear. To want to lay-low until the threats were over.

After giving birth, she'd become a shut-in with Gabby, frightened to live a normal life. Seclusion was her safety net. And she'd fantasized she could create "normal" apart from the world. In fact, she'd even decided to resign from the SWC to avoid adding more stress and danger to her new reality. But by chance, or maybe fate, she'd agreed to go on one final mission.

And that's when her eyes opened to the truth.

She understood now: fear had tricked her. *Safe* didn't happen by itself. Didn't happen when people hid indoors, frightened and inactive. *Safe* happened when people lawfully protected and defended their right...to *be* safe.

Insley had journeyed through a similar transformation. But on the fear-spectrum between the polar-ends of retreat and attack, he'd chosen attack. He had pledged his allegiance to an untreated PTSD-stricken war-hero who'd morphed into a sociopath. Who'd become worse than the enemy he used to fight. A person who hid a nefarious scheme behind a patriotic-mask that displayed power-to-America on its surface. And power to a Marine equated to securing safety.

By coincidence or fate, he had been left with Ruby in the captain's quarters of the USS Simpson, where he now admitted his distortions were challenged for the first time. And now Ruby suspected he understood: *power* didn't happen when people exchanged a fair system with corruption. *Power* happened when a country and its military lawfully protected and defended their right to have sovereignty.

Inaction and corruption were the evils of their time.

Both extremes led to lawlessness.

In the darkness of the trunk, she decided not to resign from the SWC. Instead of leaving, she'd exert herself—exert her rights as an American in service to her country—*on* the Council. Hopefully, Insley would choose to inspire other Marines (as well as defenders in all the branches) to understand they didn't have to betray the military to elevate America...or themselves.

If people like her and Insley could alter their perspectives, to find middle ground on the spectrum, then the world was *not* damned. The world had hope. Survival was in their reach.

Insley's vehicle stopped and seconds later, he opened the trunk, helping her from the car. As her feet touched the pavers at the Gonzalez's house, the front door opened. Clay emerged, pointing a shotgun at Insley. Lollie barked at his heels.

"Get away from her!" he shouted. "Get away now or you're a dead man."

Tomas joined Clay's side.

"It's okay," Ruby hollered. "He's with us. Ox is dead."

Clay handed Tomas the shotgun and raced to her. She fell into his arms, exhausted.

"My God! You're okay!" he said, holding her like he would never let go.

"And Gabby?" she asked, as Lollie licked her legs.

"Perfect. Margo has her and she's fine."

A helicopter thrummed in the distance.

61

STANDING ON THE driveway, Clay held his wife close. The helicopter transporting the SEAL squad landed on the lawn.

Eyes exited from the aircraft and ran toward them. For the next ten minutes, his wife explained how she and Insley had worked together. How she'd eventually killed Ox. As she spoke, Clay kept his arm around her, sensing her weariness. Listening to her story, he was overwhelmed with gratitude that she'd survived. And he wondered if he'd ever forgive himself for leaving her behind at the docks. His only solace was that she'd been right: if he hadn't left with the baby after Ox agreed to her deal, they'd all be dead. And Gabby's life could never be gambled.

While they stood on the pavers, Eyes contacted President Newton about the briefcase. The President, shocked by Ox's mystery serum, agreed to send Em by the house that evening. No doubt Em would discover what the turncoat bastard had been planning to inject his wife with. He balled his hands into fists thinking about how close she'd come to getting the shot.

When the syringe—and whatever serum it contained—was no longer in their care, he'd feel relief. Big time.

The SEALs loaded the fallen MARSOC operatives into the chopper. Eyes could barely contain his fury over the six lives lost. He took a breath, calmed himself, and said it was time for his squad to head out.

Not surprising, Insley was taken into custody. But the Marine divulged where *The Cause's* tactical operations center was located. In fact, the other SEAL squad, the one which had collected Ox's body, was already en route to arrest Ox's accomplices.

With their goodbyes, Ruby promised Insley she'd convince the President to pardon him. The two had clearly bonded.

As the chopper lifted, he and Ruby went inside the house. Her eyes looked heavy so he convinced her to lie down, suggesting Gabby nap in her arms. She didn't resist.

He walked her to the guest suite and helped her to bed. Margo placed Gabby in her arms, before leaving the room. Sitting on the edge of the mattress, he moved strands of hair from his wife's face as she held the baby. Lollie jumped on the bed, snuggling beside them.

His family was together. Safe at last.

Ox had gotten what he deserved, and the threat—thank the Lord—had died with him.

"I have to say it," he said, still feeling guilty, "to make sure you...make sure you know that I..."

She placed her palm on his cheek. "I already know, Clay. You never would've left me at the docks if you didn't believe, as I did, that Gabby's life was in danger."

"I need you to know that."

"Of course I do. And thank you for trusting me."

She segued into her decision to continue serving on the SWC. Instead of *her* leaving, she asked if he'd consider resigning. He didn't hesitate. He'd gladly stay home with their daughter. And he could serve as a consultant to the SWC when needed.

Leaning over, he kissed her. He loved her more deeply than she'd ever know. Than words could ever convey.

"Get some sleep," he said, giving her a parting peck on the forehead. "I'll check on my girls every now and then."

"When is Em expected to arrive?"

"Tonight, like eight-*ish.*"

"I'll be up long before then."

"I think you'll be surprised."

62

Saturday, July 17, 2032
The Gonzalez Residence: Annapolis, Maryland

RUBY SLEPT INTO late evening as her husband had predicted. Hearing a knock on the bedroom door of the guest suite, she opened her eyes. The room was already cloaked in charcoal gray. And Gabby and Lollie were no longer with her on the bed.

The door opened a crack. "Em's here," Clay said, almost in a whisper. "Is it okay to turn on a light and have him come in?"

She was still dressed in her day clothes. Scooting into a sitting position, she rested her back against the pillows and headboard.

"Sure. No problem," she said.

He walked to a small table and lamp near the doorway, turning on the light. Em followed him in. The lamp cast a soft yellow-hue within the room. Grabbing the briefcase from a chair, Clay handed the case to Em. "Please let us know what's in the syringe."

"Absolutely." Em walked to the bedside. "How's my girl doing?"

"Fine. I was tired, that's all." She managed a weak smile.

"Not every day you have to take-on a thug like Quinton Oxford." Em turned to her husband. "Mind if I catch up with Ruby for a couple of minutes? Cover some Council business?"

"Not at all." Clay looked at her and tapped his smartwatch. "Call me if you need anything. We'll be in the music room. Tomas has a new jazz CD he wants me to hear. And Margo has Gabby."

She nodded. He left the bedroom, closing the door behind him.

"Hey, may I sit down on the bed?" Em asked.

"Oh sure. Sorry."

He sat sidesaddle on the edge of the mattress, near her hip. Placing the briefcase on his lap, he rested his forearms on it.

"Did Clay share our decision with you?" she asked. "That he'll be leaving the SWC and I'll be staying on?"

"Yes! Great news you're staying. I'm stoked. Ava will be too."

"Ava?" She raised her eyebrows. "So now you're besties with the POTUS? Should I be jealous?"

He smiled, somewhere between guilt and innocence. "Sometimes she asks me to call her Ava. And it's hard to shut off that mental programming. Pavlov conditioning, I guess."

"Still in a lab coat? Do you ever wear civilian clothes anymore?" She tugged on his sleeve. "You're going to burn yourself out."

"I know, right?" He chuckled. "In fact, I just came from work. And I brought you something to make you feel better."

"For me?"

He put the briefcase on the floor and reached into his lab pocket. When his hand emerged, it held a syringe. She flinched. Syringes weren't in her comfort zone. Especially after the day she'd had.

"Relax," he said. "It'll take the edge off. You've been through a lot, and I thought you'd appreciate it. The shot will help you drift into la-la-land, on a fluffy carefree cloud."

"Em…" She was confused. "You know I don't like meds unless I really need them. And I'm fine. I've rested *all* day. Besides, I was almost injected with a mystery serum today. Don't you think you're being just a little insensitive?"

"You've been lecturing me a lot lately," he said, tilting his head.

"What?" Her heartrate elevated. His voice wore an unfamiliar timbre. One she'd never heard before.

"Seriously. I've been playing nice," he continued. "But your attitude is starting to piss me off."

"Piss *you* off? What are you talking about? You…*you* kept me and Clay in the dark."

"There you go again." Flicking the cap from the needle, he pressed the plunger to expel any air bubbles. "Anyway, it's rude to reject a gift, especially from a bestie."

The man sitting next to her on the bed wasn't her best friend. Not even his eyes looked the same. They were darkened with hate. Hate for *her*. Panic raced from her brain, coating every cell in her body. A metallic taste soured her tongue.

"Stop it," she gasped. "You're scaring me."

He lifted off the mattress, planting his feet firmly on the floor. With the leverage he gained, he struck down on her shoulder, forcefully sliding her flat on her back. Before she winced or moved or resisted, he pressed the same hand on her chest, restraining her on the bed while digging a knee deep into her abdomen. With his right hand, he fisted the syringe and thrust it toward her arm.

She felt helpless.

Until rage and terror combined, feeding her muscles.

Swinging to the right with her left fist, she blasted his arm, the one holding the needle. His hand jerked away, but the syringe remained in his fist. She fought to rise against the pressure crushing her chest, crushing her gut. Her fingers extended, grasping for contact. Reaching, stretching for his face and eyes. For his throat. Anything.

She gulped in air. *"Cla..."* she started to scream.

Lifting his hand from her chest, he slapped it onto her mouth, piercing her cheek with his fingernails as he clamped.

Her nerve-endings screamed.

Eyes bulged from her sockets.

The needle plunged into her left arm. The serum burned under her skin. She consciously breathed, waiting to feel the effects.

Her heartbeat no longer pounded in her ears.

Was the serum a sedative as he'd claimed? Or a muscle relaxant? Narcotic? Or worse...was he trying to kill her?

Within ten seconds, she could no longer blink.

Her eyes were frozen open. She tried to move her hand: nothing. Her toes: nothing. Her breathing slowed like a tanker had parked on her lungs. Everything was heavy. But her mind still worked, still processed.

There were no fluffy clouds. Only the sharpest edges of fear. Of panic that was trapped inside.

Em propped her head with a pillow and lowered her eyelids. Her world transitioned to the dark side of a curtain.

She wanted to scream, but nothing moved. Nothing came out.

"Easier if you don't fight it," Em said seductively. "I've given you succinylcholine or SUX. Remember learning about the drug at Johns Hopkins? It's a neuromuscular paralytic drug. In other words, it paralyzes your muscles, without sedating you. I know, I know...most people given SUX asphyxiate. But they don't know dosing like I do.

"You're probably wondering...*how could he do this to me?* Well, girlfriend, even though you were going to receive the injection one-way-or-another, you've earned it. Such a selfish little bitch you've become. I mean, the world is about to crash-and-burn, and you want to pull the plug on our project for three lives—three nobodies—who might die during testing? Yet you'd gladly watch the whole of humankind perish? Such a hypocrite!

"More than that, you still have no clue what's *really* going on. To think you graduated second, under me. Somehow you've managed to make first-in-the-class meaningless."

Her mind raced. She'd missed something. No doubt trust had blinded her.

She heard a click. He was opening the briefcase with the syringe! If her heart *could* have accelerated, *could* have burst through her chest, it would have.

"You're not going to like this," he continued, "but Ava and I invited Ox—that's right, Quinton Oxford, embittered Marine *numero-uno*—to join our dark-science project. Ava called him when you were on the USS Simpson, while you were meeting with him in the captain's quarters. Small world, no?

"Truth is: we had to invite him to join *our* party. He was becoming quite a nuisance by interfering with your whereabouts. Ultimately, screwing with our project timeline. You know what they say: keep your enemies close. Come to think of it, one of the differences between you and me is that you don't know who your enemies are. I've always agreed with Clay; you're way too trusting, girlfriend.

"Anyway, after we proposed a...collaboration, Ox found the prospect titillating. He was promised a huge sum of money and a position on Ava's Cabinet. He accepted, of course. I mean, his notion of becoming the world's supreme ruler wasn't going to happen. Talk about...duh! For starters, his theory of using your blood for a cure was flawed. Come on, people: leave science to the scientists.

"So he abandoned you on the USS Simpson to come Stateside, to wait for the *real* formula from yours-truly. To execute *our* plan. And we got the added benefit of his Marine moles. Surprising, right?

"I could've qualified for an Oscar when Ava and I met with you and Clay at the White House, upon your return. Everything has been a perspicaciously executed plan. Imagine how baffled the MARSOC operatives were when our moles snuffed them at the Gonzalez's. Of course, we didn't count on you and the red-haired Marine killing Ox at the docks. If you had gotten the injection from *him,* which would have been optimal, we would've kept you in the dark about our involvement. I'd still be your bff. And sure…Ox's early death was a temporary ripple. But we had planned on killing the asswipe anyway. Ava never liked him."

Ruby willed her blood to boil, but she had no control.

"Yes, everything was a setup, except the SEALs sweeping-in for cleanup. They thought the situation was legit…when they got the order. Can't believe you bought that the SEALs would take two hours to respond. Two *hours?* And we knew that you wouldn't follow orders to stay put. That you'd head to the docks."

Em took a deep breath. "I'd warn you to brace yourself for another needle, but I think SUX dulls the nerve endings. Probably won't feel a thing."

He said nothing for a few seconds.

"There. It's done." She heard him slowly exhale.

"In case you haven't figured it out," he continued, "*you* have become the ultimate human test-subject—our Hail Mary—for a project that's been failing thus far. Rather ironic.

"Because the girl who rejected the project so dramatically is the only one who has the potential to save it! Isn't that poetic justice?

"Here's the problem: you probably won't survive the ride. I've calculated a twenty-percent chance of survival. But then again, you *are* Ruby Never-Dies, the one-and-only. If anyone can wake from this, it's you, girlfriend. But if you don't, at least we're rid of the squeaky, hypocritical wheel. Besides, I still have a pint of your blood if my formula needs tweaking. Even though you left a blood bag behind in the Situation Room, did you really think it was *your* blood I had returned? Please. You underwhelm me as an adversary.

"Now don't get hopeful when your hubby discovers something's wrong with you and calls nine-one-one. We have moles in all the right places. The Ox-man taught us that. You'll get no help outside of these residential walls."

A feeling of doom blanketed her thoughts. Heavy and dark.

With a click of the briefcase, it sounded like he was about to leave.

"By the way, I kissed your forehead for old-time's sake. I also rolled you on your side to make you more comfortable. I'll turn off the light and tell Clay you're sleeping like a baby. Don't know if I'll see you again. Happy travels, bestie."

Ruby was trapped inside her body, poisoned with something that only gave her a twenty-percent chance of survival. But did she really *want* to live anymore? Because if she survived, what would the serum do to her?

She still couldn't fathom that Em had concocted a dark-science project and forced her to be the test-subject.

Her heart jolted. Physically jolted. But she couldn't move.

In quickfire fashion, her mind began flashing images of her life. Scenes from her childhood, with her loving parents, played in her mind like fast-forward film, racing from the past to the present—in hyper-speed.

Her heart ached from the images and scenes of her present-day life. Clay and Gabby were and always would be the loves of her life.

She was unraveling.

And she could do nothing to stop it.

63

Saturday, July 17, 2032
The Gonzalez Residence: Annapolis, Maryland

CLAY WALKED EM to the door, happy the briefcase and syringe would no longer be in his and Ruby's possession. Twisting the knob and opening the door, the breeze greeted them. Low tide added a pungency to the air. It didn't help that the humidity had returned. Night was thick and slurry.

"Get home before the electricity shuts down," Clay said.

"No worries. Anyway, I'm heading back to the White House lab."

"What? No blackouts on Pennsylvania Avenue?"

"Gotta be connected, man!" Em turned and faced him on the other side of the door's threshold. "By the way, Ruby was still exhausted. She fell asleep while we were talking, like snore city. Didn't even say goodbye."

"Yeah, stress was off-the-charts today. Especially for her. I'm going to crash super hard myself."

"I'll contact you in the morning. Let you know what I've discovered about the serum. Accept my call. No matter what, okay?"

"Sure. We want to know about the serum more than you do! And hey, thanks for stopping by. Appreciate your help, my friend."

"Tomorrow is a new day, brother. Peace out."

Clay locked the front door, said goodnight to Margo and Tomas, and headed toward the guest suite. Lollie followed closely. He couldn't help himself. Stopping in front of the nursery, he opened the door, peeking in on Gabby. She was on her back, rhythmically breathing, with arms over her head like she was signaling a field goal.

Life would settle. Find its rhythm again.

In the bedroom, his wife was on her side, still in her shorts and sleeveless blouse. Not wanting to disturb her, he left the lights off. He carefully climbed into bed and snuggled behind her, spooning. Her skin was clammy and hot, so he threw off the thin blanket, leaving only the bedsheet.

"Dream of sailing *The Gem* to exotic places," he whispered, nestling behind her—a perfect fit. "I love you, Ruby."

Sometime in the wee hours, he woke sweating, like a heating blanket had been turned to the highest setting: as in, ten-inches-from-the-sun. Even the mattress was soaked. His eyes adjusted to the dark. Lollie stood in between him and Ruby, licking her face.

"Come on, Lollie! Lick in the morning. Not now." He glanced at his wife; she was in the same position as when he went to bed. "Hey, are you okay?" He touched her arm. She was burning up.

Fumbling on top of his night table, he grabbed a flashlight and pressed the button on its shaft. He stared at her in disbelief.

She was lobster-red, coated in beads of sweat. Her hair was drenched, stringy. The fitted bedsheet was soaked. "What the..." Leaving the flashlight on the bed, its beam illuminating her like a spotlight, he leapt off the mattress and raced to her side of the bed. Lollie barked.

"Wake up, Ruby! Wake up! What's going on?"

He opened an eyelid. Her pupil didn't dilate.

Raising his wrist, he commanded his smartwatch to contact Margo. He noticed it was three-thirty in the morning. The device emitted one ring after another, all unanswered.

Maybe if he screamed, the baby monitor in the nursery would pick-up his voice. He shouted, begging Margo to call him. The baby started to cry. Lollie barked. Seconds later, his watch rang.

"Margo! Something's wrong with Ruby. She's burning up. I need ice. Do you have any?"

"I keep frozen water-bottles in the freezer for the blackouts. Tomas and I will bring them to you. Is she okay? Is she conscious?"

"No." His heart was pounding. "Are you on city water or is water still running?"

"Still running. Fill the bathtub. We'll be right down."

Lifting his wife from the bed, he couldn't believe a body could get so hot. He was frightened. Fever this high could cause seizures or brain damage. Even death.

With Ruby in his arms, he snatched the flashlight and headed to the bathroom. Lollie whined.

Laying her on the tiled floor, he started the tub water, turning the dial to the coldest setting. Water roared from the faucet.

"Don't leave me, Ruby. Don't you dare."

Margo and Tomas raced into the bathroom, carrying frozen water-bottles in a trash bag.

"Dump them into the tub," Clay said, "then we'll lay her on top. Hurry! Please hurry…"

They dropped the bottles into the tub. Water splashed over the sides.

Clay picked his wife up by the shoulders, while Tomas lifted her legs. They lowered her into the frigid water.

"My God," Tomas said. "She's on fire."

As Clay held his wife's head above the water, tears raced down his cheeks. "Margo, please call nine-one-one. We're losing her!"

64

CLAY'S WORLD WAS drowning. The oxygen was being sucked out of it. His lungs threatened to implode.

"Has she been sick?" Tomas asked. "Or could she have gotten infected? During the assignment maybe?"

"Her blood was cleared Friday! And she avoided Ox's injection—whatever it was. So I don't know what's going on. Except...except Em said she fell asleep while he was visiting. Which was strange because she'd slept all day. And when I came to bed, she felt warm. And now...now she's burning up..."

Margo re-entered the bathroom. "Nine-one-one has dispatched an ambulance. Should be here soon."

Tomas shined his flashlight on Ruby, while Margo turned off the water. The redness which had colored his wife's skin was gone, leaving an ash-gray tone. His heart pounded in his throat.

"Is the water too cold?" Clay asked. "Should we take her out?"

Margo knelt and touched her skin. "She's freezing now. Her lips are blue. Let's move her onto the rug in the bedroom. Quick!"

He and Tomas lifted her, carried her to the bedroom, and lowered her on the rug by the bed.

"Is she breathing?" Margo asked. "Does she have a pulse?"

Clay's hands shook. His wife was slipping away.

Pressing his fingers on the artery in her neck, he couldn't detect a pulse. And she wasn't breathing. "Damn it, Ruby! Breathe. Gabby and I need you." He straddled her and began compressions. "What did you shout at me? In the prison? You told me to get back into my body and fight through it. It's *your* turn to fight!"

After thirty compressions, he administered two breaths. Her lungs expanded and released his air. He administered thirty more chest pumps. "Where the hell's the ambulance?"

"I'll check the driveway," Tomas said, running from the room.

He pressed his fingers to her neck again, checking for a pulse. None. He looked at Margo. "We're losing her." He was desperate, crying. "What should I do? Tell me…tell me what to do!"

She touched Ruby's skin. "Keep compressing her chest."

He pumped with force. Over and over again. For fifteen minutes.

"Let me take her pulse this time," she said.

He stopped his compressions. She placed her fingers on his wife's neck. Then she bent over with her ear by Ruby's mouth and nose. Raising her face toward him, she was crying. "Clay, I don't know what to say. I think she's…I…I think…she's gone. We've lost her."

Standing, he yanked at his hair, feeling helpless. Desperate. Confused. Margo was right. His wife was gone. No one could survive being that hot. Not even Ruby. But why would he lose her *now?* After they'd survived so much together? *Why?*

He raised his chin, squeezed his eyes shut, and released a scream of frustration and anguish. The baby cried louder from the nursery. Pacing, he took a deep breath. He had to get a grip. Had to stop from losing it. His daughter would depend on him, and him alone.

"Please leave us," he said softly. "And could you calm Gabby? I'll get her in a while. But first, I need a minute with my wife."

Margo nodded. She took the dog with her, closing the door.

Clay lifted Ruby's body from the floor and moved her onto the bed. He lay next to her, sobbing. "I can't face life without you. You're my rock. My foundation. My everything."

He cried beside his wife for at least an hour.

Daybreak cast its pinkish-orange glow in the bedroom.

Still, the ambulance never came.

And Ruby Pearl Airily Spencer—the girl his mother-in-law called her little superhero *(by land, by sea,* and *by air)*—had vanished, leaving behind an empty shell. And his shattered heart.

65

RUBY FOUND THE experience surreal. She floated, or should she say... *her spirit*... floated above the bed. Below her, she watched her husband sob while lying next to her. She had wanted to return to her body, to fight back like he had pleaded. But she couldn't get any traction. Feathers couldn't control where they floated. They were at the mercy of forces greater than themselves.

At least she was no longer in pain.

That's how she determined she had died. Because before her heart stopped, liquid fire had raced through every capillary, torching every nerve ending. Whatever Em had injected her with, it was hell. Fire-blinding HELL. She had mentally cried out, non-stop, entombed within her skin. But internal screaming had done nothing to extinguish the pain. So although she felt guilty accepting a fate she'd never wanted, a fate she'd run from her whole life, in the end, she welcomed death. With opened arms.

If not for the physical relief death brought, no doubt she'd be wallowing in despair. Clay and Gabby, and Lollie, meant everything to her. They were life itself. And now she couldn't touch them, feel them, smell them. They were separated, existing on different planes.

The mystery was why she hadn't passed on. There was no ray of light showing her the way, like near-death survivors always testified about after their resuscitations. And she clearly wasn't in Heaven.

Something was wrong.

Even though she couldn't touch or smell from her vantage point floating near the ceiling of the guest suite, she could hear. Acutely, in fact. Like she heard Margo and Tomas crying in the master bedroom upstairs. She heard the soft crinkle of sheets. Margo had lifted her back off the mattress, sniffling. Ruby heard her girlfriend place her bare feet on the walnut flooring, before whispering to Tomas that she was heading to the kitchen. That she'd call nine-one-one again to find out why an ambulance had never been dispatched. Or why it had never arrived.

In the nursery, Ruby heard the air moving above the baby. Gabby was no longer crying; she was cooing. A breeze had picked up and was probably spinning the mobile over the crib, making the farm animals go around and around. She could *hear* each revolution.

Clay's heartbeat was strong; each beat resonated in her eardrums. His breathing was slow and heavy. Since she had died, he hadn't left her side. If only she could place her arms around him, she'd tell him everything would be okay.

The feeling of longing grew powerful. Overwhelming.

The rhythm of her husband's heart was unnerving. She listened to valves open and close in his veins and capillaries. With each heartbeat, blood raced from the chamber, carrying and delivering oxygen to cells throughout his body. She heard it all. Every detail.

She struggled to identify the intensity of her reaction.

Then, as if someone had turned on the power-switch to an industrial vacuum cleaner, her spirit felt pressure, like a G-force. Like a tornado had swept her up into its vortex, swirling and tossing her. She didn't know where she'd land.

Without understanding why, Ruby's lungs inflated.

She opened her eyes.

66

Sunday, July 18, 2032
The Gonzalez Residence: Annapolis, Maryland

HIS WIFE MOVED as if she'd taken a breath. But as a scientist, Clay understood decay. Gasses were produced when tissues broke down; gasses could move a corpse. Even though calling the coroner would induce agony—beyond what he could handle, he couldn't deny the time had come. Ruby's body needed to be moved to the morgue.

For the last hour, he had planted his face in her chestnut-blonde hair. The floral fragrance of her shampoo still lingered. How could he live without the smells that were his wife? The sounds and actions that were Ruby? Lifting his head, he wanted to gaze at her face one more time, before he had to accept that she was gone forever.

Green eyes gazed at him. Blinking rapidly.

His heart lurched like combustion moving a piston.

"Am…am I alive?" she asked, looking up at him, her face pale and smooth. A China doll. The bruises which had colored her injuries were gone. Not even a freckle marked her skin.

"Ruby?" He propped himself up by an elbow and touched her face. His hand was shaking. Her cheek was unnaturally cold. "Are you *okay?*" Confusion furrowed his forehead. "Because you didn't have a pulse. And you weren't breathing. For close to two hours…"

She touched his face. "I think…I think I survived. Against the *odds*. I made it, Clay. I did!"

Tears raced down his face. He had no clue what odds she was

referring to. And it didn't matter. "You've come back. My God, you're alive!" He lowered himself next to her, taking her into his arms. His sobs could not be contained.

Nestling her face in the crook of his neck, like she always did, she cried as well. Tears wet his neck.

He needed to gaze into her eyes again to convince himself he wasn't dreaming, that life coursed through her veins. When he lifted his face, fear assaulted him, took his breath away. Resembling his Grandmother's old hands, swollen purple-veins rose from Ruby's skin—under her eyes, on her cheeks, and up her neck. And the tears she'd been crying were blood, staining her face.

What the hell was going on?

He jolted back, moving away from her. Stepping off the bed, he slowly moved toward the door, never turning his back or taking his eyes off her, like he was retreating from a wild animal ready to attack.

"What's wrong, Clay?"

"Your face." His heart pounded in his ears. "You're crying blood, and veins are raised on your skin. See for yourself." He pointed to the mirror.

She leapt from the bed as easy as someone launched by a trampoline. Landing in front of the mirror, she raised her hands to cover her mouth, which she had dropped open. After a minute of staring, she turned to face him.

"The serum. Last night when Em was alone with me, he injected me with SUX, against my will. The shot paralyzed me and then…" She squeezed her eyes shut. "And then he injected me with the serum from the briefcase." Opening her eyes, she glared at him, as though she saw into his soul. "Clay…Em, the President, and Ox became partners in some twisted, dark-science project. Whatever is happening to me is their doing."

"You can't be serious." He swallowed hard, trying to fight back the bile. "So what is the serum? Did he tell you what it does?"

"No. But I'm scared."

Clay clenched his teeth. He was going to kill Emory Bradshaw. Kill him if it was his last act on Earth. Betrayal from a friend—of this magnitude—was the worst kind of evil. For now, he'd table his anger. His wife needed him. Needed to know that he loved her no matter what. No matter what freak-aberration Em had turned her into.

With arms extended, he approached her.

"Stop!" she pleaded, holding her hands in front of her. "I think...I think I'm hungry. When my face was next to your neck, my brain couldn't stop imagining the taste of your blood—of the oxygen coursing through your system. Something's wrong with me. I was salivating for your blood—like a zombie would."

His smartwatch pinged with a request for videofacing from the mad-scientist himself.

"What the fuck have you done to my wife?" Clay snapped, scowling at the image of Em on his watch screen.

Em smiled wide. "Figures Ruby survived. Only she could pull it off! Always one-upping me."

"I'm going to kill you."

"Calm down, man! You're going to blow a gasket. I've got a package on its way for delivery. It'll explain everything." He disconnected.

While they waited for the package, Clay agreed to move the baby to another section of the house, as a precaution, until they understood what they were dealing with. He'd also update Margo and Tomas. Ruby, on the other hand, would stay in the suite and take a shower, while trying to analyze how she felt physically and emotionally.

In the kitchen with Gabby in his arms, Clay updated their friends on what was happening. Like him, they were confused and concerned, but at the same time elated.

As Margo took Gabby and Lollie to the right wing of the house, where the exercise and billiard rooms were located, Clay heard a knock. Walking through the foyer, he opened the front door. A delivery guy—a government worker, no doubt—handed him a large Styrofoam cooler and told him no signature was required for the delivery.

Clay took the package to their suite and placed it on the bed. Dressed in jeans and a T-shirt, Ruby joined him by the bedside. Removing the tape which sealed the lid to its insulated container, he lifted the top. A letter lay on a large cardboard box, which rested on dry ice. A misty fog rose from the bottom of the container, creeping over the edges as if alive.

"It's blood. I can smell it," she said.

"Wait. What?"

"The serum must have turned me into some kind of hybrid. I can tell I need blood, like an undead." She lifted the letter, turning the paper over as if inspecting both sides. She handed it to him. "Bastard. I hate him."

"You've finished reading already?

She nodded, and crimson tears bled from her eyes.

"Let me catch up." He read the letter, at human speed.

Dear Ruby,

By now you know two things: 1) you've beaten the odds once again, and 2) you crave blood. Inside the box are a dozen blood-bags and a tall Yeti tumbler with a stainless-steel straw, to make the experience more appealing. Go ahead...enjoy! Compliments of the United States government.

Let me start by affirming the dire crisis. Humans are indeed heading toward extinction (and I'm not ready to check out yet). Which is why our mission is to eradicate the bacteria by destroying the undead: a global shoot-and-burn campaign. Initially, we lacked a weapon. Until I figured it out: the only way to defeat ZOM-B is to create warriors—a specialized immortal army—who can walk among the undead.

You are the progeny of Project Voodu—the SWC's brainchild, with yours-truly blazing the path toward this new frontier. Voodu is an acronym for the Vampire Offensive: Operatives for the Destruction of the Undead. Which makes you a vampire operative, our very first. What are vamp-ires? Vamped Immortals Restoring Earth. Confession: the acronyms are all me. Clever, humorous, and deadly—all at once. Admit it: in a twisted sort of way, I made you smile!

Remember when I told you I was attempting to create hybrid bacteria, that if injected into an infected, might preserve brain functions and sustain human life? Another Oscar performance! I led you to believe that the serum was being engineered for the infected. I mean, it's a no-brainer that you'd want to help the poor souls who were already infected. Seemed like a slam-dunk.

Must admit, though, we had no idea you'd get hung-up on using human test-subjects. I thought you'd do anything to save your baby. You got me on that one. So now you know the truth: the hybrid is designed for a healthy human. After all, we want to destroy zombies, not sustain them, girlfriend!

Splicing human blood with ZOM-B presented quite a challenge over the months. In the end, YOUR blood was the only blood sample that worked; believe me, I had hoped someone else's blood could've done the trick. But somehow, our efforts to save the world always come back to you.

Same with test-subjects. We tried the serum on at least a dozen healthy humans—of all ages and ethnicities, but they all died—horrible deaths, actually. (Cat's out of the bag: when we asked for your permission to use human test-subjects, we were lying again. We'd already done it. Another epic performance! Who knew I was such a good actor?)

Lying is a hard habit to break, once you get started. But let's try more truth. When you were in Taiwan, I had an epiphany. If you—the one and only—were the vessel for the hybrid, rejection would be least likely since your blood helped create it. And you're alive to prove my theory was brilliant! The dynamic duo strikes again!

Ava and I would've preferred that you were kept in the dark about Project Voodu and our involvement—right through your transformation. In fact, when we accepted that you had to be the Guinea pig, we asked Ox to join us, like I mentioned last night. He was our front-man, tasked with administering the injection. But then you killed him, so I had to execute the job myself.

Here's the thing, girlfriend: you can't survive without a hefty supply of blood. So unless you want to start draining your loved ones, or stealing from blood banks, or sucking humans dry like your inferior relative (the zombie), we're going to have to work together. A symbiotic relationship of mutualism. We're going to have to place our goals of destroying zombies and saving humankind ahead of our blistering dislike for each other. If I can do it, you can!

As a scientist, you might appreciate the exhibit, highlighting the differences between you, a zombie, and a human. Really quite fascinating.

	Vampire:	*Zombie:*	*Human:*
Food:	Oxygenated blood	Oxygenated blood	All food groups
Life Expectancy:	Immortal	Unknown	83 years
Death Induced By:	Unknown (though incineration is likely)	Bullet to the brain and incineration	Infinite causes
Predator of (what the species hunts):	All living things with oxygenated blood	All living things with oxygenated blood	All living things
Prey for (what hunts the species):	Nothing	Vampires	Vampires, zombies, and carnivores
Strength:	Superhuman	Powerful	Basic
Agility (on land):	Superhuman	Inadequate	Effective
Speed/movement:	Superhuman	Variable	Effective
Intelligence:	Superhuman	Inadequate	Effective
Breathing:	Temporarily effective when needed	None	Required for life
Underwater— Breathing/Agility:	None required/ superhuman agility	None required/ effective agility	Will drown without oxygen source / effective agility
Injuries:	Superhuman healing	Injuries sealed with lava-like crust to prevent bleeding, but injuries do not heal	Healing is dependent on type and severity of injury
Ability to infect/time lapse for transfer:	Unknown/unknown	Bite from zombie infects humans / zombiism occurs four hours after contraction or three-minutes after death	Humans infect other humans with communicable diseases common to the species/transfer times vary
Ability to Breed:	Unknown	Unable	Able
Sleep:	Selective, but not required	Unable, though dormancy preserves life source	Required (8 hours preferable)
Senses:	All senses: acuteness is superhuman	Smell and hearing: acute	All senses: dull
Muscle tone:	Highly defined	None	Varies with human
Reaction to sunlight:	None	None	Skin can burn with extended exposure

Vampire stats are based on my predictions, since you are the first. But as you can see, you're at the top of the food chain. First-in-the-class at last!

And now your country needs you—our one unstoppable warrior.

The next SWC meeting will be on Wednesday, July 28th. Same time, same place. We'll have your first mission outlined and ready to execute. In the interim, get comfortable with your new abilities. (And yeah, you can thank me later!)

Before you receive another supply of blood, I'll need confirmation that you're on the team. Call me today. Tomorrow at the latest. And remember: you carry an embedded GPS chip. Wouldn't want our vampire warrior running off on the wrong side of the war or hiding from the action, without us knowing exactly where to find you. Hope there are no hard feelings, girlfriend. If there are, you'll get over them. The SWC has more important things for you to focus on!

One more clarification. Your kind does have one predator: the United States government. Don't do anything stupid, Ruby. Choose to use your abilities to save the world. It is your destiny.

Peace out, Em

Clay put the letter down. "We'll get through this together, like everything else."

"But he took my life away. I'm not *human*. He robbed me, never giving me a choice."

He approached her for a hug.

"I can't," she warned. "Not without...without...eating."

Opening the cardboard box, he grabbed a blood bag, tumbler, and the cup components and headed to the bathroom. Slicing the bag with scissors, he emptied the blood into the cup, trying not to gag. After twisting on the lid, he lowered the stainless-steel straw into the opening. He walked back into the bedroom.

"Here." When he handed her the full tumbler, the veins returned on her face. "Drink it and see what happens."

She finished the cup in seconds. So he emptied another bag and then one more, watching her suck on the straw until each refill was emptied. Finally, she was full. The veins receded.

After washing her face and brushing her teeth, she emerged from the bathroom, looking beautiful, with a hint of color on her cheeks. Somehow, she looked feline—gorgeous and sleek, but deadly. Every beautiful feature was exaggerated. Her green eyes seemed to glow.

"Are you ready to see Tomas?" he asked.

"What about Gabby?"

"Let's try Tomas first. We can build from there."

"You're right. And after that?"

"Then we make hard decisions."

67

Monday, July 19, 2032
The White House Oval Office: Washington, D.C.

THE PRESIDENT SAT behind the Resolute desk in the Oval Office, tapping her nervous fingers on the desktop and waiting for Emory, who sat facing her, to offer his interpretation of the delay.

"Like I said, Ava: no way was Ruby going to call me yesterday. It was inevitable that she'd keep us waiting up to the deadline. I mean, she detests being controlled. But she'll call today. And she'll join us. My record's nearly flawless so far, right?"

She'd never met anyone so skilled at turning ice into water. And most of the time, Emory was indeed spot-on accurate in his assessments. That's why she had elevated him from the SWC's lead microbiologist to her senior advisor. Of course, he continued to spend most of his time in the White House labs, but when she needed him for counsel, he was at her beck-and-call.

"If she resists being controlled, why would she join us?" the President asked.

"Her desire to retreat from this rising war has been squashed. As a vampire, her every instinct is designed to fight. To be an unstoppable killer. And as the FIN report becomes reality, she'll have no choice but to use those skills to save the world, to keep her family alive. And in the meantime, she needs us. She needs blood to survive. And she's not the type to drain people herself, despite her new thirst for self-preservation. What did Ox call her? A people-hugger."

"But will she agree to turn others? To form a vampire army?"

"First things first. Baby steps. We've had a tremendous victory and there *will* be others. She'll help us. And soon the world will bend-a-knee to you…and me."

"Before I forget," the President said. "How is surveillance going at the Gonzalez residence? Any activity?"

"Nothing important. Last night, a SEAL visited them—Lieutenant Commander Dexter Marks. For about a half-hour. We both know him; it makes sense. No one else visited. She called her parents, but we didn't listen in. They're harmless, believe me."

"Eyes visited her? He was my CO for the Moscow prison evac. I was aware you all were acquaintances—back from the mission to extract the original F8 cure. Nevertheless, best not to get lax in our surveillance. In fact, maybe I'll task Justine with activating Ruby's smartwatch when she has visitors or communicates with anyone."

"Be very cautious. Remember, her senses are now off-the-charts. And if she catches on, she could resist just to prove she's in charge. Don't know about you, but I'd rather have the only vampire on Earth drinking from *our* bottomless well."

"Good point."

Emory's smartwatch pinged. The President raised her eyebrows.

"Speak of the devil," he said. "She's requesting a videoface." He raised and lowered a finger to his lips before accepting the call.

It was frustrating that the President couldn't see the girl herself, but at least she could listen to the exchange.

"Girlfriend!" Emory said. "How are you feeling?"

"Call me Ruby."

"No problem. Now how about answering my question?"

"I'm feeling hungry, but you probably anticipated that."

"I have a fresh blood-supply waiting to be delivered. All I need is your commitment to join Project Voodu and the SWC's efforts to save the world."

"Let me recap the choices," the vampire said. "I can…use my superhuman abilities to defeat the enemy or stand idle as everyone, including my family, dies or turns zombie. Did I sum up the choices accurately?"

"When you consider the options, it really is a no-brainer."

"No-brainer? I've already read every book in this house, Em. And every choice I make from here-on-out will engage my expanding intellect. So more like an *all*-brainer."

"And what does your growing intellect advise?"

"Join the SWC, of course. And fight the zombie bastards to save this world."

The President smiled as her heart fluttered with excitement. Silently, she mimicked hand-clapping, like a school girl. Feeling downright giddy.

"Say hello to President Newton," Ruby continued. "I can hear the acceleration of her heartbeat."

"Good afternoon, Ruby," the President said. Holy hell: the vampire could hear a pin drop. "I'm so pleased you'll be joining us and that you aren't harboring any hard feelings. We desperately need you to save the United States and then, of course, the world."

"What are your plans until we meet on the twenty-eighth?" Emory asked. "Because I have some ideas on how to spend your time."

"Not to be condescending, but you're no longer the smartest tool in the shed. I'll be spending my time reading-up on warfare, preparing for my role as a vampire warrior. My marksmanship will be flawless, as will my knife skills; I'm not worried about those. What I need is to get comfortable with my new agility. So I'll be inviting over experts trained in the deadliest forms of martial arts. I'm sure we'll have more enemies than simply zombies."

"Will you stay at the Gonzalez's? Or head home?"

"Are we pretending I don't have a GPS chip now? Anyway, we're staying with Margo and Tomas for a spell. They can help with the baby. At least until I master my new...circumstances."

"So what types of martial arts are you considering?"

"The Israeli Defense Force's Krav Maga; the Marine Corps' LINE; the unconventional Japanese warfare of Ninjutsu; Peruvian Bacom; and Hawaiian Kapu Ku'ialua. For starters, anyway."

"Any thoughts on explosives?" Emory asked.

"Set me up with a Navy Explosive Ordnance Disposal technician. Someone can pick me up and transport me to a training site. And I'd like to meet with an expert on AI, like from the firm which spearheaded the President's DEPE Justine."

"Why?" the President asked, feeling her level of anxiety increasing.

"Madam President, artificial intelligence may be the next weapon-of-mass-destruction."

Emory nodded, in full view of the girl, encouraging the President to accept the vampire's request.

"Okay. Sure," the President agreed. "I'll arrange for both and contact you."

"Girl," Emory cooed, "you're going to be so badass."

"Did you see that Eyes visited me last night? On your surveillance cameras positioned in this home and on the Gonzalez property?"

"Actually, we did. A little surveillance can't hurt, right?"

"Eyes came to check on me. And to update me on Insley. I hope the President appreciates what a loyal and exceptional Commanding Officer Eyes is."

"I certainly do," the President said.

"Since I'm playing nice, I have two requests that'll balance the give-and-take in our mutual collaboration. How about promoting Eyes to the Deputy Secretary of Defense, under Secretary Kilgore? Within the week?"

This is what the President feared. That Ruby, with her new superhuman-*ness*, would begin to exert charge over the government. The line in the sand between appeasement and refusal hadn't been clearly drawn yet, though she knew with every fiber in her body that she, Ava Newton, was and always would be the only one in command. For now, she'd appease the girl. Until she needed—or wanted—to play hardball. Because down the road, she wouldn't hesitate to imprison the freak and starve her. Watch her shrivel up.

If it came to that.

"The appointment of Eyes to Defense Deputy would require Senate approval," the President said, testing how committed Ruby was to the request.

"Does your hesitation mean that the most powerful political-figure in the world cannot make such a simple request happen expeditiously? Do you need my assistance?"

The President's cheeks flushed. "I can make it happen."

"Perfect. Vext me when confirmation is official."

"Your second request?"

"Madam President: I need Lance Corporal Eugene Insley to be

pardoned and released from prison. I'm requesting this happen today. You can understand why. Anyway, I'd like to make him my personal bodyguard."

"A human to protect *you?*" President Newton rolled her eyes. Such a pointless request. "Sure. Consider it done."

"Thank you. Now, about my nourishment…"

"The blood should arrive within the half-hour," Emory stated. "Let me know if you need anything else."

"How is this blood being…"

"Don't worry, girlfriend. We aren't killing anyone to feed you. We're just borrowing from blood banks. And Ruby? You won't regret your decision to join us."

68

ELEVEN DAYS AFTER Ruby turned vampire, she had effectively learned to control her hunger around Clay, Gabby, and Lollie. Even Margo and Tomas. And her parents, as well as human instructors and experts. But during the SWC meeting, she'd be surrounded by a dozen humans—all in one confined room. Beating hearts would serenade her, entice her to submit to her natural urges—to her lethal vampire impulses. That's why she had feasted on four blood-bags at breakfast, instead of one. To avoid the slightest onset of bloodlust. Because she was already anxious. Why complicate her new supercharged emotions with hunger?

Walking into the Situation Room, she noticed a short table had been added, positioned perpendicular to the rectangular conference-table, forming a capital T. Unlike meetings in the past, name tags indicated where members were to sit. Not surprising, Ruby and Clay's seats were located at the short table, facing the other members, providing a perceived separation between them. Internally, she laughed. Did President Newton really think the table arrangement would hinder a strike, if attack was on Ruby's mind? They had created her, knew she was superhuman and highly trained, and yet, didn't comprehend how deadly she was?

She sat in her assigned seat, the one closest to the door.

President Newton remained standing, her armpits dripping sweat. Ruby literally heard the droplets race down the woman's skin and absorb into her bra's fabric.

"I know Clayton will be leaving the Council," the President said, glancing at the empty chair where he was slated to sit, "but my understanding was that he'd attend this meeting, as his last. Is he coming? Or should we start without him?"

"Oh, please...start. Clay will be joining us momentarily."

"The Council has been briefed regarding your training regiment," the President said. "On behalf of the SWC, we'd like you to know how very impressed we are. Your initiative has been stellar."

"Thank you, Madam President. But while I'm feeling...*satisfied*, would you mind jumping into the details of my first mission?"

Members fidgeted and squirmed. She heard the uptick in their heartrates, smelled the acid in their perspiration. Most people's hands were trembling.

The President took several steps back from her. "Certainly. The first mission is an exercise designed to furnish members with an opportunity to witness your superhuman skills. On Friday, we will release a horde of two-dozen zombies into the baseball field of Nationals Park. We'll observe how effectively you can slay the undead. The information gleaned will be used to organize your next mission to Wyoming. Because Jackson has reported a ZOM-B outbreak, our nation's first."

Ruby had no-doubt the zombies she'd encounter in the baseball stadium would be government-made.

She locked eyes with Em. "Will I be the only vampire warrior, or have you made progress on turning others?"

"At this point, progress is limited to a plan. But I'm confident the plan is viable."

"I'm all ears..."

"When humans donate a pint of blood, it takes eight weeks before they can donate again. But if my calculations are accurate, *you* can donate a pint every hour, as long as you are feeding."

"Let me guess," she said. "You've given-up on injecting humans with the serum derived from my blood. Human blood—excluding what was once my own—is resisting the invasion of the hybrid. Instead, you plan on extracting six-to-eight pints of my assimilated blood, enough volume to provide for a human transfusion. Meaning my blood will completely replace a human's. This might eliminate the problem of rejection, thus allowing you to create a new vampire. If you repeat the cycle every day, you could eventually propagate a vampire army. How am I doing so far?"

Em's eyes widened. "That is precisely the plan."

"And all this bloodwork with humans…will it be done in the West Wing lab? Here at the White House?"

He paused for a millisecond. "Yes."

"*Yes?*" Ruby shook her head. "When you answered, your eyes drifted from left to right. Your pupils narrowed. Your voice changed an octave. Your brain's amygdala experienced an uptick of activity and your blood pressure increased."

"Your point?" the President asked, sounding irritated. "Besides a medical assessment?"

"Her point," Em answered, "is that she knows I'm lying."

Ruby locked eyes with him. "I'll ask one more time. Is all the lab work for Project Voodu being conducted in the West Wing?"

"No," he corrected. "Too much potential for West Wing traffic to become suspicious. We're utilizing the underground bunker, beneath the White House. It's safer anyway."

"And who has access to the bunker area?"

"The President and I, as well as my technicians."

"How is access to the bunker obtained?" she asked Em.

"With eye scans." He clamped his hands together. "Are you asking because you'd like to tour the facility or are you simply curious?"

"Both. I don't want to be kept in the dark about anything. In the recent past, secrets have caught me off guard." She stood, reaching for the doorknob.

There was a knock on the door as she opened it.

69

Wednesday, July 28, 2032
The White House Situation Room: Washington, D.C.

AS THE DOOR opened to the Situation Room, Eyes gave a quick glance to his team, signaling *ready or not, game on.* He walked into the room first, leading the others.

"I hope you don't mind; I've invited a few friends to join us," Ruby said, ushering the group into the room before closing the door. "You all know my husband Clay." She pointed to the next guests in line. "And of course, Vice President Baldwin and Majority Leader Mumford. With us is also our newly appointed Deputy Secretary of Defense, Lieutenant Commander Dexter Marks, whom we call Eyes…"

"Stop with these silly introductions," the President snapped, while beginning to stand from her chair. "I'm in charge of these proceedings, and this is out of order."

Eyes sensed rising temperatures in the room. Veins on Ruby's face raised from her porcelain skin, resembling tree branches in winter. If he was Ava Newton, he'd clamp his mouth shut. Pronto. That is, if self-preservation meant anything to her.

The President must have noticed Ruby's face. She changed her mind and sat back down, releasing a huff, then thinning her lips.

"Next to Eyes is Lance Corporal Eugene Insley, my personal bodyguard." She and Insley exchanged a smile. "And beside him are five members of SEAL Team 86. Eyes? Would you do the honors?"

"Absolutely. From right to left, we have Boomer, Hornet, Blade,

Target, and Launch." As he said their names, he felt great pride. He was introducing the best-of-the-best.

"What is the meaning of this?" the President asked, with sharpness in her voice. "Why are these people here? In our classified meeting? And if you don't explain yourself this minute, Secretary Kilgore will call security to remove you all."

"Relax, Ava," Luther Pennington said. "I was aware they were coming. Listen to what they have to say. It's rather important."

"This is bullshit, Luther," she snapped. "You have no authority, not as chair or my National Security Advisor, to invite others to this meeting. I am in charge. I am your Commander in Chief." She glared at the Secretary of Defense. "Call security. Now."

As Henry Kilgore lifted his wrist to make a call, Eyes nodded to Target and Launch. His SEALs took two steps toward the Secretary. The move served as a warning.

"On second thought," Secretary Kilgore said, lowering his wrist, "I believe security is now being handled by our visitors, Ava."

"I'd have to agree," the Director of Homeland Security said.

"Justine," the President called to her DEPE, which could be accessed through the voice-activated two-way speaker system. There was no response. "Sweet Mother of Jesus…answer me, damn it!" The President sounded desperate. "Justine…"

Nothing.

"Justine," Ruby said.

"Yes, Ruby?"

The whites of the President's eyes enlarged, and skin-trenches formed on her forehead. Served the crooked ice-queen right. Presidents needed balls, and no one would refute that this one was well equipped. But more importantly, Presidents needed respect for human rights. For the law. But this POTUS had a slow leak that had finally emptied her of all integrity.

Bottom line: Ava Newton disgusted him.

"Justine," Ruby repeated, "would you explain why my team has joined the SWC meeting today?"

"Certainly. Your team has joined the meeting to arrest the members, except for Luther Pennington who has served as a valuable resource regarding this matter."

Em threw back his chair and lunged for Ruby. He placed his hands around her neck and looked like he might pop his own blood vessel as he squeezed.

Eyes remained still, knowing full-well how this was going to play out. When his SEALs looked at him for direction, he shook his head to stand down. No point getting involved.

"Remove your hands from me," Ruby said, with icy calm.

The guy kept squeezing.

Her neck became tattooed again, looking like a purple spider-web of veins. With jaws clenched, she flashed her teeth.

A predator ready to strike.

For being called a genius, the jerk doctor wasn't using any smarts. He kept squeezing her neck.

She placed one hand on his left forearm and snapped the bone. Just like that. The guy dropped to the floor crying, whimpering. His good hand clutched his twisted limb.

"Fuck you, Ruby," Em shouted from the floor, grimacing.

"What's the charge?" demanded the President, ignoring her wounded partner.

"Murder and attempted murder for starters," she seethed through her snow-white incisors.

The President hurled water at her, glass and all.

Seeming to leave a trail of color, like when a camera captures motion-blur at night, Ruby whirled from the front of the room to the President's side, before the glass ever struck the cherry paneling. She clasped the woman's chin, yanking her head back faster than a blink of an eye. "Justine: can someone already-dead be convicted of murder?"

"Currently, there are no federal or state laws which address that scenario, Ruby."

She released her. "No. I'd rather watch you rot in prison."

Returning to the front of the room, Ruby appeared to regain her composure. "Here's what you need to know. Ava Newton is no longer President."

Eyes un-holstered his Glock as a precaution and the other SEALs simultaneously followed his lead. At this point, he liked to say *the mission got real…real fast.*

"Congress," Ruby continued, "under Article II/Section Four of the United States Constitution, has impeached Ms. Newton on the allegations of treason and high crimes. Based on the evidence, the Senate voted to convict, officially removing her from office. The forty-ninth President of the United States, who has already been sworn-in, is our former VP: now President Fletcher Baldwin."

SWC members looked like fish out of water, gasping for air.

"Except for Luther who has been pardoned," she said, "you've all been removed from your governmental positions. Eyes is our new Secretary of Defense. As such, he and his SEALs will escort you to a chopper waiting on the South Lawn, ready to transport you to U.S. Penitentiary, Lee in Virginia, where you'll wait for your individual trials."

"Team," Eyes said to his SEALs. "Handcuff this scum and remove them from the White House."

"You'll regret this, Ruby," Ava Newton snapped. "We're fighting a war to *survive!*"

"You can't prevent the loss of humanity by stripping people of their *humanity!* Fighting fire-with-fire only builds an inferno, where everyone becomes a monster! No, we'll find a different way to defeat zombiism. We have to prevail with a conscience—it's what makes us human."

"You've sealed our demise," Em retorted. "Way to go, girlfriend. Humankind is officially doomed."

"We'll see about that...*boyfriend.*" She paused. "Now Eyes, please get this filth out of my sight."

70

Wednesday, July 28, 2032
The White House Situation Room: Washington, D.C.

RUBY HAD ONE more order of business before she would leave the SWC meeting, return home, and begin packing. Tomorrow, she and Clay would leave from their Annapolis marina for a seven-day cruise on *The Gem*—their honeymoon getaway with Gabby and Lollie. She would've scheduled a longer trip, but a week's supply of blood required a lot of space. Thankfully, an additional refrigerator had been installed in the yacht's galley.

After helping to load the former SWC members onto the transport chopper, Eyes returned to the meeting, minus the five SEALs who would personally escort the prisoners to the USP, Lee.

Now that Eyes was back, she could continue.

"Are we ready for the final move in this war game?" she asked her trusted friends who had taken seats at the table. Clay was closest to her, nodding.

"Whenever you're ready," President Baldwin said.

"Justine..."

"Yes, Ruby?"

"Please call Vladimir Volkov and stream his image on the screen."

"Certainly."

Five minutes later, Vladimir's image was projected on a wide-screen mounted to the far wall in the Situation Room. He was still held-up at his mountain compound in Sochi National Park.

"My dear," Vladimir cooed. "Such a pity we did not say goodbye at the prison. But now our paths cross again. You are looking…how do I say…ravenous. Yes, ravenous! My moles have told me of your…transformation."

"Moles burrow in all sorts of places, don't they?"

"Indeed." He lifted a lowball glass in agreement, filled with chilled vodka, no doubt. He sipped slowly and lowered his drink. "May I ask, my child, about the nature of your call? You see, Alyona and I were conducting *private* business and would very much like to resume our…negotiations."

"I believe you have some…items of mine. I want them back."

He looked around the room, like an actor in a D-movie, exaggerating his movements to indicate he was clueless. "See for yourself. I have nothing!" he said, talking and laughing simultaneously like the troll that he was.

"Ahh, but not all Russians are loyal to Russia, Vladimir. Some are loyal to opportunity. See, I have moles as well."

She detected a hitch in his breathing. An uptick in his heartrate.

"I want my blood back," she demanded. "You have two bags in the refrigerator, and I want them returned. Today."

His eyes narrowed slightly, as though he was trying to analyze who might have betrayed him. "I have nothing of the sort," he said, with Russian *umph*.

"But Vlad," Alyona whined, entering the room, wearing sheer lingerie. Her hands were behind her back. "You have two bags full in the refrigerator, my pet! Did you forget?"

He whipped his head around to face her. "Shut up!"

"Vladimir?" Ruby asked. "Do you hear footsteps climbing the staircase of your chalet?"

He resembled a panicked animal, with eyes darting around the room. "Quick, Alyona! We must escape."

The Russian female exposed the pistol hidden behind her and pointed the barrel at him. "Not so fast, Vlad. It would be rude to leave when we're about to welcome company."

Vladimir lowered his wrist before the watch's camera displayed footage that abruptly swept around the room as he struggled. Ruby heard the click of handcuffs. Finally, someone—Alyona by the sound of her breathing—unclasped the watch and held it to the Russian

President's face. Several armed guards flanked the troll.

"You are a clever American woman, Ruby Spencer," he said.

"You mean: a clever American *vampire*. The one-and-only."

As the call disconnected, her mind flashed to Gabby. Children, not zombies or vampires, were the future of humanity. A future she had to protect.

As she reached for her husband's hand, she accepted once-and-for-all that the lantern-sock from Shifen had depicted a flawed prediction. The world was *not* damned. Or cursed. Not as long as people remained engaged in the planet's wellbeing.

And her mission as a vampire warrior was to make sure humanity thrived for as long as she walked the Earth. Because safety and justice required action. Required a voice.

ଓ END OF BOOK 1 ଓ

ACKNOWLEDGMENTS

COMPLETING A NOVEL is rarely a solitary endeavor, which is why acknowledgments are so important.

First to my readers: please know how much you are valued! Words have no meaning, no impact, until they are read. Thank you for reading mine. And if you are so inclined, writing a book review for THE ONE AND ONLY would be equally appreciated. Vendors make it easy to provide reviews on the book's Detail Page (the online page where you purchased the book).

My husband Rick has been my rock in this process, listening to paragraphs as I read each aloud and offering feedback. And long before I earned my first royalty, he regarded my writing as a passion *and* profession. Thank you for respecting what I do!

Despite being busy people with busy lives, beta readers delve into a manuscript and furnish critiques because they are passionate about books. My beta readers are incredible. Thank you, thank you, thank you to Dena Baker, Deborah Faroe, Jed Faroe, Mary Lee, Martha Mitchell, and Cheryl Tomlinson. I will be forever grateful!

Before my novel was ready for release, Ashlynne Meiklejohn proofread the manuscript. Her time and efforts have been invaluable. Thank you for your help, my beautiful niece!

Author and developmental editor Kerrie Flanagan has been my number-one mentor. Her advice—from outline to manuscript—was priceless. THE ONE AND ONLY is a better product because of her guidance. She is the best!

Gratitude is extended to my adult children: Brooke—for being addicted to books and always recommending great reads; and Mitchell—for believing, in his youth, that everything imagined could one day exist on Earth! They constantly inspire me. Their feedback along this journey and with this project has been deeply appreciated.

Thank you to *Damonza.com* for a fantastic cover!

Last but not least, I'm blessed with author friends who have helped nurture my growth—from the beginning, especially author, fly fisherman, and cocktailer extraordinaire Brian Wiprud. Thank you!

WHAT IS NEXT...

RUBY SPENCER'S STORY
continues in the second installment
of The ELI Chronicles, to be released in 2019.

The Tether

ᔥ ᔢ ᔥ ᔢ

For updates on
THE TETHER
visit: https://juliaashbooks.wordpress.com

ABOUT THE AUTHOR

JULIA ASH is author of her debut novel THE ONE AND ONLY. Prior to fiction writing, she held positions as a public relations coordinator for a school system, an internal publications editor for a leading poultry company, and an accounts manager for a graphic design firm.

Ash lives with her husband Rick and two Brittany bird-dogs on Maryland's Eastern Shore.

For a complete biography, please visit her website. And please join her on social media.

https://juliaashbooks.wordpress.com

Facebook.com/JuliaAsh.Books

@Author_JuliaAsh

Goodreads.com/julia_ash

Reviews

Please consider providing a review of

The One and Only
by Julia Ash

Vendors make it easy to provide reviews
on the novel's Detail Page
(the online page where you purchased the book).

Authors appreciate reviews more than you know.

Thank you!

CPSIA information can be obtained
at www.ICGtesting.com
Printed in the USA
BVHW031450020520
579082BV00001B/12